MW01257527

A Volcanic Eruption

Yunnie squinted at the heap of burning rock in amazement. If the lava pits had coughed up viscid rock, it would not run along like a thing alive!

Curiosity drove him closer until he reached the brink overlooking the steaming apertures.

"What are you?" he whispered. Suddenly a creature easily topping his six-foot height reared up and thrust out thick arms that glowed like the heart of a campfire. In the center of the featureless face opened a mouth, *revealing* a white-hot interior.

Yunnie cried out and staggered away.

Every breath stabbed a dagger of sulfurous gas down his throat and into his chest. His eyes watered and began to play him false. He thought he saw a path before him—and tumbled over a cliff.

Cartwheeling in air, Yunnie prepared to meet his death!

Look for
MAGIC: The Gathering

Published by HarperPrism

ATTENTION: ORGANIZATIONS AND CORPORATIONS

Most HarperPrism books are available at special quantity discounts
for bulk purchases for sales promotions, premiums, or fund-raising.
For information, please call or write:
Special Markets Department, HarperCollins*Publishers*,
10 East 53rd Street, New York, N.Y. 10022.
Telephone: (212) 207-7528. Fax: (212) 207-7222.

DARK LEGACY

Robert E. Vardeman

HarperPrism
A Division of HarperCollinsPublishers

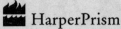 HarperPrism

A Division of HarperCollins*Publishers*
10 East 53rd Street, New York, N.Y. 10022-5299

If you purchased this book without a cover, you should be aware
that this book is stolen property. It was reported as "unsold and
destroyed" to the publisher and neither the author nor the
publisher has received any payment for this "stripped book."

This is a work of fiction. The characters, incidents, and
dialogues are products of the author's imagination and are not to
be construed as real. Any resemblance to actual events or
persons, living or dead, is entirely coincidental.

Copyright © 1996 by Wizards of the Coast, Inc.
All rights reserved. No part of this book may be used or
reproduced in any manner whatsoever without written
permission of the publisher, except in the case of brief
quotations embodied in critical articles and reviews.
For information address HarperCollins*Publishers,*
10 East 53rd Street, New York, N.Y. 10022-5299.

ISBN: 0-06-105697-9

HarperCollins®, 📖 ®, and HarperPrism®
are trademarks of HarperCollins*Publishers,* Inc.

First printing: December 1996

Printed in the United States of America

Visit HarperPrism on the World Wide Web at
http://www.harperprism.com

❖ 10 9 8 7 6 5 4 3 2

For Patty. Always.

ACKNOWLEDGMENTS

So many people helped me through the storms while I wrote this book that I am sure I will inadvertently leave some out. Sorry.

Those who cared, encouraged, and fought so hard alongside us:

Dr. Amy Tarnower;

Amy Antle, Dorothy, Mary, and all the others in the chemo room;

Molly Brown, Anna, Terry, and the legion of others on the NW 4th floor whose names elude me;

Max Mottram.

And the greatest friends in this or any universe:

Fred and Joan Saberhagen, Kathy and Danny O'Connor, René and Bill Hallett, Craig Chrissinger, Kate Keefe, Sue and Dennis Keefe, TJ and Maclean Zehler, Dennis and Lou Liberty, Steve Donaldson, Petra Heger, Patricia Rogers and Scott Denning, Mike Stackpole and Liz Danforth, Stephanie Boutz, Dan Maccallum, Sal DiMaria, Rabbit, Mike and Marilyn Kring, Mike and Denise Wernig, Bill McClellan and Eric Klammer, Jodi Stinebaugh, Audra Struble, Roslee Orndorff, Pat Weber, Raina and Sean Robison, Jennifer Roberson, Simon Hawke, Martin and Laurie Cameron, Geo. and Lana Proctor, Mike Montgomery, Al Sarrantonio, Victoria Lopez; Rose Fehr, Steve Dolch, Alicia, Martha, Carol, Matthew, and the others at Van Buren; Sherry Rohrig, Allison Almquist, Caroline Alexander, and the others at Wherry; Sue Kramer; Geoff Comber.

A tip of the hat for understanding to Kathy Ice, Kij Johnson, and Jana, too.

And extra special thanks to Gordon Garb and Hildreth Garb. Words are not enough to express my gratitude for your kindness and generosity

DARK LEGACY

CHAPTER

1

POWER FILLED THE NARROW VALLEY ALONG with the dense, swirling white vapors rising from twin fumaroles. Yunnie shivered as the energy crept into his bones and brain, giving him a vitality he had never experienced before. Strong hands pushed away a shock of flaxen hair as he turned his face upward to the warm sun, absorbing its strength. Azure eyes closed, sun baking his already weathered, bronzed skin, he wished he could stand there forever letting the power flow through his tall, rangy body.

The feeling lasted only seconds. Uneasy at the notion of something beyond his control taking him over, Yunnie restlessly shifted his weight from one foot to the other on the narrow ledge. He moved from the fifty-foot declivity into the fumaroles. Such a drop made him giddy. Or was it the nose-biting fumes? Or the energy flow that rattled his senses?

It was all that. And more.

Beside him, Mytaru's nostrils flared as he snorted like the fumaroles below. Unconsciously, the Urhaalan minotaur made pawing motions at the stony ledge with his big feet as he crossed his heavily muscled arms over a broad chest and closed his large brown eyes. Yunnie turned his attention from the precipice to his friend. Mytaru was incredibly strong and had a strength the human envied, but the minotaur's belief in an external force guiding him bothered Yunnie. He had learned through his short, difficult life that the only one he could depend upon was himself. True, Mytaru had saved his life more than once, but Yunnie knew he dared not believe the minotaur would always be there for him in times of danger. He, alone, had to cope with the adversity fate sent his way.

Savoring the feeling of omnipotence flowing from beneath, he knew he was capable of doing that. Vague uneasiness assailed him anew as he realized this place provided a different sort of external aid and was not to be relied on. The sensation rippling through him was too potent to deny or question, though.

"Do you feel their power?" asked Mytaru in a hoarse voice. "The spirits of the earth funnel energy through those vents and send it into the air for us to possess!"

"I feel something," Yunnie said. He shuffled his feet again. "The earth trembles beneath us." Try as he might, he could not force himself to acknowledge what he truly felt. Yet there *was* something greater than the power and skill locked within his breast, and it supplied a confidence that was as humbling as it was exhilarating.

"This is more than a minor earthquake, my friend," Mytaru insisted. Round brown eyes turned to Yunnie. "You experience it, also. I read it in your face. You want to take to wing and fly, no matter that you have no wings like a Serra angel. You want to run faster than any centaur. There are noble deeds to do, and only you have the skill and strength to do them. Power builds within you and consumes you. Admit there is a power greater than the one locked in here." Mytaru reached out and tapped Yunnie's bare chest.

"The steam rising from the ground might bring us some noxious gas that deludes us, blurs our senses, makes us think we are greater than we are." Even as he spoke, Yunnie knew he argued against his innermost feelings. The white vapors laced with sulfur fumes choked him and burned his eyes—they were not the cause of the ebullience or sensation of vigor filling him like water flows into a jug.

"This is a Place of Power," Mytaru insisted. "We Urhaalan come here to cherish it. By letting it touch us, we can know a little of what can be achieved by the intervention of the gods."

"I feel the power," Yunnie finally admitted. He closed his eyes and let the energy quaking under his boots filter up to his ankles and calves and thighs, and finally to his heart and brain. "Are you sure it is not spawned by magic?"

The minotaur shrugged and shook his head, carefully burnished black horns gleaming in the bright light.

"Does it feel evil? You worry too much about magic gone awry. The Brothers' War is a thing of the past, and it did not touch us as it did the rest of Terisiare."

"This is not right," Yunnie insisted. "We should not take delight in such feelings of power. It seduces us into thinking we are more than we really are."

His words fell on closed ears. Mytaru stepped to the ragged edge of the cliff, faced the venting steam, and began a mournful lamentation that added to the sense of invulnerability Yunnie experienced. The baritone lament spoke of past deaths and future sorrow that caused a catch in Yunnie's throat when he tried to speak. He moved from the ledge where Mytaru stood and climbed to higher ground. As he hiked up a rocky incline, he found a different perspective on the venting fumaroles spewing forth their feathery clouds.

"A face," he said, looking down to trace out the head of an enormous minotaur shoving its way from the bowels of the planet. "And nostrils expelling the breath of the world." The huge rock head lacked eyes, but Yunnie's imagination furnished them to either side of the vent holes. Two large boulders, both gray multifaceted, composite rock, gave a cockeyed glittering appearance to his make-believe minotaur. A river of crystal-clear water parted from its course and ran to either side of the volcanic arca, giving the illusion of silvery ribbons of hair and providing definition for a face. Under the craggy chin the waters reunited, this time bubbling and boiling before dropping over a steep waterfall into a pool beyond.

He glanced back to his friend trumpeting his sorrowful song. How the minotaurs suffered! His life had been difficult and so different from the Urhaalan during his youth along the coast of the Ilesemare Sea. Years ago the tough, finny leer fish the village of Shingol depended on so heavily had migrated south and never returned. The loss of their diet staple required many of the fishermen to find new professions, some not too successfully. Yunnie had felt no loss at remaining on shore to seek other ways of fortune while the few members of his family continued to work backbreaking hours at the deep-sea nets pulling in less worthy fish. Unlike his older sister, Essa, and her husband, one-eyed and shortsighted Heryeon, he felt no psychic bond with the restless sea.

He had found his destiny inland, with the Urhaalan minotaurs and the war they fought, without even realizing it. He had come to the mountains to find solitude and had found friendship—and more. Mytaru was the brother he had never known. Mytaru's one-horned uncle, Mehonvo, had assumed the role of father, and Yunnie had come to think of Mytaru's mother, Usru, as his own and Noadia, Mytaru's wife, as a sister. He smiled as he remembered how fate had changed his life that bitter, rainy spring day when he had left Shingol months ago.

Mytaru's and his paths had crossed in the foothills, and they had found an instant mutual admiration more miraculous than even this place. He had not rescued Mytaru that day, not really. Yunnie had watched Mytaru and three other minotaurs drive off a small band of elves venturing far from their forest on a raid. The elves had stolen a few lengths of carefully forged chain and some of the minotaurs' best, sharpest spear tips. The minotaurs had routed the elven party, recovered their stolen goods, and then Yunnie had pointed out the presence of the lurking goblins to Mytaru, who had chased them off. For his help, the minotaurs had invited him to share supper with them.

For two weeks he had walked the guard circuit to protect the valley where the minotaurs lived, and with every day he developed a closer bond with Mytaru. They had shared their lives, bit by bit, and Yunnie had tried to convince Mytaru that a few thieving elves were not the Urhaalan's problem. If anything, alliance with the forest folk would do more to drive away the goblins who pilfered and killed at every turn like the cravens they were. Mytaru had never agreed that the elves might be useful allies, but Yunnie had convinced the minotaur to watch more carefully for goblins.

Being allowed now to see this Place of Power showed how completely Yunnie had been accepted by the Urhaalan minotaurs and Mytaru in the last six months.

Yunnie sucked in his breath and held it when he saw movement near the vent holes. Shielding his eyes against the bright sun, he tried to make out who—or what— moved there. The intense heat near the lava-filled pits and fumaroles melted ordinary rock. How any living being could cavort there puzzled him and made him think his eyes played tricks. Yet he saw *two* people moving about, one dark and indistinct, the other glowing with the white-hot intensity of melted rock itself.

"There," Yunnie called, seeing shadows slipping rapidly past the vent holes. "Mytaru, do you see that? It looks like a goblin."

The minotaur continued his low chant without pause. He might not have heard his friend's outcry, or he might have chosen to ignore it in favor of completing his ritual.

Yunnie knew better than to interrupt Mytaru again. The Urhaalan were devoted to their elaborate and often secret rituals, and he had learned never to anger one of the bulls. A minotaur, once aroused, fought with the strength and ferocity of a half-dozen humans.

He squinted as he tried to make out the fleeting figure beside the vent holes. He had thought a goblin gamboled about there, but this was not possible. Even this high on the hill, sweat caused by the intense heat beaded on Yunnie's forehead. Another glimpse revealed—what? The darker mass had vanished as dancing shadows do, but the other?

Yunnie squinted at the heap of burning rock. If the lava pits had coughed up viscid rock, it would not run along like a thing alive. What living creature cast shadows independent of the bright sunlight, as if it burned with its own light?

Curiosity drove him closer until he reached the brink overlooking the steaming apertures. Again he saw strange, inexplicable movement that piqued his curiosity even more. He had to investigate, or the mystery would work at his brain like a nettle until it drove him crazy. Starting down the steep slope proved more difficult than he anticipated. There was no path leading below.

He let out a yelp as the verge gave way beneath his feet.

Rocks turned under his feet and sent him sliding. He clawed and grabbed futilely to slow his descent as gravel beneath him gave way. For a moment he was distracted by the shallow grooves and deep gashes on his chest and arms as he slid. He ignored the pain of his minor wounds to entwine his fingers in dangling roots. The sudden jerk and ripple of pain in his shoulders as he stopped almost caused him to let go. He kicked at the rocky incline and looked directly down, realizing at last the foolishness of his excursion. Climbing back to the top of the bluff seemed impossible because of loose dirt and gravel. That left only one direction, unless he chose to hang until Mytaru finished his ritual chant.

Rather than slide into the lava pits, Yunnie angled his tortuously long slide and ended up a few yards away from the infernally hot holes in the earth.

Yunnie wasted no time getting to his feet and racing from the pit. The steam billowing forth choked him, and the heat threatened to boil the flesh from his body. Rivers of sweat ran down his naked torso and worked its way under his tough leather leggings.

As eager as he was to put considerable distance between him and the fumaroles, Yunnie slowed and then stopped. He swung about, shielding his eyes against the glare from the molten rock bubbling in the pits near the fumaroles.

"What are you?" he whispered as a creature easily topping his six-foot height reared up and thrust out thick arms that glowed like the heart of a campfire. In the center of the featureless face opened a mouth, revealing a white-hot interior.

Yunnie cried out and staggered away. This small effort caused him to suck in vile fumes that turned his throat raw. He coughed and dropped to one knee, gasping for air. The sulfurous fog seething from the rocky ground almost blinded him.

"Who?" he choked out. Yunnie tried to wave to the faintly seen shadow drifting at the edges of his vision. If the creature saw him, it paid no heed.

Knowing he would choke to death if he lingered, he stumbled from the area. The power he had once felt surging through his veins now fled. Every step he took turned him weaker. The shortest breath stabbed a dagger of sulfurous gas down his throat and into his chest. His eyes watered and began to play him false. He thought he saw a path before him—and tumbled over a cliff.

Cartwheeling in air, Yunnie prepared to meet his death.

The rush of water around him caught him by surprise. The hot, clear water washed away the poisonous miasma that was blinding and suffocating him. Yunnie instinctively stroked for the surface of the gently bubbling pool where he had fallen, tossed his head to get the long flaxen hair from his eyes, took a deep breath of welcome air, then swam hastily for the bank. His arms and body smarted from the combination of hot water and myriad cuts.

"A curious time to take a bath," Mytaru observed, standing tall above Yunnie as he pulled himself from the hot pond.

"You don't enjoy swimming for recreation," Yunnie said, shaking like a wet dog. "Neither do I when the water is scalding, but this saved my life." He shook off hot droplets and rubbed his reddened skin. Here and there white blisters popped up, but if this proved his only injury, Yunnie knew he could consider himself extremely lucky. Stretching his long legs in front of him revealed new aches and cuts from the fall. He rubbed his muscles and vowed to let Noadia tend him with her secret healing herbs when he returned to her house.

"How did you get down here so fast? I fell," Yunnie asked.

Mytaru turned serious. "I saw you slide down the slope. I thought you would die. Why did you so foolishly embark on a journey so few survive when you needed only to take the path?" It never occurred to him Yunnie might have slipped. The minotaurs were too sure-footed to understand how he might have lost his balance.

"I saw someone near the fumaroles," Yunnie said, not wanting to admit he had been careless. He experienced a passing dizziness from his fall and escape, but he distinctly remembered seeing two people near the jetting plumes both before and after his excursion.

He looked across the pool of hot water, up to the water cascading from above. The river rejoined just under the chin of the rocky face he had imagined before tumbling into the pool. Luck had been with him in that this pool was heated only by the water from above and not from beneath. If the lava had heated the pond, he would have been boiled to death in seconds. As it was, the waterfall allowed some of the warmth to leave the water before it joined the pond.

"Impossible. No one survives long there." Mytaru turned pensive and asked, "Who might it have been?"

Yunnie smiled crookedly at his friend's confidence in him. No one *could* live for more than a few minutes, yet he was sure he had seen one—no, two figures. Since he was convinced, so was Mytaru.

"A goblin, or so I thought," Yunnie said, "but when I got closer, it bore no resemblance to any of the thieving cowards I have ever seen."

"Perhaps one of the Scavenger Folk? Our sentries have reported seeing bands of them moving this way. The cities along the coast must be driving them away again."

"Some Inquisitors think the Scavengers are dealers in magic artifacts or even might be sorcerers." Yunnie laughed harshly. "Those red-cloaked fanatics see evidence of magic wherever it is safe or expedient."

"You follow a strange religion," Mytaru said. "It is not founded in strength and heroism as is ours. Rather, you deal in fear and guilt."

"You do me a great wrong thinking the Inquisition is embraced by everyone. Their coin is fear, and in that currency I am completely bankrupt."

Yunnie stared again toward the tall cliff where the waterfall began its plunge. He squinted a little, as if it might allow him to see through rock to the strange creature he had witnessed so near the lava pits and fumaroles.

"We Urhaalan are content to defend our boundaries and keep such human foolishness far enough away so as not to trouble us."

Yunnie saw an opportunity to renew his long-standing argument and said to his friend, "You should speak with the elves and try to forge a peace."

"What? Why?" Mytaru pawed a little at the ground. His broad chest expanded as he sucked in more air and tossed his head in mock combat, horns darkly menacing. "They steal from us. How much longer before they leave their forests and come to kill us? We live in a paradise compared to their pitiful, puny, leaf-blighted groves."

"They are not like that," Yunnie said, choosing his words carefully. He saw how Mytaru's nostrils flared at the mere suggestion that the elves might not be vicious, intent on driving the minotaurs from their home. Yunnie had spent enough time among the elves before finding refuge with the Urhaalan to know they were decent, if a little difficult for him to associate with owing to their clannishness. With the minotaurs he felt an immediate bond of friendship; elven brotherhood was more difficult to cultivate, even if he did feel he understood them better than the minotaurs.

He laughed harshly at that thought. His village of Shingol was equally clannish, and the minotaurs, with their intricate rituals and precise ways of doing things, even more so. Perhaps it was their tight-knit community and selfless devotion that made him appreciate the elves so much. In any fight between minotaur and elf, both sides would be losers.

"We will never deal with the elves," Mytaru said harshly. "Unless it is to gore them!" He tossed his head to display his horns, then strode off without waiting to see if Yunnie followed.

Yunnie hesitated, then wound his way through the wooded area surrounding the pool to catch up with his friend. He wanted to convince the minotaurs that peace with the elves was to their mutual benefit—and what *was* it he saw by the fumaroles?

CHAPTER
2

DARKNESS. DARKNESS SO THICK IT ENWRAPPED
Peemel like a warm, inky blanket as he stepped onto the
balcony from his quarters. Never before had he seen fog
blanketing the city so completely. Strong hands gripped
the railing before he clamped shut his pale eyes and then
opened them slowly. No difference, closed or open.
Darkness. Even the comforting patterns of stars he had
known all his life were missing from the nighttime sky. It
was as if the gods dropped the fog on Iwset to focus his
attention and blot out his petty concerns in the city
beyond.

Gone was the Spiked Serpent writhing in stellar glory
from the zenith across the sky to curl around the Pole
Star. Nowhere did the handsome, well-built ruler of Iwset
see the gauzy white patch of the Maiden's Curls or the
distinctive pattern of the dozen stars forging the Broken
Sword of Ennea. Or the Lost Rat hunting its hole, or the
Two Dryads, or even the most distinctive of all summer
constellations, the Arms of Elysium blazing so brightly it
often blotted out lesser patterns after it rose above the
eastern horizon.

"Darkness, darkness, be my guide," Peemel muttered.

Light from his chambers spilled out to pool at his feet. Futilely, he tried to kick away this faint yellow circle cast by his reading lamp. He did not want any glimmer, not tonight, when he sought a sign, an omen, something to show he had chosen the proper direction for his soaring ambition.

"Give me evidence I am not following a fool's pathway." Peemel started to fling out his arms in supplication when across the foggy dome of sky blasted eye-searing lightning. Peemel instinctively threw up his robed arm, not in humble prayer, but to protect his face from the raging brilliance that had so quickly replaced the featureless dark. He felt his fine plush red velvet sleeve begin to smolder. The lord of Iwset beat out the tiny fires ignited by the sudden display from above. In the courtyard below his balcony where the bolt had struck bubbled a pool of churning molten rock. Blinking away the yellow and blue dots dancing in his eyes from the dazzling bolt, Peemel saw pasted onto the forbidding, utter black void above his head the familiar outline of the two moons that had always shone so cheerily on the continent of Terisiare.

As was its wont, the larger moon whose name could never be spoken aloud hid behind a veil of dancing, shifting mist. Its crescent beauty might have foretold rain as it tipped to one side to spill its watery load. Peemel shook his head and turned his attention from the moon to its smaller companion. Such folk tales of rain and wind did not serve him now. He dealt in facts—in power—not superstition. What did it matter if rain *did* fall on Iwset? Weather meant nothing when the fate of the entire continent was at stake.

A sign. He needed a sign. For this he studied the lesser moon of Iontiero.

The small moon with rugged, shadowy features had produced the effulgent lightning that had set his robe to smoking and singed his eyebrows. Peemel tossed his head and smoothed out the long black hair caught into a ponytail by a jeweled ring at the back of his neck. No embers threatened his carefully tended hair, and disease did not fall from the heavens.

"Again," he whispered, intent on the tiny moon as it raced across the sky. Did Iontiero move more quickly than usual on its endless journey this night? Peemel thought it did. As it raced like a frisky thoroughbred, it spat tiny green and blue sparks. Those sparks touched the fabric of the sky and changed it subtly. Was it purple he saw instead of black after the electric caress? Or could it be that the very sky itself caught fire and burned like that massive active volcano far to the south, the Anger of the World?

"Give me another sign," Peemel said forcefully, demanding complete acceptance of his plans before he committed himself to a course from which there could be no turning.

He staggered as another cascade of sparks from Iontiero rolled and twisted sinuously into thicker cords of energy and, joining into knotted cables, exploded anew. They writhed like snakes given hideous life greater than anything on the planet.

The sky parted, and for a moment Lord Peemel saw only the two score stars comprising the Arms of Elysium. Then the constellation vanished behind renewed assault by Iontiero. Now the snapping whips of energy grew brighter and cast light as bright as day—but only on the courtyard below him.

Lord Peemel stared down, and a sneer twisted his lips. In the courtyard, face raised to the heavenly display, Abbot Offero stood next to the rapidly cooling crater of lightning-struck flagstone. The Inquisitor Magnus in his blood-red robe appeared barely human as the scintillant light from the pool at his feet cast light upward and bathed his face in shifting shadows.

The abbot's dark eyes locked with Peemel's colorless ones.

"My sign," Lord Peemel said. He opened his hands and gestured carefully so there would be no question about his benefaction. Abbot Offero bowed deeply, pulled up his cowl, and vanished into the night. The die was cast.

The die was cast in darkness, and it pleased Peemel.

He glanced at the sky and saw Iontiero's feverish

activity dwindle and finally cease. From the darkness billowed leaden storm clouds to replace the sight- and sound-deadening fog. Within seconds a steady, bone-chilling cold rain fell. The spot where Abbot Offero had stood sizzled and hissed, clouds of condensed steam rising into the downpour.

Peemel laughed long and deep as he swung about and strutted back into his chambers.

"The abbot has been given his sign from above and has acceded to my authority. I am now both secular and religious leader of Iwset," Peemel said, settling into the chair behind his writing desk. Before him stood his two most trusted advisers.

"This is wrong, Lord Peemel," spoke up Apepei, a mountain dwarf barely tall enough to look his liege straight in the eye, even after Peemel sat. The dwarf walked forward on his bandy legs and pounded a massive gnarled fist on Peemel's desk, causing pens and other implements to bounce. "He will bring only death to our citizens."

"Death to traitors bothers you, Apepei?" Peemel asked in a deceptively mild voice. A lesser man would have been cowed by the implied threat. Not Apepei.

"Offero puts to the question any who opposes him! His fear of all things magical burns out reason in his pea-sized brain." Seeing Peemel remained unmoved by this, Apepei changed his argument. "The Inquisition brings fear and hatred of *you*, milord."

"A ruler," smoothly cut in Digody, Peemel's other adviser, "can govern through love or by instilling fear in his subjects. Love is far riskier, because who can know the changing tide of a citizen's goodwill? A friend today can become an unsuspected and implacable enemy tomorrow. Fear, on the other hand, remains a constant principle, giving a firm and immutable foundation for sensible rule."

"You would turn the people of Iwset against him!" shrieked Apepei. The dwarf jumped up and down, his hands curled into huge fists. He thrust out his lantern jaw and glared at the much taller Digody. Stepping forward belligerently, it appeared that Apepei would swing at the other adviser.

Burning red eyes peered down at Apepei, and Digody's thin hand reached out deliberately to close around the hilt of a dagger shoved into his belt. Apepei's barrel chest rose and fell faster.

"Go on, draw on me in your ruler's presence!" cried Apepei. "Spill my blood, you foul backstabber! I am willing to die for my opinions! Lord Peemel," Apepei said earnestly, his jutting chin pointed directly at his liege, "do not give Offero the power he seeks. He will slaughter thousands of innocents in your name. The Inquisitor carries a sickness in his breast. This sign tonight carries many interpretations. Do not let it begin slaughter of innocents in your name!"

"What's this?" Peemel frowned. "Abbot Offero is ill? Not the Tes Fever?" Try as he might, Peemel could not keep a shudder from racking his muscular frame. He feared no one in battle. He did not even fear Digody and his endless intrigues, subtle poisons, and occasional assassination attempts. Dealing with them was a mere inconvenience compared with tapping Digody's brilliance as a political tactician. But Peemel did possess a great terror of sickness. A blight could sweep across him and reduce his power to that of a mewling infant, or decay his strong good looks with pox, or even cause his potency to diminish.

Disease brought too many things to fear to a man of his puissance. He opened a drawer in his desk and ran his fingers over the handy cloth soaked in cleansing carbolic acid. It stung his flesh, but destroyed all chance of infection. Trying not to be too apparent, Peemel wiped his hands on a dry cloth and shut the drawer.

"There is sickness of the mind as well as of the body," Apepei said. "Offero tastes blood; desire for power becomes insatiable. There will never be enough citizens put to the question. Not enough will scream for mercy and be shown none. It matters naught if he finds any trace of evil magic. Every death feeds his vileness. And he will plunge downward to commit ever more excesses . . . in your name, milord. He will do it, and the people will blame *you*."

"My esteemed companion forgets one salient point," Digody said in a voice wrapped in silk and oil. "Abbot Offero is a valued ally. Who among us can spit in the eye of the Inquisition and survive? The power of the Church is immense and extends far beyond the borders of Iwset. We cannot offend those wielding such power. The sacred warriors might not be able to defeat Iwset's fine army, but to embark on other ventures would be folly."

"I intend to expand my borders soon," Peemel said thoughtfully. "The sign this evening shows the truth of that move. See that the witch who predicted this impressive display is rewarded—by turning her over to Abbot Offero!"

He hardly listened to his advisers squabble over this order. This was not the first time they had disagreed, nor would it be the last. Yet each had splendid ideas, given the proper guidance from the throne. His throne.

Peemel sucked on his teeth as he thought of the intense darkness that had been ripped apart by the lightning from Iontiero. He interpreted this omen to mean he would rise from a sea of mediocrity to stand preeminent along the coast—after he waged a successful war against the island fortress of Jehesic. And war it must be, he knew after this night. Lady Edara would never seriously entertain his offer of marriage, even to avoid conflict.

"Yes," he said, more to himself than to either Digody or Apepei, "beyond the borders of Iwset. I must reach out to others. What better instrument to use than the Inquisition? And Abbot Offero? He will be loyal for some time, after witnessing tonight's omen."

"Omen? A rain storm drenched him, nothing more," complained Apepei. "Did it also wash away all your good sense, milord?"

"You skirt treason, Apepei," Peemel said, his colorless eyes fixing on the mountain dwarf. "I value your opinion. I am not bound by it, however. In this, you are wrong. Digody speaks with greater clarity and purpose. We will encourage the Inquisitor to perform his religious tasks, and if he oversteps, it might become necessary to remove him."

"And when you do so—if it becomes necessary, of course," Digody said easily, "you will be seen as the savior of our people, Lord Peemel. That will leave you in complete control of both civil and religious forces."

"This is what you want? You desire command of Abbot Offero's sacred warriors?" Apepei gaped at such audacity.

"The sacred warriors fight well," Digody said.

"They fight like mindless fanatics," Apepei said angrily. "Using them is like swinging a sword by its blade. It can be done, but will eventually cut your hand to bloody ribbons. The more vicious the fighting, the more risk you run with such a tactic."

"They would prove a worthy addition to our own crack troops, if they are used judiciously and well," Peemel went on, ignoring Apepei. "The war with Jehesic will not be easily won. Lady Edara's marine forces are considered the finest for half a thousand miles north or south along the coast."

"You see not only loathsome alliance with Offero, but also war with Jehesic in a lightning storm?" Apepei shook his head. A shock of unruly red hair tumbled into his eyes. He tugged on it until the pain forced him to stop. He brushed it from his wide-spaced green eyes so he could stare unblinking at his liege.

"Interpretation of this sign shows why I am better suited to the throne than you, dear Apepei. Now go, both of you. Go and prepare for the arrival of the Inquisition—and Abbot Offero's revered assistants, the Wizards' Bane."

Apepei snorted in disgust and stomped indignantly from his lord's quarters. Digody watched the dwarf leave, then turned to Peemel. He held his hands together in a bony tent in front of his chest, as if he sought to share a prayer with his ruler.

"What is it, Digody? I dismissed you as well. There is much to do, and I see I must rely more heavily on you in the days to come. You are feeling unequal to my growing dependence on you?"

"No, Lord Peemel, not at all. Never have I shirked any task you set me, and this is one I cherish. Rather, I have another matter to discuss, one not suitable to mention in front of any other."

"Even Apepei?" Peemel laughed. He knew his advisers hated each other. That pleased him; it had taken years to find precisely the right mix of counselors. Apepei provided a much needed brake to Digody's raging ambitions for rule, just as Digody prevented Apepei from being too conservative in his decisions. One checked the other and allowed Peemel to rule more effectively.

"The dwarf shows a righteous streak that might cause both of you great uneasiness in the future," Digody said.

"What are you saying?"

Peemel pushed upright in his chair and studied his adviser more closely. He had never identified Digody's race, nor did it matter. Peemel valued good advice and ruthless ambition, both of which Digody had in great quantity. His advisor's skeletal hands with a hint of proto-finger nubs at the sides bespoke of something other than human, as did his fierce, feral red eyes. Seldom did Digody push back his cowl to reveal his hatchet-thin face with its large, straight nose, stringy mustache, and ludicrous goatee. There was something slightly . . . wrong . . . about his aspect. Perhaps it was the full lips, or the way the ears were pinned back along the sides of Digody's head. Peemel chose not to consider the matter at length.

"This is a delicate matter, milord," Digody said, choosing his words with great care. His red eyes focused on Peemel, Lord of Iwset, who would rule the coast of Terisiare for limitless miles in both directions, as if taking the man's measure and finding him wanting.

"Delicacy be damned!" raged Peemel. "This night I have been given a sign of victory. Alliances are being forged. War will be declared should Edara reject my offer of marriage, as we both know she will. These are not matters to be bandied about carelessly."

"Do not allow your displeasure to rule you," Digody said, more sharply than before. "I bring you news only recently discovered about Lady Pioni."

"Pioni?" Peemel frowned, trying to place the name. Slowly running his fingers down the front of his velvet robe, he stroked across his groin. Memory returned. "Yes, Lady Pioni. My wife, my fourth wife, she was. What of her?"

"She was your wife for almost a year, milord," Digody said. "While this was fully two decades ago—"

"Twenty-two," Peemel said, memory flooding him now. Pioni of the corn silk hair, the azure eyes, the lissome form. She had possessed great beauty, as did all his wives, but little more. Pioni had not been clever enough to even try to assassinate him.

"She cared little for you, milord," Digody went on, as if Lord Peemel had not interrupted. "Lady Pioni was as unfaithful as she was fruitful."

Peemel sat straighter and fixed his adviser with a cold stare. "There was no get," he said.

"Ah, milord, we have recently uncovered evidence that there was a bastard."

"Impossible. Pioni would never have—" Peemel clamped his mouth shut. It had been too many years, and he had only faint memory of the woman. He had no idea what she would or would not have done. A minor noble's daughter, Pioni had married above her station. Had she brought along a commoner lover? Peemel could not say.

"What does it matter?" Peemel said finally. "She died." He had executed her to marry his fifth wife, Lady Dylees, who had died under mysterious circumstances only a month after the nuptials. Lord Peemel thought she had died of poison meant for him, though he had never uncovered any specific plot.

"She, as you say, died, but after giving birth. You were less than attentive to her, milord, or so it is reported," Digody said quickly.

"Even if she gave birth while my wife, the bastard has no claim to Iwset." Something deep inside told Peemel that Digody would not have brought up this matter had it not been more serious.

"An elf stole away the child to protect it," Digody said.

"Elves, pah," grumbled Peemel. "Meddlesome, they

are, but they are merely annoyances, not true difficulties. Wherein lies the proof of this bastard's claim to my throne? No one would believe an elf."

"The sigil, milord, the elf carried away both child *and* sigil."

CHAPTER
3

THE ONLY SOUND IN THE BURIAL GROUND WAS the soft slip of shovel into freshly turned dirt. Deguhe worked slowly but steadily under the dim light of the mist-shrouded crescent moon whose name could never be uttered. Smaller, electrical nimbus-ringed Iontiero had yet to rise, but the grave robber did not need its illumination for his grisly work. All day Deguhe had waited for the funeral party to leave so that he could get to work. The grieving widow and her two burly sons had lingered so long the robber thought he might have to find another cadaver. He had heaved a sigh of relief when the old hen and her cackling brood finally left the cemetery a few minutes past sundown.

Then Deguhe had only to fight off the Scavenger Folk for his prize. He had not spent much time chasing them away; they were frightened of their own shadows. A true grave robber need not compete with them and lose a jot of treasure if he showed enough truculence.

Deguhe showed enough—and more.

His sharp-edged shovel struck the metal lid of the coffin. He dropped to his knees and hurriedly brushed off the spot until he saw a mirror finish reflecting his own image. Deguhe smiled, revealing broken, blackened teeth. He canted his head this way and that, pushing back dirty strings of braided hair to reveal a flat face with a mashed nose, watery eyes, and a furtive expression.

"Looking good," Deguhe said to himself. He climbed to his feet and started digging with a feverish urgency that soon uncovered the entire coffin top. Deguhe again dropped to his knees, this time using the flat shovel blade to pry open the sealed coffin. A tiny puff of fetid air gusted forth.

The grave robber inhaled deeply. This was the stuff of dreams, this sigh of the dead. He took another breath, then wrestled aside the lid to get a better look at the corpse inside, decked out in simple but clean clothing. Deguhe reached in, using sharpened fingernails to rip away cloth, revealing a necklace of gold links, a bracelet set with a semiprecious stones, boots of decently cured leather and solid soles, and a belt with small prayer slips hidden inside pouches.

Deguhe pulled the prayers from the secret pockets in the belt and tossed them aside in a wild paper shower. The belt, now emptied of its blessings for a swift and easy transit to the netherworld, circled the grave robber's scrawny middle. The belt hung loosely about his frame, but Deguhe hardly noticed. He had found enough wealth this night to justify his work.

He stood and turned in a full circle, examining the cemetery for those he knew were spying on him. Deguhe's cracked, bleeding lips curled into a smile when he saw dark movement. He rushed across the burial ground and waved his arms wildly.

Crouching behind a rundown mausoleum, Maeveen O'Donagh whispered to her companion, "What's he doing? Who is there?"

"Hush, my dear," Vervamon said as he pushed past her for a better look. His sinewy hand lingered for a moment longer than necessary on her arm, then slipped free. He hastily scribbled a few notes on a sheet of folded foolscap. "We are only observers, not participants. As such, we must never meddle as the ritual theft unfurls for our edification."

Maeveen snorted in disgust at this and lifted her pug nose. It offended her that the grave robber stole the few baubles from the dead, and it galled her even more that Vervamon refused to put an end to the pilfering in favor of making interminable notes. Within shouting distance, her company of seasoned soldiers lounged about their campfire, swapping improbable and probably obscene stories. Any one of her crew could easily dispatch this thief and allow the dead to make a safe journey to the netherworld.

For all that, Maeveen was willing to do the chore. She had fought far worse battles in her day.

She knelt, settling her sword and making sure her dagger did not rattle against the wall of the marble mausoleum as she spied on the grave robber. Tugging her dark green cloak about her shoulders, she watched the grave robber yammer at shadows. Maeveen squinted a little and made out dim shapes. Her gorge rose as she recognized the other occupants of the cemetery.

"Ghouls," she said. "The grave robber strips the corpse of its valuables, then lets the ghouls eat it."

"A symbiosis, a perfect union for both parties," Vervamon said, chortling. He scribbled until one side of the foolscap held his tiny curlicue observations, then flipped it over and continued to write briskly.

"The sound of your pen against the paper will alert him," Maeveen said in disgust. "Or *them*." She pointed to the trio of dark silhouettes drifting like puffs of vile mist toward the open grave.

"What does he do with his ill-gotten gain?" mused Vervamon. "Deguhe, I heard him called back in that quaint village. What was it called?"

"Tondhat," said Maeveen. She sat on her haunches and watched the ghouls begin their awful dinner. Gobbets of newly dead flesh vanished into their gaping maws and turned her stomach. For years she had waged war and seen death, some violent but none easy. She never quite became inured to it, but she accepted it as a hazard of her chosen profession. She was a good soldier and a capable leader.

Watching these creatures devour their gruesome meal turned her belly more than any clean death ever could.

"Back in Tondhat he has others who depend on his expertise at robbing the dead," Vervamon rambled on, his baritone voice taking on barely suppressed excitement. "Deguhe is a one-man industry keeping dozens alive on this impoverished coast, such it was when I came this way two decades back, and it has not changed one whit. Fascinating that the economical underpinning of the area remains so stable. How can it be explained?"

"It wouldn't be in such a sorry way if their lord didn't tax them into oblivion. Peemel and his wars." Maeveen spat some of the gumweed she chewed to illustrate her opinion of the lord of Iwset. She had traveled widely with Vervamon and on her own, and always the petty tyrants sucked the life juice from honest, hardworking men and women through taxes for unwanted wars.

Vervamon did not hear her. He moved from behind the mausoleum and slowly went to where the ghouls feasted. Vervamon clucked his tongue, unconscious that he did so, sidling closer and closer until he stood over the beasts.

Maeveen drew her sword and strode out to stand beside him. The academic was almost a head taller, but what bothered Maeveen more was that he possessed an animal magnetism that caused everyone to notice him no matter how many others surrounded him. The thick thatch of snowy white hair helped, as did his height, but the set to his firm chin, the way he held his broad shoulders and back as stiff as an Ironroot, his very being demanded attention.

For all her years in military companies, Maeveen knew such charisma, such command presence, was impossible to learn. And she had tried. Her soldiers obeyed her through earned respect and the knowledge she had gotten them out of dangerous situations safely, not by the unreasoning obedience Vervamon commanded so easily. Her soldiers listened to her, but if Vervamon walked into the room, all eyes went immediately to him.

Maeveen both hated and admired that. She had been drawn to Vervamon like so many others. She had learned about the academic's priorities the hard way: through experience. Maeveen's hand tightened on the hilt of her dagger as she considered how easy it would be to slide it into Vervamon's back.

She made no move to draw her sword either, like all the other times this idea had occurred to her. She had loved him once. Now she alternately hated and grudgingly respected him.

"This will complete my study of the scavenger culture. Jenns and Boyzen will eat their own hearts out when they see how my findings contradict theirs—and mine are backed up with solid field observation and detailed interrogation of the subjects."

"You're going to talk to *them*?" Maeveen would rather use her sword on the ghouls. That would keep her a decent distance from them and their gore-smeared faces. The only drawbacks to such a scheme that Maeveen saw were having to clean her shining steel blade later to keep it from corroding and that the ghouls would fall into the same grave as a decent person.

"I say, you there. I would have a word with you!" Vervamon revealed himself to the hungry ghouls. They shied and started to bolt. If they had seen only Maeveen, they might have. The commander of Vervamon's company sneered when she saw the ghouls fix their round, sooty eyes on the academic. Again that personal magnetism of his ruled the day—and night, she thought with a touch of bitter memory.

"Got to get over this," she muttered to herself. She moved to the foot of the grave and stood, trying to hold in her loathing for these despicable creatures Vervamon was speaking easily with for his infernal essay. Her attention drifted from the academic and his flesh-devouring beasts to the periphery of the cemetery. Not a quarter mile distant her soldiers camped. A single blast on her combat whistle would bring them to her aid.

Maeveen frowned, wondering why such thoughts bothered her. She and Vervamon were alone in the cemetery with the scavenging ghouls, but perhaps the grave robber remained behind, foolishly thinking to waylay them. The woman tapped her short fingers against the wire-wrapped sword hilt, then took a firmer grip and went to reconnoiter. Something was not right. Only a few steps into the dense forest surrounding the cemetery showed her the reason.

Those spying on Vervamon were inept at hiding themselves, once Maeveen decided to look. They stepped on twigs, brushed against rustling leaves, scrapped along rough-barked trees, and made more noise than a squad of recruits passing in review at a full-dress parade. Maeveen sheathed her sword and drew her dagger, preferring the shorter length for killing in the tangle of undergrowth surrounding her. She dropped to her belly and wiggled forward. For once she was glad she was not as tall as Vervamon. Her short stature allowed her to wiggle into tight places the white-haired academic could never manage.

She came out of a thicket directly behind two spying men. Maeveen inhaled deeply, catching the scent of votive candles, and knew the identity of those spying on Vervamon. Moving like a whisper of summer breeze, Maeveen shifted forward. Her dagger point came toward the first novice's heart and stopped after pricking the skin enough to draw blood and a cry of surprise.

"You both die if you try anything," Maeveen said. The other robed man tried to flee. Maeveen O'Donagh kicked out and caught his ankle, sending him to the ground face-first. She stuck her dagger a little deeper into the novice's chest. He stiffened and gulped.

"You have nothing to fear from us if your heart is pure," the novice gasped out.

"You have much to fear from me, you—" Maeveen bit off her detailed description of the novice Inquisitor's character and improbable lineage. Her sharp ears caught the sound of others coming through the forest toward them.

"You are a child of evil," the fallen cleric shouted. Maeveen kicked him into silence so he would not warn the approaching party of Inquisitors. She had little respect for their skill as fighters, but like biting flies on a lion, they could swarm and overwhelm her.

"He is right," said the novice as her dagger tip edged toward his heart. Maeveen took such an argument as a sign he was recovering his courage and would soon be willing to die for his church if it meant he brought a heathen to sacred justice.

Maeveen jerked him around to use as a shield. A quick step back and she felt the solidity of a tree to prevent attack from behind. From the darkness came three men, then four more, then a dozen to ring her completely.

"The life of a novice is nothing to us," came a resonant voice. Maeveen tried to identify which of the hooded figures spoke, but could not. "His death only strengthens our resolve."

"He's one less to torture innocents," Maeveen shot back. She gauged her chances of escape and didn't find them too good. Killing a few Inquisitors might give her some satisfaction, but escaping to argue with them later, both verbally and over the length of a sword, pleased her more. Maeveen realized the wisdom of living to fight another day.

"What is the meaning of this incredible impudence on your part?" boomed Vervamon. He strode up, pushing his way noisily through the bushes to stand beside Maeveen. He grabbed the novice by the cowl and shoved him forward. Maeveen pulled away her dagger.

"You have infernal gall to interrupt my research!" bellowed Vervamon.

"Infernal research?" cried the vicar leading the Inquisitors. "You freely admit your interrogation of those godless monsters is an abomination in the eyes of the Church?" The glee of vindication burned in the Inquisitor's voice. He stepped forward and threw back his hood, revealing himself for the first time, the golden badge of office dangling around his neck.

Maeveen considered a cast of her dagger and decided against it. Killing an Inquisitor General did nothing to alleviate the threat posed by the others, whom she counted at thirteen. Keeping her dagger allowed her to kill more than one; never throw away a perfectly good weapon.

"You twist my words to your own misguided end," Vervamon countered in an equally menacing voice. "Finding those unable to endure your tortures is the true diabolical behavior. How many have you slain this week, you bloody-handed butcher? I have documented the Inquisition's course across Terisiare and can show you seldom badger those most able to contest your charges."

"Your entire infernal company has been taken prisoner," the cleric said proudly. "How many of them carry the seed of evil in their heart? We shall discover this when they are all put to the question."

"You could never have taken my soldiers so quietly," Maeveen said hotly. She forced herself to calm. The Inquisitor taunted her, wanted her to angrily expose her views as heretical so he could justify the coming torture. He had not captured her company without a long and bloody fight; Maeveen had trained them personally. Her chief lieutenant, Quopomma, would have never surrendered, no matter the odds. Her other lieutenant, Iro, would go fighting to her own grave if a cleric so much as approached her with a drawn sword. Iro's entire family had been slaughtered by the Inquisition. The tall, gangly woman hated them with a passion matching Maeveen's own.

"The sacred warriors are prepared to strike and die for their belief. Can the same be said of your godless mercenary killers?"

"They aren't godless, or for hire to the highest bidder," Maeveen said, "but they are killers." She turned the dagger in her grip to prepare for the fight she knew to be forthcoming. The Inquisitors had not shown any weapons, but their threats convinced her they were ready to skirmish. She hoped she acquitted herself well before they brought her down.

"Arguing with the like of this one is pointless," cut in Vervamon. "Who leads your pack of jackals? I would speak directly with the one who sent you to nip at our heels."

"Silence," ordered the Inquisitor. "Do not tempt us to a hasty decision. You have commerce with grave robbers and ghouls. We know who has shown true piety this night."

"They intend to murder us," Maeveen told Vervamon. She moved closer to him to better defend the unarmed academic. As little as she regarded him as a person, she respected his devotion to knowledge and truth. And duty compelled her to defend him. She and her company were more than baggage carriers. They had been contracted to protect Vervamon during his travels.

"You will be put to the question for determination of the true extent of your sins. Then you will be executed," the Inquisitor General said, with some glee entering his tone.

The circle began to draw tighter around them. Maeveen shifted the dagger to her left hand and drew her sword to fight. For the first time she saw the gleam of the clerics' weapons as light from the crescent moon filtered through the leafy ceiling and glinted off naked blades.

"Stop!" The command echoed through the forest. All turned, Maeveen, Vervamon, and the Inquisitors, to see who spoke so forcefully.

CHAPTER

4

ISAK GLEN'DARD LIKENED HIS JOB TO WALKING across quicksand. A single misstep and he would vanish tracelessly. Even if he performed well, without mistakes, he ran the risk of coming away befouled with the vile muck all around him. As he pondered this, a smile came to his pleasant face, giving it light and affability. He even broke into an off-color song with gusto as he strutted along Iwset's main street, leading from the city-state's walled byways northeast to the Eln Forest, which was infested with noisome elves.

He dealt with the most disreputable of all denizens and relished the challenge.

"Top of the morning to you, good sir," Isak said to a man who turned to stare at him, politely touching the felt brim of his floppy gray hat. The liquid white Serra angel feather thrust into the woven hatband rippled languidly from the motion. Isak received a sour glance in return for his amiable greeting, but it troubled him little. He had nothing but contempt for those who lived in Iwset under Lord Peemel's thumb, but he had nothing but admiration for the vast wealth flowing through the port and into the lord's coffers. Some of that treasure would rattle soon enough in Isak's purse for doing what he did so well.

He was a go-between, an intermediary, a diplomat without portfolio, and was well paid for his services. Isak drew his fine cape around him and settled it squarely on his shoulders to hide the panoply of weapons he carried. Over the years, the ability to reach out in any direction and find a dagger waiting had saved his life more than once. It never paid to trust those who paid him any more than it did to have sympathy for those involved in his intricate negotiations.

"You, the one with the feather," came a grating challenge. "What is your business?"

Isak turned and faced the red-robed Inquisitor. He responded to power; there was no reason to deal with this minor functionary.

"My business is with the Inquisitor Magnus, and I fear I am late. The abbot does so show his irritation when he is denied my timely presence, you realize. Now what is it you require of me?"

Isak watched the flow of emotion on the young cleric's face. Isak wanted to laugh uproariously but held back. Such fear! It had taken only a split second to find the precise point of vulnerability in this one's armor. When he spoke with Abbot Offero it would be no different. It never was.

"Why, nothing, good sir. Blessings upon you," the cleric said, actually bowing as if Isak were an Inquisitor General.

Isak watched the young man blunder along, then almost run when he reached the street corner. Such fear emboldened him. Then, Isak sobered, realizing how dangerous was the game he played. Arrogance might spell his death, no matter how well connected he was in the circles of the rich and powerful. Somewhat subdued, Isak walked along with deliberation until he reached the cathedral at the end of the Street of Six Holy Virtues. Rather than enter the massive front doors, he went to the eastern side, where Offero and the other Inquisitors made their offices.

He walked through unguarded corridors directly to the abbot's office. He rapped twice, then once, and entered. Abbot Offero sat in a well-padded chair, staring out the window at the endless, hypnotic motion of the surf off the Ilesemare Sea. Isak wondered at the thoughts being entertained in the cleric's brain.

"I have brought the information you required," Isak said, dropping a packet of papers on the Inquisitor Magnus's table. Offero nodded without turning from his scrutiny of the sea's whitecapped waves. "Is there any further service I may perform?"

"You have been paid well for this treachery. What do the papers say? The ones you brought."

"It is a breach of etiquette for a courier to—"

"What do they say?" Abbot Offero turned and fixed his gaze on Isak. Seldom had the go-between seen such desolation on the face of anyone wielding the power this man did. "You are no fool. I do not employ fools. You know what is contained in those documents."

Isak saw no point in lying. He cleared his throat, framing the information in the best possible light.

"Lord Peemel wishes for the Inquisition to destroy his enemies in Iwset and beyond. He would use the sacred warriors as his own, and will do so once the populace begins to fear and loathe you for your diligence in pursuing heretics."

"He gives me license to persecute heretics, then uses that against the Church," Abbot Offero said in a tired voice. "It is as I thought. I find myself caught on horns sharper than any minotaur's. Move to crush the heretics and I will become the focus of the people's hatred. Refuse and my Church will suffer, vile magic running rampant among the unrepentant and destroying the foundations of our world. We cannot permit such devastation as that which occurred during the Brothers' War to happen again. What do you suggest, Isak?"

The question took Isak by surprise. He fought to retain a neutral expression—and his current body's shape. Being a shape-changer had advantages and, as he knew so well now that he faced a man devoted to wiping out any hint of magic, disadvantages. Isak covered his confusion by knocking the packet of papers to the floor. The time it took to kneel, face shielded from Offero's gaze, allowed him to control his emotions once again.

He laid the packet back on the table.

"I have always found it expedient to solve the most immediate problem first," Isak said carefully.

"Expediency." Offero spoke the word as if it were a curse. "Perhaps you are right. We have a sacred duty to enforce the Church's will and hold down the use of magic in order for the masses to benefit the most. The wrongs suffered by the people through careless use of magic must be avoided, even if means garnering their hatred." He took a deep breath and turned back to watch the eternal sea's waves. "Even if it means Peemel will turn those I protect against the Church."

Isak almost spoke again, to tell the cleric of the need to send his own spies into Peemel's ranks. More than the soul of Iwset was at risk with the lord's plans for war, and more than religious belief had to be employed. But he did not. It was not his place. A go-between never took sides.

He turned and left without another word. He had warned Abbot Offero truthfully of the danger he faced, giving documented proof as he had been instructed to do.

Now he had another mission. Isak touched the single sheet of instructions hidden in his clothing, then patted another pocket to reassure himself he still carried the map showing the way toward the Forest of Eln and the elves. He had to get on the road quickly or Digody would be irate. Isak had learned quickly not to anger the feral-eyed adviser. Few suffered the consequences of such folly and lived.

CHAPTER
5

YUNNIE'S CLUB WHIRLED THROUGH THE AIR TO smash into the elf's sword arm. The elven warrior grimaced in pain and clutched the injured biceps. He snarled and reached around awkwardly to grab at his dagger sheathed at his left hip—but he never made it. From the other side of the game trail, where the elf had worked to lay his intricate, deadly trap, Mytaru lowered his shaggy head, bellowed, and charged. The tip of his right horn caught the elf in the gut and lifted him high. Mytaru tossed his head and sent the forest dweller sailing through the air to land heavily in a thorny shrub a dozen feet away.

"Finish him, Yunnie. Don't let the marauder get away!" The minotaur struggled to regain his balance, his legs tangled in the net dropped by the elf.

Yunnie had no stomach for killing the severely injured elf, but it was obvious the warrior was the scout for a larger war party intending to invade the Urhaalan's valley. Too many minotaurs had been caught in the net traps laid by the elves over the past month, some had broken legs, and two other minotaurs became so seriously ensnared that they strangled to death in the elaborate

traps. Any chance at negotiation had died when the first
minotaur perished from a noose-like netting around his
bull neck.

Retrieving his gnarled war club, Yunnie went to do as
his friend and new blood brother requested. For all his
distaste for slaughtering an injured elf, Yunnie had additional pressures on him to do so. Increasingly, he had
been accepted into Mytaru's clan, at first living apart
from them, then invited into their homes, and finally
sharing household responsibilities as a junior family
member. After sharing his Place of Power, Mytaru had
accepted him as a blood brother and promised to recom-
mend to the clan elders that Yunnie be adopted into Clan
Utyeehn, the proudest of all the proud Urhaalan minotaurs. With such commitment, Mytaru ought to be given
as much in return. It was his due as a blood brother.

Yunnie looked down at the injured elf, who clutched
his belly as blood from the deep horn wound oozed out.
Only hatred flashed across the elf's thin face. He sneered
and tried to move so he could kick out at Yunnie.

"Why are you doing this?" asked Yunnie, easily avoiding the feeble movement. "We mean you no harm."

"Traitor to your own kind," spat the elf. "What do you
know? The minotaurs lie to you, and you let them. They
invade our forest and ambush us without mercy. Do you
know what it is like to be burned to death? We must
carry this war to them, or we will die. Of course you
mean us harm. You mean to kill us all!"

"They have no interest in your forest. They find the
woods too boring, and there is not enough farm and pasture land for them. No Urhaalan minotaur has left the
valley to invade your homes," Yunnie said, knowing this
for the complete truth. The time of the ascendant full
double moons approached, a most holy time for the
minotaurs, the Celebration of Tiyint. Under the light of
the twin moons, young minotaurs were accepted into the
herd as adults, wedding proposals were issued—and challenges of honor were made.

Clan Utyeehn might declare war on the elves under the
bright illumination of small Iontiero and mist-shrouded

Fessa, but they would never leave their valley on a raiding party. That would come one week later, after the moons' sacred glow faded and the Time of Resolution demanded action on all covenants made.

"I do not lie. No minotaur has invaded your forest in the past two weeks. We prepare for holy times."

The elf coughed and tried to spit at Yunnie again. "Like your masters, you lie, too! Who killed my wife and two sons? Who killed my brother and sister? In the last week, they all died at the hand and horn of minotaurs!"

"You've seen this with your own eyes?" Yunnie was astounded. He could not deny the elf's sincerity or righteous anger. He would soon die of his wound and had no reason to lie. The time he had spent with elves had convinced him of their basic honesty—and their hardheadedness. In their way, they were as bullheaded as a minotaur.

"I was with a hunting party when the minotaurs attacked. Food grows scarce in the forest. Even the Ironroots become restless and begin to wander away in search of better forests. But the Forest of Eln is mine! And my family's. And my people's. Would that I had died with them killing you and your filthy bull-headed monster allies!"

The elf struggled to sit up and draw his dagger again. He sank back, too weak to fight anymore. His eyes blazed angrily at Yunnie, then the light faded in them.

Yunnie reached over and closed the elf's eyelids, the sight of blind, dead eyes disturbing. He took it as a sign, an omen of a violent and fruitless future unless he acted to bring peace between minotaur and elf.

"He's dead? Good," Mytaru said with satisfaction. He limped from where the elven net had cut into his leg and stumbled away into the clearing. "We can expect others to follow soon. I'll sound the alert." Mytaru threw back his head and vented a deep-throated bellow that caused the very ground to shake with its intensity. Yunnie felt the vibration pass from the ground up his legs and resonate within his chest as Mytaru communicated all they had found using the minotaurs' wordless song.

Yunnie glanced at the dead elf and then followed

Mytaru, waiting for his friend to end his baleful communiqué.

Mytaru sagged with the last note, then sucked in a deep breath, expanding his barrel chest to the point Yunnie thought it would break. The minotaur shuddered and turned to Yunnie.

"The others have been alerted," Mytaru said.

"We should declare a truce so we can talk with the elves. This is a great misunderstanding."

"Is that what you call it?" Mytaru snorted, nostrils flaring wide. "I am glad we 'misunderstood' him to death." Mytaru rubbed his injured leg. "The net might have ended up around my neck, or yours."

The implication was obvious. If a minotaur with a bull's neck could die in an elven noose, Yunnie's life would be forfeit with a single snap. He took no offense at Mytaru's insinuation of weakness.

"He said he came in retaliation for a raid that killed his entire family." Yunnie watched Mytaru's reaction. "The elf's entire *clan* was murdered while he hunted," he said, changing it to a concept Mytaru might better deal understand.

"It was a sad time for him when his clan was slaughtered," Mytaru said solemnly. "I regret I was not the one to do it."

"He said minotaurs were responsible—this past week."

"When none leaves the valley because we prepare for the Celebration of Tiyint? What a liar that elf was. But they are all like that. They say we want to steal away their forest. What good is Eln or any like it to a minotaur? We need our mountains, our valleys, our farms and pastures. What are we without our Places of Power? No elf was ever born who could speak without lying."

"I know none of Clan Utyeehn raided the elf's village," Yunnie said. "What of other clans? Perhaps one of them decided to take the war directly to the elves."

"No Urhaalan would leave the valley now, regardless of clan. There is much you do not know, Little Bullock," Mytaru said, using Yunnie's clan name to show mild rebuke coupled with affection.

"Tell me now, Mytaru. Why isn't it possible that one Urhaalan warrior ravaged the elf's community? One minotaur is more than a match for a dozen elven warriors, after all." Yunnie did not try to hide the harshness in his words. Mytaru seemed oblivious to such sarcasm.

"You are almost one of us in Clan Utyeehn," Mytaru said with carefully chosen words. "All adult males purge themselves before the Celebration of Tiyint. This requires continual ceremony, carefully chosen foods, and nocturnal vigils. While our souls would not be forfeit if we left the valley during this purging, it would be foolish to risk it." He shook his head slowly. Yunnie saw dried elf blood glint on his right horn as Mytaru rocked his head from side to side. It would remain there until after the forthcoming rituals. "None of Clan Utyeehn would risk a foray into elven forests, since we will declare war at the Celebration of Tiyint. We are not so impetuous that we cannot wait for the Time of Resolution."

Movement caught Yunnie's eye, and he returned hastily to the elf's body. In the few short minutes he had been away, the elf's bow and arrows had been stolen. A quick study of the ground showed no footprints.

"Goblins," he muttered, knowing how quickly they could sneak in and rob a corpse fallen in battle. It might be Scavenger Folk, but they were not as sly in their gleaning. Yunnie started to shout to Mytaru, but the sight of a dozen minotaurs trooping from the woods along the path the elf had been booby-trapping stifled any outcry on his part. The minotaurs walked with determination, weapons cradled in their arms or slung across their broad backs. They saluted Yunnie silently when they saw the dead elf, then picked up the pace and vanished in a few minutes as they sought the remainder of the elven war party.

Yunnie ought to have been proud at this victory, satisfied with the day's excursion, and eager for the Celebration of Tiyint to begin. Instead, he felt a gnawing hollowness inside.

Anticipation of war was never pleasant.

CHAPTER

6

"WHO ORDERS THE INQUISITION'S RIGHTEOUS servants to halt in their sworn duty?" The crimson-clad Inquisitor General whirled about, his robe hem softly rustling against the ground as he thrust his sword at the woman who had spoken.

Maeveen O'Donagh scowled and edged closer to Vervamon to protect him. He had no sense when it came to dangerous situations, never seeing peril, but only opportunity to learn more about esoteric topics. As far as Maeveen was concerned, the newcomer was scant improvement over the Inquisitors. The tall, regal, dark-haired woman was decked out in lavish purple velvet robes, jewels sparkling from gold and silver rings on each of her slender fingers. The clasp holding a fur-rimmed cape at her swanlike throat harkened back to the days of antiquity with its craftsmanship and ornate design. Everything about the woman bespoke wealth and power—and easy acceptance of others instantly obeying her every whim.

Maeveen did not fail to note, under the regal finery, a more functional outfit suitable for rougher conditions. Even on those clothes, gold medals and parti-colored ribbons marched up onto one shoulder showing the woman's penchant for adornment.

"Do put away your holy weapon, my Lord Inquisitor," the woman said expansively, moving forward as if she walked on air rather than the littered forest floor. "In this night air, it might become . . . rusty." Hand gestures more in line with dismissal than acceptance shooed away the cleric, causing his face to redden in anger. Such insolence did not distract Maeveen, who recognized the old tactic of diverting attention to gain control.

"I am no lord," the Inquisitor said tartly. "I am only a servant, as are we all." Steel-edged words were intended to put this interloper in her place. The attempt failed.

"When next I have tea with him, I really must get Abbot Offero to explain your ranks to me," she said, sniffing, as if this rebuke inconvenienced her. "You are— what? The commander of a company of sacred warriors?"

"You speak with the abbot?"

"Of course. All the time. And Lord Peemel, also. He sent me to fetch these daring explorers." She smiled radiantly and glided forward, hand outstretched. The smile on her lips failed to reach her indigo eyes, Maeveen thought. Maeveen lowered her sword point to stop the woman's advance, but her employer easily sidestepped the blade and accepted the woman's hand, kissing it in a courtly fashion.

"It is *so* good to find formal manners have not died, even in the wilds far from the center of Iwset."

"One so lovely forces manners upon even barbarians," Vervamon said, casting a sidelong glance at the Inquisitor General. The cleric fumed, swishing his sword back and forth in the air, obviously wishing he could place the academic's neck under its keen edge.

"I am Vervamon, a simple traveler and investigator of cultures, customs, and curiosities on our glorious continent of Terisiare."

"A simple traveler?" The woman laughed. The sound set Maeveen's teeth on edge, though it was meant to be lighthearted. "You are so much more. You are *famous*, Sir Vervamon."

"If I can be nothing more than your humble servant, my fame would surely be immortalized." Vervamon bowed deeply, still holding the woman's bejeweled hand.

"I am Ihesia," she said, as if introducing herself as the queen of all Terisiare.

"You say that Lord Peemel sent you?" Maeveen interrupted. She now worried about more than this woman and the pack of Inquisitor wolves yapping about. Her troopers ought to have overheard such byplay and rushed to her side. They were not camped on the other side of the continent, after all. When she found who had slacked off on sentry duty, she would have their ears on a decorative necklace.

"You might say that," Ihesia said, smiling. The chill Maeveen felt froze her bones. "Then again, you might simply say I am doing him a favor, since my own travels brought me in this direction. Who can deny a ruler such a small favor?" She turned her charm on Vervamon again. The silver-haired explorer basked in the glow, though Maeveen knew it was as cold and insincere as the light from Iontiero.

She glanced through the leafy canopy to the sky. Iontiero shone with its reflected light, and to the east rose a three-quarters waxing greater moon. This promise of a double full moon was not a good omen, if Maeveen believed in such things. Luckily, she did not.

"What would *you* say if we find our current studies too demanding to abandon on a whim?" Maeveen shot back.

"That would be most unfortunate, especially since the rest of your company has already begun the trek to Iwset."

"What? My soldiers left their posts?" Maeveen stared open-mouthed. Her soldiers did not abandon their post because some court harlot ordered it. Maeveen had fought beside most of the company and trusted each and every one with her life. Those whom she had not saved in the heat of battle had saved her. They were not of such weak mettle to flee, leaving Vervamon and her to their own devices. Still, Maeveen felt a curious satisfaction that her company had fallen prey to this trollop rather than the Inquisition's soldiers. Ihesia obviously commanded more than the artful toss of her head, her knowing wink, and her outthrust chest.

"What are you saying?" cut in the Inquisitor, as outraged at this as Maeveen.

"Why, nothing save that Sir Vervamon's party has graciously accepted my lord's invitation to join him at the royal court in Iwset. You will find the city a delightfully quaint place, I am sure. Nothing like other fabulous places you have visited, but certainly . . . amusing." She held out her arm for Vervamon, who took it. "You simply must regale me with tales of your travels and your bravery."

"You will never believe this, but I have seen the Pillars of Dawn, a sight few have ever witnessed," Vervamon said, as if launching into a lecture at a university class. He warmed when he saw an appreciative audience in Ihesia. "Those milky cylinders march like obedient soldiers from horizon to horizon, but only on certain days of the year. They are whiter than any marble and stretch from the churning surface of Ilesemare Sea to the very top of the sky."

Vervamon rattled on, portraying as miracle what Maeveen considered nothing more than a clever mirage. She had been there and seen them at the same time as Vervamon two years earlier, but she could never describe them in such poetic terms. The pillars were bred by poisonous fumes venting from fumaroles underwater less than a mile out to sea. While their rising steam in its orderly pattern might be picturesque, the stomach-churning stench was all she remembered.

She turned to the Inquisitor General.

"How many troops accompany you?" She watched him carefully for any hint of a lie. He was too taken aback by his failed attack and failure to defend his faith to build a falsehood successfully.

"These," he said, indicating the score of red-robed troopers slipping from the darkness of the forest to form orderly ranks behind him. "No more."

"I had three score fighters and bearers," Maeveen said. "They would not easily surrender."

"Three score?" The Inquisitor's eyebrows rose in surprise. He quickly hid his reaction. "You bring massive barbarity to our enlightened shores. The question must be put to many of your rank, I am sure, to determine the true depth of their heresy."

Maeveen spat at the cleric's feet and strode off, following Ihesia and her new conquest. She wished Vervamon would think more with his brain and less with other parts of his anatomy. It would be far safer for them all.

CHAPTER
7

YUNNIE'S BELLY GRUMBLED FROM LACK OF food. He clutched the few miserable blades of grass he had been given to live on, then threw them aside. For six days and nights he had not eaten and had slept only in short naps, worse than not sleeping at all. But he had made good progress up the steep valley walls and along the rugged terrain rimming the Urhaalan domain. He knew others enduring this initiation ceremony had not fared as well.

What Yunnie lacked in strength he made up for in agility and ability to climb sheer rock cliffs. The minotaurs following him found the going increasingly difficult. For them this was truly a rite of passage. For him it was simply going without food. He rubbed his growling belly again as a sharp pain lanced into him.

Sitting on the edge of the precipice he had just scaled above fuming pits of molten rock, Yunnie stared out across the paradise that would be his permanent home once he was accepted into Clan Utyeehn. Then truly Mytaru would be his brother—and he would be Mytaru's brother. Yunnie let the idea roll about in his head, spinning and whirling from lack of food though it was. He liked the idea of having a family. He remembered nothing of his parents. They had died when he was very young.

Yunnie frowned as vague, hazy memories intruded. Memories of elves—or a single elf. He could not grasp it firmly and bring it into full recognition. Small, he had been so small, but the elf had protected him. Or was it only the lack of food bringing him visions?

Visions were a necessary part of the rite. He had to listen to what went on within himself and use it to bring new purpose to the clan. Only through the young bulls would Clan Utyeehn advance, or so said the elders. At this Yunnie had to laugh. The minotaurs were steeped in hidebound tradition. How any new member of the clan could change centuries of ritual and tradition, he did not know. The males gathered for their spiritual debates while the females conducted their own more pragmatic rituals, preparing for birth and life.

This gave Yunnie pause. Marriages were determined by the females through some esoteric method that he had never heard discussed. Would he be considered a likely candidate, or would he be like many of the bulls and never be chosen, for whatever reason? He thought of Mytaru's Uncle Mehonvo, a wise bull, but never selected for marriage because he lacked a horn and had no strong female clan member to plead his case. Perhaps if Mehonvo had lost the horn in battle it might have been different, but the bull had been born with only the one horn. No one wanted to mate with a mono-horned minotaur.

Yunnie rubbed the sides of his aching head. He need not think of marriage into another clan, he knew. He had no horns at all, those most prized of minotaur attributes. He closed his eyes and wobbled a bit, pulse thundering in his temples. For some reason, his eyes shot open, and he peered down at the base of the cliff.

Huge tongues of flame shot skyward, making Yunnie break out in a sweat. He stared, eyes wide, at the sight of a creature far below him, moving about and shooting gouts of fire with every gesture. From where he stood, Yunnie thought the monster opened its mouth, revealing the fiery bottom of Hell as it tipped its head upward toward him.

Eyes like living coals fixed on him. A bulky finger pointed and flames leapt upward. Yunnie threw up his arms to protect his face from the blast of hot air gusting past. He rocked and almost fell. Catching himself, he pulled back from the edge of the cliff and tried to find the flame creature again. It had vanished—as if it had never been there.

Perhaps lack of food caused Yunnie to be lightheaded and to hallucinate.

"It wasn't there. It was a vision," he said, but in his gut he knew this was not right. He had seen a similar creature earlier when Mytaru had shown him Clan Utyeehn's Place of Power. Or had it really been the same? Had he imagined this one?

Holding his head and listening to his stomach yowl in hunger, he no longer knew what was real and what was a product of his starved brain. Getting to his feet, he stumbled on. He had to reach the clan caves before sundown for the final part of the ceremony.

Tonight the two moons would be ascendant and full in the sky.

Yunnie and three young minotaurs stood shoulder to shoulder across the mouth of the cave. From the rocky depths came a mournful howling that caused gooseflesh to ripple along his neck and upper arms. He knew this was part of the ritual and that the worst part lay behind him. He had shown endurance by circling the valley in the allotted time and returning with the seven sacred flowers. Yunnie clutched them tightly, as did the other survivors of the ritual. There had been five who started. One had failed to arrive at the designated time and place.

Yunnie wondered what might happen to that one—or what had already happened to him.

Then new bellowing erased all thought but of what lay ahead in the darkness.

"Only those who are stout of heart and loyal to Clan

Utyeehn need advance. To all others, *death*!" came the resonant words.

Yunnie shivered again, but stepped forward quickly. The other minotaurs followed him—in time to avoid a heavy log studded with spikes that slammed down from the darkness above. If any had hesitated to enter, he would have died.

New dread filled Yunnie. He had thought the ordeal reaching this place, the starvation and the hunt for the sacred blossoms, had been the end. Now he feared he might not survive. Was that the meaning of the flame monster he had seen? Was the vision warning him of his death and eternal damnation for thinking he might ever belong with the Urhaalan minotaurs?

Memory of Mehonvo's advice to him a month ago rose to torment him. "Panic kills, only not as slowly as indecision." Yunnie realized any half-heartedness on his part would have meant his death. How could he quell the fright rising within? Looking left and right at the others did nothing to settle his rising terror.

"We are minotaurs and will not flag," Yunnie heard one mutter, using this simple phrase to focus his courage. "The herd survives, even if individuals die."

"We'll all become members of the clan," Yunnie said softly. His quiet words did much to ease the harsh fear he felt. "Never doubt that."

The three glanced at him, clutched their sacred flowers more firmly, and walked forward with more determination. Yunnie kept pace with them, never flinching as feathery, sticky *things* fluttered across his face, dragged over his bare chest, tangled in his hair. Light touches turned to sharp pain as unseen knives slashed at him.

Yunnie kept walking, never turning to meet his attackers. He realized this was another part of the ceremony: he had to show faith in the herd and stay with the other three. To stop to fight alone spelled disaster. He had to overcome his human instincts in an effort to think and act like a minotaur.

Unexpectedly entering a large chamber, Yunnie and the minotaurs with him stopped and stared. Two immense shafts cut with cruel power through the roof, which opened on the clear night sky.

"The time is near," came an echoing voice. "Enter the Chamber of Truth and await your destiny in the hallowed light of the moons."

Yunnie found a worn spot on the cave floor and stepped into it, feet apart enough to brace him against any attack. As he looked up, Yunnie knew he need only wait. Iontiero already filled one shaft and bathed him in its brilliant, reflected light. In the other rocky chimney angling away to his right he saw Fessa slowly working into full ascendancy.

He stiffened slightly. In Shingol he had been brought up to believe it was blasphemy to speak the larger moon's name. Minotaurs had no compunction about speaking of it and its power in their society. Yunnie fought old habits and superstitions. The name "Fessa" formed on his lips as it fully entered the opening. Its brilliance became ringed by the darkness of the nighttime sky.

Twin beams illuminated Yunnie, pinning him to the spot in the middle of the vaulted cavern. He closed his eyes and wobbled slightly from weakness—and exultation.

"Have you the sacred flowers?"

"I have the seven left as our legacy by our forefathers," Yunnie said, following the text of the ritual Mytaru had drilled into him.

"How do you see?"

"I see truly by the sanctified light of the twin moons," Yunnie replied.

And so it went, Yunnie never pausing in his replies. After each response, another member of Clan Utyeehn entered and slowly circled to issue a challenge and question. Seven circuits passed before a blossom was plucked from Yunnie's hand. With his forty-ninth and last reply went his final flower.

"Welcome to the herd of Urhaalan, Clan Utyeehn, House Mytaarun," welcomed his blood brother. Mytaru clasped Yunnie to him, then pushed him away and passed over a sword and bundle of grasses. For a moment,

Yunnie worried he was supposed to eat the grass. Sidelong glances at the other three minotaurs convinced him this was purely symbolic of the herd providing fellowship for its members.

"With the sword you will defend your brothers, with the grasses you will feed your sisters," Mytaru said solemnly. "Do you accept these burdens?"

"I accept these burdens with full knowledge and joy."

"May your life benefit the herd," Mytaru said. The other minotaurs echoed this sentiment. "As a member of the Urhaalan herd, what are your innermost thoughts? What did your vision tell you, Brother Yunnie, our Little Bullock?"

Yunnie swallowed hard as he remembered the fiery prophecy revealed to him. He swayed slightly, then knew he was obligated to speak the truth.

"The herd should seek to parley with the elves. It is wrong for minotaur and elf to fight. If we do not follow this course, we will all die in fire."

Silence fell like a heavy blanket on his shoulders. In the dancing light of the twin moons Yunnie saw his apocalyptic vision failed to match that of anyone else in Clan Utyeehn.

CHAPTER

8

"PRISONERS," MAEVEEN O'DONAGH GRUMBLED. She used her whetstone to sharpen her dagger for the hundredth time since Ihesia had beguiled Vervamon into accompanying her to Iwset.

"Well-treated prisoners," said her second-in-command, Quopomma. The ogre used a shining cloth on her sword until the smallest scratch vanished. "They do not march us far every day, for which my aching feet thank them. And food? I've killed better, but their food is free and tasty enough." Quopomma let out a belch to emphasize her opinion of the provender supplied by Ihesia's quartermaster.

"Prisoners, nonetheless," Maeveen said. She cast her dagger underhanded, to sink it half a blade deep into a tree a dozen paces distant. Satisfied, she retrieved it and carefully removed the sap from the keen-edged weapon.

"We seldom have eaten so well," Quopomma said, "and Vervamon keeps to himself."

"He keeps to Ihesia's bed," Maeveen said angrily.

"I thought you were over him," the ogre said. She grunted and scratched her head, finding a nit. Strong, blunt fingers plucked it from her tangled, ropy hair and crushed it wetly. "I cannot see what you humans find attractive about him. Certainly not his physique, and brains are overrated."

"You've given this some thought?" asked Maeveen, amused in spite of herself. "You prefer a stupid man to a smart one?"

"Vervamon has certain analytical qualities, granted, but common sense? Where is that? Why would he require your services—or mine—if he had a speck of good sense?"

"His thoughts soar beyond what he sees," Maeveen said, not wanting to defend her employer and former lover, but finding herself compelled to do so. "More than this, he fits everything together to reveal the truth. His observations of the local burial customs are nothing less than brilliant."

"Who cares about any grave? Excepting our own, of course."

At this Maeveen had to laugh with a bitterness she made no effort to conceal. "At least we have avoided ours for the time being, thanks to Ihesia snaring us so easily."

"That one hides much—between her ears, at least. I cannot say she hides anything physically, dressing as she does in such thin gowns. Haven't seen her in decent clothing since she got rid of those fancy-dress fatigues she wore."

Maeveen bit at her lower lip. She hated Ihesia more every day. Ihesia did nothing to hide her tempting beauty from Vervamon, who snuffled after her like a bull in rut. Worse, the Iwsetian woman was not simply a beautiful slut. She was as good a tactician as she was pretty. Interrogation of Quopomma and Iro convinced Maeveen that Ihesia had been responsible for the Iwsetian soldiers' deployment and the easy capture of Vervamon's entire expedition.

Maeveen knew, even outnumbered, her soldiers would have fought if there had been even a hint of a chance to escape. Ihesia had cut off every avenue completely and wrapped this defeat in silken threads that bound more securely than any chains. What soldier would protest decent food while being allowed to keep his or her arms?

She looked up as Vervamon and Ihesia emerged from the ornate tent where the two spent much of their time. Too much. Vervamon motioned her over. Maeveen glanced at her lieutenant, who smiled crookedly and shrugged her massive shoulders. The ogre seemed to be saying, "What can any of us do?"

"What is it?" Maeveen asked Vervamon, walking slowly toward them.

"We will enter Iwset on the morrow. Keep the company in top condition, Captain."

Maeveen wanted to ask him if that was all he required, but bit back the sarcastic question. She always kept her soldiers in fighting trim.

"What of our captors?"

"Captors? Captain, please. Dear Ihesia does not hold anyone prisoner. Rather, she protects us."

"*Protects* us?" blurted Maeveen. "From what? The Inquisitors?" She spat at the mention of the clerics. The red-robed sadists had trailed some distance behind Ihesia's mounted company, only slowly falling back and finally vanishing when they discovered a small knot of possible magic-using heretics along the way.

"War brews in Iwset, despite its peaceful appearance," Vervamon said, as if precisely repeating Ihesia's words. "Lord Peemel desires an audience with me to discuss what I have seen in my adventurous travels."

"I can muster a bodyguard and—"

"No!" snapped Ihesia. More calmly, she said to Vervamon, "There will be no need for this, Sir Vervamon. My protection is all you need in our fair country. The people of Iwset are no threat to you."

"Of course, my dear, but Maeveen—Captain O'Donagh—accompanies me everywhere. She is an astute observer and quite handy when I need to obtain certain intelligence from the locals."

"None of this will be necessary," Ihesia said in a sharper tone. "Lord Peemel requests only *your* presence on a very secret and important matter, a matter only a man of your stature and intelligence can deal with effectively." She ran her long-fingered hands up and down Vervamon's arm.

"Very well," Vervamon said. He cleared his throat as he gathered his thoughts. "Captain, tend to our company. We shall continue our journey in the morning—wherever it might take us."

"What?" sputtered Ihesia. "You cannot! Lord Peemel—"

"Then Captain O'Donagh and another officer will accompany me. You cannot expect a gentleman of my station to entertain a ruler of a city-state with less than this for an entourage. Unless I am considered some sort of prisoner, as Maeveen suggests so incautiously."

Ihesia chewed at her lower lip, realizing Vervamon had trapped her. She had to either admit they were her captives, or permit Vervamon to act like the honored guest she claimed him to be. In a few seconds, Vervamon had put the situation into focus and forced her hand.

"Very well. You and two officers," Ihesia said. "More might be considered . . . provincial."

"We would never be so . . . provincial," Vervamon said, smiling broadly.

"Wait! Just like that, you'll dance off into the heart of this, this *person's* power?" Maeveen sputtered, words refusing to come to make her point. Vervamon had chosen to accede rather than fight. She longed to whip out her dagger and remove Ihesia permanently. A single slash would cure most of their problems.

Then she realized Ihesia's death would start a bloodbath. The Iwsetian general's troops still surrounded Vervamon's smaller, less well-armed company.

"We come in peace," Vervamon said. "There is no reason Lord Peemel will not deal in a straightforward manner with me. Twenty years ago, perhaps more, now that I reflect on it, his hospitality was lavish, and he put me up in his palace. Can he respond with any less civility now?"

"He wants only to greet a true hero, Sir Vervamon," cooed Ihesia, adapting quickly to her small defeat.

"Why, yes, of course he does. The stories I have to relate to him! Why, there was the time—"

Ihesia and Vervamon returned to her tent, the flap softly sighing after them. Maeveen growled, stared with cold anger at the closed tent, and slowly lifted her eyes to the twin moons. Iontiero slipped under a bank of thin clouds and the greater moon, with its foggy shroud, showed concentric, pale bands around it like some celestial bull's-eye on the early morning horizon.

Maeveen O'Donagh counted that as a truly evil omen.

CHAPTER
9

THE MECHANICAL CONTRAPTION CLANKED AND rolled precariously, causing Isak Glen'dard to grab the vibrating controls for support. He craned his neck and poked his head up from the front of the rusted, magically motivated device. His eyes went wide when he saw he was heading for a sheer drop off the road and into the Ilesemare Sea.

Working frantically at the wheels and pedals, he tried to steer the conveyance away from the cliff. He saw he was not going to succeed. For a moment, he shape-changed from human to something more snakelike, allowing him to slither up and out through a narrow hatchway. Atop the conveyance, he reasserted his human form and got his feet under him. Strong legs propelled him from the doomed device. He hit the rocky ground as the sputtering mechanical device tumbled over the cliff and fell into the sea.

Isak brushed off his fine clothing and checked his pockets for the packets of paper containing his permits for safe passage—and a letter of marque from Peemel, should it be necessary for him to commandeer a vessel and attack any ship from Jehesic. He snorted in contempt at such a notion. He was no sailor. He preferred to have both feet firmly on the ground. At this thought, he walked to the edge of the cliff and stared at the twisted wreckage a hundred feet below in the surf.

"Close," he muttered to himself, then his usual good humor returned. He had come far using the now wrecked device. It had taken hours of hard work to animate it and learn its complicated controls, but the machine had brought him to the edge of the Eln Forest. The conveyance had provided speed and comfort unlikely to be supplied by even the finest coach service from Iwset, had one existed.

Isak sauntered along, whistling a tune he had learned in a Sarinth brothel about a wandering minstrel, two bawdy lasses, and a magical device. The song took away some of the inner conflict he experienced over this mission. He had already betrayed his employer by delivering the details of Peemel's plot against Abbot Offero— another one of his employers. Isak chuckled, trying to order those lined up to pay for his inestimable services.

"For Digody do I come north," he said, stopping his song long enough to lick dried lips. A cold breeze belied the warmth of the summer sun burning his flesh. So it always was along the coast. "But he pays in coin of silver, while my other employer uses gold—and more." Isak touched his weighty purse.

An easy task, this one. He need only find the dark sorceress in Digody's employ and relay orders to her from the skeletal, red-eyed adviser. Or were Digody's orders also those of Lord Peemel's? Isak frowned, trying to make sense of politics in Iwset, then gave up. It was none of his concern. He relayed messages, he dabbled in some diplomacy, but mostly he collected vast wealth from any willing to pay for his services.

As he walked, the sun dipped lower into the sea, and his senses warned of a watcher. Isak's stride never lengthened, nor did it slacken as he maintained his path. The bonfires in a small fishing village, mayhap Shingol, if he remembered aright, cast a glow to push back the twilight. The odor of searing fish caused his nose to wrinkle in distaste. When he returned to Iwset with his report, he needed to treat himself to a decent meal.

Isak abruptly spun and faced a patch of darkness within darkness.

"I would deliver my message and leave this insignificant land," he said to the shadow. Small movement convinced Isak he was not merely speaking to a phantom. The inchoate darkness shifted and flowed, then took shape as the reason for his journey presented herself to him.

Isak bowed deeply, in his most courtly manner, knowing such courtesy was wasted. From the depths of the woman's cowl glowed two eyes, silver and catlike. Other than this small concession to humanity, she betrayed no hint of belonging to any race Isak had ever seen. No wonder she and Digody conspired. They were a strange species adrift on this wild coast. This did not bother Isak; he often dealt with those far less human than this shifting mass of shadow.

"You come from the south?" a soft voice asked, drifting on the sea wind and turning it even colder.

"I bring you greetings from our lord and master," Isak said, trying not to smile as he spoke. "From Lord Peemel I bring greetings and the wish that you act as his emissary, preventing any alliance between elf and minotaur and human."

"I should set them at each others' throats?"

"How you accomplish your task is of no concern to me." Isak handed over the thick envelope containing a single sheet of paper, waving whitely in the wind for a moment. With a pass of a shadowy hand that never approached his, the instructions vanished. It took no talent on his part for Isak to recognize a wizard of surpassing power. Her casual use of magic told him she held no fear of the Inquisition, Lord Peemel, or him. Caution descended on Isak like a veil of calm, ordering his responses and guiding him through dangerous shoals. He bowed a little deeper this time.

"No alliance," mused the figure with the bright eyes. "Why?"

"War brews between Iwset and Jehesic. Lord Peemel would not like an alliance capable of joining with Lady Edara's forces to line his northern border. A dispute, however insignificant, prevents a unified front to thwart him. Already his legions fight in the south. When war with Jehesic is declared, Peemel will fight on two fronts. He does not need a third to sap his city-state's strength."

A faint red nimbus grew around the dark figure, forcing Isak to use more of his magical skills to thwart it. He made no mention of her attempt at beguiling him with mind-numbing spells. That was not his place as go-between. However, he now knew Peemel had a more able lieutenant doing his bidding in the Forest of Eln and beyond than even the lord of Iwset realized. To whom should Isak report this potential for trouble? To Lord Peemel? Or to his other employers?

To all of them, should the price for this delectable tid-bit be sufficient?

"There will be some small dispute along Iwset's border," the dark shape assured him. With that simple state-ment, Isak knew Peemel need worry long and hard about more than Jehesic. This one had designs of conquest of her own, and they did not include sharing power with any upstart conqueror from Iwset.

"I will return to report this most excellent assurance," Isak said.

"Who receives your first report?" came the disarming question.

Because of the compulsions the dark woman had laid upon him in spite of his efforts, Isak found himself speaking the truth.

"Digody," he said, the name slipping all too quickly from his lips. He bit his tongue to prevent further revela-tions. He need not have worried. The sorceress laughed in such a fashion as to freeze Isak's blood, then she stepped back to disappear into the suddenly chilly sum-mer night. She had learned what she wanted and had no more need of the courier.

Isak stood for several minutes after the wizard's depar-ture, finally recovering his usual good humor. A smile bent his lips slightly, and he turned back south, his gait loose-jointed and easy as he walked. He had been sent to deliver that sheet of paper in its well-sealed envelope, for whatever reason. Perhaps the paper contained a slow-acting poison to kill anyone touching it. This might be Peemel's way of controlling an agent beyond his power to control. Isak was certain of nothing but that there would be other couriers sent from Iwset to report on this dark agent provocateur's dealings.

It mattered naught to Isak Glen'dard. He would report to Digody, then to Lord Peemel. And then he would deliver a more detailed report to the employer he valued above all the others.

The song rising to challenge the moons tumbling across the sky was one of Isak's composition and, as a result, bawdier than the others in his repertoire.

CHAPTER
10

CAPTAIN MAEVEEN O'DONAGH STRAIGHTENED her tough green-and-brown splotched field uniform, acutely aware of its drabness amid the gaudy peacocks in the honor guard escorting them into Lord Peemel's presence. She tried to tell herself none of those uniforms were useful in a swampy or thorny terrain where camouflage meant more than show. A hand drifted to her breast and noted the lack of medals there. In her day she had done many heroic acts, but seldom had anyone noticed, any save those she rescued from certain death. That was the price she paid for not swearing allegiance to a lord and, instead, serving as a private soldier for those who impressed her most.

A slow smile curled her lip. That freedom and the knowledge she had won loyalty through devotion and unfailingly honorable action might be better a reward than any hunk of metal with a dollop of colored ribbon attached. No, it *was* better.

"Don't worry your head about it. They shouldn't scare you, my pretty. You are so lovely, you put them all to shame," Quopomma said beside her, but Maeveen knew the ogre was not speaking to her. The ogre often talked to nonexistent creatures she counted on for friendship and aid. Others in the company laughed at Quopomma's fascination with her invisible friends, but Maeveen had learned not to scorn another's belief, especially anyone as filled with common sense as Quopomma. For all Maeveen knew, the creatures existed, and if they did not, no one was hurt by the ogre's occasional dialogue with them.

The military commander in her caused Maeveen to pay strict attention to the shining weapons swinging at the guards' sides and the other soldiers lining Iwset's main street. Ahead, Ihesia waved to the gathered citizens crowded behind the soldiers as if she were a returning conqueror, and perhaps she was. The way Vervamon grinned stupidly as he walked alongside Ihesia showed how he was a human prize collected in combat softer than Maeveen preferred. All that remained was for his silver-haired head to be mounted on the wall of Ihesia's trophy room.

Ihesia might be a dangerous conniver, but the guards around her were more dangerous, Maeveen saw. For all the shine to those fine weapons, they were well used. Contrary to her first impression, they were no mere peacocks, these guards. Maeveen guessed they might be Lord Peemel's personal bodyguards, ready to defend their liege at the first sign of any threat. Her feeling of walking into a trap increased as she saw the other guards along the route. If the lord's guard was comprised of veteran soldiers, these watching had seen recent, hard battle and were hungering for more souls to steal. More than one of the fighters made as if to draw and rush forward, only to be held back by hard-bitten officers.

"The company," Maeveen whispered to Quopomma. "Are they safe, do you think?"

The ogre shrugged massive shoulders. "I saw them laughing in the camp, but they were so easily taken I have no faith in their skills or good sense anymore. If only I had not been away from camp with the hunting party . . ." Quopomma snorted in disgust at Lieutenant Iro and how easily her sentries had been overcome.

"Those soldiers along the street are fresh from battle. Who does Lord Peemel fight?"

"Everyone," the ogre said in disgust. "Anyone, from what I have heard from his soldiers. He expands his southern borders constantly, honing his men in preparation to fight Lady Edara since she refused his offer of marriage."

"Edara of Jehesic?" Maeveen let out a whistle of disbelief. Peemel played a very dangerous game if he thought to attack the island of Jehesic. Maeveen had spent a few months there early in her career learning marine tactics. Never had she seen, before or since, such elaborate works to hold back attack, or such highly trained warriors who fought out of loyalty for home and monarch.

"None other. With Jehesic added to his crown, Peemel sees nothing between him and control of the entire coast. Inland from Iwset, who can say? Rumors abound of battle between minotaur and elf. But Peemel cares nothing for that, since he will be preeminent on the sea and able to force all to pay exorbitant harbor fees."

"He's nothing more than a pirate," Maeveen said, watching the troops from the corners of her eyes. The column led by Ihesia marched directly into a gleaming palace, fashioned from a white stone Maeveen could not identify. With streams of uninterrupted wealth flowing through his ports, Peemel stood to grow even richer and more powerful.

"A pirate he may be, but one with force of arms behind his corruption," Quopomma said. She shrugged her shoulders again, settling the bandoliers holding her swords. Deep in her throat grew a rumble that caused Maeveen to place a hand on her own sword hilt. Such a sound from the ogre always meant trouble.

"The cleric over yonder," Quopomma said, explaining her . "Another of the damned Inquisition lackeys."

"That one's an abbot, if I remember their garb," Maeveen said, knowing she'd accurately identified the prelate of Iwset. She forced herself to relax in spite of wanting to draw her sword and run the man through. Dark eyes fixed on her fleetingly, then dismissed her to fall on Vervamon. In that glare she saw no hint of mercy or forgiveness. "An Inquisitor Magnus, one of the Church's worst butchers."

"I can take him out with a knife toss," Quopomma offered.

"Later," promised Maeveen, "unless I decide to kill him myself and fail." She had no more love for the Inquisition than did Vervamon, if for different reasons. He opposed them on a purely philosophical level, as much for restricting free travel across Terisiare as anything else. Her hatred ran deeper, with more emotional conviction.

Maeveen walked faster, leaving the abbot behind. She passed under a low arch, having to bow her head to keep from banging into the spiked lintel, then straightened and found herself in an immense audience chamber. Gold leaf decorated the walls in what she considered salacious patterns. Her nose turned up at such public display of lewdness better hidden behind drapes than shown to all who entered. It was a measure of the lord's contempt for his visitors, she decided.

"Welcome!" boomed Lord Peemel from his throne. He made no move to rise, keeping his hands curled around the emerald-studded armrests and his posterior on a plush purple cushion. Peemel shifted his weight slightly, crossed his legs, and lounged indolently against the ebony throne. "Your fame precedes you, Vervamon!"

"Delighted, I am sure," Vervamon said. He walked forward and bobbed his head slightly, his piercing eyes never leaving the lord. A darkness came and went from Peemel's face at this impudent failure to show proper fealty. An amused smirk replaced the ire.

Maeveen looked about to be sure Peemel had not ordered the archers stationed high on mezzanine to fire. Any ruler who forced all entering his throne room to bow their heads to prevent banging their foreheads was capable of ordering those same heads chopped off. For all her anxiety, Maeveen saw nothing to indicate that Lord Peemel was inclined to slay Vervamon, in spite of his obvious irritation at the academic's irreverence. Even the

dozen advisers standing silently around the room showed
no inclination to speak up.

The only positive sign in the entire room, other than
Peemel's seeming amusement at Vervamon, was the
absence of the Inquisition's minions among Peemel's
advisers. The last people Maeveen wanted to deal with
were the Inquisitors and their vicious torture instruments designed to pry forth their version of the truth.

"Ihesia speaks highly of you, and I have never heard of
any scholar with greater standing," Lord Peemel said. The
smirk never left his lips, as if he found everything he said
amusing. Much to Maeveen's relief, this contempt was
not lost on Vervamon.

"I seek truth, no matter where it might lie,"
Vervamon said, green eyes locking with the Iwsetian
lord's. "I seldom find it in such lavish audience chambers. You seem not to remember my earlier visit, but
your hospitality was adequate then. Now it is nothing
less than sumptuous." Vervamon made a sweeping gesture, encompassing not only the audience chamber but
the rest of Iwset.

"You need only remain here for an audience with my
people. Then you would hear truth, both spoken and
implied."

"I am sure," Vervamon said dryly. He rubbed his hands
together in an unconscious gesture, showing that his
attention wandered. Vervamon needed something more
intellectually challenging than banter with a petty warlord
to keep him engaged.

"Milord," broke in Ihesia, ignoring the angry glare from
her liege, "your time is too precious and other matters
press us all. I am sure Sir Vervamon would be most interested to hear of your intriguing offer."

Maeveen O'Donagh saw the byplay between Ihesia and
Peemel, wondering at the tension. Were they lovers?
Probably. A woman such as Ihesia held her position using
many silken strands. Maeveen could not, however, decide
what that exact position in Peemel's court might be. The
soldiers deferred to Ihesia, as did the Inquisitors, but
Peemel was competing with the tall, dark-haired woman.

He tried to impress her with his power, as if that were in doubt.

A courtly coup? Maeveen would have to send Quopomma bar-hopping to listen to the soldiers and their concerns, to find out alliances and pitfalls.

Even as this thought crossed her mind, Maeveen sighed in resignation. Ihesia had snared Vervamon's entire company with no trouble. Getting involved in politics would only entrap them further, as if they fought quicksand sucking them ever deeper. She counted on Vervamon's quickly aroused sense of boredom to get them free of the city-state and its intrigues.

"Offer?" asked Vervamon. "You kidnap us and force us to come here to listen to what you so blithely call an 'offer'? I am outraged at such behavior!" Vervamon straightened and presented his best "offended academic" face to the lord of Iwset.

"I hardly call your accompaniment of Lady Ihesia a kidnapping, Vervamon," Peemel said. His fists banged on the arms of his throne, yet he held a more visible display of temper in check. Maeveen wondered if Ihesia's presence was the reason, or if some other motive controlled this impetuous, wrathful man.

"We were not free to continue peacefully on our way. My studies of Terisiare burial customs were interrupted by those red-robed thugs—"

"Sir Vervamon encountered a patrolling band of Abbot Offero's sacred warriors," Ihesia cut in smoothly. "It was unfortunate that they thought Sir Vervamon's *study* of grave robbers somehow implied he *approved* of such activity." Ihesia smiled. Maeveen preferred dealing with the grave robber and his ghoul friends.

"Ah, yes, the good abbot is ever vigilant," said Peemel. "We must thank him for finding these expert explorers. For, Vervamon, you see I, too, am interested in many things."

"Ah, you are giving me free passage from your city-state so I may continue my explorations? Good. Thank you, Lord Peemel." Vervamon started to go, but found his way blocked by Peemel's bodyguard. Maeveen moved closer, then glanced to the mezzanine and saw archers with arrows nocked and drawn, ready to fill her with deadly shafts if she interfered.

"Why, yes, of course, but not as your expedition is now composed."

"I do not want your troops with me. Captain O'Donagh provides ample protection, thank you."

"I am sure she has her finer points," Peemel said, never looking at Maeveen, "but that is not at issue. Financing. Do you not require funds to continue your quest?"

"Why, yes," Vervamon said carefully. "It is well known that my sponsors are eager patrons of knowledge, more eager than moneyed."

"Then it is settled!" cried Peemel, swinging around and planting both feet on the floor in front of his polished black throne. He leaned forward, hands gripping the inlaid emeralds until his knuckles turned white. "You will engage in an exploration for the Kingdom of Iwset!"

"Kingdom?" muttered Quopomma. "Iwset is hardly more than a dung heap. He might expand his borders, but he is far from being a king."

"Hush," Maeveen said, wondering at both Peemel's tenseness and Vervamon's response to the offer of funding. The Academy of Egaverral sought answers Vervamon was willing to unearth, but their endowment had been spent in full months ago. Only living off the land and careful maintenance of both personnel and matériel had allowed them to travel this far for Vervamon's detailed study of burial practices.

"Nothing is settled," Vervamon said, his resonant voice booming clearly for all to hear. "My first duty is to the sponsors of my expedition. I cannot take money from you. I am not a mercenary, nor is Captain O'Donagh's company for hire. We will not become engaged in petty regional squabbles."

"You mistake my intent, Vervamon," Peemel said. "I will fund your studies in return for your promise to find an artifact stolen from Iwset's vaults by another explorer."

"No." Vervamon's denial came sharp and without equivocation.

"You can continue your work for years with what I will give you to find this trinket!" bellowed Peemel, patience gone.

"No."

"This could be the start of something serious," said Quopomma, hands resting on her sword hilts. The ogre prepared to rush the guards standing between her and Peemel. Without knowing it, Maeveen had already positioned herself to take advantage of her lieutenant's assault so she might kill Lord Peemel. The archers might find a target in her body many times over, but unless they launched poisoned arrows, no single shaft would stop her. Peemel would pay for his high-handed ways. Maeveen hoped Vervamon lived long enough to notice the sacrifice she and Quopomma made for him.

"Why not, Sir Vervamon? Are you not curious about a symbol of power from Iwset's distant past?" Ihesia smiled, but it appeared to be strained. Her lips hardly curled and the coldness in her eyes never strayed far.

"What symbol?" Vervamon asked, hooked by the hint of archeological import.

"We should not tell him until he accepts my commission," Peemel said.

He and Ihesia engaged in a silent battle of wills, staring hard at one another. Finally, Peemel wilted slightly and sank back onto his throne in resignation. "Very well, very well. I had hoped never to divulge such information."

"Is it embarrassing?" asked Vervamon.

"I do not like to discuss the failures of my soldiers," snapped Peemel. "The artifact spirited away from my vault was nothing less than the Sigil of Iwset, the symbol of rule in my own city-state."

"Is this Sigil of Iwset akin to a scepter?" asked Vervamon. Maeveen had seen him like this before. A simple question led to another and another until he was enmeshed in a problem of surpassing complexity that would hold even his soaring imagination.

"It is. I . . . I need it back." Peemel glanced at Ihesia, who no longer smiled.

"You see, Sir Vervamon," she said, "if it is discovered that the sigil is missing, civil war might ensue. Lord Peemel, of course, is hereditary heir to the throne, but any usurper desiring to lay claim must at least have the Sigil of Iwset. It is only used for ceremonial matters of extreme importance, such as coronations, weddings and—"

"The sigil and a drop of Peemel's blood flowing in the veins," Vervamon said, nodding. He rubbed his hands together as he thought. With an abrupt motion, he stepped away and violently shook his shaggy leonine head. "I have no reason to become involved in civil matters. I will not yield to your wishes, no matter how much you offer."

Silence reigned in the audience chamber. Maeveen O'Donagh heard the hard pounding of her own heart as the full import of Vervamon's declaration struck her. Better to have accepted Lord Peemel's offer, then won free of the city-state's walls before denouncing the scheme. The archers could kill them all.

This thought stopped her from pulling her sword. She laid a restraining hand on Quopomma's shoulder.

"A moment," she whispered. "What is wrong with Peemel's confession?"

"What ruler wants it known he lost the symbol of his authority?" said Quopomma. Then the ogre understood what her captain meant. Her eyes turned upward as she counted the archers, then the bodyguards arrayed about the chamber. A dozen advisers also stood silently around the walls.

"Yes," Maeveen said. "This is hardly a secret that, should any find out, will foment civil war. He lets even his lowly archers know of the loss."

"Please, milord, let us not be hasty," said a skeletally tall adviser, drifting forward. Bony hands clasped in front of his body, blazing red eyes fixed on Vervamon, the robed man cleared his throat again before speaking. "Allow me to give this man more information in strictest confidence."

"Very well, Digody. Do so," said Lord Peemel, dismissing the lot of them.

"Does this seem too convenient?" Quopomma asked as the guards herded them from the audience chamber and down a narrow corridor to the side of Peemel's throne.

Maeveen did not answer. The same thought had come to her when Digody had advanced, like an actor responding to a well-rehearsed cue. If true, Ihesia played a role along with her liege—strictly for their visitors' benefit. She walked a pace behind a grumbling Vervamon.

"Damned inconvenience," Vervamon grumbled. "And Ihesia. What does she think she can wrest from me? I am no sleuth, finding lost pets and stolen trinkets. I am the foremost scholar of Terisiare! How dare Peemel suggest . . . "

"Please be seated," Digody said as they entered another chamber, indicating a single chair across from a desk littered with scrolls, books, and oddments. The hatchet-faced adviser noted Vervamon's interest and said, "I, too, am a scholar of sorts, though not in your league. Many things interest me."

Vervamon sank into the chair, letting Maeveen and Quopomma stand behind him. Maeveen inventoried the items on Digody's desk, but could not decide if there was any underlying theme to his collection. Vervamon, however, seemed more at ease, being assured he was in the presence of another like himself.

"It would be going too far to suggest that I was insulted by your lord's offer," Vervamon said, "but I am not a finder of lost objects. Only the memory of charity he showed a younger, poorer scholar years before holds my indignation in check."

"Ah, but I think you are intent on seeking lost objects," Digody contradicted. "You seek antiquities lost from view. Is that not the reason burial customs intrigue you so? What is given over to the netherworld in each grave? More than a simple soul, in many cases."

"Well, yes, I have found that . . ." Vervamon launched into a discussion of items buried with the dead in various Terisiare cultures. Maeveen stepped back a half pace and

tried to fathom Digody's reaction to the lecture he
received. Lord Peemel's adviser betrayed no emotion. He
might have been as intrigued as Vervamon or as bored as
Quopomma.

Beside her, Maeveen heard the ogre begin whispering
to her invisible friends. Maeveen's attention shifted from
Quopomma and Vervamon to the desk and the man sitting behind it. Outwardly Digody might be human, but
his fierce red eyes put that to the lie. His thinness and
seaweed-fine goatee hinted at nonhuman blood, but she
could not be sure, since he lacked any distinctive col-
oration. All that was certain was Digody baited Vervamon
as surely as Ihesia had—and waited to reel him in.

Maeveen hoped it would not take long for Vervamon
to realize still another trap lay ahead.

"Fascinating work, Vervamon," Digody said when the
explorer stopped to take a rare breath. "I wish we had
more time to compare notes. I have studied burial customs in the region for many years, and it is a pity Lord
Peemel failed to tell you the full importance of the Sigil of
Iwset."

"Full importance?" Vervamon shook his head, silvered
hair in wild disarray. "What could be of greater importance to a ruler than the symbol of his position?"

Digody laughed. "Lord Peemel is a complex man. He
prefers to tell people what he thinks will fascinate them
most. I am at a loss to explain how he thought you two
were not kindred spirits in this matter. The Sigil of Iwset
is a symbol of rule, true, but it is also a key."

"A key to power? One needed for the war against
Jehesic?"

"A key to knowledge," Digody said, pitching his voice
lower, into an almost conspiratorial whisper. "Peemel is
an archeologist, as I am—as you are, Vervamon. We
share more than a thirst for knowledge, however. We all
want to be the first, to be the only ones to have ancient
knowledge revealed to us."

"What are you saying? This Sigil of Iwset is a key to
what?"

"Peemel desires to be the first to enter, but if you can

recover the sigil, *you* might be the first in centuries. I admit I lust after the opportunity, but archeology is only a pastime for me, not a profession."

"What are you going on about? Tell me. Now!" Vervamon slammed the flat of his hand against Digody's desk. Artifacts jumped with the impact.

"Peemel needs the sigil to unlock the Tomb of the Seven Martyrs. But if you recover it, *you* can be the first to enter and catalog the secrets locked there."

"The Tomb of the Seven Martyrs?" Vervamon's voice carried a hint of awe—and lust.

"A crowning achievement for any archeologist. Peemel desires it, but so do I. Through you, I can bask in some of the reflected glory. If Lord Peemel enters . . . alas, he is a great man, but one unwilling to share the fame such a discovery will bestow."

"The Tomb of the Seven Martyrs," marveled Vervamon. "You know where the tomb is?"

"Yes, but the Sigil of Iwset is absolutely necessary to open the vault door," said Digody. "One mistake, one failed attempt to open the sealed entrance, and ancient magical spells will destroy everything within. All would be . . . lost." He leaned back and tented his bony fingers under his chin. The thin goatee dragged along the sides of his fingers as he nodded slowly.

Maeveen knew the bait had been cast, and now Vervamon was hooked.

"Whoever opens the tomb will not be a footnote in history," Digody said in a beguiling tone. "Whoever opens the tomb *makes* history."

The light blazing on Vervamon's face was nothing new to Maeveen O'Donagh. Every time a new discovery beckoned, the explorer's heart pounded faster, and he glowed with excitement.

He was very definitely hooked and now being reeled in by an expert angler.

CHAPTER

11

THE SENSATION OF SOMEONE WATCHING MADE
Yunnie uneasy. He hiked along the edge of the meadow
passing near a stand of trees, then quickly dived into a
cluster of low-growing bushes. He hit the ground and
rolled, coming to a prone position so he could look out
across the open space. On the far side of the meadow he
made out the dim outline of a black-cloaked figure. A tree
limb swayed and allowed a ray of sunlight to shine
directly on the spy. As quickly as the light illuminated, so
did it conceal. Yunnie blinked; whoever had been watching him so intently vanished into the thicket.

He came to his feet and made his way through the forest, more clumsily than most trained in the ways of the
forest, such as the elves, but less awkwardly than Mytaru
or any of his other new minotaur clan members. Yunnie
regretted having spent so much of his life in Shingol. A
fishing village was no fit place to live, not when fragrant
forests and vast open expanses like the Urhaalan's valley
beckoned so.

Reaching the spot where he had seen the intruder, he
dropped to one knee and studied the soft ground. The
grass had been cropped recently, possibly by a young

minotaur. The dirt had been cut up by several others passing by, but one set of prints held his full attention. Minotaurs did not wear boots.

The foot was thin and long and most of the wearer's weight seemed to go back onto the heel. The style of footwear was unusual and nothing Yunnie had seen before.

"So, someone *is* spying on us." He considered this for a moment, then changed his mind. "Someone is spying on *me*."

Asking the others in Clan Utyeehn if they had seen any interlopers had produced a vehement denial. The males spent much of their time training for the war they intended to wage, and the women worked diligently to store food and lay up supplies needed for a long confrontation, though no one thought a war against the elves would last more than a few weeks.

In that, Yunnie was not so sure. His memories— possibly hunger-induced hallucinations from his rite of passage he mistook for reality—carried him back to early childhood. An elf had tended him, or so he remembered, feeding him when he was hungry and singing songs like the wind through tall trees when he was meant to sleep. The iron will and indomitable spirit shown by this half-remembered—or purely imagined?—elf convinced him any war would be lengthy and hard-fought. In spite of their superior strength, the minotaurs could not defeat the elves easily.

"I can negotiate a truce," Yunnie said to himself as he followed the tracks into the wooded area. "I can prevent needless bloodshed." Yunnie was not sure of his motivation when Mytaru and the others of his new clan sought only to defend their precious valley. To the Urhaalan minotaurs, this land was sacred. Any intrusion by elves or other beings meant war, complete and without quarter. For it was here that the sacred caves introduced new minotaurs to their clans, rituals were performed, grazing areas belonging to the females of the herd were tended. In the valley of the Urhaalan minotaurs grew the seven sacred blossoms.

Here were the Places of Power.

Better to protect it all with words than by force of arms. Yunnie did not want to see Mytaru or old Mehonvo or any of the others die needlessly. But the utter hatred in the elf's eyes as he had died haunted Yunnie as much as the vision of a creature dancing about in the fire and fume of the lava pits—or the unknown lurker following his every movement.

The trail he followed vanished when it crossed a rocky patch. Yunnie sought a continuation of the tracks on the far side of the stony section to no avail. He sighed deeply, worried at his failure to discover the identity of the spy, and abandoned his hunt reluctantly, turning back to the course he had begun earlier. Long, loping strides devoured the distance as he made his way from the valley of the Urhaalan and onto the broad plains leading toward the distant Forest of Eln. By shielding his eyes and using a bit of imagination, Yunnie saw the emerald sheen that marked the westernmost entrance to the forest.

He had walked less than an hour when he saw bright flashes to either side of his path. Yunnie slowed and finally found a comfortable spot to wait for the elves to approach. He recognized their signaling mirrors, if not the messages sent using reflected sunlight. Spreading out his travel rations, he ate until he heard the velvety sliding approach of feet shod in soft fabric. Elves usually made no sound when they moved; they alerted him to their presence intentionally.

"Welcome," Yunnie said, not bothering to look up. "I would share my meal with you."

"There are many of us," came a voice high-pitched with fear. An elf showed herself and advanced cautiously.

"I am willing to divide what I have," Yunnie said, knowing the challenge was more in line with warning him of innumerable fighters rather than out of concern for his food supplies.

She came over and squatted down, staring at him with wide brown eyes. Her pointed ears were tucked under soft chestnut hair pulled back and fastened behind her neck with a ring carved from shining white bone.

At her side dangled a dirk with a worn leather handle and across her back was slung a bow. She carried no arrows, telling Yunnie that she spoke the truth about others nearby.

She had been chosen to speak for the group. Should he prove dangerous, her life might be forfeit, but her arrows would not be used against the rest of her band. Instead, they would be used to end *his* life.

"I come from Shingol," Yunnie said in way of introduction. She cut him short with an angry gesture.

"You are the human who ruts with the minotaurs," she said hotly. "You make war with them against us!"

"I seek to avoid war because I dislike seeing innocent blood spilled," he retorted. "I am a member of Clan Utyeehn, true. I was raised in Shingol, true. But I bear no malice toward you or any other elf. I seek a parley so that any differences between elf and minotaur can be discussed and resolved."

"Why should we believe you or any of *them*? They seek only to burn our forest and turn us out!"

"No," Yunnie said, astounded at how deeply the elf held her mistaken conviction. "On my honor, I—" He stopped in midsentence when a war lance whistled through the air and impaled the elf. She gasped and tried to pull the heavy shaft from her chest. Her brown eyes turned to him, first in surprise, then in hatred, before she died.

From all around came loud cries as the elves jumped from their hiding places. Some Yunnie had identified. He was appalled at how few he had found before the skirmish began. The elves shot their arrows with deadly efficiency against the band of attacking minotaurs, but they were outnumbered and in no position to retreat.

"Mytaru, wait!" cried Yunnie, seeing his friend and blood brother leading a large company of minotaurs. The bull-men charged forward, lances stabbing and short swords slashing.

One elf spun and tried to shoot Yunnie, but Mytaru killed him before he could draw back the bowstring. Mytaru bellowed in triumph and raced on, hunting more elves.

"Good work, Little Bullock! You decoyed them perfectly! Come, come with us for the kill!" Mytaru grunted
as he used his impressively strong arm to heave a lance
through the air. Yunnie cringed when he saw it spit
another elf. "To the attack! Come, Yunnie, come!"

Mytaru did not slacken his headlong run or even glance
back. He assumed Yunnie would accompany him in the
slaughter.

Yunnie started to join his blood brother and the others,
then fell back and finally stopped. As if another walked in
his skin and guided him astray, he returned to stare at the
fallen elf at the edge of the forest. He had offered her
food. He had desired no harm to come to her and now
she lay dead, a minotaur lance thrust completely through
her body. Without knowing it, Yunnie had brought the
elves into a trap sprung by Mytaru and the others of Clan
Utyeehn.

He felt unclean and betrayed. Jumping to his feet, he
roared wordlessly, but the cry was swallowed by the triumph voiced by the minotaurs. This day they had killed a
score or more enemy warriors.

Yunnie started to confront Mytaru and tell him how
angry he was being used as bait for their traps, then knew
he could not speak without igniting Mytaru's wrath,
accomplishing nothing. Yunnie had to wait until he was
better able to speak his concerns without the fire of anger
and ferocity of battle yielding heat but no light. He
backed away from the dead elf, then rushed into the
woods to gather his thoughts.

How long he ran, Yunnie did not know. The ground
under his feet turned marshy and insects began buzzing
viciously around his ears, seeking a blood dinner. When
he began swatting at them more than he was running, he
realized he had outdistanced some of his fury.

When one of his feet sank into the mire, Yunnie
backed away and took a closer look at his surroundings.
Tiny frog noises gave way to a deeper-throated croaking,
nothing like Yunnie had ever heard before. He touched
the dagger at one hip and the sword at the other as liquid
sucking sounds came closer and closer in the dusk.

"Who's there?" he called.

No answer.

He slipped his sword from its sheath and found a thick-boled tree for his back. He waited to rob the advancing creature of its dinner.

"You need not parry with steel," came light, mocking words. "Your wit and good intent are enough."

"Who are you?" Yunnie tried to identify the woman who so easily cornered him.

"I am called Sacumon by some. Less complimentary names by others. I would be your friend for what you have done this day."

"What have I done, besides get lost in a swamp?" New sounds came from Yunnie's left and right, hungry sounds of swamp-bound night denizens beginning their quest for fleshy sustenance.

"What, indeed!" Sacumon laughed. Yunnie shuddered at the sound. It reminded him of glass grinding against rock. "You tried to bring peace to the elves, peace to your minotaurs. You know the goblins are to blame."

"How do you know this? Are you the one who has been spying on me?"

"I am," came the simple, chilling admission. Yunnie wondered what he faced. Sacumon had shown incredible cleverness in hiding her tracks and moved through the muck as easily as Yunnie crossed an open meadow.

He tensed when he saw Sacumon make small, intricate hand gestures in the air before her. Did the unknown woman use a spell to bind him to the spot? For all the evidence of a spell being cast, Yunnie detected nothing. His arm felt as strong as ever and his brain as clear. Picking up one foot and shaking it betrayed no weakness. His coordination seemed untainted.

"Is this some ritual I have never seen before? Perhaps of Shingol, or is it a minotaur-fisherman hybrid?" She seemed amused at his attempt to find what the spell accomplished.

"You know much of me and I nothing of you," Yunnie said, stepping forward. He wanted to be away from the tree so he could fight more effectively, if necessary.

"I listen and I learn, Yunnie," came her words. Sacumon stepped forward. A patch of dangling luminous moss cast a pale green light on the woman's face, betraying angular planes and a sharp nose like a hatchet. Her lips were pulled back in what she thought was a reassuring smile but what appeared to Yunnie as more like a knife slash across the woman's lower face. She was about his height and thin, as he could tell from the way the dark robe clung to her body.

"What do you want?"

"Why, the same as you, Yunnie. I want peace between the minotaurs and elves. There has been so much distrust. Blame the goblins for all the woe in the land."

"You can speak to the elves and arrange a talk?" Yunnie gripped his sword harder when he saw Sacumon tense at his question. Muttering accompanied new gestures. Magic enshrouded this one, but to what end?

"Of course I can, as you speak so *eloquently* with the minotaurs. Together we can create a permanent peace in this land and allow all to live in harmony." Sacumon laughed sardonically, but at what jest?

Sacumon's words said one thing, but Yunnie heard another. Her unctuous phrases carried no desire for true peace, only hints of power gained and force wielded. In spite of this, he still heard himself saying, "I will talk with the Urhaalan. We must have peace at all costs."

"Yes, Yunnie," came Sacumon's honeyed words, "we must pursue a treaty between such great powers at all costs. The goblins are to blame."

He turned and walked away in a daze, sword still in his hand. Before he realized it, night had fallen, he had returned to the clan, and he sat at the bonfire with Mytaru and the others, celebrating their victory over the elves—and wondering how he could bring them to the peace parley suggested by the mysterious Sacumon.

CHAPTER

12

"WE CAN NEVER CARRY THIS MUCH IN OUR packs," complained Maeveen O'Donagh. She eyed the mountains of supplies Lord Peemel had sent them. Day after day wagons rolled into Vervamon's camp and dumped still more matériel, until it would require a company ten times their size to make use of it all.

"You fret for no reason, dear captain mine," Vervamon said, strolling along, a large leather-bound book open in the palm of his left hand. His right finger worked down the rows of complex arcane symbols, translating with some effort, attested to by the slight wrinkling of his high forehead. "We will take what we need and leave the rest."

"To them?" Maeveen indicated the hordes of Scavenger Folk circling their camp like vultures waiting for something—or someone—to die.

"What difference does it make? We're not paying for any of this. The Academy of Egaverral will be delighted for us to eat another's food and drink another's wine."

"What about swearing allegiance to another master?" Her brown eyes flared with indignation at having to sew the insignia of the Army of Iwset on her uniform,

especially after she discovered, by accident, that Ihesia
was Peemel's general-in-chief.

"Our only allegiance is to the truth. You know that.
What we say to Peemel is one thing, what we do when
out from under his vigilant gaze is quite another."

"How honorable," Maeveen grumbled.

"The search for truth need not be virtuous, it need only
be exhaustive and published where nitwits like Boyzen and
Jenns can die of jealousy when they read it. Surely, even
they can recognize brilliant research and astounding discovery when they see it." Vervamon turned back to the tome
he deciphered, muttered to himself, and wandered off.

"At least he isn't still wrapped around Ihesia like a
hungry southern boa," observed Lieutenant Quopomma.
The ogre grunted as she dropped a huge crate of supplies
to the ground with a loud crash.

"What do you have?"

Maeveen did not comment on Ihesia's absence. The
battles along the southern frontiers had taken a turn
against Iwset, or so said the tavern pundits, and the
woman's presence was required to insure victory.
Maeveen was never one to wish for another's death in
battle, unless it was a sworn foe's on the tip of her own
sword, but she hoped the enemy captured Ihesia and held
her prisoner for a good, long time. The indignity of
imprisonment would go far toward subduing her over-
weeningly haughty manner.

"Not foodstuffs, that is a sureness," said Quopomma.
"Looks illicit to me." She used her blunt fingers to pry
open the lid. Inside lay peculiarly shaped instruments
whose function baffled Maeveen. She reached for one,
only to have her wrist grabbed.

She reacted instinctively, twisting free and spinning
about, her fist ending up in the man's belly. His lungs
emptied fast as her fist buried forearm-deep in soft flesh.
Maeveen stepped back, considering the need for either a
second punch or her dagger. Either would end the
attacker's life.

"Don't," the man gasped out. His face had gone white,
and he made weak gagging sounds.

Maeveen studied him as she waited for him to recover
his breath. He was a youngish man, with dark hair thin-
ning prematurely. From the lack of tan, he seldom saw
the light of day. Indeed, his hands showed no sign of
work of any kind. While he might have been an academic, he was not of Vervamon's class. Vervamon never
failed to pitch in when work needed doing, no matter
how arduous.

"Who are you?"

"The owner of the rubbish in this crate, I'd wager,"
Quopomma said.

"Not rubbish. Needed . . . equipment," he got out.
Some color had returned to his cheeks, although he was
still pale. He struggled to his feet. "I beg your forgiveness.
I had not meant to arouse your ire. I did not want you
meddling with my property."

"Yours?" Maeveen let an eyebrow drift higher. "Why
should you have anything sent to our camp?" She already
knew the answer, and it irritated her. This one had the
stench of the Inquisition about him, but she held back
making the accusation. Small details did not fall readily
into place. One thing she knew, he was a spy for someone
if he thought to accompany Vervamon's expedition.

"My fellows and I come with you on your journey to
find the sigil," he said.

"Over my dead body," snapped Maeveen. "I have trouble enough wet-nursing Vervamon and my own company
without adding to the burden."

"Lord Peemel recommends it," the young man said,
finally able to stand upright again. He rubbed his belly
and sucked in air until he returned to normal. "I am
Coernn."

"And I'm damned if I let you come along. Tell Peemel
to take back all his worthless supplies and we can—"
Maeveen bit off her tirade when she saw Vervamon
speaking with five others, dressed similarly to Coernn.
Their clothing was hardly suitable for the trail yet was of
tougher fabric than the usual city dweller's. While the
coloring and patterns for each of the six were different,
they all seemed to be uniformly similar, as if someone had

started with the same pattern and thought to confuse any stupid observer with tiny variations.

"Maeveen, my dear, do see these gentlemen are situated properly. They will be accompanying us," called Vervamon. "They are experts on the seven martyrs and wish to confirm the discovery after I enter the crypt."

"Where are we going to find the Sigil of Iwset?" she asked. Coernn's eyes hardened, and she knew whatever came from his lips would be a lie. Any chance she had of learning the truth had passed when he regained his breath.

"Sir Vervamon is the expert in this matter. Digody has told him in general how to further his quest, though I have certain documents to use when we get closer to the site. When I recognize landmarks, Sir Vervamon will be the first to know. Lord Peemel himself would be hunting for the sigil if it were not for Lady Edara's declaration of war."

"*She* declared war?" Quopomma laughed harshly. The ogre turned to empty space, no doubt addressing her imaginary friends. She asked them, "Do you believe such bilge?" Quopomma turned back to her commander. "He tried to force her to marry him. For her that would be like mating with one of the Scavenger Folk."

"He is my liege, and you should not speak ill of him." Coernn faced the ogre squarely. Although Maeveen was inclined to let Quopomma reduce the upstart to a pile of broken bones, something in the young man's attitude warned her this might not be the outcome of any fight. He lacked the calluses of a swordsman. He moved well, but not with the power of a boxer. As far as Maeveen could tell, he wore no armor under his loose-fitting clothing.

Quopomma was the company champion at wrestling and could hold her own with her double sabers against all but the finest fighter. Maeveen had seen the ogre clean out a tavern all by herself, then return to drinking as if nothing had happened. She was a fighter, a brawler, and the perfect second-in-command.

But Coernn presented a definite, if unknown, danger to

the ogre. Maeveen O'Donagh stepped between the two, pushing Quopomma away.

"You have work to tend to," she said. "See that Iro isn't malingering again. When she gets with the two sergeants from your squads, she is worthless for the rest of the day."

"I can take out the garbage first, Captain," offered the ogre. She clenched her fists, loud cracking noises echoing through the camp. For all the menace in her pose, Quopomma did not faze Coernn. This worried Maeveen even more. Did he feel he had the Inquisition on his side and death would free his spirit from its imperfect mortal body, or was there something more?

"Tend to sorting through the supplies for what is useful and judge what we ought to leave behind," Maeveen said. "Whatever goes with these six is their responsibility alone. None of our soldiers is to aid them in lugging about such a huge pile of equipment." She glanced back into the crate at the odd instruments and edges of books poking through packing material. Coernn moved to shut the lid and cut short her examination.

"That is acceptable," Coernn said in a soft but menacing voice. "That is even preferable." He bowed slightly, his eyes never leaving Quopomma, then he turned and walked away, head held high.

"An arrogant one," observed Quopomma. "It's a sureness he has not the sap to make it stick."

"I'm not so certain," Maeveen said. "Tell me, Quopomma, where is that pub you favor?"

"The one frequented by Peemel's bodyguards? They are a loose-tongued crew, after a few tankards." Quopomma laughed, remembering the nights she had spent swapping lies and rounds with them. "It's the Singing Geoduck, down on the Street of Six Virtues and a Sin."

Maeveen marveled at the high-blown names villagers placed on their thoroughfares. She watched Coernn join his five comrades and their brief discussion of her. Coernn occasionally glanced over his shoulder in her direction, his expression neutral. Maeveen wished she could use her skills at lipreading to find what he said to

the others, but Coernn managed to keep a hand over his
mouth as he spoke. She shrugged it off. Once on the
road, these six would be left behind quickly. They could
never maintain the pace she intended to set, not if they
insisted on lugging their heavy boxes.

She made a circuit of the camp, roused Lieutenant Iro
from an afternoon nap, then turned toward Iwset, satisfied the company neared readiness for departure.
Maeveen had only a few details to figure out before heading up the coast in search of Lord Peemel's bauble—and
to feed Vervamon's insatiable hunger for knowledge.

When she, Quopomma, and Vervamon had first
entered Iwset a week earlier, the city-state had seemed
almost festive. The soldiers lining the street as an honor
guard had been stately in their fine dress uniforms, but
the snarling veterans fresh from the wars, with their hard-
bitten looks and avid desire to use their weapons,
remained in Maeveen's memory. Iwset had drifted more
toward the latter in appearance and spirit in the past few
days.

Now everywhere she looked she saw battle-ready soldiers marching along in squads and companies as they
prepared to depart. She paused to watch how their officers commanded, how the soldiers responded. A grudg-
ing respect rose for Ihesia, or whoever she had placed in
charge of preparation and training. These were no green
fighters marching off for an ideal, only to find a grave
rather than glory. Whatever enemy these troopers faced
would know they had met a valiant and well-drilled
force.

Making her way through the marketplace showed her
something else about Iwset. The vast supplies pouring
into Vervamon's camp were not available to the ordinary
citizen. Fresh fruits and vegetables were absent in their
carts, and what meat was presented for sale looked old
and tough. The best of the produce had already gone to
the soldiers.

From the dour expressions on the vendors' faces, this
diversion was not overly acceptable. Maeveen wondered
how the people of Iwset might respond if Ihesia had more

than a single setback in battle. A series of defeats might bring down the haughty general, as well as her ruler.

Passing a seller of Aeolian harps moaning out their tunes as the afternoon breeze blew off the Ilesemare Sea, she entered the Street of Six Virtues and a Sin. Everywhere she looked she saw evidence of the sin, but nothing of any virtue. Maeveen sniffed at this moral decay, set her eyes straight ahead, and marched off hunting for the tavern Quopomma had frequented with Peemel's soldiers.

She found it at the end of the street, only a narrow cobblestone path separating the easternmost seawall above the littoral and the pub. Ships moved with the wind and tide, heading seaward from the harbor a half mile farther north along the coast. She thought she spied a few brightly colored pennons far out at sea, but the salty mist and wind caused her eyes to water.

Maeveen pushed through the heavy door into the Singing Geoduck and inhaled deeply of the scents of roasting meat and spilled ale. Who of the motley crew assembled here would most likely know the identity of the six joining Vervamon's expedition? She saw one junior officer in Peemel's guard, who might know something of palace intrigues, and started toward him when a coldness ran up and down her spine. Many times she had ignored this warning to her deep regret. This time she turned and pulled open the tavern door and peered into the darkening street. Storm clouds blew in and hid the sun.

The lack of warmth she felt was not from this natural event. She saw Lord Peemel's tall, thin adviser, Digody, walking down the street, speaking confidentially to a well-dressed servant in pale blue-and-green striped livery. The silver escutcheon identifying his house was hidden from Maeveen's view. The servant averted his eyes several times, giving Maeveen the impression Digody was unhappy with the report delivered him. She tried to read his lips, but the man kept turning his head and bobbing it up and down with nervous gestures. When the adviser's red eyes seemed to glow with an inner light, the servant threw up an arm as if to defend himself. Maeveen considered coming to the poor man's assistance, then decided it would prove more instructive if she followed Digody.

What brought Lord Peemel's powerful adviser to this poverty-stricken section of Iwset? And who would the servant report to when he was finished with delivering his message?

Maeveen O'Donagh decided she might find out those answers quickly enough when Digody shoved the servant ahead of him and strode off at a brisk pace. Almost running, Maeveen kept up as Digody and the servant twisted through back streets and alleys, always heading closer to the harbor to the north. She had hardly broken a sweat by the time they reached their destination, but the servant was gasping for breath.

To her surprise, Digody seemed unaffected by the rapid trip through Iwset. A man of such skeletal body ought to have been winded. Maeveen knew there was more to Peemel's adviser than met the casual glance. She backed into a doorway to survey the area without being seen. Like the other doors, this one was painted a vivid red to frighten off evil spirits, or so she had been told in complete seriousness. For all the disrepair evident in the buildings, she thought it might be true, but would have to ask Vervamon for confirmation. There was little he did not know of strange cultural quirks and obscure superstitions.

A cart rattled by. Maeveen closed her eyes and let the second one go past without staring at its contents. The dead wagon carried those out of the area who had died during the night. From the stench, Maeveen guessed some of the corpses had lingered more than a day or two. Disease ran rampant everywhere, but more in this part of Iwset than others, if the bodies were any indication.

"Where is she?" The words came drifting toward her on the rising wind. She pulled her cloak tighter around her sturdy body as she found herself able to overhear Digody and the servant's conversation.

"She comes, sire."

"Begone," Digody said. Even from across the street

Maeveen saw the adviser's fierce red eyes blazing like tiny suns. In the gathering darkness brought by heavy thunderstorm clouds blowing in overhead, those eyes took on a life of their own. She shivered, and it was not from the increasingly cold wind.

"There, sire, there she is." The servant bobbed his head and backed off. Maeveen tried again to see the coat of arms on the man's chest and failed as he backed from Digody, then hurried away, vanishing down the street.

Maeveen peered around the recessed doorframe and tried to see what Digody did now. The adviser fumbled under his long robes and grumbled. When he began pacing, Maeveen slipped back into the shallow safety of her painted portal. She tried to press herself further into the shadows when she sighted a woman coming from down the street. She need not have worried about being seen; the well-dressed newcomer had eyes only for Digody.

"Your choice of meeting places lacks much in the way of comfort and shelter," Digody said without any greeting.

The woman laughed. The sound caught on the wind and carried musically, like distant buoy warnings in the harbor. Maeveen listened intently, fighting to pick out words amid the whistle of the rising wind. The woman was stunningly beautiful and dressed opulently for such a poor section of town. The gems dusted throughout her dark hair reflected the distant lightning and gave her a surreal aspect. The tall woman turned elegantly, letting her sable-rimmed cape float away from her body and be caught on gusts of wind. In that instant Maeveen saw that the lavish clothing and throat-tightening beauty extended deeper than the surface. Trim, athletic, the woman moved well, and Maeveen thought she might be capable of using the two daggers which were sheathed in an ornately hand-tooled, ruby-studded leather belt.

"You worry so, Digody. Do not. All is well."

"The only advantage is that Peemel would never come here," Digody grumbled.

Again the woman laughed. "Ah, yes, the fear he has of disease. It is quite a debilitating condition for one in such good health." She tossed one side of her cape over her shoulder, more fully revealing her clothing. Maeveen sucked in her breath. The woman was dressed in the style of Jehesic, the island kingdom against which Lord Peemel so recently declared war. Why was his chief adviser speaking with a high-ranking noble of that distant island?

Peace? Formal conditions of war? Neither struck Maeveen as logical. If this meeting reflected the policies of either ruler, it would have been conducted in more formal setting, not in the middle of a windy square as a storm blew off the Ilesemare Sea.

As if realizing she had revealed too much, the woman pulled the cape back around herself and moved closer to Digody. They exchanged heated words for several minutes, then Lord Peemel's cadaverous counselor stamped his foot, spun about, and stalked off. The woman laughed again, but this time the sound carried no amusement. She watched Digody hurry away, then went on her own way, heading toward the nearby docks.

Maeveen considered following Digody, then decided he had nothing more to offer in way of information. Instead, she sought the identity of the woman as a lever against Peemel's obvious treachery. She had no love for Peemel, but all information proved worthwhile, and force of arms was not the only way to wage a war. If Vervamon's expedition was financed by Peemel, and the city-state of Iwset embarked on a war that might affect Vervamon's free passage, it behooved Maeveen to learn what she could. She closed the distance between her and the rapidly retreating woman, not sure what to do when she overtook the Jehesic noble.

By the time Maeveen reached the docks, the storm blew with gale-force intensity. All but one of the ships had furled its sails, fighting to keep from smashing hard against their moorings. The one vessel preparing to brave the storm carried neutral markings, but Maeveen had not expected a Jehesic spy to sail into the harbor of a sworn enemy flying its banner: orange-and-blue with a black sea kestrel rampant.

"Ferantia, hurry. We must leave soon," the ship's captain

shouted to the woman at the foot of the gangplank. She lithely vaulted onto the deck and swung around to give the captain a jaunty salute.

The captain bellowed orders as the woman joined him at the wheel. The sails were dropped partially and the lines cast off. Maeveen caught her breath, thinking the ship would be dashed against the dock as it tried to leave. The storm wind was no ally to a boat this afternoon.

Maeveen stepped out into plain view to be sure her eyes did not play her false. Although the ship's sails were only catching a fraction of the wind, it built speed and shot from Iwset's harbor like an arrow. Maeveen rushed to the end of the dock and stared. The ship sailed directly into the wind, in complete defiance of the storm.

"Magic," she said softly. "Digody meets a Jehesic spy—and sorceress. What else are you, Ferantia?"

In minutes, the ship carrying the lovely spy disappeared into a low-hanging haze. A strong current flowed from Iwset to Jehesic, and it contained as much danger as it did magic.

CHAPTER
13

"IT WAS DECIDED DURING THE CELEBRATION
of Tiyint. The Time of Resolution nears and *we must
wage war!*" The shaggy minotaur swaggered about, nostrils flaring, finally crossing strong arms belligerently
across his bare, broad chest. He dipped his head and performed a few quick, expert hooks with his horns, showing what would be done to the elves once they engaged in
formal warfare.

"Wait, Little Bullock," Mytaru cautioned Yunnie as he
started to shout out a protest. "Aesor is not finished. It is
rude to interrupt before he has had his say."

"He speaks nonsense," Yunnie said heatedly. He
refused to allow Aesor to continue with such explosive
talk. "The elves are not the cause of our woe. It does not
matter what was decided during the Celebration of Tiyint.
What matters is the truth!"

"I caution you in the name of Clan Utyeehn," Mytaru
said sternly. "There will be no blasphemy. Decisions made
during the celebration under the light of the double moons
are sacred. You were brought into the clan then because it
was a favorable time for major transitions in our lives. The
herd prospers under the holy light. Do you deny that?"

"No, but I—"

"Other matters, secret and revealed only in rituals you have yet to learn, were decided. War against the elves is but one of them."

"Too many of our herd will die, and for nothing!" raged Yunnie. "The elves think *we* are the enemy. We think *they* are. Both sides are wrong."

"How is that possible?" asked Mytaru, looking uneasily at Aesor. Such discussion while another spoke was both rude and cause for individual challenge to combat. "They lay traps that kill our clan," Mytaru said in a low voice. "We kill them when they trespass on our territory. The elves are moving supplies closer to the valley, readying to bring war into our sanctuary."

"I cannot deny that," Yunnie said, anxious to convince his blood brother, "but we should be fighting the goblins, not the elves."

For a moment, Mytaru said nothing. Then he burst out laughing. The others gathered in the Circle of Discourse glared at him. Aesor had not finished prancing about and brandishing his newly metal-tipped horns. Many murmured at Mytaru's rudeness.

"I beg your forgiveness, clan brothers," Mytaru said when Aesor moved to stand directly in front of him. "I thought to instruct our newest clan member in our ways of etiquette and foolishly violated the very precepts I sought to teach."

"Let him speak to the circle," Aesor said. "Let him tell us of how great our victory will be against our sworn enemies, the elves."

"My blood brother is—" Mytaru began, but cut off his words when Yunnie rose and moved into the center of the circle.

"I thank my esteemed brother, Aesor, for the honor he grants me," Yunnie said. His heart jumped into his throat when he realized how big a chance he took. He was the junior member of the circle, but by herd tradition his word carried as much weight as the eldest. Only in spiritual matters, in which the Three Chosen spoke with absolute authority, was any individual clan member unable to debate.

"I speak with all my heart when I say the elves are not our enemies. I saw goblins sniping at our patrols, fighting from hidden positions and then running before our valiant warriors could capture them. They also incite the elves by similar cowardly attacks, then stand back and let minotaur and elf kill one another."

"How do you explain the elvish nets? My cousin Hoty was strangled by one near the Lycoh Wash. No goblin strung that trap. They are not smart enough for that." Aesor pawed at the ground and snorted fiercely. Yunnie could not take his eyes from the shiny metal horn tips. Aesor had sharpened the small ridges on those metallic sheaths to razor sharpness. Even if Yunnie was not ready for war, Aesor was.

A humorless laugh billowed up from deep in many minotaur throats.

"I sorrow for your loss. Hoty's death diminishes the herd," Yunnie replied, mind racing. He needed solid proof to convince them of the true source of their grief. "I agree that the goblins are not smart enough to lay such traps, but they are cunning enough to set elf against minotaur. The goblins steal elvish weapons and use them to kill us. I am certain they do the same to the elves."

"The elves think to burn us out of our homes!" raged another minotaur. Yunnie knew he was the leader of Clan Helmhein, but had never heard his name. "Can you deny the fires that raged along the ridge for three days! They were set by elves."

"The elves accuse the Urhaalan of burning them out, too," Yunnie said. He knew he dared not follow this thread of argument very far. The goblins relied on rock, not fire, for their weapons.

"They are liars. If they tell you the goblins are responsible, they are doubly liars!" raged the clan leader. "They say such things to lull us. They are not fighters. They can never stand against the might of the Urhaalan!"

"The elves are more than able to defend themselves, but they fight the wrong enemy, as do we. We must eliminate the goblins."

Yunnie stepped from the Circle of Discourse and waited for several minutes for someone to respond to his impassioned plea. The silence weighed heavily, then Aesor stepped back as truculently as he had left it. He ignored Yunnie and began his declaration of war against the elves as if nothing had been said to contradict his assertions of elvish treachery.

"He can't—" Yunnie was silenced by Mytaru's stern glance. He settled down and listened to the others in Clan Utyeehn whip themselves into a fighting rage.

Fighting rage against the elves.

Yunnie stood on a rocky butte above the entrance to the valley and looked down on the gentler grassy slopes where soon the minotaurs would fight the elves. Until dawn Aesor and the other bulls had laid their plans, deciding how best to fight the elves. Yunnie shook his head, knowing war was wrong. Who else but the goblins could be the source of their woes?

Aesor had brought up a good point about the goblins. More cunning than smart, such calculated, coordination, pitting minotaur against elf, seemed beyond their limited mental ability. Yunnie knew that they stole weapons and ambushed minotaurs with elvish arrows and elves with minotaurs' lances, but why did they bother burning down both elvish and minotaur dwellings? It would only increase the chance they would be seen.

"Underground," Yunnie said to himself. "Yes, underground is where answers lie. I can get proof, show Aesor, Mytaru, and the others, and put an end to the fighting before it gets out of hand."

Less than an hour earlier he had watched the first band of minotaurs marching out, ready to slay the elves massing at the mouth of the valley. The Time of Resolution demanded it; war had been discussed and declared under the light of Iontiero and Fessa.

Yunnie shivered. Even thinking the name of the greater moon caused him some discomfort. He had to get used to the minotaur way of life, or such small details would haunt him forever. And he had to shake the feeling he was only stirring up hatred rather than quenching it by his insistence that the elves were not their true enemy. Every word from his lips seemed subtly wrong and insincere, enough to convince the minotaurs a dozen times over that he was wrong and the elves were indeed their problem.

He began walking, not sure where he was headed. If the goblins sneaked out from their underground realm, they had to have entrances nearby. Otherwise, the keen-eyed bulls patrolling nearby when the Clan Helmhein houses had been destroyed would have spotted the scuttling little monsters.

Yunnie sniffed the air and detected the acrid odor of burned wood—and flesh. He was out of breath by the time he climbed a ridge and peered down into the grass-lined bowl of this section of the Urhaalan's valley, where many of Clan Helmhein had lived. He sat and studied the topography, finding no fewer than eight houses left smoldering after the attack, all secluded, not one in sight of another. Curiously, for a herd animal, these minotaurs valued their individual privacy, perhaps too much. It had permitted easy attack.

"There," he said to himself, tracing out a path leading into more rugged terrain. Something about the way the sun shone off the rock caught his attention. Yunnie scrambled down the slope, wondering what was not right. Staring at the ground, it took him several minutes to realize what he saw.

"Not goblin footprints," he said, puzzled by the strange shapes he found, "but there is plenty of soot and burned grass. It's as if they dragged their fire pots behind them as they went."

Eyes downcast and following the charred trail, he crossed rock and grass, soil and wetland without losing sight of the black smudges. Almost guiltily, he stopped and looked up. He had come to a stand of trees. The lower branches had been scorched, impossible heat passing near them. Yunnie jumped and grabbed hold of a limb, using his weight to break it free. He dropped it and frowned as he studied it. It had been burned as if a large fire had been set directly under it. He found no trace of an old campfire.

He had heard of sieges against walled cities conducted using inflammable mixtures of pitch and other secret ingredients that burned fiercely, yet could be concentrated into a small missile. For all that, how did a goblin carry an ignited ball—and why?

Stride lengthening, he fell into an easy lope as he pursued whoever carried the fire pot. Did the goblins conduct some bizarre ritual of their own, taking embers from the minotaur houses back to their underground kingdom?

Spires of rock rose along the trail, and Yunnie struggled to make his way through the Urhaalan foothills. The scent of sulfur came strongly to his nostrils. He neared fumaroles thus far unrevealed to him by Mytaru. He hoped he did not violate herd custom by looking upon them without observing the proper ritual, whatever it might be.

He came to a narrow divide, the rocky walls forcing him to turn sideways to squeeze through. His chest and back brushed sooty spots where his quarry had left evidence of recent passage. Yunnie popped out into a rocky arena where a fumarole spat forth yellow clouds of sulfur mixed with white steam. He put his hand over his mouth to keep from choking.

It did no good. The vapors set him to coughing hard. His eyes watered, and he started to return through the rocky notch when a deafening roar of anger spun him around. Through the rising clouds of sulfur and steam he saw a creature wreathed in flame lumbering toward him.

"No, no!" he shouted, sucking in a lungful of noisome gases. He wobbled and fell to his knees. His eyes tried to focus on the burning giant approaching him through the gases spat forth by the fumarole. No living creature could survive such heat and fumes.

This one did.

Yunnie groped feebly for his dagger to defend himself.

He stared up into burning yellow eyes and a mouth that opened to show the blazing pits of Hell. Loud cries came from all around, echoing in his ears, calling his name. Then he passed out, dagger tumbling from his feeble grip.

CHAPTER

14

"FERANTIA, HURRY! WE MUST LEAVE SOON," called Captain Oseltei as he struggled to throw off the rear mooring line before running to the *Slippery Eel*'s steering wheel. He yanked off the rope securing the wheel and looked aloft to where crewmen struggled with the bucking sails.

"Belay the sails!" Oseltei shouted into the teeth of the wind. "They won't help us in this tempest."

"There will be no need for sails this trip, my captain," said Ferantia, lithely jumping onto the deck. She cast a single glance behind at the green-and-brown-clad soldier who had dogged her steps after Digody departed. The solider was not of Iwset, therefore posed no threat to her or her mission. Still, she wondered who carried such curiosity or interest to the very end of the dock. Ferantia heaved a sigh. So little was secret these days, especially in Iwset. She wished Lord Peemel would keep a better grip on the spies rushing about—or perhaps she ought to let Digody know of this.

Ferantia decided to let the Iwsetians tend their own stewpot of trouble. She played a deeper game, and it only casually involved them.

"Then be about your magic. We need to leave this port right away," Oseltei said, putting his back into whirling the wheel and aiming the *Slippery Eel*'s prow out to sea.

Ferantia smiled wickedly, then clapped her hands twice, muttered a small spell, then clapped her hands three times and was almost thrown from her feet as the impetus spell grabbed the *Slippery Eel* and pushed it along. Oseltei gave a cry of joy and worked furiously to aim the ship's prow directly into the waves rolling in from across the Ilesemare Sea.

"To Jehesic, my good captain, as fast as this fine ship of yours can take us," she ordered.

"It's your spell that propels the *Eel*, not my sails," grunted Oseltei. "I'll be well and glad to slip back into a decent harbor. Those land-gripping barbarians might be expert at breeding mules, but they know nothing of taking care of their harbor."

"Breeding mules?" Ferantia laughed. "That's good, Oseltei, very good. I shall remember that one."

She went to the railing and peered ahead into the storm. Heavy sheets of rain battered the heaving sea. Ferantia closed her eyes and formed a picture of calm water and easy sailing. The ship no longer tossed high into the air to crash down into foam and mist; it now slipped along as if the water had been greased.

"We'll make port within a day at this speed," Oseltei reported. "Is your message of such importance?"

Ferantia could only nod. It took immense concentration to maintain the spells propelling the ship and giving it an easy voyage through the storm-racked sea. Sweat beaded on her forehead and some of her beauty faded as she concentrated. Ferantia's hands shook as she renewed the propulsion spell after pausing a moment to urge a sea leviathan to seek other fare for its dinner. And so it went for the rest of the tiring, taxing trip.

"We're in sight of land, land ho!" cried the captain.

Ferantia relaxed all her spells and for a perilous moment thought the *Slippery Eel* might be capsized by a

cresting wave. Oseltei fought the wheel and brought the
ship about in time to keep it from breaking apart. He
glared at her. Ferantia knew the captain had little regard
for such magic and its results, but she wanted to report
quickly to her liege. She saw the bright orange-and-blue
banner snapping in the brisk wind blowing across the
island, the storm still miles from Jehesic. The battlements
along the beaches seemed little more than seawalls, but
Ferantia knew them for the massive fortifications they
were.

Peemel was a fool if he thought he could land marines
on those beaches and take the island. He was even more
a fool if he thought to defeat Jehesic's fleet. Captains
with more skill than Oseltei showed at the *Eel*'s rudder
commanded the frigates and cruisers—and Oseltei was
one of the most capable captains Ferantia had ever sailed
with.

She heaved a sigh. The world was in such turmoil, and
she felt caught in a vortex sucking her ever downward.
But she had risen from the lowliest of fishmongers in
Jehesic's market to become second in power only to Lady
Edara. Ferantia smiled slightly at the thought of her liege.
Lady Edara, spoiled and never certain about what to do.
She needed someone to steer her on a steady course,
avoiding the reefs and shoals of poor advisers and those
who sought only riches at her expense.

Ferantia had loftier goals than mere gold.

"There's our berth," Oseltei said to her. "We'll be
docked in a few minutes. Never have I made the run from
Iwset in such a short time, milady."

"Soon you will be hauling more cargo than ever—to
Jehesic's colony on the mainland," Ferantia promised. She
smoothed her expensive cape and adjusted her silken
blouse and flowing skirts, then patted her gem-strewn,
windblown hair into place. By the time she finished this
simple toilet, Captain Oseltei had gently touched the *Eel*'s
hull against the dock. Eager hands fastened the mooring
lines and reached down to aid Ferantia's departure from
the ship. She ignored them all. She had risen from their
rank. She need never have anything to do with them

again. Light as a feather, Ferantia jumped to the dock and walked briskly toward the battlements running from the harbor toward the peninsula where Lady Edara now camped behind fortified walls. The citadel commanded the harbor entrance as well as the sweep of the island all the way to the Enrys Reef. At sunrise the hulls and masts of invading fleets could be seen poking up from the reef, a monument to a dozen and more failed attempts over the years to wrest Jehesic from its rightful rulers.

Ferantia knew such an assault could never succeed. The people of Jehesic were too secure, both behind their battlements on the beaches and in their massive citadel. They traded well up and down the coast and brought great currents of wealth flowing into this single island, allowing for the expansion of their fleet until no one who wanted a job need look any further than the navy.

Most able-bodied citizens joined either the merchant marine or the navy, giving the island protection. Such safety enticed wealth from the mainland and so its banks flourished. Lady Edara presided over a paradise in a wretched sea of the Inquisition, which brought fear and outright loathing for magic on the mainland.

"Sergeant, please inform Lady Edara I have returned," Ferantia said to the guard at the citadel's main gate as she strode past, never slowing as she went. The sergeant saluted her but said nothing in reply. Ferantia knew the message had been sent as soon as the *Slippery Eel* hove into view. Nothing sneaked past the watchful eyes of Jehesic's coastal guard.

Servants drifted through the fortification lighting torches against the gathering gloom. The storm that hammered Iwset bypassed Jehesic, but the island could never escape nightfall.

All around bustled guards and servants, working to ready the citadel for the night. There was little to guard against from the citizens of Jehesic, but the head of Lady Edara's security worried about assassins sent by Peemel. Ferantia could put her ruler's mind at ease on this point. She had been promised no such attempt would be made against Edara's life. This was only one of the messages she brought from her meeting in Iwset.

The hangings on the walls told of great prosperity, but Ferantia made mental changes to the tapestries and paintings. When rule passed in Jehesic, she would see that more modern artwork replaced this ancient, dusty display. The woman made her way through increasingly narrow hallways, finally winding up a turret staircase to emerge on the high battlements overlooking the sea. For a few minutes, Ferantia stopped to gaze out over the heaving, tumultuous water.

Its ceaseless motion never failed to hold her mesmerized. Now and again she thought she saw creatures break the surface, bellow, and dive back to the safety of their watery realm. How she envied them—how she feared them. Ferantia's hands moved in intricate patterns in front of her, casting new spells she had learned from sorcerers in hiding from the Inquisition near Iwset. The wards would not hold a monster at bay, but they made Ferantia feel better for the casting.

Straining, Ferantia thought she saw lights on the horizon, showing where Iwset lay. But this was absurd. Iwset lay many days' journey away and would be hidden behind the storm. Her spell had hastened the *Slippery Eel* on its way faster than any Inquisition-blessed ship could travel.

Ferantia was considering Abbot Offero and his power in Iwset when a door opened, letting out a gust of warm air. She turned and let the soft, fragrantly perfumed air waft against her face. The brisk wind that always blew across Jehesic quickly erased its heady effect.

"You have word from Iwset?" came Lady Edara's petulant voice.

"Yes, milady, I do," Ferantia said, walking through the door and into the dimly lit bedchamber. All around the chamber diaphanous azure curtains moved restlessly, caught by the wind. Lady Edara seemed disinclined to shut the door and stop the nervous flow of the silks. Ferantia's liege returned to a small writing desk, its lamp spilling wan illumination.

She made a new gesture to ward against evil spirits. The dancing shadows caused by the rippling curtains made her uncomfortable. With every unexpected snap of fabric, she jumped instinctively to fend off an attacker. How Edara lived in such a room gave Ferantia pause.

"What of your trip?" asked Lady Edara. She tossed back her head, sending a coppery banner of hair fluttering in the draft. Her sea-green eyes shone with a feverish light, made all the more intense by the paleness of her face. She seemed hardly more than a child in stature, but Ferantia knew better than to underestimate her. More than one pretender to the rule of Jehesic had made such a mistake. All wore heavy irons around their ankles—at the bottom of Jehesic Bay.

"I bring word from Peemel," Ferantia said, bowing slightly. She tried not to stare, but she heard movement behind the curtains in the direction of Edara's sleeping quarters. A lover? Ferantia thought so. She chewed on her lower lip, considering her words even more carefully. A witness to what she said proved inconvenient.

"He retreats from his absurd position?" asked Edara.

Ferantia snorted and shook her head. "Not at all, Lady Edara. He reiterates his desire for your hand in marriage. Such a marriage would cement relations between Iwset and Jehesic, and insure peace for—"

"*No!*" The denial of Peemel's offer rang loudly, causing Ferantia to jump. Lady Edara leaned forward, her petite form shaking in anger. "I will never wed that son of a sea crab. Just thinking of his touch makes my skin crawl. And how long would I share his bed before an unfortunate accident befell me?"

"It would not be that way," Ferantia said, mind racing. She had not expected such emphatic rejection. "He needs you and your influence to—"

"He needs my fleet. He lusts after the gold in Jehesic's banks. His bloodthirsty treatment of those foolish enough to marry him is history I have learned, as well as how to use my fleet to protect Jehesic's wealth!" Rosy spots came to Edara's cheeks. She pulled her thin wrap around her shoulders as if to shut herself off from the world.

"It need not work that way. We can remove Peemel before he finds a way of killing you, milady," Ferantia said. "Then *you* would be ruler of both Jehesic and Iwset!"

"I will not sleep my way to power. Such is for whores."

Ferantia held back an angry outburst. Her plans slipped through her fingers. Rejection at first had been expected, but Ferantia thought she could persuade her liege to talk with Peemel about dowry, on matters of military alliance, of ventures proving useful to both rulers. She had not expected Edara's resistance to the offer of marriage to be so adamant.

Movement behind the curtain convinced Ferantia they were not alone. She had to guard her tongue even more closely.

"Do not think he will accept this refusal, Lady Edara," Ferantia said carefully. "Peemel will declare war."

"He intended to fight before he sent his offer of marriage. He makes a mockery of a sacrament. How dare he!" Edara shook her head again, then ran her fingers through coppery strands.

"Are you willing to see your subjects' blood flow into the sea?"

"Yes," Edara said hotly. "Better to die in battle than live under the heel of a tyrant. If necessary, I will command the flagship personally, but fight I will. Peemel must not prevail."

"I—" Ferantia clamped shut her mouth, realizing her course took her through increasingly perilous seas. "You are right, Lady Edara. Should I order the fleet to prepare for war?"

"The order was given before you returned," Edara said, startling Ferantia. She had thought her counsel worth more to Lady Edara. It was time to solidify her position, or she might be returned to vending fish.

"As you wish," Ferantia said. Edara made a sweeping motion, dismissing her. The rest of the report on conditions in Iwset could wait for another time.

As she stopped at the door to pull it closed behind her, Ferantia saw her liege push aside a hanging curtain. She could not make out who lay on the grand bed, but there was no denying Edara's passion for her mystery lover.

CHAPTER

15

FIRE BURST IN FRONT OF YUNNIE'S FACE. HE tried to escape the searing explosion, to scramble even a foot away, and could not. His tortured lungs strained for fresh air and found only poison. He saw an incandescent fireball blazing above his head, turning solid rock to seething liquid. Droplets of molten stone spattered on him and sent shocks of pain throughout his body. This more than the fear thrusting through his body forced him to action.

He rubbed his eyes to remove the thick sulfurous fog from them and thought he saw a tower of burning stone. A yawning chasm opened and belched fire, but all Yunnie could stare at were the twin beacons of blistering hatred blinking fiercely above the mouth. He whipped up his dagger and made a clumsy toss at the advancing monster. A deafening roar rewarded his effort.

"Yunnie? Are you hurt?"

"Mytaru, be careful! It . . . it's a behemoth like nothing I have ever seen." Yunnie forced himself backward until hot rock pressed at his back. He tried to draw his sword, but the danger had passed. The indistinct but deadly creature had vanished as if it were only a nightmare and he had awakened. He watched a darker, less luminous shape move through the yellow fog. Mytaru stood above him, hand outstretched to help him to his feet. Yunnie took the strong grip and got to his feet. After a wobbly moment, he felt better.

"I see nothing but the fumaroles," Mytaru said, tossing his head about.

"It was there," Yunnie said, but he was no longer so sure. The fumes might have clouded his brain and eyes. "Let's get out of here."

As he turned, his hand touched hot rock. He flinched and saw he had not been hallucinating. The flying fireball had touched the boulder and burned a foot-deep hole. The stone was still somewhat soft.

"Why did you stray? We prepare for war. The rituals must be observed."

"I've had enough purging," Yunnie said. His belly growled from lack of food, but he had not imagined the monster. He whirled around and said, "A moment. I dropped my dagger." He went back into the poisonous fog and knelt, scrabbling about to find his weapon.

His hand closed on the hilt. The blade looked as if it had been thrust into a crazed smithy's forge until it turned buttery. Yunnie peered through the fog at it and finally tossed aside the ruined weapon.

"That's one dagger that will never serve me again," Yunnie said, amazed at the heat required to destroy steel. Mytaru ignored the weapon in favor of grabbing Yunnie's shoulder and steered him out of the rocky gorge.

"You can get another from our armory. Do not rely on inferior human-forged weapons. They will dull every time on you. Clan Utyeehn has the finest daggers and swords of any in the Urhaalan herd," boasted Mytaru. The mino-taur pushed Yunnie through the narrow passage and into the fresh air of the valley. Yunnie sucked in pure air, try-ing to remember why he had ventured into the cul-de-sac in the first place.

"Footprints," he said. "Not a goblin's. I followed the trail of soot from the burned houses."

"The elves will pay for their treacherous attacks," vowed Mytaru.

Yunnie did not bother arguing with his friend over their true enemy. He was too confused to offer decent arguments. He had been certain the goblins were responsible, but the *thing* he had faced was no goblin, unless they had grown tall, snorted flame, and threw fireballs.

"Where are we going?" Yunnie asked.

Mytaru's buoyant mood darkened. The minotaur straightened and placed his hands on his hips. He pawed at the ground, then said in a resonant voice, "You are a member of the herd, Little Bullock. I sought you out for a reason. The time has come for you to experience the most sacred of the Urhaalan Places of Power."

"At the far end of the valley?" Yunnie's strength returned slowly, but he did not yet feel up to a long trek to reach another Place of Power. He glanced over his shoulder in the direction of the fumaroles where the monster had attacked him—and had retreated after destroying the Clan Helmhein homes.

"The Shrine of Tiyint is not far, but it will be an arduous climb." Mytaru pointed up the rocky slope forming the valley's barrier wall, which had isolated the Urhaalan from other cultures for many generations. Mytaru set off at a stately pace, easy for Yunnie to match. "Tiyint is the most revered of all clan heroes, a sorcerer of incredible power, and a warrior second to none in our history."

"Even you?" joked Yunnie. He immediately regretted his lighthearted jibe. Mytaru's face reflected only anger. No one made light of minotaur heroes.

"Tiyint was greater than any other Urhaalan, and for this he shall be venerated forever. He fought enemies no longer walking the earth, using sword and spell so that all minotaurs would live. He gave himself up for the good of the herd. There can be no greater destiny."

"I meant nothing by my words," Yunnie said in way of apology. Mytaru hardly heard, lost in the telling of the legend of Tiyint.

"The times were different before the days of Urza and Mishra. Now, only a few dare cast feeble spells, and the

Inquisition eagerly opposes any practice of magic. Tiyint's enchantments were of cosmic power. It took a hero to cast them and a minotaur of unsurpassed integrity to direct them properly."

"He fought the orcs?" Yunnie knew the story, or thought he did.

"Tiyint fought the orcs with sword and lance. Tiyint fought the diabolical machines and merfolk with magic. Tiyint brought to all a wisdom never seen since." The words carried the ring of litany, and Yunnie knew better than to interrupt Mytaru.

"Our Celebration of Tiyint pays homage to our greatest of heroes. We bring new members into the herd, hoping they will follow Tiyint's path to honor and thereby give total devotion to the clan. If only one stands in the radiance of Tiyint's nobility and reflects it onto the herd, the Urhaalan can always reign supreme."

They continued to climb, trooping along until even Yunnie was out of breath. Mytaru resolutely marched up the path, eyes fixed on something more than the jagged rock and rocky trail. Yunnie had seen this expression before, usually during intricate minotaur rituals.

All day they walked until they came to a small canyon leading back into the hills. Lack of volcanic activity here put Yunnie's mind at ease. He was coming to believe something more menacing than either elf or goblin rose from the bowels of the earth to bother the minotaurs. But here in this quiet canyon, with sheer, towering red rock walls, he felt a curious peace. At the other Place of Power, excitement and energy had risen within his breast. Not here. Here he felt at peace with himself and the world for the first time in years—perhaps during his life.

He wondered if Mytaru shared this sense of tranquillity. From the set to his shoulders and the expression on Mytaru's face, it seemed unlikely. If anything, the minotaur reacted in a completely opposite manner. He snorted and looked as if Tiyint's presence fed the drive to wage war.

"There," Mytaru said in a choked voice. "There is the Shrine of Tiyint."

Yunnie stepped to the side and looked past his friend toward the end of the narrow canyon. He sucked in his breath and held it until his lungs strained. Only then did he let out the trapped air. Yunnie walked forward, as if this would bring him greater peace, but his sense of well-being was overcome by awe. Carved into the side of the mountain was a gigantic minotaur, ten times larger than life.

"Tiyint," Yunnie said, certainty in his voice.

"Tiyint," agreed Mytaru.

Mytaru did not stop him, so Yunnie made his way through the tumble of rocks to stand immediately below the overwhelming statue of the most heroic of all minotaurs. How long it had taken to fashion this statue, Yunnie could not say. It had been carved with loving care. Every surface was polished to a gleam almost painful to stare at, yet the feeling of harmony held him firmly. The statue's eyes were blind, but Yunnie knew Tiyint saw everything.

"Begin the ritual chant," Mytaru said. He widened his stance, took in a chestful of air, and let out a mournful cry that echoed down the canyon and through Yunnie's mind.

Rather than join the chant, which his throat could hardly fashion, Yunnie settled down and stared at the stone idol, letting his thoughts run wild. Somehow, in the presence of the statue his thoughts came more easily, more lucidly, with greater speed.

What battles had the real Tiyint seen? Yunnie knew Mytaru's brief recitation only hinted at the sorrow and sacrifice Tiyint had made for the Urhaalan minotaurs. Closing his eyes, he imagined Tiyint striding onto a battle-field, decorative ribbons showing clan affiliation fluttering from his shiny horns. A toss of the head, a snort, the low-ered horns, and a frantic charge into the ranks of his enemy. A jerk of powerful neck muscles could bring the horns to bear. Muscles rippling in his arms, Tiyint hurled his lance. Words shaping a spell, he cast magical death among those who dared oppose the Urhaalan.

His breath came faster, and he imagined himself thrust-ing with lance and taking the life of the herd's enemies.

He could run for miles and never tire. He could fight and kill and be drenched in searing blood and rise above it all because of Tiyint's example.

"It's almost as if Tiyint can step out of the mountain and join us," Yunnie said in a low voice filled with raw emotion. He had come to this most sacred of all minotaur shrines with peace in his heart. Now his nostrils flared and he wanted to drink his enemies' blood!

To his surprise, Mytaru responded. "He can, given the proper ritual. It is written that Tiyint will return to defend the honor and life of the herd, when needed."

"Is it needed now?" asked Yunnie.

"We await a sign," was all Mytaru said, returning to his chant.

Yunnie found himself clumsily joining in the chant, being carried to distant blood realms by its power. In the back of his mind, he realized Tiyint reflected the purpose of the chant, magnifying its message. If Mytaru had come here seeking peace and had prayed accordingly, Tiyint would have granted it. But the minotaur had sought war, and aggression became the overwhelming sensation filling Yunnie.

The sun vanished behind the rocky rim of the canyon wall and plunged the area into chilly premature night. The flowers that had blossomed so brightly a few hours earlier closed their petals and went to sleep, letting more fragrant night blooms open and hold sway. Their heady perfume made Yunnie giddy.

He reached over and plucked a trumpet-shaped white bloom and inhaled deeply. Its sweet fragrance sent his heart racing and pulse pounding. Any feeling of well-being experienced earlier vanished totally now. Whether it came from the night blossom, Mytaru's chanting, or a sense that something about the stone idol was changing, Yunnie could not say.

He paced nervously, occasionally looking up at Tiyint's graven image. The stone seemed to suck up all light now, turning into pitch-black rock. With light went emotion. Yunnie was being drained of his optimism and sureness that war could be avoided. Power exuded from the stone like condensation on a cold pane of glass. Power and something more that made Yunnie restless. No longer able to simply stand or sit, he paced like a caged beast, anticipating—what?

He jumped a foot when Mytaru bellowed, "There! There is the sign!"

Above the stony Tiyint rose Iontiero. The lesser moon boasted an annular rainbow of pale yellows and whites that, for a brief instant, showed as a halo around the statue's horn-crested head. As quickly as the halo formed, it disappeared as Iontiero rose furiously in the black sky.

"The herd will triumph," Mytaru said breathlessly. "Minotaur will win over elf in the coming war!"

Yunnie gaped. His vision had been completely different.

CHAPTER
16

EVEN HER WATERPROOF CAPE LET SOME RAIN sneak in, soaking her clothing. Maeveen O'Donagh tried pulling the cloak closer around her, but the clever wind from the sea-born storm proved too aggressive. Tiny eddies gusted about her ankles and sent the cape flying outward for another sheet of rain to blast against torso and legs. Head down and resigned to the drenching, Maeveen made her way through Iwset's now deserted streets and back to Vervamon's camp. She considered partaking of the warmth and cheer at the pub Quopomma had found, the Singing Geoduck, but she cared little for congregation or drink right now.

Sloshing through mud brought her to the Iwsetian defense wall. Sentries huddled under thin metal sheets for respite from the storm, the rain hammering loudly against the iron. Maeveen made a mental note that Ihesia's stalwart soldiers could be driven from their posts by inclement weather. If Lady Edara chose a time to launch a successful attack, this would be it.

Maeveen wiped rain from her face, hoping against hope the water would wash away her hated freckles. She knew it didn't. Her thoughts turned from the impossible to the change occurring in Iwset. More crept through the streets than the dead wagon and its lonely driver.

Ferantia, or so the ship's captain had called her, provided a curious riddle to be solved. From Jehesic, without a doubt, she met Lord Peemel's chief adviser in secrecy. What treachery did Digody plan with Ferantia? Who was being sold out? Both Edara and Peemel? Maeveen O'Donagh had seen senior advisers plot against their masters more than once. How did their plotting affect Vervamon and his expedition? What malevolence did the Inquisition bring to this combination of Iwset and Jehesic's advisers?

The Sigil of Iwset was no fit treasure to recover, she thought, and this Tomb of the Seven Martyrs only diverted Vervamon from his true research. It served as adequate lure to the ever curious explorer, but it held unknown danger if found. As much as she hated lurking around cemeteries watching grave robbers and gore-hungry ghouls, such work was cleaner than dealing with politicians and clerics bent on the domination of others.

Dark masses rose in the storm, alerting Maeveen to the camp's nearness. The supplies were spoiling in the weather, but that was Peemel's doing. If he had inquired, she could have given him a small list of items truly needed for a research expedition. Instead he had lavished tons of useless matériel on them, along with six spies. Six spies. This was another curious occurrence requiring considerable thought.

As Maeveen worried about the confrontation between Quopomma and Coernn and what it meant, her chief lieutenant appeared from the storm, an avenging force of nature herself. She muttered constantly to herself, or to her invisible companions, and stopped only when she saw Maeveen.

"Captain, glad you're back. When are we going to leave this miserable place? It's a sureness it can't get worse if we hike inland from here on the morrow. Get away from the shoreline's storm track, I say."

"Quopomma," she said in greeting, "I need to speak

with Vervamon. I have some concern about departing just yet."

"Why's that?"

"Treachery," was all she said. Could it be Digody and Ferantia plotted to waylay the expedition? A few extra days enjoying Peemel's fresh food and resting under his eye might be the tactic to pursue. It would surprise their enemies and might force a mistake, revealing the extent of the plot against them.

"Always that," grunted Quopomma. The ogre shook herself like a dog, sending sheets of water flying. "He's in his tent, all safe and dry, reading that Uncle Istvan-damned book of his."

Maeveen set off through the encampment, noting the way the guards were posted and alert, even in this downpour. For once, Iro did not have to be badgered into doing her duty. Maeveen took this as a good sign that they would get away from Iwset safely. All her soldiers fought well. It remained for their officers to do as good a job leading them and setting an example.

She stopped in front of Vervamon's tent. The reading light inside made the entire tent glow, dark water running off the sloping canvas roof in steady rivulets. She settled her thoughts, then entered. Vervamon looked up, a distant expression on his face. She knew he was lost in the wonders of the text he studied so intently.

"I need to discuss our departure," she said, thinking to edge into the subject. Vervamon's face lit up like a torch in the night.

"Ah, yes, of course, my dear Maeveen. Departure shall be at dawn, if we can determine when that is with this foul weather socking us in."

"No, that's not what I meant," she said. Maeveen settled an angry impulse. He could be so dense at times. "The unrest in Iwset affects us."

"What? Impossible. What do we care for internal politics in a nothing of a city-state? Knowledge. That ought to be our only concern. We are scholars hunting for the wisdom of the ages."

"If we leave, we might find ourselves beset by Jehesic

soldiers. Iwset and Jehesic go to war, and within the walls of Iwset there is a plot brewing. Digody—"

"Ah, yes, Digody. A learned man, that one, rare to find in a politician and bureaucrat. He has studied history and knows much, though not as much as I, naturally. He put me on to this fine volume about the Tomb of the Seven Martyrs, *Explorations in Antiquity*, by Sten El-rohar of Vhati."

"We place ourselves in danger between warring factions if we leave without knowing more of the situation," Maeveen said in exasperation. She cared nothing for Vervamon's academic pursuits right now. "Digody and Ferantia of Jehesic conspire. We need to know of this alliance and how it affects our studies." Maeveen tried to maneuver her reasons for remaining, if only a few more days, in a course Vervamon could appreciate. He blinked at her as if he had heard nothing.

"Politics means nothing. Knowledge is all. You may quote me on that in your journal."

Maeveen started to ask how Vervamon knew she kept a journal, then decided he must have seen her penning her daily thoughts of their travels.

"That is less important than the safety of my company—and you."

"We leave at first light, even if this dastardly rain does not let up. First light, the light of knowledge," Vervamon said, rolling the words off his tongue as if savoring a fine wine. "A nice turn of phrase. You may not use it. I reserve the right to include it with my monograph on this expedition."

The expedition left at dawn.

The rain slackened to a drizzle, but the all-night downpour had turned the roads to ankle-deep mud. The only other traveler on the road was a solitary man trudging through the mud toward Iwset. Maeveen shouted orders and Quopomma put her powerful back to pushing a supply wagon out of the mire. Iro scouted ahead with three of her platoon, and Vervamon strode along as if this was the finest day Terisiare had ever seen. He whistled a jaunty tune, and Maeveen wanted to strangle him.

She remembered the solitary traveler had been whistling cheerfully, too. A pox on them all!

As she worked to find a path through grass and rock that would not spell immediate disaster and a sore back for Quopomma, she eyed the six men who had joined the expedition. Inquisitors, she thought, though she usually had a stronger sense of the clerics than she did now. The way Coernn had faced Quopomma without a trace of fear bothered her. The ogre was imposing—Maeveen was glad Quopomma was her friend and comrade-in-arms rather than an opponent, and Maeveen usually feared no being.

She worked her way closer to Quopomma and asked in a low voice, "What of Peemel's 'observers'? Do they show any interest in this expedition so far?"

Quopomma shrugged her massive shoulders and wiped mud from her hands and arms. She glanced in Coernn's direction and pursed her lips before answering.

"He is a quiet one. Unusual for an Inquisitor. They can never be silent when you utter a blasphemy in their presence."

Maeveen did not have to ask if Quopomma had. It would have been only the first of many attempts on the ogre's part to provoke Coernn into a fight.

"As your captain, I must warn you against rousing Coernn's ire. He is a mere slip of a lad. I'd have to try you for murder, even if he struck the first blow." Maeveen wondered anew at the outcome of any fight between ogre and observer, choosing this way to warn Quopomma off from any squabble. They both needed to take Coernn's measure before proceeding against him and his five colleagues.

"The weather clears. I see patches of sky through those infernal clouds," Quopomma said loud enough for Coernn to hear. He took no offense at her mention of "infernal sky."

"We will follow the coastline toward Shingol, but cut inland two dozen miles south of that fishing village," Maeveen said.

"Is that where we will Vervamon's Tomb of the Seven Martyrs?"

Maeveen shook her head. She had no idea where the academic led them now. Before they left Iwset, Coernn had insisted he knew the location of the tomb, yet he had spent almost a day in his tent muttering and being tended by his colleagues before proclaiming their path of travel. Going from burial plot to ossuary to crematory to those who conducted ceremonies over the recently departed had framed the better part of her life for two months. Changing now to pursue Peemel's new infatuation did not please her.

"Do we dawdle, or do we find the hidden lore of the ancients?" cried Vervamon cheerfully. He laughed and set off at a clip impossible for the soldiers to maintain, burdened as they were with the supply wagons.

Maeveen wished Lord Peemel had seen fit to furnish them a few beasts of burden, but Ihesia had insisted all were needed for the war effort against Jehesic. The four soldiers pulling each of the four wagons tired quickly and had to be replaced with another, more rested, foursome. Maeveen worried that this would exhaust her company and limit their ability to fight, should the need arise.

She heaved a sigh of relief when, on the third day, they left the rugged coast and turned inland. This relief lasted only a few hours.

"Have your scouts cut faster," ordered Vervamon. He paced back and forth, wringing his hands. "This delay is intolerable when there are tombs to be unearthed."

"Graves to be robbed," grumbled Quopomma. Maeveen O'Donagh shot her lieutenant a cold look that did little to silence the ogre.

"We cannot push on any faster," Maeveen tried to explain. "The forest turned to jungle on us. It is unusual to find growth like this along the coast."

"We're miles inland," said Vervamon, as if lecturing a dimwit. "Why is there such a swamp, such tangled undergrowth, such delay in finding the Tomb of the Seven Martyrs?"

"It's not the scout's duty to carve us a path. Slyfoot ranges far and wide hunting for the best paths. He cannot be expected to hack through this with the knife he carries."

"Give the scout a bigger knife!" raged Vervamon. "There must be some in all those wagons we drag with us."

Maeveen did not answer directly. Her company traveled better, smarter, and faster with only a backpack to furnish their basic needs. Hunting as they went kept their skills honed. A soldier with an empty belly fired an arrow more accurately the next time a rabbit showed itself. Even better, a hungry soldier was more likely to notice slight movement in the brush, hoping it was dinner. All too often that rustling turned out to be an ambush otherwise ignored.

"More than supply wagons impede our progress," Maeveen said, staring at the six observers sent by Lord Peemel. Coernn argued with three others, then one left and Coernn continued his dispute with the two remaining. They had kept apart from Maeveen's soldiers and even turned down requests from Vervamon to dine with him. If she had to have spies in her midst, at least these had the good sense to be unobtrusive and keep out from under foot. The only things she wished from them were longer turns at pulling the supply wagon laden with their arcane equipment, and for them to be gone.

"Take care of it. I am anxious to find the Sigil of Iwset and enter the tomb," Vervamon said. "From my research, I am certain we can unlock the secrets hidden by time and too many petty conquerors. What do we truly know of the artificer twins and the Brothers' War? The answers lie with the seven martyrs in their eternal repose."

"What happened to the grave robbers?" asked Quopomma. "Why have you gone from studying them to being one?"

Maeveen silenced the ogre with a gesture, then waited to see if Vervamon was offended. He had not heard Quopomma's angry comment. She took the ogre's immense arm and led her to one side.

"I'll deal with Vervamon," she said. "Tend to hacking a path through this jungle."

"Not jungle," grumbled Quopomma. "I smell magic here. This growth is not natural, and that is a sureness even Vervamon ought to see."

Maeveen had to agree. The vines dangling across the path had dropped to the ground as they penetrated deeper into the woods, until dozens of roots sank into the soft earth, making travel increasingly difficult. Then, when shrubs went berserk in their growth and viciously thorned bushes spread across the trail, they might as well have been slogging through the Fuwallian Jungles in search of the rare night-blooming elf orchid.

"Get Iro to move the wagons to one side and let all the company work on clearing the route," Maeveen said. "If that doesn't get a better path for us, take what we need from the wagons, then abandon them."

"Your friends won't take kindly to that," Quopomma said, jerking her thumb in Coernn's direction.

"Don't call them my friends," Maeveen said with some rancor.

Resenting Coernn and his fellows did nothing to change the situation, but Maeveen could do nothing. Vervamon insisted they remain with the expedition—with their wagonload of enigmatic equipment. She started to argue with Vervamon again over the course their expedition was taking, then stopped as hideous shrieks reverberated through the jungle to chill her soul.

"To the living wall," Quopomma bellowed. "Iro, bring your squads. You, sergeant, get one of my squads. All forward with full arms!"

Maeveen had no dispute with her lieutenant's orders. She drew her own weapons and made her way through the litter of supplies and wagons to the solid wall of vegetation blocking their path. Maeveen lifted her sword between her and the writhing plant. A gray-green tentacle slashed at her, wicked barbs showing on the underside. Maeveen judged the distance and coldly hacked. The limb fell to the ground, still thrashing about.

"Iro!" cried Maeveen. "Watch out!" She saw her

lieutenant turn her attention from one plant to another—
allowing a barbed protuberance to loop around the gangly woman's legs. The plant spasmodically jerked, pulling
Iro from her feet. Kick as she might, she could not free
herself as the hungry plant pulled her along the ground
toward a gaping maw low on the stalk.

"Carnivorous plants!" shouted Maeveen. "Be wary.
Barbs on the branches." She covered the distance
between her and Iro in a flash. Her sword sliced at the
tough vine. For a breathless second Maeveen thought her
razor-edged sword was not equal to the task of saving her
lieutenant. Then the vine yielded.

Iro scrambled away, clawing at her legs. Her face con-
torted in pain. "It burns. There must be poison in the
barbs."

"Healer, attend her!" shouted Maeveen. She spun,
swinging her sword in a wide arc to hold other probing
tentacles at bay. Maeveen found herself fully occupied
keeping other vines from looping around her and finishing the job already started with Iro.

"You swing your sword like a sissy," came a deep
voice. A great sword whined past Maeveen's ear to lop
off a long section of ravenous plant. Quopomma stepped
forward, muscles turning to cables on her back and
shoulders as she worked to kill the tenacious vegetation.

"You move as if you had your feet in a bucket,"
Maeveen countered, lithely jumping over a tentacle and
cutting downward to prevent it from wrapping around
Quopomma's trunklike leg.

Together they fought until the ground was sticky with
sap. Maeveen and Quopomma saw Iro being carried from
danger. Slowly, they retreated to reform their company.

As Maeveen gave the orders to her soldiers, she saw a
curious sight a dozen yards to her right. Three of the
observers sent by Peemel approached the wall of carnivorous plants—or, from the way it looked to Maeveen, two
approached, dragging the third. They heaved their comrade forward. Vines lashed out and the wickedly barbed
underside curled about the man's legs. He screamed as he
slipped toward the open maw.

And vanished inside.

Maeveen lowered her sword, wondering why two of Coernn's companions had fed the third to the ravenous plant. Then she was fighting for her own life as the wall of green death renewed its attack on her.

CHAPTER
17

ISAK GLEN'DARD PULLED HIS CAPE CLOSER
around his slender body, musing on the lack of con-
veyances available along the coast. He wished the rattling
mechanical conveyance that had plunged over the cliff
into the sea had a mate. Even sitting in a burned-out husk
of a magically powered transport would be superior to
slogging along the dreary road in mud and storm. Still, a
lightness of heart kept him moving. He had accomplished
his bothersome task easily and well and had information
for his employers.

Lord Peemel would be happy that he need not fear an
elven-minotaur alliance along his northern border. Isak
had not lingered after giving Sacumon the instructions
from their liege, but he did not need to do so. Sacumon
brimmed with more than ambition to obey Peemel's
orders—and this would be reported, but not to the lord
of Iwset. Digody would learn of the sorceress's barely
hidden desire to rule on her own.

Isak muttered to himself. Digody was a dangerous
employer, more than Lord Peemel with his sudden flights
of anger and constant fear of disease. Isak had seen rulers
come and go, and they always fell from power for the

same reason: they ignored the perfidy of those around
them. Peemel had no idea that Digody hired his own
couriers to serve purposes different from his own.

A broader smile turned up Isak's lips. Digody had no
idea still another commanded this diplomat without a
portfolio. An alliance between this employer and
Sacumon might prove profitable in the future for all parties concerned, save for Digody and Peemel. Isak broke
into song in spite of the driving rain. Head high and
thoughts on the reception he would receive in Iwset, Isak
noticed a column of soldiers struggling to pull supply
wagons with wheels sinking into the sucking mud.

He touched the brim of his hat as the commander of the
company passed within a dozen paces. She hardly noticed
his courtesy, bent with the weight of her command. She
muttered constantly and occasionally shouted orders to a
huge ogre Isak thought he had seen before in one of
Iwset's many pubs. He continued to watch as they struggled past, the mud impeding their travel. Trailing behind
the soldiers came six others with a supply cart precariously
laden with crates. The six were dressed similarly, but in a
fashion and color differing from the others in the column.

Isak pulled up his cape and turned to keep his face
from being recognized by the six. He had seen them poking about Peemel's palace. Unsure of their allegiance,
Isak chose caution to boldness now. They might accompany the military column to further Peemel's plans—or
Digody's. He chewed his lip as he tried to remember who
else he had seen with the leader of this small band.

"Coernn," he said, finally summoning the pale young
man's name. "You go north for Lord Peemel and . . . who
else?" Isak frowned, trying to place Coernn with another
in the palace and failing. There was something he had
overheard or seen, and it had slid past his attention. Most
unusual, Isak decided. It was not like him to forget any
meeting, however insignificant it seemed. Through such
casual encounters he traced the strands of power running
like a drunken spider's web through any palace.

A gust of wind almost blew him from his feet. Isak
pulled his floppy-brimmed hat down to keep the rain out

of his eyes and lengthened his stride. The sooner he reached the comfort of Iwset, the sooner he could dry out, sip a glass of fine wine, and enjoy the pleasurable society of a companion of his choosing.

"She accepted the letter of instruction?" demanded Digody. "With her own hand she accepted it?"

"Sacumon took it from me," Isak said, easily skirting what he knew to be the truth. The envelope had been plucked from his grip magically. This insistence on Peemel's adviser's part convinced Isak the letter contained some magical device to hold Sacumon in check.

"Good, good," Digody said, bony fingers flexing in a tent under his chin. "You have done well. Here is your pay." Digody reached into the folds of his dark robe and came forth with a pouch laden with coins. It clattered to the table in front of him. Isak bowed, moving closer to the pay for his mission.

"What do you require me to say to Lord Peemel?"

"Tell him anything that makes him happy," Digody said. "My agent in the north will produce enough disruption to keep alliances from forming. That is all I require."

Isak knew Digody sought more. He wanted to insure Peemel's victory in the south before turning his own attention northward. With Sacumon stirring up a minor war, this gave Digody time to formulate his own plans for conquest there. Divide and conquer. It was an ancient but trusty tool in any ruler's workshop. Perhaps Digody even intended to use Sacumon against Peemel when the time came for the lord of Iwset to be deposed.

"Sacumon might prove difficult to control," Isak said. "She has goals beyond those of serving your honor."

"I am sure she thinks she can forge a new empire, but she is wrong. Never reveal everything to a truckler, Isak." Digody laughed harshly, and Isak knew that advice applied to simple couriers, also.

Isak Glen'dard took the pouch from the desktop, backed away from the adviser's presence, then settled his damp felt hat on his head. Isak reached up and ran his fingers over the Serra angel feather, wondering if he

ought to find another. Two feathers would be even jaun-
tier in appearance. Striding away, whistling softly, Isak
headed to one last stop within the city walls.

The audience with Lord Peemel had been quick and to
the point. A few coins jangled in his purse from that.
More from Digody kept Isak's lips sealed as to the trans-
fer of the envelope with its letter. But Isak had one last
employer to visit before considering where next to wander. Iwset's war with Jehesic would prove disastrous, of
that he was convinced. It would not benefit him to
remain in a city about to be sacked by marines bent on
revenge for dishonoring their ruler.

Hardly realizing he did so, Isak made his way through
the city in such a way that any following him would
become obvious. Neither Digody nor Peemel thought him
important enough to examine further. Isak might have
been offended by this seeming dismissal of his importance, but he was not.

"They are too ignorant to realize my true value," he
said to himself, stopping by a locked door in a narrow
alleyway. One last glance in all directions convinced him
no one was watching. He opened the door using a small
golden key from a chain around his neck. Ducking inside,
he made his way to the cellar and down a hidden tunnel
that wended its way through a rat's maze of subterranean
corridors. Any following this far would need more than
luck to track him.

At last he came to a narrow flight of steps leading up.
He spiraled around and around, past a ground floor, past
a second and third and even fourth, and finally opened a
hidden panel into a bedroom on the fifth floor of a stone
tower. A narrow window opened to give a spectacular
view toward the sea. A second presented a panoramic
view of the countryside to the south of Iwset, but Isak
had eyes only for the stunningly exquisite woman
stretched languorously on the bed.

"You took your time with Digody," the dark-haired
beauty said. Her indigo eyes danced with lust. She pulled
a thin wrap around her sensuous body as she sat up in the
soft bed, long, trim legs nakedly inviting Isak.

"I had to make a full report."

"Not too full, if I know you," she said, reaching out and pulling him to sit beside her. Slender fingers worked to free Isak of his expensive clothing. "I hope it was not too tiring."

"Not that tiring," Isak said. "Sacumon was—"

"Later, my darling. Later." Isak allowed Lady Ihesia to silence his report until later. Much later.

CHAPTER

18

"DID YOU SEE THAT?" MAEVEEN O'DONAGH called to Quopomma. The ogre swung her great sword with deadly effect against the wall of plants. "It's as if two of them fed a third to these things."

"Thoughtful, aren't they? Can't let nice foliage like this go unfed too long, or they turn prickly." The ogre grunted and jerked hard to pull her heavy blade from its juicy berth in the stalk of the carnivorous plant. "Mayhap Coernn will feed the others to the accursed monstrosity, then shove his own head in its maw." Quopomma kicked to keep a barbed tentacle from curling around her legs. She added, "We should be so lucky, and that's a sureness."

"Don't bother trying to save any of them, if it means putting yourself in danger," Maeveen said, using her own sword double-handed now to increase the strength of her blows, the once-sharp edge blunted by the tough vines.

"Me, in danger? Not me, Captain. I know how to play safe." Quopomma laughed, fending off a new attack.

Maeveen made her way from the wall of increasingly active vegetation and found Vervamon a few yards behind her. The white-haired scholar scribbled furiously in his notebook, looking up to fix details of the ravenous plant in his mind, then turning it into written description for their expedition log.

"Work your way back to safety," she told the academic. "Something aroused the wall, and it is trying to engulf us now. We have to retreat."

"Leave the supply wagons," Vervamon ordered, still writing in his crabbed hand. "They will only slow us in our advance to the rear. Take what you need from them first. Peemel was such a fool giving us trivial goods we could never use."

"We'll be lucky to get out of this with our hides in one piece," Maeveen said. She grunted as her sword bounced off a tough tentacle sporting fishhook-shaped barbs on it. She used her dagger to slice off a small tendril of the deadly vine as it flopped and flailed toward them. Trying to guess how fast the wall of plant life moved proved difficult as it moved swiftly on their flanks to block retreat while remaining stationary in front.

"It's trying to encircle us!" she called to Quopomma. "Keep it from closing."

"Aye, Captain," shouted the ogre. "Iro's on it. She's hobbling about, but then she never fought all that well before, either." Quopomma's great sword broke. She tossed it aside and drew her two sabers, using a scissors motion to slice at the writhing plants.

From the direction of the supply wagons came Iro's snarled protest. "You hunk of gristle, you don't know the first thing about combat. All you do is swing that flagpole of yours and think you do battle. Let me show you real fighting!" With a shout, Iro sent forth three soldiers, two orcs, and a mountain dwarf to use their axes against the encroaching barrier of plant life. The lanky lieutenant's own battle-axe chopped hard and fast into the smaller fronds threatening those in the rear of the company. Coernn and his four companions stood passively, neither speaking nor seeming too upset over the vegetative assault.

"We should get out of the circle of the attack," Maeveen urged Vervamon. The scholar nodded absently and walked off as if unaware of all that went on around him, yet he agilely leaped over a sweeping tentacle of green and stomped down hard on it. Pulp squashed under his boots and spattered up his legs, but he had escaped being trapped. Vervamon walked on as if nothing untoward happened.

"You, Coernn, you others, get out of here!"

"My supplies need to be moved first," Coernn said, indicating the wagon laden with equipment.

"Try moving it and you will die!" Maeveen had no time to see if they obeyed. She had a company to command and lives to save. The harder her soldiers fought, the more agitated the plants became. It was as if opposition forced them to grow and respond more vigorously.

In spite of this observation, Maeveen was not inclined to tell those in her company to put down their swords and simply watch. The ominous encroachment on their flanks told Maeveen that the carnivorous greenery would not rest until it digested the entire party. Where had it come from?

She hesitated long enough to see Coernn and the others frantically sorting through their crates, dragging out curious machines and books. One dour observer fumbled as he thrust bottles of what looked to be herbs and elixirs into his backpack. Coernn worked more methodically, drawing forth books and carefully sorting them, discarding many and keeping a few for his own pack. In spite of her inclination, Maeveen rushed back to sever a groping tentacle trying to loop around Coernn's throat.

He looked up, mildly surprised at her action. He tipped his head slightly and smiled. This was all the thanks she received. Maeveen grunted and ran back to the edge of the clearing, where Iro fought to hold open their escape route.

Shoulder to shoulder with her lieutenant, Maeveen fought until her arms ached and her armor floated on a river of perspiration. She lost all sense of time, though it seemed the sun crept with surprising speed across the sky, dipping low in the west. With twilight came even more frantic activity on the part of the plants.

"How many are free of the circle?" Maeveen tried to do a quick count of her command but failed. Sweat blinded her.

"Only you and me left, Captain," came Quopomma's gruff voice. "We can get free any time we want."

"Out!" Maeveen wanted to spend no more time than necessary fighting the inexorable wall of plants. With the ogre she edged toward the small opening that afforded their only escape route. Throughout the day, the hungry foliage had almost entirely ringed them.

"Comes night, it will go to sleep," said Quopomma.

"It's in a sunset frenzy now," Maeveen said. Her shoulder muscles refused to lift the sword more than a few inches. As she dipped the blade point, she saw they were not going to escape. The last paroxysm from the growth would cut them off—unless their daring proved greater than the plants' hunger.

"Get out and don't try to free me," Maeveen ordered her lieutenant.

"What? I can't let you die in here! Not when we're so close!"

"Obey, Lieutenant!" shouted Maeveen O'Donagh. "No disobedience now, or you'll get twenty lashes!"

Quopomma grunted something Maeveen did not catch, then backed through the narrow opening won by Maeveen's swinging blade. But when her slashing and hacking lessened, the small doorway to safety closed. Maeveen heard the ogre's bellow of outrage and frustration. Resting her sword arm, Maeveen went toward the supply wagons, hoping to put her back against one and savor a moment's respite.

The tentacles crept under the wagons in their hunt for flesh. She used her dagger to slice away small groping tendrils.

Setting fire to the supply wagons might drive back the growth, but Maeveen had no time to waste fiddling with her fire-making kit. The flint and steel required a specially whittled fuzz-stick for easy lighting. There was no time, no time remaining at all.

Maeveen hopped to the top of the nearest wagon and

balanced precariously on the crates. A few half-hearted slashes kept the groping plants away from her ankles, but she knew the creature would soon realize only she remained in its clutches. The wall of green would become an ever tightening ring of death.

Taking a deep breath settled her nerves. Maeveen sheathed her sap-drenched sword and knife and waited. Seldom had she done anything so hard as bide her time, watching the dim shapes of barbed tentacles approach, as a blind man uses a cane to tap his way through a maze.

"Maeveen! We're coming for you!" came the faint cry from the far side of the death wall.

"Don't," she called back. "I can escape. Give me another few minutes." Maeveen wiped her sweaty palms on her leather britches, dug her toes into the supplies underfoot, then launched herself through the air. A vine brushed her cheek, igniting pain unlike any she had ever felt. The poison exuding from the two-inch-long thorns threatened to paralyze her face and neck—and brain. She shook off the pain and concentrated on grabbing a tree limb free of the carnivorous plant growth.

Fingers straining, she clawed at the rough bark. She slipped and dangled by one hand, then pulled herself up and over the limb. For a few seconds she had eluded the hungering plant. Running along the thick limb took her almost to the periphery guarded by the living wall. Aerial shoots swayed to and fro, keeping her within the ring of death.

Maeveen licked her lips and tasted salty blood. She had bitten her lower lip when she jumped from the supply wagon to the tree limb. She rubbed her mouth on her sleeve and regretted it immediately. Acrid sap from the cloth burned her tongue. She spat, wishing she had a mouthful of gumweed to mask the bitterness.

Dancing lightly along the limb, she avoided the questing tendrils until she saw another branch above her. She jumped, caught hold, and scrambled upward into the tree. From here she leaped to the limb of an adjoining tree. She hit with bone-bruising force, and her arms refused to grasp. She had reached the end of her strength.

Downward she plunged, through cutting limbs and tiny twigs and slashing saw-toothed leaves and finally to the ground. She lay flat on her back, gasping vainly.

Through fogged eyes she stared up and saw a mountainous body looming over her.

Then she was plucked upward as easily as a child lifts a toy and thrown heavily over a broad shoulder.

"You're safely beyond the damned plants' gropers, Captain," came Quopomma's jovial words, "but you owe me an extra ration of whiskey for this chore, and that's a sureness. You owe us all, but especially *me*."

Maeveen O'Donagh was in no position to dispute Quopomma's claim to the liquor, as long as she got her share.

CHAPTER

19

YUNNIE FORCED HIMSELF TO WAKE UP, THOUGH
his eyelids stayed half closed. The rituals leading to war
were exhausting and lengthy and, for once, his agility did
not benefit him. Mytaru's endurance proved far greater
than his during the all-night chants, the hard runs from
one end of the Urhaalan's valley to the other, the long
vigils watching for signs from spirits.

He had survived the skirmishes with the elves. He was
not sure he would survive the preparation for war with
the forest dwellers.

"Let him sleep," Mytaru suggested to his wife. Noadia
knelt and pulled the blanket up over Yunnie's shoulders.
He stirred and rolled onto his back, staring at her. He had
been half asleep and now came fully awake, but how he
ached! His body screamed for rest.

"The rituals," Yunnie said, rubbing sleep from his eyes.
"We have to continue."

"You rest. What good will you be in combat if you fall
asleep on your lance?" Mytaru laughed, slapped Yunnie
on the shoulder, then ducked his head so his horns
avoided the delicately carved lintel, and left his wife's
house. Noadia watched Mytaru, then vented a deep sigh.

"War, it is always war," she said. "Why can't you tend our pastures? The weeds grow high and need cropping. There are so many more important chores to do." Noadia sighed heavily again, resigned to life with a warrior. "But no, I prepare the jerked meat for our fighters to give them strength in battle."

"I think we are getting ready to fight the wrong ones," Yunnie said. "The goblins are the enemy, not the elves."

Yunnie felt a tickle of memory and tried to grasp it more firmly. Something was wrong with this flat statement. A dark figure, a stinking swamp, talking, forgetting, it all jumbled in his head. The harder he tried to bring it into focus, the more tenuous his thoughts became. He held his head. Only peace between elf and minotaur would work, but the more he worked for a parley, the less he achieved. If only he could find the right words, but he never—quite—succeeded. He felt hollow inside, worrying that his words only added fuel to a small fire, causing it to flare out of control. Why did he always speak the wrong words? What if he had said nothing?

"No," he said to himself. "I am not the problem." Enmity between the two factions would soar to a dangerous level, no matter if he were here or in Shingol. When the minotaurs finished their ritual at the end of the Time of Resolution, they would march off to war. With him or without him. It did not matter.

He could not shake the horrible feeling that his protests spurred the minotaurs on. And that Sacumon relished that fact.

"Sacumon," he said, the shadowy figure coming into focus. "Who are you?"

Yunnie remembered bits of their conversation now and caught the hints of contradiction in what Sacumon told him. Did she truly believe the goblins were responsible, or did she say that to spur him on in a false direction? Her talk of peace rang hollow. Her ironic tone was more memorable than her actual words.

"What is that, Yunnie?" asked Noadia, working on a religious amulet, weaving colored yarns through carefully

carved wooden struts. Yunnie had seen many of the
females wearing these after their own secret, separate ceremonies, perhaps the only outward show of religion
Noadia displayed.

"I have to prepare food packs before Mytaru marches
off to kill elves. Would you like to help?" Her tone was a
mixture of contempt and anxiety.

"I was thinking out loud," Yunnie said. "What can I
do?"

"Gather the meat, and I will put it into the bags for
travel," she said. Yunnie nodded and went about the
four-room structure finding the various storage places.
Minotaurs left no cranny unfilled in their homes, giving a
solidity to furniture never found in human dwellings, as
much to support their extra weight as for distaste for
wasted space. Over every window blazed Mytaru's clan
emblem drawn in blood to ward off enemies.

Yunnie stepped closer and peered at the symbol beside
it. Noadia had placed her former clan emblem next to it,
to insure domestic serenity and prosperity under this
roof. Yunnie paused and wondered what Noadia used for
the careful delineation. She kept her house spotlessly
clean, but as he touched the clan emblem, his finger came
away black.

"Soot." He tried to piece this together with everything
else rattling in his brain. The footsteps he had followed to
the fumarole had been caused by intense heat—and the
overhanging tree limbs had been burned, too. He had
been attacked by some hideous fire creature and had
fought his way free. The melted dagger proved the searing intensity of his opponent had not been imagined.

But it had somehow slipped from his mind. Why?
How?

"Yunnie? I have to go out for a few hours."

"I should go, also," he said, knowing Noadia hesitated
to chase him out, yet was loath to leave him in her home
alone even though he was a clan member and Mytaru's
blood brother. She took her responsibilities seriously, and
household security was a part of that duty. He ducked out
the door facing east, as did all minotaur entrances, to

prevent the spirits of the dead from entering from their home from the west.

He stepped into the bright sunlight, an immense tiredness washing over him like the waves of the sea. He needed rest, but most of all he needed to meditate and piece together the mental images assailing him. Walking slowly, he went down the grassy slope outside Noadia's house. From near the small stream meandering along the middle of this branch of the main valley, he looked uphill to Noadia's house.

She had built well and could be proud of her home. Yunnie smiled a little, thinking how lucky Mytaru was to have a wife able to provide such a fine house and so much love to fill it. The slanted roof was tightly shingled with wood shakes, and the walls were decorated with dried fronds from medicinal plants giving a faint, agreeable odor to the entire area. The doors were secure against both wind and invader, though the windows were too wide for safety inside should the elves begin firing their deadly arrows.

"The roof," Yunnie said aloud, "it will burn. The elves used fire arrows. Aesor's clan was burned out." He stared at Noadia's house, but he saw the charred remnants of Clan Helmhein in its place. The shingles would burn, no matter how Noadia might have treated them, and nothing Mytaru could do to protect her and the house would work. The elves need only stand off a hundred paces and shoot their fire into the roof.

Knowing the danger ahead, vowing to prevent it, Yunnie started walking. At first he had no clear notion where to go. He walked and thought, his resolve hardening. Then he realized where he headed. Back to the fumarole where he had been attacked by . . . whatever it was.

The heavy yellow pall hanging over the land convinced him he neared the spot where he had been trapped before. This time, he approached by climbing over the rocky ring around the pit, avoiding the narrow passageway that had trapped him before. His azure eyes watered as he peered over the rim into the smoldering pits. The fumaroles quietly spewed their filthy vapors and covered the rock with lacy sulfur crystals, but other than this, Yunnie saw nothing out of the ordinary.

"Rock, some water bubbling up from a spring and—" he said, catching his breath "—a cave entrance." Hidden behind an outcropping of rock lay deep shadow, but within the shadow Yunnie saw only ebon darkness hinting at something more. He wiped sweat from his eyes and pushed his hair back across his high forehead, then realized he only postponed what had to be done.

Like a snake, he slithered over the rim and dropped into the circle of stone, forcing away an irrational dread. He knew it was only because of his experiences here a week ago. Even as he used this rationalization to wash away his fear, his booted toe kicked the remnant of his dagger.

The blade had struck the monster and had melted. What good was the sword at his side, or the new dagger Mytaru had given him from the clan armory against such a creature?

Yunnie's gaze turned toward the curtain of rock hiding the cave entrance. If he left now, he would never know what lay in that cave. It would be cowardly, but no one would ever know. No one but himself and the dreams that would stalk him every night of his life. He stepped forward, ready to use his sword, even if it melted against his enemy.

He expected heavy sulfur fumes to gust from the mouth of the cave, but he felt only cool air against his face. He closed his eyes and used other senses to penetrate the darkness. He smelled life, community, more than a single creature dwelling in the depths. More than this, he heard grinding and grating of rock against rock, as if someone struggled to drag huge boulders along stony trails.

"Goblins," he said, knowing their favorite weapons were boulders pushed down on their enemies. No one who lived in the foothills was safe from goblin attacks.

Yunnie slipped forward, hand reaching out to touch the curving cave wall for both support and guidance. Stepping into the darkness, he found himself blind within ten paces. He swallowed his fear and forced himself to keep walking and not retreat to comforting sunlight. He needed proof to present to Mytaru and the others before the Time of Resolution ended. Blood would flow, and not just elven blood, either. As much as Yunnie disliked Aesor, he had no desire to see his herd brother injured if fighting could be avoided.

Yunnie paused, considering Aesor—and Mytaru. The minotaurs were so caught up in the rituals of war, they saw no other course. While they were never lightly started, the rituals foreordained war. No one started on such a complex ceremony without intending to complete it in blood.

Grinding noises lured Yunnie forward again. As he walked, hand sliding along the rough wall, he noticed dim light far in front of him. His stride lengthened as the illumination grew. By the time he reached the faint circle of pale yellow light, he had his dagger out, ready to fight goblins.

Yunnie cursed under his breath when he failed to see any. He had hoped to find their lair and spy on them, perhaps stealing some proof that the goblins fought a guerrilla war against both elf and minotaur, provoking them to fight each other. He now realized how foolish such a hope on his part had been. Aesor was fond of pointing out the goblins were vicious, not smart. They might plan, but it would never been laid out in a single document Yunnie could hold up as another might display a trophy head in an honors court.

The grinding sound became louder. Curiosity drove Yunnie forward. Well-trod paths spiderwebbed across a vast cavern below him. Burn marks on both rock floor and cavern wall alerted Yunnie to the recent passage of whatever monster it was that had almost killed him above. He stepped from the path and wedged himself behind a stalagmite to hide while he reconnoitered.

It took several minutes for him to make any sense out of the vaulted cavern and all within it. The trails showed constant use, but he saw no one on them. In the middle of the cave floor, a crystal clear pool seemed to sink limitlessly to the core of the planet. Around the pool were lumps that might have been benches, but for what sort of creature Yunnie could not decide. They were sloping and massive, as if some giant leaned against them rather than sat to listen to a speaker in the center of the ring.

And always came the grating noise of rock slipping over rock. He failed to locate the source as it filled the entire stony vault. He started to move deeper into the cave when he saw a dark figure drifting along the floor, fifteen feet below his vantage point. It was as if he had a balcony seat overlooking a huge rock amphitheater. Yunnie settled down to see if he could identify this solitary figure.

"Sacumon," he muttered. Memories flooded back, but he could not put it all into order. The woman had said something, and he had grown forgetful. "A spell. You cast a spell on me," he whispered. His hand tightened on the wire-wrapped handle of his dagger. Rising, he edged closer to peer down at Sacumon.

Sacumon faced away from him, toward a rock wall.

Yunnie blinked and rubbed his eyes. His vision betrayed him. The solid wall rippled and changed color subtly. Yunnie edged closer to the edge of the drop-off, not caring if Sacumon saw him. He was too mesmerized by the patterns swirling about on—in—the rock. And then the ever-changing designs firmed and stepped *from* the wall.

First one exited from solid rock, then another, and another, and still another, until ten of the strange beasts stood in a half circle around Sacumon. Yunnie kept looking from the creatures to Sacumon and to the solid wall. How had they emerged from rock so firm?

The creatures did not walk as much as they flowed, a pseudopod slipping out and the thicker body following. Of faces Yunnie saw nothing, but he had the impression of sensory organs focused on Sacumon. The semiliquid creatures flowed around, one bouncing off its neighbor and others flowing through to emerge on the far side as they propped themselves against the sloping ledges.

For such beings, the rock wedges proved perfect for relaxation.

"Select Ones, attend!" Sacumon called in a voice that resonated in the immense cave. "All proceeds according to plan."

Yunnie peered at Sacumon, wondering how the woman fit into all this. She had seemed to be an ally of the Eln Forest elves, and now she spoke to the restlessly shifting, indistinctly shaped creatures with easy familiarity.

"When?" came a voice carved from rock. The grating noise might have been what Yunnie had heard earlier, but he did not believe so. He could not tell which of the rock beings spoke. Sacumon had no such trouble. She turned to the creature on the far left and faced it.

"Select One, soon. The minotaurs prepare for war through ritual even now. The elves fear the minotaurs and move supplies to the mouth of the Urhaalan lands."

"Goblins?" ground out the rock creature.

"They are alerted and will serve in the manner already decided. You must guarantee their participation."

"They will obey. They have no choice. We rule their underground domain now."

"So it has been for forty years," Sacumon said, bowing deeply and spreading her hands in front of her in mock supplication. She straightened and folded her hands again in front of her.

Yunnie tried to make sense of the exchange. Sacumon directed the gathering storm clouds of war with the precision of a general, but to what end? The rock creatures on their sloping ledges smoked slightly, showing how hot their bodies were. Even as he tried to make sense of the situation, one stood and returned to the solid rock wall. The creature pressed against the bulwark, then flowed along the surface and eventually merged with the stone.

Yunnie had seen enough to plead his case with Mytaru and others in Clan Utyeehn, even if he had to bring them into this cave to see the outlandish stone creatures with their own eyes. And Sacumon somehow proved to be the common thread running from elf to goblin to minotaur aboveground.

He forced his way out from behind the stalagmite and
started up the path leading to the surface. Yunnie
stopped suddenly, eyes widening in fear.

Ahead of him in the passage glowed a fire creature,
eyes of flaming coals and a mouth that gaped to display
the heart of a blast furnace.

CHAPTER
20

FEAR FROZE HIM, BUT THE HEAT RADIATING from the advancing monster gave strength to Yunnie's arm. He drew back and threw his dagger at the creature, as he had done aboveground. As before, the blade struck the creature's chest and melted from the intense heat. Yunnie knew better than to rush forward and grapple with the flaming giant.

Eyes like burning coals fixed malevolently on him. Blunt fingers reached out; Yunnie danced back, feeling painful blisters rise on his arm from the near touch. The blazing monster groped awkwardly for him. Its mouth opened wider, and a sizzling hiss emerged.

Yunnie had no idea if it tried to talk, or simply cried out in rage. It did not matter. The lightest touch would mean death. Backing away, Yunnie came to the rim above the amphitheater. He glanced over his shoulder and saw that Sacumon had gone, but three of the semisolid rock creatures remained. The tendrils of steam rising from them told of their heated nature. While not as fiery as the lumbering monster blocking his escape, they were hardly less dangerous.

"Back!" shouted Yunnie, hoping to startle the monster

into a mistake. The creature might not have heard for all the effect it had. Yunnie scooped up pebbles and cast them at the giant's burning face. Some of the gravel went into the wide-open mouth, hissing and popping and vanishing in puffs of smoke.

"Kill you," the creature said as it lumbered forward. Every step it took left sooty prints similar to those he had seen outside Clan Helmhein's destroyed settlement. This revelation about the identity of the minotaurs' true enemy did nothing to suggest how he was going to live to tell anyone of it.

A larger rock sailed through the air and seemed to stick on the creature's chest. Yunnie followed it with two other, bigger rocks. Like the pebbles tossed into the burning, open maw, these turned liquid and vanished in wisps of gas.

"Kill you now," the creature promised. Yunnie learned to decipher the hisses and grating sounds better. It was a skill he hoped would not be put to the test for much longer.

"I mean you no harm," he shouted, hoping to appease the fiery guardian of his path to safety. "I . . . I was looking for a lost goat. I'm from above. It wandered from its pasture." He jerked his thumb upward to indicate where he so fervently wanted to be.

The monster gave him no chance to speak. A thick, smoldering arm swung like a club, aimed squarely for his face. Yunnie ducked under the hot limb, tottered on the edge of the amphitheater, struggled to keep his balance, then fell heavily into the pit below. He crashed against hard rock, stunned. He moaned as air tried to force its way back into his lungs.

The sight of the semimolten rock beings moving off their sloping rests sent a surge of energy through him. Gasping, crying in pain, he forced himself to his feet. Fifteen feet above him towered a fire monster like he had faced twice before. Memory of the Place of Power Mytaru had shown him earlier returned in a rush. This was what he had seen around the fumaroles. . . . And had it been talking with Sacumon?

It struck him as likely. Even then, even before the Celebration of Tiyint, Sacumon had invaded the Urhaalan's valley and dealt with this strange behemoth of rock and fire.

At the sound of another hiss, he spun around to face a blank rock wall. From the surface rose a figure in relief. In front of him grew another of the stone creatures as it passed through the rock and into the open amphitheater. He backed away from it as it emerged from solid stone, only to feel the warmth from the others behind him. Spinning, Yunnie jumped onto a stalagmite and balanced.

A burning missile struck his arm, dislodging him. He fell heavily again, rubbing at the scorched spot on his upper arm where the monster above had struck him with his well-thrown pebble. Yunnie stared up and saw the burning eyes fixed on him. The mouth opened even wider as smoke and flame belched forth.

"Bad breath," he muttered. "That's enough to make me avoid you." He rolled past two of the beasts slipping toward him, their movement making the now familiar sound of rock grating on rock.

Yunnie scooped up a handful of gravel and tossed it toward the creatures. The stones stuck to their chests and then were subsumed, as if they digested his pitiful offering and hungered for more. He got to his feet, dodged another flaming rock thrown from above, and dashed down a path that seemed safe enough. A bull-throated roar of anger and defiance chased him as he ran. In that cry he heard his death sentence.

The fierce, fiery monster would never let him escape alive.

Yunnie fought a catch in his throat and a sense of helplessness. Mytaru wasn't going to save him this time. However he escaped, he had to do it on his own.

"Can't die, not yet," he told himself. "I haven't composed my death chant yet." From the time they were accepted as full members of the herd, all Urhaalan minotaurs worked on the sorrowful lamentation to be sung at their funerals. Somehow, Yunnie had never found the time, occupied with other concerns. Now he was sorry he had neglected this task. Would Mytaru sing one of his own? Mehonvo? Would Aesor?

He dug his heels in and skidded on the hard rock path. The large boulders on either side of the path ahead began to ripple. The surfaces bulged slightly, rippled again, and then the rock *things* oozed forth to block his retreat. A quick glance over his shoulder convinced him he had no chance to return to the amphitheater. All he saw were the flaring yellow eyes of fire and a mouth opening to the center of Hell. The soot-black arms waved about menacingly as stubby legs carried the creature forward.

"Aiee!" Yunnie yelled, and whipped up his sword in time to deflect a lump of flaring coal. It ricocheted from his sword blade and almost knocked the weapon from his grip. He dropped to one knee, regained his composure, then rose to face the beast.

The path ahead was filled with two of the creatures and the clomping brute filled the path behind. He gripped his sword tighter and saw no hope for eluding any of the rock monstrosities. A loud grinding behind him told of the two nearing, as well as increased warmth on his naked back. And in front?

Arms like burning logs reached for him.

Yunnie jumped from the path, crashed into a stalagmite, whipped around, banged his head against a dripping limestone stalactite, then fell to the ground. New hissing told of the creatures coming through the cavern wall after him. Yunnie rubbed the bloody spot on his head, got his knees under him, and lunged forward, avoiding their groping hands. Rock sizzled and popped wherever the monster touched the cavern floor.

Yunnie dodged a few more pieces of molten rock flung at him as he wiggled under a small rock arch and came out on another path. A steel door set in the rock wall drew him. It was the only sign of wrought artifact he had seen since descending into this underground Hell filled with smoking monsters intent on frying his flesh. He skidded to a halt in front of the door, tested the handle, and found it open.

From behind he heard rock grating on rock—more coming from within the solid sides of the cavern—and the all-too-familiar hissing of the more mobile and equally determined creature with the burning eyes. A lump of burning coal crashed into the door and shattered into a thousand stinging pieces.

"Get away!" Yunnie shouted. The monster kept coming, its slow, inexorable pace sure to pin him against the steel. He wiped flecks of hot cinders from his eyes and tugged hard on the handle. To his surprise, the door opened on well-oiled hinges. He almost took a tumble backward, recovered, and spun around the door, slamming it hard behind him.

"There is a latch that will keep them out," came a soft voice.

"Thanks," Yunnie said, dropping a locking bar in place. Only then did he turn to see who had spoken.

"Sacumon!"

"Ah, this is an interesting development. You remember our prior meeting?" The woman glided toward him, as if she rolled rather than walked. She held out a hand ritualistically scarred and decorated with intricate, colorful tattooing. Yunnie blinked. It appeared that the tattoo came alive for a moment, a snake rising from the woman's arm to strike at him.

"What is this place?" demanded Yunnie.

"This? The armory of the Niroso Stone People. Quite impressive, isn't it?"

"Not *this* place. This *place*!"

"Ah, the cavern. A curiosity of geologic proportion," Sacumon said, as if lecturing a dimwit. "A huge bubble of volcanic gas became trapped centuries ago, creating this small underground cathedral."

"Small? It's huge. I cannot see the limits, even with the light from the lava pits." Yunnie heard the creature banging outside the door. "Can it get inside?"

"The coal golem?" Sacumon shook her head. "I think not. That is why the Niroso use steel. They are quite advanced for such a young culture."

"Coal golem? What is that?"

"You have no contact at all with things magical, do you, fishboy?"

"Don't be insulting." Yunnie advanced, sword tip ready to spit the woman should she not make an apology.

"I see I have injured your feelings. If you find it offensive that you hail from Shingol, I apologize."

"Accepted," Yunnie said, realizing he had been insulted anew. He chose not to press the issue. Let Mytaru and the headstrong, prideful minotaurs worry over such slights and the retribution their honor decreed. "Now tell me about the coal golem. How do I escape it?"

"You have done well so far," Sacumon said. "It is not alive, not actually. The Niroso are adept at finding undead creatures in the earth. Their domain is underground—all the planet not exposed to the surface where we live such productive lives. They found veins of coal and, using their knowledge of such spells, freed golems from dark deposits."

"Sorcery," spat Yunnie.

"Yes, of course. I am not sure if it is their nature to flow through solid mountains as they do, or if they use some arcane and long lost lore to accomplish the feat."

"They travel through rock by melting into it and then just . . . just appearing elsewhere?" Yunnie tried to keep his mind from spinning. Such knowledge lay beyond his ken. While he had no love for the Inquisition, he shared their distaste for magic and its users. Too much destruction had been brought upon the world by sorcerers and their ill-considered spells.

"That is so. They happened upon the surface forty years ago, quite by accident. Up and down have little meaning for the Niroso. They simply . . . flow. One encountered a human graveyard, alerting others to the concept of life on the surface. Since then, they have tried to make contact and have not done well."

"They are so alien to all we know."

"True. They are unlike the Ironroots and other nonhuman beings that abound in that they have no definite shape."

"Like a stony jellyfish."

"No, not exactly," Sacumon countered. "They are different in ways I cannot explain to you. They are very intelligent and curious, and desire only the best for all races."

Yunnie wobbled slightly, bracing himself on a stone ledge as waves of dizziness washed over him. He had felt this way before when he first met Sacumon. The woman's outstretched hand seemed innocent enough, as if she offered aid, but he recoiled when he saw how the tattooed designs on her flesh writhed as if alive. Serpents spat and struck, fangs agleam, and hideous monstrosities from the depths of his worst nightmares poked out from under her sleeve.

But he resisted, and Sacumon withdrew a short dagger from her belt, drawing its wicked tip along the back of her arm. A tiny line of blood appeared, and with it came a new wave of dizziness for Yunnie. Somehow, spilling blood augmented the sorceress's power and reinforced her hold over his mind.

"Best for everyone," Yunnie heard himself repeating, as if a hundred miles distant and watching someone else perform a mime's festival play.

"Yes." Sacumon hissed like one of the snake's emblazoned on her wrist. The dagger vanished, but the wound on her arm remained, sluggishly flowing to drip onto the dusty cavern floor.

"The coal golem," he said. "It will break down the door. It is so strong."

"I fear you are right," Sacumon said. "See how hot spots appear on the metal? The golem will melt its way through soon. The door served only as a reminder to its dim brain that it ought not enter here."

"Why not?" Yunnie grabbed for any slight advantage. "What is here that it fears?"

"Fears? Nothing, the coal golem fears nothing. It is less intelligent than even a goblin. Rather, the Niroso wanted to keep human artifacts away from it to give as presents, peace offerings, a kind of courtesy when they encountered abovegrounders."

Yunnie leaned more heavily against the stone ledge as

new dizziness hit him like a war club. Sacumon lied. Every time she spoke an untruth, the dizziness racked his senses, but he could do nothing about it.

"These Stone People. What do they want?"

"Only to live in harmony with those on the surface," Sacumon said. More lightheadedness as she drew fingernails along the cut on her arm, widening the wound and causing more blood to flow. "It came as a shock and wonder to them that anything could live in the utter cold—to them—on the surface."

"What happens to them when they emerge?" asked Yunnie, sensing a distant, vague truth that Sacumon glossed over with her silky words. "Why do they need a coal golem to come to the surface for them?"

"You should look about this armory. They find many human relics as they drift through the rock," Sacumon said. "Perhaps something herein might prove useful in eluding the coal golem."

"Weapons," he said, studying the devices fastened to the walls. "And armor of all kinds. So much, and all of it useless to the Niroso. They could never wear or use any of this. It is more a museum than an armory for them."

"Presents to prove their good faith," Sacumon insisted. Yunnie almost fell over as giddiness crashed into him like a physical blow. The room spun in wide, crazy circles until he was forced to close his eyes. The vertigo passed; the nausea mounting in his belly did not.

"The door," Sacumon said urgently. "The coal golem is almost through. Here, try this on. It might fit you." The woman pushed back her long, loose sleeves, revealing more of the animated tattooing on her arms as she reached for simple leather armor.

"I would try this breastplate," Yunnie said, tapping a well-wrought suit of armor standing nearby. "It is almost my size. That is too small."

"I think not," Sacumon insisted. "Try it."

Yunnie almost vomited as compulsion seized his senses, but he reached out and took the pathetic leather armor. In his hands it came alive, writhed, and turned warmer by the second. He started to throw it away, but held it in mute fascination as it grew larger and changed shape.

"I think it just might fit," he said, pulling it closer. He tossed the leather straps over his shoulders. They fastened themselves as the armor molded perfectly to his muscular chest. He ran his fingers lightly around the middle of the armor. It pulsed with power, transmitting some to him. Gone now was all the wooziness. Replacing it came a certainty of victory. He could fight the coal golem and triumph.

He could fight all the Niroso and defeat them singly or as an army!

"Living Armor," Sacumon said in a reverential tone, as if she spoke of the dominie of the Church. "It fits you. You were meant to wear it in battle, fishboy."

Yunnie hardly heard the insult. He stood straighter and felt a vitality unlike any he had known before. Accepted into the Urhaalan herd, he had been tired but thrilled at the honor. After each ritual Mytaru had led him through, he had experienced zeal and a renewed vitality. Nothing compared to the sensation of invincibility he now savored like a delicate, subtle taste, the ineffable touch of friendship, or a lover's whisper in his ear.

Yunnie swung his sword and knew he could never die.

"The door weakens. If we are not to be trapped, you must get past the coal golem," Sacumon said. She moved behind him. He knew he had to fight his way free to save her, to escape from this underground dungeon filled with Stone People.

He flicked aside the locking bar and waited for the right instant to fling open the door. He caught the coal golem between assaults on the steel plating. The golem stood stupidly just outside the armory. Yunnie rushed forth, sword swinging. He melted off the first foot of steel as he tried to run the monster through. Then he smashed hard into the coal golem, sending up a shower of sparks and cinders.

The coal golem roared in pain and staggered away. The armor surrounding Yunnie protected him as the creature tossed bits of burning coal at him. Every touch added to his spirit, his life force, driving him onward.

He drove his sword down into the coal golem's yawning chasm of a mouth and felt the blade turn in his grip as if he had struck rock. He refused to yield. He repeatedly struck with his sword until it was reduced to hardly more than a dagger.

"Run, lead the way out," came Sacumon's urgent words. "The Niroso come to see what is wrong."

The coal golem lay on its back, writhing in obvious pain. It bucked and thrashed about, then lay ominously still. Inside its mouth, Yunnie saw the heat go from red to yellow, then to white-hot. The golem expanded and finally exploded, sending fireballs sailing in all directions.

Cringing, turning, Yunnie took the glowing barrage on his armor. The Living Armor.

"This way. I can get out now!" he shouted, running hard from the burned pit where the coal golem's remains seethed.

Yunnie bounced off a Niroso emerging from a rock wall. The Living Armor protected him and let him race on until he found the sloping path leading to the surface. He ran and ran and ran, until he burst into bright sunlight and fresh air. Even then he did not stop running until he was far from the mouth of the cave leading to the Niroso's underground world.

Gasping for breath after his frantic run, Yunnie leaned over and put his hands on his knees.

"We made it. We escaped!"

Only the soughing of wind through distant treetops answered him. He looked around and saw he was alone. Sacumon had stayed in the cavern.

CHAPTER
21

"SET FIRE TO THE JUNGLE, UNCLE ISTVAN TAKE it all!" cried Quopomma. She slapped her hairy right hand down on an equally hairy left forearm, making a loud smacking sound to show her anger, as if it weren't apparent to all around the campfire from the way she glowered at anyone daring to make the slightest noise.

Maeveen O'Donagh chewed gumweed, studying the faces of her assembled officers and noncoms. She spat into the fire. A thin white wisp of steam rose, signaling her intention to speak. Quopomma fell silent. A hard glare at Iro kept the other lieutenant from voicing her opinions before Maeveen.

"We can't go through the carnivorous plants," Maeveen said. "Scouting reports tell us it is spreading like wildfire in both directions, throwing up a barrier to prevent us from flanking it. Going through the trees on the branches as I did to escape isn't practical."

"It is," insisted Iro. "We can navigate just fine." The gangly lieutenant's eyes caught the firelight and turned them an eerie flat silver. "Leave them that can't make it behind."

"Vervamon?" Maeveen's soft naming of their leader quieted Iro. The lieutenant too often spoke first and considered afterward. "He is unable to maintain any pace through the trees, as if he were some kind of Cape Furious monkey."

"Then we must return to the coast," came Coernn's calm voice from outside the circle. "We need to find the coast, get our bearings, then continue on our mission."

"To find the Sigil of Iwset?" Maeveen asked in a contemptuous tone. She wanted to see how Coernn reacted when she named the reason for their expedition in front of her officers. Maeveen was not unduly surprised when Coernn said nothing and showed no anger at the revelation. This only gave her another bit of proof the Sigil of Iwset was the bait dangled in front of Vervamon, hoping the explorer would snap at it like a hungry fish. The true reason for diverting their quest lay elsewhere.

"We follow a path set by Vervamon, one that is inconsistent with what we know. I have, uh, decided on a different path, one of greater promise. We can reach Shingol in a week's time and—"

"Shingol?" barked Quopomma. "Why do we go to such a filthy fishing village? Captain O'Donagh is always talking about how she enjoys fishing, and even she would avoid Shingol. It is nothing but debris left after a hurricane, and the people there gasp like the bottom feeders they are!"

Maeveen watched Coernn's reaction. This time layers of emotion fluttered across his face, but Maeveen could make nothing of them. Lord Peemel's spy—his observer, she corrected herself—wanted to change their destination from the agreed-upon inland course. Coernn had done all he could to set Vervamon on this path inland, and now he wanted to waste time in Shingol. It made no sense, except that Coernn and his four remaining comrades had gone off in the night to conduct their own examination of the carnivorous plants blocking the path. They had taken much of their salvaged equipment with them, and she did not know when they returned, though it had to be within the last hour.

What had Coernn discovered that he was not revealing to Vervamon or her?

"The object of our quest must be found. The change in our route is due to . . . necessity," Coernn finished lamely.

"No change, no time to waste," came Vervamon's brusque words. "I have given the matter much thought. Scouring my journals, I found a similar barrier to progress. You remember the expedition to the Blissful Isles, do you not, Captain?"

Maeveen nodded, remembering that nothing about the exploration had been blissful. Fully half her company had been lost to cannibals. Only when the voracious natives had eaten a sergeant fallen ill with Tes Fever had—

"We poison the plant!" she cried.

"You have a good mind, my dear, though a trifle on the slow side. I have taken steps already with great risk to my own well-being, I should say in all modesty. The plant begins to wither and draw in upon itself in a most fascinating manner. I have taken the opportunity to sketch the death throes of this part of the plant, well poisoned now by a pot of the cook's stew."

Quopomma laughed harshly. "I wondered what good that slop would be, other than taking bloodstains off my dagger."

"Get your troop together, my dear. We have many miles to cover if we are to make up for this brief vacation spent lallygagging." Vervamon went off, muttering to himself and scribbling notes in his expedition journal.

"You heard him. Get your packs and form your squads," barked Quopomma.

Iro went to assemble her platoon, and the sergeants scattered to do their leader's bidding. Only Coernn remained behind, his eyes fixed coldly on Maeveen O'Donagh. She took a perverse delight in seeing him thwarted, but did not know why. He started to speak to her, then spun about and stalked off. She watched as he hailed the other four in his small band. They argued until Coernn pointed back toward the coast. One nodded and hurried off.

Maeveen smiled in satisfaction. The number of spies in her camp had been reduced by another. One had been fed to the plant by his comrades, and now another no doubt returned to Iwset with news for Lord Peemel. Whistling a jaunty song, Maeveen went to be certain her soldiers were ready for the continued journey.

An hour later, they were on the far side of a brownish, dying wall of carnivorous plants and making good time through the forest.

"Do we walk forever without rest?" complained Iro. "We are footsore, and the forest stretches endlessly, and we will never find this sigil if all we do is walk and not hunt for it."

"You mean your feet are tired," Quopomma cut in. "Your brain ought to be in the same condition, except you never use it."

"Quiet," Maeveen ordered. The ogre flashed her a wicked smile, then subsided. "We've been hiking for almost two weeks to reach this point."

"What point is that?" Iro crossed her arms over her chest and glared.

"The foothills of the mountains," Maeveen said. She had no idea what mountains these were, and it hardly mattered when an expedition's purpose was to map new territory. For all its long and colorful history, Terisiare remained virtually undocumented, its cultures fragmented and its topography a mystery. "From here, Vervamon says we climb."

"A mountain expedition," grumbled Iro. "Just what I signed on for."

"You signed on for the good pay and that's about all," said Quopomma. "If you spent less time griping and more time soldiering, we'd have arrived here days sooner."

"I don't want to hear another word from either of you," Maeveen said, her patience worn thin. "Putting up with Coernn's constant complaints that we should return to Shingol has depleted my endurance for such argument."

"What do he and the other three do with their time?" Quopomma scratched herself, then stretched and yawned. "I see them huddled about a cook pot, but they never put food into it. Just smelly liquids they bottle up later and carry along. If they are cooking,

Coernn does all the work. The others sit and watch what he prepares."

"And books," said Iro. "They read their books and Coernn chants. They are clerics, I think, come to spy on us for the Inquisition."

Maeveen nodded absently. She thought that also, though Coernn did not carry the stench of a torturer. Just what he did, other than spy for Peemel, she did not know. His insistence on returning to Shingol had grown with every footstep they took, until Vervamon had to put him in his place. Peemel had set Vervamon on the trail of the artifact, and the scholar was not one to let drop any toy for his massive intellect.

"I overheard Coernn telling Vervamon the Sigil of Iwset was hidden in Shingol, that we go the wrong way," Iro said. "If he knew where it was, why did he set us on this path originally?"

"He didn't know," Maeveen said, realization slowly coming on her. "He knew only after he and the others—"

"Captain!" yelled Vervamon. "Come here immediately. You must see this fabulous sight, you must. Hurry, my dear, hurry!"

Maeveen shrugged and left her officers, her short legs pumping hard to get her up the rocky slope to the top of a rise where Vervamon had set a tripod and telescope. He peered into it, the instrument aimed at the summit of a higher crest.

"Here, look, look!" he said excitedly. Maeveen bent over to the eyepiece and turned the knob to focus it. Her eyes were sharper than Vervamon's and required less correction. Still, for a long moment, she did not understand what she saw. Then she straightened and turned to him. A huge smile split his handsome face.

"Yes, my dear, yes! The city we seek! We will find the Sigil of Iwset there!"

"It looks immense, " Maeveen said, "but deserted. I saw no watch fires or sign of any inhabitants."

"What better place to hide the Sigil than in a city long dead? It is the key to the Tomb of the Seven Martyrs, and it has been hidden in a tomb of its own. Perhaps the sigil's hiding place will prove as thrilling a discovery as the truth about the seven martyrs and their spilled blood."

"How can you be sure we'll find anything there when Coernn has been saying the sigil is in Shingol?"

"My evidence points to this city," Vervamon insisted. "Coernn is nothing more than Peemel's lapdog. What does he know of academic matters? I found clues to the sigil in Duchess Lani Thesavert's fine work *Lost Lands and Hidden Hoards*. Coernn can prattle on all he wants about the sigil's location. I *know* it is there, in the City of Shadows!"

CHAPTER
22

"SHOW US THE WAY, LITTLE BULLOCK. LEAD the herd to victory!" Mytaru whispered with battle fervor. The minotaur tossed his head and showed the red war ribbons dangling from his horns. Yunnie lacked such decoration; he had no horns. But painted on his bare arm were five red hash marks, one for every battle he had fought.

Three of the marks of honor he had won in the last week alone. The elves began their war in earnest after the minotaurs had attacked the encampment just outside the mouth of the Urhaalan's valley. Since that day, reports of a minotaur killed, two elves killed, five minotaurs injured, a dozen elves routed and chased back to the Eln Forest, and more had poured in from every region.

"Lead us, Yunnie. You fight like a demon, and your armor protects you in the fiercest battle!"

Yunnie stared down at the plain leather breastplate he had taken from the Stone People's armory. Living Armor, Sacumon had called it, and Yunnie believed it to be true. The leather had been awkward to hold, and difficult to wrap around his body, when he first put it on, but the longer he wore it the more comfortable it became.

And the more it protected him. At first, the straps over his arms had snapped into place by themselves. Now all he need do was hold up the armor and it leaped from his hand to mold itself to his body. Once in place, it felt more comfortable than a fine leather glove caressing his hand. Every movement became a pleasure bordering on the sensuous.

When he swung his sword and wielded his lance, he was undefeatable. In some way he did not understand, the Living Armor gave him energy. The longer he fought, the stronger he became.

"I cannot, Mytaru," he pleaded. "After a fight, I . . . I cannot move. I am completely exhausted." Yunnie could not explain his soaring energy during the fight, or the horrible exhaustion afterward, a weariness of both body and spirit.

"It does not matter *after* a battle," Mytaru insisted. "What you do *during* gives us all inspiration. The elves defeat us easily—except those times you are at the front of our herd, leading us to victory. For the good of the Urhaalan, for the *herd*, you must go forth, carrying our banner!"

Yunnie looked past Mytaru to Noadia. She stood in the door of her house, struggling to maintain a neutral mien on her usually expressive face. Whether she held back sorrow for those who would die in the coming fight, or she denied a stronger emotion, Yunnie could not say. Her brown eyes, brimming with tears, fixed on him. He wanted to go to her, to assure her he would be all right, that Mytaru would return and the useless war would be at an end.

If only he could spit out the words he had to say about the Niroso, the coal golem, the other wonders he had found underground. For whatever reason, Yunnie could not speak to Mytaru or the others in Clan Utyeehn of his exploration and what he had seen. He could not even tell Mytaru how he had come by the Living Armor. Mytaru probably believed Yunnie had fashioned the leather armor with his own hands. The only words that tumbled out whenever Yunnie tried to warn them of danger from below dealt with goblins.

His continual harping on this topic had alerted Aesor and the few other survivors of Clan Helmhein to the goblins and their guerrilla tactics. Several of the subterranean monstrosities had been killed trying to strip corpses left on the battlefield. Yunnie's real warning had been left unsaid, though. And it choked him badly.

"Stone People," he grated out, invisible fingers tightening on his throat until he could not even croak.

"What's that, Little Bullock? You will lead us? Good!" Mytaru sprang straight up and let out a bull roar that echoed the length of the small valley. "Victory will be ours this day. We will drive the accursed pointed-eared ones back to their leafy Hell!"

"I'll lead you," Yunnie said, giving in to the inevitable. How else could he warn the herd of the danger posed by the coal golems and the Niroso if he was not taken seriously in the Circle of Discourse? Immediately after being admitted to the herd, he had been ignored by Aesor and the others because he was nothing more than a young bull without proper blooding in battle.

"Five," Yunnie said, looking at his arm and the battles recorded there.

"Today will be six, and we shall all acquit ourselves honorably with you at our head."

Again Yunnie tried to speak of the Niroso, and only garbled words erupted from his throat. He gave up trying when he saw Mehonvo trotting up with his long war lance gleaming in the bright sunlight. The old minotaur wore his battle ribbons on his lone horn. From the various colors, Yunnie knew Mehonvo had seen action in more than a half dozen different wars sanctioned at prior Celebrations of Tiyint. He tried to guess how many years that might be and failed. Until the next Celebration of Tiyint and a declaration of war on someone other than the elves of Forest Eln, only red ribbons would be awarded as horn adornment.

It might be two years or longer until the sacred moons were full and the Celebration of Tiyint again took place, the sacred light falling through the twin chimneys in the minotaurs' ritual cave. And then there might be no formal declaration of war to change the battle colors. As far as Yunnie knew, the Urhaalan had lived in peace for more than ten years prior to his arrival in the valley.

Mehonvo was far older than he had guessed, if his war ribbons were any indication.

"A fine day for the spirits to take our enemies to the western lands," Mehonvo said loudly, as if convincing himself the elves would die and not any of the Urhaalan. The old minotaur eyed Yunnie critically, then gave a single nod to show his approval.

Somehow, this made Yunnie feel better, even if he did not want to lead the minotaurs into battle. He would rather have held a peace talk with the elves, knowing what he did. But he could not sit by idly and let the elves slaughter the minotaurs. Whatever drove them, they had to be stopped before any parley could be called.

Hiking off, leaving Noadia behind, proved harder than Yunnie thought. He kept glancing over his shoulder at her. He was not sure, but he thought tears openly rolled down her cheeks now. For him? For her mate? For the losses that would be suffered by both sides? Yunnie saw her vanish into the house to prepare for her own rituals, praying for victory and health.

Yunnie fell into the distance-devouring stride that took him and the others of Clan Utyeehn to the rise overlooking a bowl-shaped meadow. A small skirmish had ended recently. Two minotaurs lay dead in the hot sun. Arrows protruded from the bulls' chests.

Elven archers still stood their ground, firing with deadly accuracy.

"There! There they are! We can get them!" cried Mytaru. He turned to Yunnie, waiting for the command to attack.

Yunnie reflected on how far he had come. In Shingol he was nothing but a fishboy. He shuddered at the name. Where had he heard that imprecation recently? He could not remember.

He had been an outcast there. Directionless wandering had taken him through the elves' territory, past stands of Ironroots, to sights he had never imagined while struggling

with the nets in the fishing village. The time spent among
the elves had been strained, as if he belonged and yet did
not. Yunnie could not explain it, even when dim memory
of an old elf haunted his dreams. Only in the Urhaalan's
valley had he found a home and family. He had gone from
a wandering human to a bull of Clan Utyeehn. Now he led
the herd into combat.

From somewhere deep inside came a loud cry. Yunnie
was startled to realize he had vented this resonant roar.
He lifted his war lance and motioned in the direction of
the slain minotaurs. Not only Mytaru and Mehonvo, but
dozens of others he had not realized trailed them, joined
the cheer—and the charge.

Running faster than the minotaurs, Yunnie outdistanced his clansmen and attacked the tight knot of elven
archers alone. He saw them smile, nock their arrows, and
let fly.

The Living Armor took every arrow squarely and
deflected them. As he ran, Yunnie felt the armor guiding
him, forcing him from side to side to avoid the worst of
the hail of arrows. Then he closed on the elves. His lance
drove forward, impaling the lead archer. The falling body
jerked the weapon from his hand, but Yunnie was already
swinging his sword. Blood exploded as he hacked and
slashed.

Somehow, he defeated five elves before the rest of the
herd arrived to join him.

Yunnie forced away the mindless blood lust that had
seized him and more passively allowed the Living Armor
to swing him this way and that to avoid increasingly feeble attacks. As suddenly as the fight had started, it ended.
The minotaurs had triumphed, twelve elves dead to
avenge the two minotaurs slain earlier.

Mytaru and the others, including old Mehonvo, looked
at Yunnie differently now. Awe rose in their deep brown
eyes and a certain deference entered their words when
they spoke to him. For his part, Yunnie was exhausted
and sickened by the slaughter he had caused.

He moved away from the celebrating minotaurs, thrust
his sword into the dirt, and tried to remove the Living

Armor. The straps resisted his efforts until he reached for his dagger to slash them. Only then, as if protecting itself, did the bindings open with sluggish reluctance. He pried the soft leather from his chest and let the breeze gusting across the meadow cool the sweat.

But Yunnie found it impossible to cast down the Living Armor. It would not let him release his grip, no matter how he tried. Panic rose in him even as a cheer rose from the throats of the bulls celebrating their victory.

His victory.

CHAPTER
23

"HOW DID THEY EVER GET TO THEIR CITY?" whined Iro, struggling with the ropes as she and three of her squad worked up the sheer rock face.

From ten yards away, Quopomma grunted and tugged on her climbing rope, pulling two soldiers up to the narrow ledge where she balanced precariously. The ogre wiped away sweat from her eyes, then called, "Might be the reason they died out. They got tired bringing their food up this way."

"They certainly weren't killed by enemy armies, unless they fell on them from the sky," Maeveen added.

She leaned out to study the rock for new places to drive steel climbing spikes. For a week after Vervamon had sighted the spire with the city atop it, she had scouted the base, only to find no simple way up. The City of Shadows proved to be a dark jewel impossible to reach, until she found this single face of the spire that she and the others could scale from a point halfway up the slope.

"They never had to defend," Quopomma said. "Who'd want this miserable place?"

"For once, I agree with her," chimed in Iro. The two

swung free of the ledge and began working upward. Maeveen guessed they were within yards of the summit. She turned back to tugging on the rope dangling over the side, helping Vervamon reach the ledge where she stood.

The silver-haired explorer scrambled onto the flat surface, panting hard. The altitude took its toll on him, as it did the others. Only Coernn and his three cohorts seemed impervious to the exertions. Maeveen wondered how they survived so when they showed no other sign of physical prowess. She frowned, remembering the trek to this point. Coernn had never flagged, and he and the others carried twice the weight of her soldiers. They had refused to abandon their precious books, vials, and equipment salvaged from the wagons, though at one point a week earlier curiosity had prodded Maeveen to offer her help.

If her soldiers carried the foursome's equipment, she might get some idea what was so precious about it—and what the books might be that Coernn pored over every night—but she refused to assign any of her troops to the chores of toting and spying. Maeveen had reached her own conclusions about Coernn. For all Vervamon's insistence that Coernn was no scholar, he spent too much time reading to be anything else.

"I want to be the first into the city," Vervamon said, sitting with his legs dangling out over the four-hundred-foot drop. "I can scale these last few feet by myself."

"Too late," Maeveen said, craning her neck around to see Quopomma vanish over the summit. Double ropes fell and those climbing with the ogre used long, loping strides against the rock as Quopomma pulled them up. Soon, Iro and her climbing partners were up. Then came Maeveen and Vervamon's turn.

The scholar was in a dark mood when he flopped over and got his feet under him.

"I ought to have been first. How would this look if—" He fell silent when he spied the City of Shadows. Vervamon took an involuntary step forward, his mouth open.

Maeveen studied the buildings. From a distance they seemed ordinary enough. Up closer they were constructed of the purest jet and obsidian. The sun's rays caught the walls and reflected off dark rainbows—she could not name them in any other way. The colors swirled in halos as she moved, but they were not the familiar oranges and red, yellows and greens and blues. The harder she tried to put a name to them, the more her head ached with the effort.

"It—inside. Nothing is as it ought to be. It's so strange," Maeveen said. "It's as if my brain itches."

"We must not linger here," Coernn said. He and his three comrades huddled together, as if for safety. "This is a bad place. I feel it in my bones."

"Your bones are too fragile for anything, even a decent stew," said Quopomma. "I like the view." The ogre turned from the city and peered into the purpled distance. The bloody sun dipped low behind the mountains and cast ever lengthening shadows.

Maeveen noticed how those shadows rippled slightly, avoiding those cast by the buildings as if the natural shunned the artificial. She walked forward in spite of the misgivings she shared with Coernn. The feel to the city was alien, odd, unlike anything she had experienced before. In the course of her travels with Vervamon, she thought she had seen and done everything of note. The City of Shadows proved her wrong.

"We need to explore carefully," she said to Vervamon. "Map the place. Find the use for those buildings. So many are identical. Did the builders show a lack of imagination, or are they used for some distinct purpose?"

"Duchess Lani says the center of town might not be the location of valuables," Vervamon said, rubbing his hands together in glee at his discovery. "Toward the west edge of town, where the rays of sunrise are blocked by the city itself and the setting sun is less inclined to cast shadows because of the sheer drop—that is where we should go."

"We must not stay here," Coernn said. "We can rappel to the base camp and rejoin the others. We will be safer there."

"We stay," Vervamon said firmly. "It is too difficult getting back up the face of the cliff. We must not waste a moment exploring the city—and finding the Sigil of Iwset."

Maeveen and Coernn exchanged glances. For once, she agreed fully with him. She feared nothing, living or dead, human, ogre, elf, minotaur, or other. Maeveen O'Donagh fought her sense of dread and rising panic as she trailed Vervamon into the heart of the City of Shadows.

CHAPTER

24

"WHAT VILENESS IS THIS?" RAGED LADY EDARA. "You are supposed to be my adviser, not Peemel's lapdog!"

Ferantia pursed her lips as she studied her liege. Repeatedly she had brought Lord Peemel's offer of marriage to Edara, but this was the most vehement rejection yet.

"It would be beneficial to you, milady," Ferantia said carefully. "Jehesic is an island. We can be cut off if Peemel decides to expend the military force. He—"

"In the history of Jehesic there has never been a successful invasion. No fleet along the coast is strong enough to triumph over our well-equipped, loyally crewed navy. The citizens would die to the last infant to protect their homes." Lady Edara's long, coppery hair fluttered as a sudden gust of sea breeze blew in the open window. The woman swung about and slammed her fist hard into her writing desk, sending books crashing to the floor and papers fluttering through the room, prisoners of the swirling air. "I will *die* before yielding to that rotting fish carcass who calls himself a lord!"

"I have pointed out the advantages to you, milady," Ferantia went on, knowing she swam nearer the undertow of her dismissal with every word, but Digody had insisted she apply as much pressure to Lady Edara as possible. A war was in no one's interest, in spite of Peemel's determination to flex his military muscle. As Digody said, if Jehesic collapsed easily, it would dull Peemel's expansion and give added time to replace him on the throne.

If only Digody's assassination attempt had not failed, thought Ferantia. She ought to have helped with a spell or two, and the leviathan-filled depths take the Inquisitors and their unceasing watchfulness for any use of magic. Digody lacked any skill with spells, but she counted that as an advantage she held over him, even if it meant continued disappointment in failing to kill Peemel. Still, it would make Digody easier to depose—after their respective rulers were eliminated.

"Oh, yes, yes, you have," Edara said coldly. The sudden change in tone alerted Ferantia to danger sailing down on her. "I will sleep with that stingfish and then show my poisonous tentacles," she went on. "Am I reduced to murdering a husband I do not desire solely to gain power? If I wanted power, I would have seized Iwset long since."

"The people would never have supported such a war, milady," Ferantia said, mind racing.

"Of course they would not. They have good sense—sense you are sorely lacking. I think the rumors are true, Ferantia. You have fallen in with Peemel and do his bidding rather than mine."

"Peemel? Hardly," she scoffed. "You, however, are correct, Lady Edara, that my allegiance no longer resides with you," Ferantia responded, seeing no reason to lie. Her influence had waned ever since Edara had found her mysterious lover. It was time to reassert her control.

Hands moving in an arcane pattern, eyes hooded and lips twisting in the ancient, throat-clenching words discovered by a sorcerer long dead, Ferantia cast her spell. Edara staggered as if she had been struck in the face. She gasped and tried to push away—nothing.

"Get away," Edara gasped out. "I cannot, no, no. . . ." Her protests faded, caught on the wind and thrust back down her royal throat.

Ferantia wiped sweat from her forehead. Casting such a complex, potent spell quickly drained her of energy. Ferantia sank to a low stool and continued her conjurations. It took more than a half hour for her spell to be fully cast, catching Lady Edara within its magical strands. Standing on shaky legs, Ferantia went to the door and peered out over the harbor. She had been told make sure her liege was on the battlements at the sun's zenith.

From the shrinking shadows cast at her feet, it was close enough to noon for the message to be sent. Ferantia turned and motioned, drawing Edara to her with slow, mechanical steps. Edara's expression alternated between flaccidity and savage hatred that turned her lovely face into something evil. It mattered little to Ferantia which pose her ruler accepted. From this high in the citadel, none below could read her expression. All they would see would be the surrender of Jehesic and acknowledgment of Edara and Peemel's nuptials.

"A dagger later, milady, is all it will take to place you on Iwset's throne." Ferantia smiled wickedly as she considered who pulled the puppet ruler's strings. Digody thought he controlled her, but Ferantia was too wise to allow that. She would deliver Edara for the nuptials, then deal with Digody quickly before he could consolidate his power among Jehesic nobles.

And Ihesia. Ferantia's lips curled in a snarl as she thought of Peemel's battle commander. That one was a definite problem of unbridled ambition to be solved— quickly.

"Go to the edge, climb the steps, allow your peasants to see you," ordered Ferantia.

Edara obeyed, fighting every inch of the way. Step by step Edara climbed until the strong sea breeze whipped at her thin clothing and drew her distinctive hair back in a ruddy banner highlighted with golden sparkles by the bright noonday sun. Although she had not been ordered, Edara lifted her arm in greeting.

"Good, so very good," Ferantia said derisively. She felt her strength ebbing as she fought to maintain control magically over her liege. "There is Lord Peemel's dreadnought in the harbor. Signal it with this." Ferantia handed Edara a pole with Iwset's colors emblazoned on three banners, the sign that she agreed to marriage.

Edara's hands shook as she grasped the pole and slowly raised it. The wind caught the pennons and pulled them along, showing the warship and the assembled citizens of Jehesic her surrender.

"Wave it back and forth. Make this a worthy surrender. Do it and you shall know power beyond that afforded you by this miserable island!" Ferantia took a deep breath and chanted louder, giving more force to her spell. "Wave the flag. Let them know you will be a faithful wife for Lord Peemel!"

Edara tottered on the edge of the battlements, trying to force herself to take a step forward and end her life.

"No, no, none of that. You must live, my precious queen. Yes, my *queen*. You will rule more than Jehesic and Iwset before I am finished with you. Now wave the flag as symbol of your—"

Ferantia stiffened, her dark eyes wide. She blinked, and her beauty flowed from her face and body as if snow melted in the warming spring sun. Then she sank to the stone floor, dead.

Edara dropped the hated flag and spun around, her face strained from the effort of resisting so futilely against Ferantia's magic. Her sea-green eyes fixed on a bloody blade behind the fallen woman.

"You saved me," she gasped out. "She held me utterly in her power with a spell. I had no idea she commanded such power. She made me—"

"I know, my love. It is done. At least *she* is done, but there are so many others. And I fear the war has begun." A bloody dagger clattered on the stone battlement and strong arms reached out for the woman.

Edara pushed away, returned to the parapet, and ripped the flag into narrow ribbons. She tossed the tattered pennant over the battlements, letting it flutter down as a signal of defiance.

In the distance Jehesic's defensive harbor batteries began hurling flaming pitch balls at Peemel's dreadnought, but Edara did not notice. She felt too secure in her lover's embrace to bother with anything else.

CHAPTER
25

"WHERE DID YOU GO, MY LITTLE FRIENDS? Where are you?" Quopomma spun about, vainly searching for her imaginary helpers. The sight of the ogre unable to imagine her transparent companions into existence sent a further chill down Maeveen O'Donagh's spine. She rested her hand on the hilt of her sword, but had no sense she would find an enemy substantial enough to run through.

"Fan out. Don't get out of sight of one another," Maeveen ordered as the handful of soldiers with her began to reconnoiter the City of Shadows. The black glass walls shone with a strange inner light that was not light, casting illumination for the search that was eerily worse than groping in total night.

"How can anything glow with darkness?" asked Quopomma, squarely facing an obsidian wall. "It is as if a black flame flickers within the glass. Or would that be 'unglows'?" The ogre scratched herself and glared hard at her reflection, then unexpectedly smiled. "I don't look half bad, now do I? With glamour like mine, I could be the queen of the Festival of Dried Bones, and that is a sureness."

Maeveen laughed without humor. She had no idea what Quopomma saw reflected. From her angle, it was only the ogre's usual image. The captain stopped and turned to stare when all the details finally registered in her tired brain. It was a precise image, not one reversed by the action of a mirror.

She turned away, wanting to deny anything out of the ordinary and failing. This was hardly the only curiosity folded within the confines of the City of Shadows. A disquieting silence held the city in its grip, and the stone paving under her boots yielded gently with every step, as if she walked on firm cushions. Dozens of abandoned cities had given over their secrets to her and Vervamon, but Maeveen felt this one would never speak, no matter how hard she listened.

Vervamon strolled off, studying everything with a critical eye and taking copious notes. Iro and another soldier marched a pace behind him, less interested in the city than keeping the expedition leader in their view. Vervamon was safe, for the moment. Until he found the Sigil of Iwset, Maeveen guessed there would be nothing dangerous for the scholar to embroil himself in.

But the buildings! Never had she seen their like. She craned her head and gawked like a peasant come to the county fair for the first time. Light vanished into their cheerless surface to become trapped within. But the light—unlight—Quopomma noted was hardly the bright sun released after pausing in their glass prisons. What macabre creatures had found the City of Shadows a comforting, safe home? To this question, Maeveen had no easy answer.

"Come with me," she called to Quopomma. The ogre reluctantly left her image in the wall, joining her commander.

"A pretty city, this one. Not like some of the rotted and rusting ruins Vervamon is so fond of scrounging about in." The ogre whistled tunelessly through the gap caused by a missing lower tooth, strutting about as if she owned all the real estate in view. Every step toward the center of the city caused Maeveen to grow that much more uneasy.

"Nothing watches us," Maeveen said, trying to pinpoint the reason for her discomfort. "Could it be these odd buildings are nothing more than sepulchers?"

"You mean the city entombed itself on top of the mountain?" Quopomma pushed out her lower lip as she considered this. "It doesn't feel like a cemetery. There is nothing alive, but there is nothing dead lurking, either. It is as if Uncle Istvan dropped by, frightened the fools who lived here, and then all left, going their separate ways."

"The doorways are oddly shaped," Maeveen observed, "designed for no creature I have ever seen." On tiptoe she could not touch the top of the doorway. The doorjambs curved outward, as if an immensely fat giant had waddled through on some unknown daily peregrination.

"Decoration, nothing more," Quopomma said, dismissing the design as beyond her ken. "Here must have been their barracks. Look at the bunks." The ogre entered the building, but Maeveen paused outside to look around more.

This building was constructed of glass shards toppled down from on high, piled in a jumble in the geometric center of the city. From this point the city streets radiated outward like spokes in a vast vitreous wheel.

"All roads lead to Terado," Maeveen said softly, smiling crookedly at this curious, old saying. "And it is here the roads start." She circled the building, seeing several of her soldiers scouting down the streets as she had instructed. A dejected Vervamon returned from the western edge of the city. The way he lectured Iro convinced Maeveen he had not discovered the sigil. Of Coernn and his companions she saw no sign. She thought they roamed to the north, possibly exploring the structure hanging over that edge of the mountain for a quicker way to descend.

"Beds, Captain, these have to be beds. And soft ones." Quopomma bounced on a bunk wide enough even for her massive frame. "I could sleep a year on this."

"We need to camp somewhere. The sun dips quickly behind the western peaks. I don't know where the day has gone," Maeveen said. "When we're rested, we can descend in the morning."

"You think Vervamon will be done with his hunt by then?" The ogre fell silent as Vervamon stormed into the large room.

"A fool's chase, nothing more! How could I have believed anything that lying bitch wrote? She was a charlatan, a liar, and a whore. Worse, she was a poor scholar!"

"Duchess Lani Thesavert?" asked Maeveen, amused in spite of her misgivings about this peculiar city.

"Poor research, that's what did it. She wrote half truths and outright lies in *Lost Lands and Hidden Hoards*. She had no idea she wrote fiction. That makes it all the worse! A fraud I can excuse, but an ignoramus who only *thinks* she is writing detailed investigation? I pity her."

"We came a long way for nothing," Quopomma spoke up.

"I told you this was not the place where the Sigil of Iwset would be found," Coernn said from the doorway. His remaining companions were arrayed behind him, looking dour from the time-consuming excursion.

"So you did, so you did. But how? Where were your facts?" demanded Vervamon. "If you put forth an argument, it must be supported with facts, not silly conjectures or 'gut' feelings."

"Where were yours? You believed a writer of romantic nonsense intent on entertaining her courtly friends. The sigil is in Shingol. We must waste no more time fetching it."

"If Peemel—if you—knew all this time where it was, why not send a frigate to retrieve it?" asked Maeveen. "As much as Vervamon appreciates Lord Peemel's funding for this leg of the expedition, why did he not send Digody or another to Shingol?"

"We only recently . . . learned of its location," Coernn said lamely.

Maeveen spat chewed gumweed onto the floor in front of Coernn. To her surprise, the hard black floor sucked up the juice. In a few seconds the floor was as clean and dry as when she had set foot on it earlier. Coernn took no notice of either the insult or the result.

"What else have you so recently *learned*?" she asked sarcastically. "We risk our lives for Peemel's precious sigil. It means nothing to us."

"The Tomb of the Seven Martyrs," cut in Vervamon, a tinge of passion replacing his anger, "to open it and decipher the mysteries of antiquity! That will be more than a footnote to our expedition, my dear captain. It will cause the name of Vervamon to be forever remembered!"

"What of the rest of us?" asked Quopomma. Vervamon did not hear, and Maeveen silenced her with a cold glare.

"So we leave the City of Shadows and go to a fishing village? At least we will find food for the taking in Shingol. There is nothing but dust and desolation here." Maeveen wanted to return to the expedition's original purpose, as gruesome as the study of funeral ritual and burial might be.

"Yes, Captain O'Donagh, and the sooner we do so the better off we shall be," Coernn said. He appeared to be uncomfortable. Maeveen took some small delight in the observer's anxiety.

"We need to explore more than we have," Vervamon said. "In the morning, in the light of day. It is now too dark for me to explore and properly map this place. Unless you have torches?"

"Nothing to burn in this city," Iro reported, shrugging her thin shoulders.

Maeveen had already noticed the lack of combustibles in the glass structures. They would eat a cold dinner and endure a colder night, though this room held warmth well. She eyed the rows of beds and thought it might be the first good sleep any of them had been granted since leaving Iwset.

Even as this entered her mind, some part of her warned against it.

"We can return to the base camp," Maeveen said, licking her lips as nervousness grew. It bothered her that she and Coernn could agree on this one item: apprehension. "It will be easier going down than coming up."

"We stay," Vervamon decided. "Why come this far and simply abandon a fine footnote to my expedition journal? The City of Shadows must offer some tidbit to interest even a jaded explorer such as myself."

"Good. I claim those two beds," Quopomma said, strutting off to claim the pair of bunks at the far side of the sleeping chamber. The ogre pushed the beds together and dropped down, testing them for comfort.

"Iro, take the first watch," Maeveen ordered.

"But Captain, we're the only ones in this city," the gangly officer protested. "Why post guards?"

"Do it," Maeveen said, not tolerating insubordination, especially from Iro. Her lieutenant had not shown great intelligence or common sense in the past few weeks. Without looking back to see if Iro obeyed, Maeveen went to find a bed of her own.

She sank down, relishing the support under her aching back and shoulders. She had spent too many nights with nothing but a little moss and soft dirt for a bed. Maeveen laced her fingers under her head and stared at the high ceiling. Tiny motes of dark "light" danced inside the material, one speck chasing another in endless orbit. She listened to the others settling in for the night, Coernn and his three comrades huddled together muttering about Uncle Istvan knew what. Her thoughts touched lightly on Coernn and the possibility that he reported to Abbot Offero rather than to Peemel.

Maeveen could not decide where his allegiance lay. She had started the expedition thinking he reported no farther than the abbot. Watching him on the trail convinced her that Coernn lacked the fanaticism of the Inquisition, but his clannishness and the aspect of those with him spoke of the Church and its secret ways. Coernn seemed harmless enough, save when he changed his mind and sent them on dangerous side trips such as this one. Would Shingol be any different? Maeveen hoped it would. The sooner they found the Sigil of Iwset, the quicker they could get on with the real purpose of their expedition.

Maeveen closed her eyes, just for a moment, to rest and nothing more. She had to check Iro's placement of

sentries, see if Vervamon was settled in safely, maintain
a presence to keep Coernn and the others in line. Just for
a moment.

Maeveen O'Donagh fell asleep.

Drifting. Sailing. Soaring on gossamer wings high above
the ground. Maeveen looked down on the world and
knew how petty it was. She held out her arms and caught
the wind on her strong pinions, spiraling lower, the cold
sun on her back.

Sudden buffeting almost knocked her from the sky.
The world exploded in war. Arrows arched high in the air
to erupt in flame. Tracing their fiery trajectories back to
the ground, she saw elven archers working furiously to
fill the air with their feathered death. On the receiving
end of this barrage were minotaurs, more minotaurs than
she thought existed in all Terisiare. Their black horns
flashed wickedly in the light cast by the fire arrows, but
leading them was Vervamon.

Vervamon?

No, not Vervamon. Maeveen brought her feet up and
batted hard at the air with her wings to get a better look.
The tall, straight figure was not silver-haired Vervamon.
Rather, it was a young man who looked a great deal like
the explorer. He wore his flaxen hair straight back and
held by a cloth headband decorated in the style of the
Urhaalan, but his high forehead reminded her of Vervamon.
And the blue eyes. How they burned with passion like
Vervamon's!

She marched alongside as this young man led the minotaurs in battle, his simple armor turning aside the elves'
most intense arrow assaults. For a few seconds, the thrill
of battle filled her. Then those around turned to skeletons
and she screamed. The words blasted from her lips and
broke into a thousand crystalline shards that turned to
insects eager to flutter away.

Maeveen recoiled, seeking the man who looked so
much like Vervamon for an explanation. He had vanished, replaced by sweeping battles that flowed faster and
merged into an all-encompassing struggle, spilled blood

turning into rivers that filled the Urhaalan's valley to the rim until it overflowed.

She blinked in confusion as she swam in warm liquid and saw fleets sailing from Iwset's harbor, bound for Jehesic on tides of blood. In the distance—in Jehesic?—stood a regal woman with gore-fouled hair. Beside her lay the woman Maeveen had seen talking with Digody in the poor section of Iwset.

"Ferantia?" Maeveen muttered. "What of Digody?" Even as she named Lord Peemel's adviser, he appeared, eyes as red as the blood tides lapping against the shores of his city-state. Locked in silent combat with Digody was another figure, one hidden in a mist so dense that she could not penetrate it. They stumbled and fought and tumbled into . . . the Inquisition's torture chambers.

Abbot Offero laughed loudly as he tightened the thumbscrews on Ihesia's torture device while Lord Peemel looked on impassively. The abbot gestured grandly and a black-masked assistant advanced, carrying a flaming torch that exploded in Maeveen's face. She moaned and tried to turn from the hulking, burning creature and the melting rocks laughing behind the monster.

"Coal golem," she muttered, thrashing about even more. "What of the other things?" The Stone People advanced on her as blood splashed under their sizzling feet, and behind it all stood a figure wrapped in the sable darkness of night, laughing and laughing and laughing. A tattooed arm stretched out, only to be severed.

The crazed laugh thundered through Maeveen's brain as the hand, chopped off at the wrist, fell to the ground and began walking along on its fingers—racing directly for her.

Maeveen sat bolt upright in bed, sweating, her heart pounding furiously. She took a few quick gasps, then forced herself to calm, as if she prepared to enter battle. But she knew she had just left a fight greater than any she had ever witnessed. Maeveen swung about on the bed, her booted feet touching the floor. Only slowly did her intent to check Iro's sentries return.

She got up and walked on cat's feet to the door. She hardly believed her eyes at the sight greeting her.

"Quopomma!" she called. "Rouse the soldiers!"

"What's happened?" demanded the ogre, lumbering up with both swords drawn. She looked past her commander into the street. "What happened to them?"

"I cannot say," Maeveen said, loath to approach her own soldiers. They cowered, curled up in fetal positions and gibbered fearfully. They had befouled themselves.

"Something frightened them," Quopomma said, stating the obvious. "Iro, where are you? What happened?"

Iro's mewling came to torment Maeveen further. She followed the piteous sounds and found her lieutenant wedged into a small alcove, eyes wide with fright and sweat drenching her uniform until it clung to her thin frame like a second skin.

"Snap out of it," growled Quopomma, shaking Iro hard.

"What did you see?" demanded Maeveen. "You fell asleep on duty. What did you see?"

"Awful things. Monstrosities. Centaurs doing terrible things to me. Griffins with claws gouging. My skin, ripped off! Vultures plucking out my eyes and entrails and then, them, *them*!" Iro descended again into the fright that robbed her of reason.

"Never thought she had much in the way of courage," Quopomma said.

"What were your dreams?" Maeveen asked the ogre sharply, remembering hers of blood and fire and death. Her hands shook even thinking of the nightmare that had visited her with such force. Maeveen could hardly tell the difference between it and reality, even now.

"Home, breaking arms and legs, my two brothers." Quopomma sighed. "They are dead, lost these four years. And my friends. Everywhere are my friends." Quopomma looked guiltily at Maeveen, as if revealing too much. Maeveen cared little of the ogre's imaginary companions, who had come alive in dream.

"What is going on?" demanded Vervamon. "It is nothing less than a travesty to awaken me from such a pleas ant dream."

"Pleasant?" asked Coernn, his voice shaky. "What were your dreams?" From the way he spoke, Maeveen knew Coernn's had bordered on nightmare, as had hers. He was even paler than normal and held his uncontrollably shaking hands under his cloak.

"Why, I was presenting a paper on my exploration of the Tomb of the Seven Martyrs. It was everything I had hoped. More. My triumphs were complete. Those jack-asses who opposed my expedition were sent packing, rele-gated to mere footnotes. Less! Their papers were taken out and burned as being insignificant contributions to the literature! The Academy of Egaverral unanimously voted me executive director for life. I was made a High Fellow of the academy, and they all begged for my approval of their researches, all petty and denied, of course."

Maeveen fastened her gaze on Coernn. Lord Peemel's emissary stared at Vervamon, as if he listened to a tale of horror surpassing that of his dreams. He turned and spoke rapidly with the nearest of his three assistants. The man's head bobbed quickly. He turned and rushed off, gathering his belongings as he went.

Coernn had sent another of his band away. To report this strange turn to Lord Peemel? Or did he report to another? Maeveen did not know, and she cared even less how the spy intended to leave the pinnacle-topping City of Shadows. All she wanted to do was erase the revulsion she felt for her own nightmares.

It was not to be. Maeveen O'Donagh sat on her bed, legs drawn up tightly to her chest for the rest of the night, listening to Iro and the other soldiers' wretched cries of insanity.

CHAPTER
26

"WE WILL BREAK THEIR BACKS AND BE TROUBLED by them no more," Mytaru said, large brown eyes scanning the proposed battlefield. "See how they gather along the flanks, thinking the trees give them shelter? We can rout them if we strike hard directly down the middle of the pasture, using a double line of fighters, then each half rolling out and engulfing the elves."

"A chancy plan," Yunnie said. He uneasily shifted the Living Armor on his chest, worrying about it. He had been unable to remove it for longer than a few minutes, no matter how hard he tried. Bathing had become difficult, though none of the minotaurs noticed. Their lathered chests were badges of honor, not unsanitary conditions to be resolved with soap and water. Yunnie scratched as the insects crawling between the armor and his skin decided to burrow.

The Living Armor prevented anything from penetrating it; the insects gnawed hungrily on him, making life almost unbearable.

The only thing more unbearable was removing the armor itself. It had worked its way into his body and brain in such a fashion as to become part of him. He might as well decide to lop off an arm—or his own head. If it had not protected him so well, Yunnie might have tried cutting it off.

But there was something that proved even more insidious. If he wore the Living Armor in battle, he commanded the entire herd. The power of being war leader fed his need for approval even more than being accepted into Clan Utyeehn as a bull.

Yunnie could not let down his clan or the herd. They had come to rely on him to the exclusion of older, more traditional, war leaders. He tried to hold down casualties on both sides, but it had become almost impossible due to the fierce, bloody battles. No quarter was given by either side. As much as it thrilled him, this was also the day he had feared, and he could do nothing but lead the Urhaalan down the hill, snorting and bellowing and ready to kill any elf they found. When they left the field this day, there might not be any more elves from Forest Eln alive.

"Mytaru, I want to tell you about the fires that burned out Clan Hiraago last night."

"Cowardly elves," Mytaru bellowed. He stamped his feet and snorted, working himself into a killing rage. As he tossed his head, the red ribbons signifying each battle he had fought waved like wind-tattered flags.

"Not the elves," countered Yunnie. "It was—" His throat seized shut, choking him. He gagged and bent double, almost vomiting. He dropped to his knees and tried to write in the dirt how the coal golems had invaded the sleepy collection of minotaur houses and burned them to the ground. The Stone People had sent them. Yunnie knew it, had seen it, but he could not tell Mytaru or anyone else without this reaction.

"A new vision?" asked Mytaru, more interested than worried at his blood brother's predicament. Yunnie continued to retch as he forced out words of warning about the Niroso and their coal golems. Mytaru finally came over and put a strong arm around Yunnie's shoulders.

"You see nothing but victory, don't you? The spirits inhabit your body, and the immensity of their advice shakes you. Why do they speak through you and not another of our clan?" Mytaru asked, shaking his head sadly. "We are strong and trained from birth to deal with their power. But no, they choose a weaker vessel for their inspiration. It is a good thing you are of Clan Utyeehn. A lesser human would be killed instantly by the spirits of the west."

"No inspiration," Yunnie got out. He stood and stared at the battlefield. How transparent the elves' plan was. It was as if they wanted to die on the point of a minotaur war lance.

"Sacumon," he said under his breath. Over and over he fought to remember and had mentally pictured the Stone People, the coal golem, the vast underground chamber where their insidious war council assembled. And again, as if catching a handful of drifting mist, he remembered Sacumon. Sacumon had led him to the Living Armor and had insisted he take it.

Yunnie beat his fist against the armor. It cushioned the blows so he felt nothing. What cushioned him from remembering?

Sacumon!

"The elves are betrayed by their own adviser," Yunnie said. "They have been sent into the field to die, yes, but we will die, also."

"If we kill the elves, they cannot kill us," said Mytaru. "That is simple."

"Not so simple. There is more to this than we can see— or say," Yunnie finished.

"Kill the enemy. They cannot kill us, then. It *is* simple," insisted Mytaru.

Yunnie tried to locate Sacumon. He doubted the woman would stray far if this was to be the defining battle in the war between elf and minotaur. Perhaps she had to be close by to direct the Stone People afterward when they slaughtered the weakened survivors. Or would it even be that straightforward? Yunnie guessed she was playing a game pitting all sides against one another so she would emerge the victor.

"Magic," he grated out, realizing Sacumon had laid a

geas on him so powerful he could not shake it off. He knew little of such things and wished he could be free of the vile sorcerers still wandering the land. Life among the minotaurs had been idyllic; the Three Chosen had no truck with magic. It had ruined the land and Yunnie saw why, if practitioners like Sacumon used their power to further only their own sick, limitless ambition.

"They use it against us?" Mytaru fell silent. "I have some talent in this respect, too, Little Bullock," the minotaur said solemnly. "I have not mentioned it before, but I feel strong undercurrents moving against us. Countering it would be difficult, but the power of the Urhaalan minotaur is second to none! We are strong of arm and strong of spirit!"

Yunnie felt sick to his stomach, as much due to Mytaru's posturing as the effect of Sacumon's spell.

"The signal! Our Uncle Mehonvo sends us the signal." Mytaru turned to Yunnie, waiting for the command to attack.

Yunnie decided he would no longer be a part of this senseless slaughter even though it made him feel more important than ever before. Elves killed minotaurs, minotaurs killed elves, and goblins slew both. And even more surreptitious in their war was the Niroso. They burned the minotaur villages, using their magically constructed coal golems. Only the Stone People would benefit from this battle.

And Sacumon.

Yunnie would not give the command.

He heard someone shouting to attack and realized that the cry came from his own lips. Then, against his will, his arm rose and he ran forward. A thousand Urhaalan minotaurs rushed downhill toward the stand of trees, intent on killing elves.

Yunnie sobbed and fought to lower his arm, to still his voice, to stop the headlong charge. The Living Armor did not permit it. It was his protector; he was also its prisoner.

His steps were slow and deliberate as he followed the thundering herd of bulls downhill. He saw Mytaru's plan

working. The elves split down the middle when their
defensive line failed. Two lines of minotaur warriors
curled and circled the smaller detachments of elven
archers and fighters. Yunnie doubted the tactic would
have worked had it not been for the naïveté of the elves,
surprising naïveté in the face of their sophisticated and
deadly attacks over the past weeks.

Yunnie knew the reason, and he sought it in the trees
behind the main defensive line of elves. He walked
through the carnage, his sword swinging easily, taking an
elven life here, wounding a fighter there. It made no difference to him if he stopped those he faced. He wanted
only to find Sacumon.

And reach the woman he did. The battle raged, the
coppery stench of blood rising to challenge the soft fragrance of late summer blossoms in the pasture. Without
looking, Yunnie knew the green grass was stained crimson and the footing slippery. He stared at the dark figure
huddled near a tree with immense, spreading branches.
She slashed at her arm with a short-bladed knife, produc-
ing rivers of blood. Strips of her own flesh had been cut
free and lay on the ground at her feet.

"I knew you would be here," he said to Sacumon.

"You are a remarkable human," the sorceress said,
glancing up from her bloodstained self-mutilation. "Again
and again I have cast the spell of forgetting, yet you
remember."

"How can I forget the carnage you cause?" The sounds
of battle deafened him. Elves died. Minotaurs died, but
not as many now. "You positioned the elves so they
would be defeated."

"Eradicated," she said softly. "I wanted the minotaurs
to be the victors. They are more easily slaughtered by the
coal golems. They move slower and their senses are not
as sharp. I might even say they are . . . bovine."

Yunnie let out a cry of rage and ran forward, sword
firmly held in a double-handed grip. He swung hard to
decapitate the woman. His muscles froze; he lost his balance and tumbled facedown onto the ground. He struggled to sit up. Try as he might, he could not draw his

dagger and toss it at Sacumon. No matter how he fought, his body refused to obey him.

His face was pressed into the bloody mud.

"The Living Armor is a remarkable artifact," Sacumon said offhandedly. "Whoever commands it commands a valuable resource." She drove her dagger hard into her leg, sobbing in pain. But as she drew out the shining blade, Yunnie saw transcendent power come over the wizard. From her own blood and pain she gained might.

"I will rip it off," Yunnie said between clenched teeth. "You will not control me!"

"Ah, but I do. Try to pull off the armor and you will find that your skin goes with it. The magic is powerful, but not as strong as I anticipated." Sacumon frowned. Her thin mouth pulled back to reveal teeth that were not teeth. Yunnie cringed. Sacumon had dental plates like a turtle.

"You distract me. I lose control of the flow of the battle. My spells fade because of your interference." Sacumon ripped open her robe and crisscrossed her exposed belly with the wicked tip of her blade, adding to the forest of scars already there.

Yunnie closed his eyes and concentrated his full power on a single location: the hollow at the base of Sacumon's throat. His vision narrowed and he gathered all his willpower for a single attack. He lunged forward, sword aimed at the woman's neck. She let out a bloodcurdling scream as his blade grazed her flesh. Sacumon pulled back, clutching at her wound, fingers soaked in the thin flow of blood. Red fluid from wrist and belly mingled with that leaking from her throat to mix in an imbrued pattern of gore.

He had struck—but off-target. His failure to kill her tormented him. Yunnie had missed his chance to end this hideous conflict.

"You will die, fishboy. I need you to yet make the victory complete, but I will see you die horribly ere it is over! The Niroso have ways of killing that make the Inquisition look like whimpering infants playing with broken toys!"

Sacumon faded into the shadows and vanished. Yunnie forced himself to his feet and staggered back to the battle.

That day the Urhaalan minotaurs sustained their worst defeat.

CHAPTER
27

"YOU PLAY A DANGEROUS GAME," ISAK
Glen'dard said, stroking Ihesia's long, dark hair. His
thoughts were miles distant from the warmth of the general's strong, sleek arms around him. "You should come
with me and—"

"And leave it all?" Ihesia laughed and pushed away
from him. Her indigo eyes glowed. With anger? Passion?
Even an astute observer such as Isak could not tell.

"Are you mocking me?"

"I ought to. We have it almost won, and complete victory is close, Isak dearest, so close!"

"How can you say that? You told me fighting Jehesic is
folly. Their navy is too powerful, their marines too well
trained and loyal, and through some spy in Iwset Lady
Edara learns of Peemel's every move. He is too stupid to
realize this betrayal turns many battles against him, making his position less secure by the day."

"I know that, but when a child's toy falls over, he often
leaves it for another. We can pick up the pieces and play
to our hearts' content!" Ihesia threw herself back on the
bed, arched her back and purred like a cat, but in appearance was unlike any cat Isak had ever seen. She was sleek

in her nakedness and so desirable. Too desirable. He never mixed business and pleasure.

He had never mixed the two before meeting Ihesia.

"Iwset is not a toy, and those playing with it will kill anyone reaching for it. Peemel might be deposed easily enough, but Digody will not. His power in the north is growing. You have heard the reports of Sacumon's war between elf and minotaur?"

"Of course," Ihesia said. "That bothers me. It is to Peemel's—and Digody's and Sacumon's—benefit for the minotaurs to be triumphant, yet they lost and are now at the mercy of the elves."

"Mayhap Sacumon cannot control her allies. I am uncertain who lends such devastating aid to her," Isak said. He climbed from the bed and went to the narrow window looking over the Ilesemare Sea. Colorful sails dotted the horizon, not a one of them a warship from a harbor friendly to Iwset. Jehesic would drive Peemel into the sea soon.

"Her magic is more dangerous to her than us, my dearest," Ihesia said. "She feeds her spells with her own blood. Should she require more power, she would pay the ultimate price. We have nothing to fear from her."

"I am not so sure," he replied. "We know nothing of her allies. Not goblins, no, not those most unworthy of monsters from below the fresh soil. She summons something more, something dangerous to everyone."

"I worry more about the southern front. Guerrillas harass my troopers," Ihesia said. "I've formed an uneasy alliance with Abbot Offero to put the rebels in their place, but the Inquisition is a poor tool for such work."

"He is a poor tool," Isak agreed, turning from the window. The sight of the naked woman on the bed stirred his loins again.

Everything he had always told himself about slipping away from danger was pushed aside when he had become Ihesia's lover. Peemel had no control over his own city-state, much less the surrounding territory, and everyone vied for power. Such an unstable base meant only death to an outsider. Isak had earned considerable wealth while in Iwset. It was time to leave behind the trouble brewing like an unsavory stew and find new territory to spend his deserved rewards.

But Ihesia would not leave with him. He sighed at his own stupidity, even as he returned to the bed to lie beside Peemel's scheming, power-mad, beautiful general. Her fingers flitted back and forth over his chest as she mimicked troop movements and tactics.

"We hold Jehesic at bay, if nothing more. Sacumon prevents an alliance from forming in the north. With the help of Offero, we can quell the upstarts in the south. And here," Ihesia said hotly, "*here* we engage in more intimate battle."

Isak groaned as Ihesia showed how they were going to deal with the likes of Digody, Apepei, and Peemel's other advisers. Isak wished he were as good with words.

Then it was his turn to share with the willing woman what they would do to Lord Peemel.

CHAPTER
28

YUNNIE WAS PAST CARING. HE STARED NUMBLY at Mytaru as the minotaur stormed around, thundering about their terrible defeat at the hands of the elves. His once glossy horns were nicked and dull. The proud battle ribbons he had worn only hours earlier were now gone, slashed off in the heat of battle. The stub of an arrow still protruded from his shoulder, unnoticed in the heat of his anger.

"You failed us, Yunnie. You disappeared when we needed your leadership most. Can you explain yourself?"

Yunnie shook his head. He had nothing to say to his blood brother or the pathetic few gathered around them. "It wasn't supposed to be that way," Yunnie finally said. He tried to talk about Sacumon and how she had intended for the elves to be overwhelmed, but the words froze in his throat. Everything was wrong. If he had done nothing, if he had gone along with Sacumon's scheme, the minotaurs would have been triumphant. By stopping the sorceress as he had, by fighting her powers and forcing her to mutilate herself to add power to her spells, he had diverted her attention at a critical moment. Sacumon had wanted the elves defeated; now they were triumphant and lacked the magical constraints Sacumon had intended to put on them.

Yunnie was responsible for the defeat, but not in the fashion Mytaru thought.

His head hurt and his body ached, as much from combat as wearing the damnable Living Armor. He had a hard time focusing, and even picturing the dark-clad sorceress proved difficult. But what was easy? Yunnie had fought her vile spell before and triumphed—a little. He laughed harshly at the irony of the situation. He had done the right thing, and the minotaurs had suffered grievous loss.

"We would have won if you had led us," repeated Mytaru. The minotaur tried to think of some new accusation to throw at Yunnie and could not. Like the others, he had run his race. He slumped in defeat.

"The elves were supposed to die, but the balance changed," Yunnie said. They had fought too well, those elves of Eln, and the minotaurs had been too sure of their victory. The elves had routed the minotaurs, and now the entire valley of the Urhaalan might be forfeit.

"They move in small groups, sneaking in to kill us in our sleep," Aesor said, pawing furiously at the ground. Wounds on his legs had been bound, making him look like southern racehorses Yunnie had seen once racing outside Tondhat. His eyes bored into Yunnie, trying to inflict more guilt, but failed. Yunnie had exhausted his ability to react.

"We can still win if we change our tactics," Mytaru said in a voice that caused Yunnie to look up. Energy returned to the defeated minotaur, and the hope ringing in his voice sounded an alarm in the human.

"What do you mean?"

Mytaru straightened and turned, his arm coming up to point toward the Place of Power he had shown Yunnie only days earlier. Yunnie held back a surge of fear when he realized what Mytaru proposed.

"Tiyint aid me, I can use a few spells. It will be all we need to swing victory back in our direction."

"A spell? Just a small one?" taunted Yunnie. "Then

what? A second, bigger one? You will become dependent on the magic, relying less on your strong arm and your brain," Yunnie cautioned.

"We can use it to win," Mytaru snapped angrily. "I have the skill and will not let down the herd." Mytaru closed his eyes and began muttering the spell. Yunnie shivered as if the temperature had fallen. A cold wind blew through the small clearing, chilling his soul more than his body.

"What will this spell accomplish?" he asked.

"There," Mytaru said, his huge chest heaving as if exerting himself. The minotaur pointed to the far side of the glade. "The elves will emerge from the forest, and we can take them *there*."

Four elves popped from the grove, warily looking around but not seeing the tight knot of minotaurs. Mytaru's spell masked their presence.

"Get them!" bellowed Aesor. He led the other four bulls in an all-out attack.

The elves heard Aesor but could not see him. One female elf rubbed her eyes as she turned in the direction of the attacking Aesor, but she did not see the minotaur because of the magical veil Mytaru lowered over her eyes.

Aesor's lance spitted her and pinned her lifeless body to a tree trunk. The other elves shrieked and swung their daggers in wide, silvery arcs to protect themselves against invisible foes. Like their companion, they died, also. Aesor's rage knew no bounds as he mutilated the bodies of those he slew.

Only when all the elves lay dead on the ground did Mytaru stop uttering his spell. He turned to Yunnie.

"I ought to have learned more from my great-uncle," Mytaru panted. His powerful chest was flecked with lather and sweat poured in rivers down his face, but pride and anger shone through the fatigue born of casting the spell. "Then I could kill all the elves with a single curse and would not have to merely blind them."

"Someone is blind," Yunnie said, desolate. "It was not the elves."

CHAPTER
29

"I'M GLAD TO BE GONE FROM THIS GHASTLY city," Maeveen O'Donagh said, struggling with the rope dangling over the edge of the ragged cliff. The two soldiers making snuffling animal noises bothered her, but Lieutenant Iro had recovered some of her wits after her nightmare—or whatever had visited her in her dreams. The rangy officer sat to one side, knees drawn up and looking frightened, but she no longer cried constantly like a whipped cur. Maeveen wished she could help Iro rather than simply tolerate her officer's misery.

Maeveen remembered her own nightmares all too well. She marveled that Quopomma's dreams had been so markedly different. The ogre's had been peaceful, bringing her reminiscences about her childhood and family, and life with her imaginary, or invisible, friends. Vervamon had lived a fantasy of ultimate academic power. And Maeveen had fought, watching blood drown those around her.

Worse, she had seen the entire western coast of Terisiare destroyed in warfare rivaling the Brothers' War. Magic had again run rampant, and armies vied with devastating results for less and less. Minotaur and elf, human and dwarf, and dozens of others all fell before the flame creatures in her vivid, frightening vision.

"It has a nice view," Quopomma said, coiling the rope as Maeveen fed it over to her. The ogre stared over the edge of the five-hundred-foot precipice on the north boundary of the city. They had dropped a message to the base camp at the other side, ordering them to circle the base of the spire to meet. The descent here would be easier than working their way down the rugged face that had afforded them scant foot- and handholds on the way up.

"What's wrong?" asked Maeveen, seeing her lieutenant's puzzled expression. "Is the rope frayed?"

"What? No. I see something curious far below. There. See it?" Quopomma pointed, but Maeveen knew the ogre's eyes were sharper than hers. She shook her head, her short hair flopping about. She needed to cut it still shorter, or it would be in her way even more when the battles began—the battles she had seen in her dreams.

She shook herself like a wet dog, hoping to throw off those dreams; they might be nothing but the product of her innate pessimism. Maeveen did not know if she had received a true divination. Nightmares did not have to come true.

"Might be nothing," said Quopomma, but her tone told Maeveen it was something more significant than she chose to describe.

"What do you think you see?"

"Elves," was all the reply she got. Quopomma looped the rope once around a stanchion, possibly built by the city's populace for just this purpose, and indicated for Iro and the others to be lowered. Maeveen put her lieutenant and the other soldiers in the sling, letting the immensely strong Quopomma lower them swiftly.

"Not so fast. You're scaring Iro."

"Give her something to take her mind off her bad dreams," grunted Quopomma, but she slowed the breakneck descent. When the rope went slack, the ogre waited, then hauled it back by the time Vervamon strode up.

"A beautiful day to head for the coast," the explorer said jauntily. "I can almost smell the sea air from this lofty aerie." He tossed his head back and drew a deep breath, then noisily exhaled. "No sea air, but there will be. I want the Sigil of Iwset in my hand so we can open the Tomb of the Seven Martyrs."

"Where is this tomb?" asked Quopomma. "After you get the key, where do we have to go?"

"Ah, that is why Coernn has accompanied us. He knows the location, having been briefed fully by Digody."

"You mean we have to depend on *him* once we get the sigil?" Maeveen's eyes widened in astonishment. "What makes you think he will ever tell you? He has led us in circles so far. We come to this city, but no, he says before we arrive, it is in Shingol. When we reach the fishing village, what then? Does Coernn decide it is in Argoth? Why do you think he will ever reveal the real location to you? If he even knows!" Maeveen was exasperated. She had risked her life in the mistaken belief Vervamon knew where the tomb was located and all they need do to snare the Sigil of Iwset was enter its locked vaults.

"Why, Lord Peemel and his adviser promised it. They are quite keen on archeology and exploring the ruins left after the war. My knowledge expands constantly, and finding the tomb will be a highlight of a fabulous career, I assure you, my delightfully suspicious Maeveen."

"You don't know where the tomb is?" She shook her head. Lord Peemel had fooled Vervamon completely. She had no doubt the Sigil of Iwset existed. That it opened the Tomb of the Seven Martyrs now lay in doubt. "How is it Coernn only recently decided the sigil was hidden away in Shingol? A fishing village is a peculiar hiding place for such a valuable relic."

Vervamon shrugged. "I do not question his ways. I suspect they might be . . . arcane," he said in a soft voice. "I have little love for those following sorcerous paths, but I have even less for the Inquisition. At least, sorcerers expand knowledge. The Inquisition strives to stifle it in any form not acceptable to their narrow mentalities. Now, is this hoist ready for me?"

"Hop in. Next stop, the rest of our expedition," said Quopomma. She rapidly lowered Vervamon, taking a small pleasure in letting the rope fall freely, then stopping it only feet from disaster at the bottom. The ogre smiled, showing her gapped teeth, and then shrugged.

Maeveen let Quopomma have her fun. She faced the dark buildings of the City of Shadows and marveled at the deathly silence. The dancing motes of black within black intrigued her, but memory of the night and the phantasms it brought drove her away. If she never set foot in this city again, it would be a thousand years too soon. She let Quopomma lower her next.

"Get the spies below, then you can descend," Maeveen told her lieutenant before the downward rush made her gasp. The side of the cliff flashed past, then the sudden stop almost tossed her from the harness. She scrambled free before Quopomma pulled it back up. Maeveen smoothed her uniform and tried not to look flustered. It was bad for discipline if the commander showed too much trepidation over such matters.

Maeveen wasn't sure if she was irritated that no one noticed her plight. A dozen paces away, Vervamon held forth on some esoteric subject and the other soldiers pretended they were acutely intrigued. They were intrigued only to the extent it got them out of work, or so Maeveen hoped. Vervamon *did* have a charisma that hypnotized those within earshot.

Maeveen listened for a few seconds, then chased her soldiers back to their chores. By the time Coernn touched down, she had the expedition ready to march. When Quopomma dropped to the ground and dusted off her hands, Maeveen gave the command to head for the coast.

"Lost? Impossible," Maeveen thundered. "You are no green scout learning his craft. You know how to find a path through the densest of forests. This one is hardly worthy of that name." She looked around the sparse trees and burned undergrowth, wondering what had thinned the grove so drastically.

"I tell you, I head out and get all turned around," the scout protested.

Maeveen eyed the soldier, a slender youth named

Slyfoot, usually capable of ferreting out the faintest of spoor, thinking he merely made an excuse to malinger. He was, after all, one of Iro's soldiers. He met her gaze squarely, and Maeveen knew the affront to his talent far outweighed any desire to shirk his duties.

"Fetch Quopomma. The three of us will find the trail to the coast," Maeveen decided. The timberland around them gave meager cover for any possible ambush by goblin or any other predator. She worried more about turning in circles until precious days were gone, wasted.

Slyfoot disappeared without a sound. Maeveen wished she could walk through a forest like that. In comparison, she walked with both feet stuck in a tin bucket. She could shrug off this inability on her part, but there was much she could not. It was her job to worry, but leaving the City of Shadows ought to have lightened her mood. If anything, she felt as if she stood still and the world rushed toward her uncontrollably. Nothing in her nightmare had come true, but she felt it all would—soon.

Maeveen jumped when Slyfoot and Quopomma returned. The ogre moved lightly for one so large.

"Jumpy, Captain?" the ogre asked, a wicked grin crossing her lips. Quopomma quickly sobered as she delivered her report. "I had the feeling we were on the wrong trail, but Slyfoot denied it. I think he and Iro are in cahoots, wanting to rest up a few days longer before pressing on."

"I could use the rest, too, but Vervamon insists we keep moving. And there is something I don't like about these woods."

"No sign of anyone willing to fill us with arrows," Quopomma said, looking about. "I've sent some of my own scouts out—no offense, Slyfoot. Of Iro's worthless platoon, you are the best."

"I would thank you for your compliment, Lieutenant, should I ever decide if I have been insulted," Slyfoot said, not concerned about the ogre's assertion in the least. Without another word, he started into the woods, moving like a puff of wind and only half as loud. For ten minutes they hiked, only to end up where they had started.

"See, Captain? It's always like that. I head out in any direction, then end up back here as if I'm an iron needle and this place is a lodestone."

Twice more Maeveen insisted they try, but Slyfoot proved accurate in his appraisal. They returned to the same spot, no matter which direction they had started from. She had stopped to ponder this when she saw a scrap of cloth poking out from under a mound of leaves. Dropping to one knee, Maeveen tugged gently. The leaves shifted to reveal a body.

"That's the one from Coernn's band who left us back in the City of Shadows," Quopomma said, staring at the half-rotted face. "Didn't get far, did he?"

"Do you want me to tell Vervamon? Coernn?" asked Slyfoot.

"There's no hurry. We seem fixed to this spot, and I want to know why without getting a lecture, or being told it is none of my business," Maeveen said. She pulled the body into view. "He had the bad luck to be a target for elvish arrows. They are remarkable shots, aren't they?" She ran her fingers over the three shafts buried in the man's back, all within a finger's length of one another.

"He was alive when he burrowed under the leaves. He got away from them and hid here, only to die later," Quopomma said, studying the lay of the body and the physical evidence around it. "I underestimated him. I would've thought he'd die of fright simply seeing an elf pointing an arrow in his direction."

Maeveen tugged hard and got the man's rucksack out from under him. He had removed it and laid facedown atop it. She opened it and peered inside.

"Is that wise, Captain?" asked Slyfoot, frowning. "The other one, that pasty-faced Coernn, might consider this his property now that his coadjutor is dead."

"Is it our fault the backpack spilled its contents?" Maeveen asked, opening the canvas flap and turning the rucksack upside-down. A torrent of debris to the ground, but one item caught Maeveen's attention. A lamp without any obvious power source shone forth with a clear white light.

Quopomma let out a low whistle between her teeth, and Slyfoot backed away.

"That's magical," the scout declared. "I want nothing to do with it."

"We have no choice," Maeveen said, pawing through the other items. She was no expert, but knew enough of magic to realize the bearer of the lantern had to know its power source was not approved by the Inquisition. That put to the lie any idea that Coernn and his friends were Inquisitors. If anything, they would avoid the red-robed clerics while carrying such a magical artifact.

She touched it gingerly, then recoiled when the white light changed to green. Maeveen calmed herself and picked up the lamp carefully. The pure light bathing them spread in all directions.

"What might it be?" asked Quopomma, as wary of magic as Slyfoot, but trying not to show it.

"A beacon, a guiding light."

"What good it is when it shines in all directions?" asked Slyfoot. "You have to know where you are going to use it, just as you do any other lamp."

"It would be useful, a lamp without oil or wick," said Quopomma.

"Perhaps it did shine forth on a single path—while he was alive," said Maeveen. "He died of elven arrows. If he lost control, the light might shine in all directions—"

"—and magically draw us back to this spot," finished Quopomma. "I hate magic."

Maeveen reached out and ran her hand over the glass envelope of the magic lantern. She pressed her fingers into the shallow depressions on one side and the light winked out. She dropped the lamp, startled by the sudden death of the illumination.

"Think we can continue on our way to the coast?" asked Quopomma. The change in her voice pulled Maeveen's attention from the magical tidbit.

"No, I don't think so," said Slyfoot. The wiry scout stood, attention on the trees around them, hand on his dagger, but he did not draw. He was too intelligent for that.

Maeveen looked up and saw the ring of elven archers ready to feather them as they had already done to Coernn's assistant. She stood slowly, wondering how she was going to talk her way out of this, for parley it had to be.

No force of arms would overwhelm so many elven fighters obviously fresh from a battle.

CHAPTER

30

ISAK GLEN'DARD STOPPED OUTSIDE THE BLACK
wood door and straightened his clothing in a self-conscious
gesture. He smoothed back his hair and tucked his stylish
hat with the Serra angel feather in its brim firmly under
his arm, in deference to Peemel's adviser. Isak knew he
had been wrong remaining in Iwset overlong, but Ihesia's
beauty drew him as if she conjured a spell binding his
heart to hers.

Isak knew that was impossible. Secretly, Ihesia might
use others who could cast spells, but she had no ability of
her own. All the "spells" cast by the lovely general were
of a gentler, more natural kind—but nonetheless powerful for that.

Still, he worried about Digody and how Ihesia dismissed him as a minor inconvenience in her drive for
power in Iwset. How long before the strange, dark
adviser to the throne realized he did not have a loyal servant in the man knocking on his door?

Isak knocked and heard angry voices within. He ought
to have waited for a clearer command to enter, but he
pushed in, knowing he could justify his hasty entry.
Digody leaned forward on his desk, face gray with rage.

The source of his anger bounced about on short, steel-spring legs.

"Digody, Apepei," greeted Isak. "I thought you bade me enter. I shall wait—"

"The mountain-born was on his way out," Digody said in a voice barely controlled.

"You shall not be rid of the matter as easily as this," Apepei shouted. The mountain dwarf bobbed and bounced, then pushed past Isak. He muttered to himself all the way down the hall. From the snippets Isak overheard, Apepei and Digody fought over the progress of the war with Jehesic. It was hardly a secret that Apepei argued against the war and favored alliance of a friendlier nature with Jehesic. Nor was it a secret of state that Apepei and his allies were gradually being removed from Lord Peemel's inner circle of advisers in favor of those supported by Digody.

"An irritating little worm," Digody growled. He straightened and took a deep breath. Isak thought of leather bellows straining in a smithy's forge. Peemel's adviser fell heavily into his chair, chin resting on one fist. His other bony fingers tapped restlessly on the arm of his chair, and his feral eyes focused somewhere past Isak.

"Shall I return, or—"

"Close the door," ordered Digody. His attention turned to Isak, as if seeing him for the first time. "You are late."

Isak did not argue. He was early for this appointment. He bowed deeply, as much to hide his face and the emotion playing there as to show his deference to Digody's opinion.

"How may I make up this affront, milord?" Isak tried not to smirk as he spoke.

"Your reports concerning Abbot Offero have been informative. He uses his sacred warriors to considerable effect in our battle to the south."

"The guerrillas find no refuge from those loyal to the abbot," Isak said carefully. "And in each victory, the Church expands its sphere of influence."

"There is no reason to believe Offero has ambition to mount the throne, is there?" asked Digody.

"He is an earnest, devout man with sincere belief he

must stop the use of magic. To this end he forces the
Inquisition onto the land. For your purpose, he is only an
innocent ally. He knows the futility of anyone seeking the
throne who lacks royal blood in his veins."

"Innocent," scoffed Digody. He pushed aside papers
and looked up. "No man who puts so many to torture and
death is innocent. But the blood on his hands is righteous
and ours is not."

Isak stiffened. He waited for the orders from Digody
that he knew to be forthcoming after such a comment.
Depending on the exact content of the command, he
might have overstayed his welcome in Iwset by days. For
Ihesia he had lingered too long, and now he might pay
with his life for his lust.

"Sacumon is too independent," Digody said. "She was
to permit the minotaurs to win and she failed. Worse, the
elves are talking with the human villagers along the coast,
feeling out possible alliances. We lose control because of
her mistakes."

"There is more brewing to the north than the elf–
minotaur skirmish," Isak said, hoping to sidetrack
Digody. "Rumors of peculiar beings from underground
ravaging entire villages are not to be denied. These are
not just clever goblins. No known race sets fires the way
these do. Some call them coal golems."

"Coal golems," muttered Digody. "Further reason to
remove Sacumon from her position of power, if she has
unleashed them on the land. Who can control such
monsters?"

"Does she still retain Peemel's trust?"

Digody snapped his gaze upward to Isak and said
sharply, "What Lord Peemel desires in this matter is of no
concern to you. You will obey *me*."

Isak bowed again, hiding his face from the enraged
counselor. Apepei had stirred more than simple anger
this time. The dwarf must have brought Digody such
news that the ripples would spread from one end of Iwset
to the other. Isak made a mental note to tell Ihesia of this
and have her seek information, if not alliance, from the
dwarven adviser.

"Sacumon has failed. That is all you need to know. I want her removed so another may be sent, one totally devoted to *my* rule." Digody leaned back and a smile crossed his thin lips. "Perhaps *you* will be that emissary, Isak. Fancy being duke of the northern lands. You have a knack for diplomacy and speaking honeyed words to soothe even the most inflamed, a skill valuable to me."

"A duchy? You are too generous, milord."

"Yes, I know. But after you have taken care of Sacumon so that she is no longer such a discommoding presence, you may bring together the factions into a stronger bloc, under my orders, naturally."

"Naturally." Isak's mind raced. "How and when do you want Sacumon removed as a pawn in your vast game, milord?"

"When? Immediately. As soon as you can get to the Forest of Eln, or wherever she makes her headquarters." Digody made a gesture dismissing this as done. "How is easier than you might think. The envelope given her carried a strong but invisible dye. Tracking it is facilitated by a peculiar stone brought to me from Tondhat. Given her location, you can contrive some small . . . accident for her, I suspect."

"She is a powerful wizard," Isak pointed out.

"You are not without resources," Digody shot back. "This is something Abbot Offero might find interesting, should I remember to mention it to him. A shape-changer is always suspected of sorcerous intentions."

"This is my nature, milord, not an ability learned or controlled."

"Split hairs with the abbot. He is always interested in such philosophical argument—before he applies the torture and asks the question."

A threat without real menace, Isak thought. Offero was more likely to side with General Ihesia than Digody, should it come to choosing public sides in the battle for the throne of Iwset.

Queen Ihesia. It had a nice ring to it, but one which would remove the lovely lady from Isak's bed. She needed him now, but not after she mounted the black wood throne. He had so many avenues stretching in front of him, and death lay waiting for him at every destination. Should he refuse Digody's order, he would expose himself to the adviser's wrath. Digody would prove especially vindictive, because failure to assassinate Sacumon would leave a danger to the north and possibly reveal all the adviser's plots within the walls of Iwset to Lord Peemel.

A simple word to Apepei would seal Digody's fate and rip apart Iwset for years to come. Peemel was not strong enough to crush Digody, Abbot Offero, Apepei, Ihesia, and all the others vying for power, not with the ill-conceived war against Jehesic raging, rebels in the south meting out daily setbacks—and Sacumon with her flaming allies to the north.

A juggler with a dozen eggs circling endlessly in the air could not be more careful, Isak knew. A single mistake would cause a mess beyond redemption.

It was time for him to leave Iwset, but he could not yet. Not without Ihesia. And Isak doubted she would accompany him.

"Removing Sacumon's threat to both Iwset and you will be my delightful duty," Isak said, cursing himself for a fool as he spoke. He would kill Sacumon, if only to remain with Ihesia a while longer. After all, the renegade sorceress presented as much a threat to Ihesia as she did Peemel and Digody.

Isak Glen'dard would be doing his love a favor. It would be her coronation gift from her most adoring servant. He backed from Digody's chambers and settled his floppy-brimmed hat on his head in the hallway. Starting off with a long stride, Isak whistled a jaunty tune as he planned Sacumon's demise.

CHAPTER
31

MYTARU GLARED AT YUNNIE, SILENTLY accusing him of vile crimes against the herd. In a way, Yunnie knew he not only stood convicted of such an unspoken charge, it was true. He tried to scratch at a bleeding bug bite, but the Living Armor got in his way. He cursed the leather breastplate and the crushing burden it placed on him—the burden he was not equal to meeting any longer.

"We attack, not at the small force the elves think has us locked into our valley, but past them, into their heart!" cried Aesor. The bull pranced about, tossing his head and sending his score of red battle ribbons fluttering with every jerk of his powerful neck. He stopped in front of Yunnie and glared at him, challenging him to speak, silently demanding a personal challenge.

Yunnie said nothing. He had nothing to say in his own defense, or against Aesor's desperate plan of attack. He was sick at heart and unable to fight with the best of the minotaurs. Endless campaigns had taken something out of him, but he knew it was more than simple battle fatigue. He could have led the minotaurs to glorious victory when Sacumon primed the elves for terrible defeat.

Instead, he had fought Sacumon and made her lose concentration.

The fierce elves had carried the day and had taken the war to the minotaurs in a battle beyond anyone's planning. Never again would the Urhaalan be able to match the elves in direct conflict. House after house had fallen—and mysteriously burned after being abandoned by the elves. Yunnie alone knew the reason for this senseless arson. The coal golems sent by the Stone People grew bolder, entering the valley and ravaging at will. The elves fought, and the coal golems burned what remained, making it unusable by either side.

If only he could get Mytaru and the others to see that their enemies numbered more than the elves, but Sacumon's curse still clogged his throat and prevented the words from coming out intelligibly, even if the others would believe him. This reckless excursion into Forest Eln to tear at the heart of elvish society smacked of suicidal tactics, but he could not speak against Aesor, or any of the others advocating such an assault. It might be the only hope for the minotaurs.

It might be their last hope for survival.

He tried to put his warning about the coal golems and the Niroso into words and felt his throat tightening, still the prisoner of Sacumon's vile spell. Neck muscles clamped down on his windpipe and choked him. Once Mytaru had thought this was a sign of the spirits of the west trying to speak through Yunnie. Now he ignored his blood brother entirely, attention fixed on Aesor's battle plan.

Yunnie stopped struggling to speak and his throat relaxed immediately. None of the minotaurs even knew of Sacumon, and if they had, she would have been dismissed as a human lackey for the elves and therefore beneath contempt. How Yunnie wished he could free himself of her spell!

"How do you intend to sneak past the elf sentries? They have us bottled up in the valley," Yunnie pointed out. He had scouted with the best of the minotaurs and knew how completely they were imprisoned in their homeland.

He started to protest when he read the answer on Mytaru's face. The bull sneered, his thick lip curling upward to expose his teeth. Mytaru had been preparing for battle, eating meat and leaving the small pieces caught between his teeth. But it was the expression that frightened Yunnie.

"You dare not use magic against them," he protested. "You are not trained. It will turn on you." He tried to say that Sacumon would turn it against Mytaru. He proved strong enough to remember her, in spite of the geas of forgetfulness she tried repeatedly to weave around him, but of the Stone People and their magical constructs and Sacumon he could not speak without gagging to death.

"My skills grow every time I cast a spell," Mytaru said, pounding his chest and prancing about. "My brother is unwilling to lead Clan Utyeehn and the herd against our enemy. I will! My magic benefits us, while his protects only his own hide." Mytaru visibly forced himself not to say "worthless hide."

Yunnie was not sure if he appreciated this small concession to his feelings. Better to break clean. He might have gained acceptance into the herd, but every battle since the great defeat had seen him pushed farther to the side, his influence dwindling. They even turned their hindquarters to him as he walked past, contempt usually reserved for outcasts from the herd.

"You need not accompany us," Aesor said haughtily. "It might be better if you stayed in the valley where you will not be hurt."

Yunnie angrily bumped against Aesor, challenging him. He had to duck to avoid a sweeping slash of the bull's metal-sheathed, razor-edged horns. Dancing away, Yunnie started to draw his sword, but found his arms held to his sides by the armor's magical force.

"My armor. Let me get out of it," he said. He fought to get free, but the Living Armor seized him in a powerful embrace that prevented combat. Yunnie stopped struggling and felt the leather relax and return to its usual tough but malleable design. This was the first time the Living Armor had worked to protect itself from battle. It did not bode well for his future if the magical artifact now directed attacks away from itself, but not necessarily from his flesh.

"You are beneath contempt. You are not worth bloodying my horns." Aesor snorted, tossed his head proudly, and stalked off. The other minotaurs joined him, leaving Yunnie alone in the middle of the meadow. They began their chants, the intricate and unchanging rituals necessary for combat.

Tears came to Yunnie's eyes as Aesor's bull roar filled the valley with challenge and bravado. He had been accepted here, but found himself as much an outcast as he had been back in Shingol. He wiped his nose and mouth and knew what he felt now was worse. He had been accepted fully into the herd, and now no one sought his counsel or heeded his dire warnings. He was scorned and reviled, but it was not his doing.

To one side of the gathered Clan Utyeehn knelt Mytaru, his hands working through complex movements that trailed burning runes. He conjured spells of invisibility and Yunnie knew not what else. Whatever Mytaru sought to bring forth, it meant only death and destruction for the Urhaalan.

"The coal golems," Yunnie muttered, his mind racing to discover how to regain his lost stature and keep Mytaru from injuring himself beyond redemption with his ill-formed spells. "The Niroso. Attack underground, not above. Remove them and the threat is gone." Even as he whispered this to himself, he knew it was not the solution to Urhaalan problems. That lay with Sacumon and her schemes, pitting elf against minotaur, then letting the coal golems have their way with the wounded.

The Stone People sought domination over more than their subterranean world. He wondered what Sacumon had promised them for their allegiance. Did the Niroso realize the sorceress would turn on them when the elves and minotaurs were dead? Or did such double-dealing have any meaning for a race capable of passing through solid rock? He knew nothing of their hopes, dreams, and abilities.

The minotaurs danced in a wide circle and began pawing the ground, waving decorated war lances high in the air and tossing their heads in fierce circles, showing how they would gut their enemies. Bloodred battle ribbons fluttered in the gentle breeze blowing across the glade. If he had tried to get a profane glimpse into Hell, he could not have succeeded better.

Then came utter silence as the last of the Urhaalan laments died. Mytaru stood. He drew brilliant yellow symbols in the air with the tip of his darting finger. Yunnie was impressed at the display of such power, even if he disapproved. But Sacumon was an able sorceress and would detect any use of magic against her or her allies, be they elven flesh or Niroso stone.

The yellow runes expanded and encircled the tight knot of minotaurs. Yunnie had to rub his eyes when both rune and minotaur vanished in a wild explosion of searing light. He knew Mytaru's spell fooled his eyes, but even so, locating the minotaurs proved difficult. He saw grass bend under the weight of the moving war party. As if pulled along on a string, Yunnie followed them to the mouth of the valley.

He wished Mytaru would use the spell to bring fighters against only small bands of elves. Chipping away at the enemy might convince them to retreat and parley, but a minotaur never thought in gradual terms. All or nothing. Rage or peace. He decided on their most likely route from the valley and made his own way past elven sentries.

Yunnie was not certain if he was on the same road until he saw a muddy patch cut up by the recent passage of many fighters. He took time to look around and sucked in his breath. He had jogged constantly most of the day and found himself at the extreme edge of Forest Eln. The grove was thin and had been chopped down in past years for fuel, only now reforesting after long decades.

"Kill Sacumon," he said over and over to himself, trying to believe it might be possible. He knew nothing of the sorceress, her powers or ambitions. Killing her might not be possible, not with any weapon he commanded. Still, Yunnie saw no alternative. Fighting the coal golems or their masters seemed an impossibility. How did he kill something at home in the middle of a smithy's forge?

"Chop off the head and the body dies," he said, knowing Sacumon was the mastermind behind this war. She did so well at diverting his energy, making him hunt down goblins when the coal golems were the menace, letting the minotaurs battle the elves when the Stone People sought true dominion, keeping him from alerting the minotaurs to their real danger.

Yunnie drifted through the periphery of the fragile, over-forested woodlands, sensing others watching him. He skirted the trees, then worked deeper into cool shadow when he found no one. Still, the feeling of being spied upon did not change and made him progressively edgier. He stopped and drew his sword, turning in a full circle. Only then did he realize the source of his discomfort came from higher up. His blue eyes rose along the trunk of a huge Ironroot and fixed on sad brown eyes.

"You are not wanted here," the Ironroot told him in its deeply resonant bass voice. "You are human and will not be harmed, but you must leave Forest Eln right away or suffer the consequences."

"The minotaurs are my brothers," Yunnie said, not willing to lie. "I would stop them from their foolish attack."

"It is too late," the Ironroot said in a booming voice. "I watched them enter, and now they fight a futile battle."

"They were invisible."

"A magic spell of such fragility," the Ironroot said slowly, "is scant impediment to my vision."

"What of—" Yunnie gagged. He could not bring Sacumon's name to his lips, even in front of this wooden giant. Her damnable spell still held him in thrall.

"Go, leave. The minotaurs will remain. Forever, their bodies fertilizing the sod of Forest Eln."

"No!" shouted Yunnie. "They are my friends, my blood brothers! I am of the herd!"

A tree limb swished down and knocked him through the air. He crashed into another tree, not an Ironroot, and lay stunned. With glacial slowness, the Ironroot turned.

Yunnie scrambled to his feet, but he would not fight the ancient warrior.

"You cannot prevail. The elves have convinced all us Ironroots we must defend our woodland. You cannot invade us, you human who claims to be a bull."

Twigs lanced through the air. Yunnie staggered as the Living Armor deflected them. Each wooden dart was hurled with prodigious strength. He withstood the increasing barrage from the Ironroot until he felt a subtle change in the way the Living Armor reacted.

He winced as a sharpened twig cut through his flesh, missing the edge of the armor by a fraction of an inch. The Living Armor increasingly protected itself now, taking some damage but sharing as much as possible with Yunnie.

It was a coward's route to tread, but Yunnie turned and fled rather than stand against the Ironroot. He had no quarrel with the majestic tree, but he realized his mistake immediately when the forest echoed with warning sounded by the Ironroot. Any elf within miles now knew another had entered their precious forest.

Yunnie ran, sword drawn and ready to skewer anyone trying to stop him. He lowered his blade when he met Mehonvo rushing out of the forest. The old bull saw Yunnie and motioned to him.

"Defeat, terrible defeat. Too many elves. Traps. Even Mytaru's spell did not give us the advantage we needed."

"The Ironroot could see through the spell," Yunnie said. "And the Ironroots are allied with the elves. Neither of them wants the forest to become a battlefield."

"Mytaru might have escaped. Aesor and his son, Pardano, also. But the others—only one in ten got away. Clan Utyeehn is gone, gone!" Mehonvo's dirge for the lost minotaurs rose, but suddenly cut off. The one-horned minotaur pushed Yunnie aside.

"By Tiyint, what is that?"

Yunnie spun about and gasped. Sizzling footsteps brought a coal golem taller than Mehonvo ever closer. He tried to warn the minotaur, but the words froze in his throat. He heaved his sword like a spear. The coal golem batted it aside contemptuously, the metal tearing like rotted fabric.

"You can't fight it," Yunnie said. "Run, Mehonvo. Return to the valley. There must be peace with the elves. This is our real enemy!"

Mehonvo let out a roar, lowered his head, and charged. His single horn caught the coal golem squarely in the chest. Powerful neck muscles lifted the magical construct high and threw it to the ground, but the coal golem rolled to its feet and began pelting Mehonvo with lumps of fiery coal. One seared the old bull's chest. He moaned and tried futilely to remove the burning lump. A second fireball of coal crashed into the bull's side, setting his clothing on fire. Then Mehonvo let out a cry of anger and charged again.

"No, Mehonvo, no, you can't fight it!" cried Yunnie, helpless in the face of such power. He watched the minotaur grapple with the coal golem. Both exploded in a fiery column that reached skyward and set fire to a dozen trees. Yunnie listened to Mehonvo's death cries, sickened by the stench of burning flesh, ashamed at his own inaction, desolated by the utter defeat of such a valiant warrior, friend, and uncle.

The coal golem expired with Mehonvo, but that was no comfort.

Fire crackled and popped all around, set by the eruption of the blazing golem. In the distance Yunnie heard the Ironroot giving voice to a new warning, but another sound caught his attention. Heavy footfalls drew him from the ring of fire toward the road leading from the woods.

"Mytaru! You got away!"

The bull turned a bloodied face to Yunnie. His expression was one of utter hatred.

"We were slaughtered by the elves and Ironroots," Mytaru said. "Clan Utyeehn is no more. The herd is sorely wounded."

"Let me help."

Mytaru swung his broken war lance at Yunnie in a wild, unfocused attack. The Living Armor protected him from the worst of the blow, but the impact sent him stumbling.

"Mytaru, please. I can help!"

"You are no longer Urhaalan," Mytaru said in a cracked voice. "You are not my blood brother or friend. You are banished forever from my sight! Do not ever darken my home with your cowardly presence or speak to those in Clan Utyeehn!" With that, the minotaur stumbled away, leaving Yunnie aghast.

He wanted to cry out for Mytaru to take back the ugly things he had said, take back the banishment, take back all the hurt and ill-feeling, but that would not be possible. Yunnie was no longer a minotaur in the clan ruled by Mytaru. That meant he was adrift and clanless. Any bull cast out of his clan could petition others for membership. Some clans were comprised mostly of outcasts—but even they would not take Yunnie, not after today.

Without a clan, he was cut off from all others. The herd had forsaken him.

The fire raging in the forest forced him off the road and deeper into Forest Eln. All day he stumbled along, lost in his misery and pain. When he came to a fork in the road, one circling back to the Urhaalan's valley and the other toward the coast and his old village of Shingol, with tears running down his cheeks Yunnie hesitated only an instant before deciding which way to turn.

CHAPTER
32

"YOUR WOUNDS AREN'T SO BAD," HERYEON
said, peering at Yunnie with his one good eye. "Mostly
healed and no obstacle to walking about acting like you
had good sense. How long did you say it took you to get
here from Eln?"

Yunnie shrugged. He hardly remembered. So much
flowed together in his head, the waves lapping against the
shores of memory and slowly erasing anything giving definition to his life. Inside he felt hollow and worthless. He
had tried to save the minotaurs and had failed. He had
fought the elves to escape the forest, hating every instant
of it. In some way he could not fathom, he felt as if he
killed his friends every time he took an elven life.

Again came the faint memory, niggling and teasing,
dancing just beyond his grasp. This was not the result of
Sacumon's magical geas to forget about the Niroso and
their magical constructs, or even to forget Sacumon's
very existence. Returning to Shingol had aroused this old
memory, and it had to do with elves. But what?

"You never were a social cuss, but you turned down-
right close-mouthed after tom-catting around."

"It wasn't like that," he told his brother-in-law.

Heryeon spat a gooey red gobbet of blood-seed at his feet. Yunnie paid no attention. He had been humiliated and scorned more by his brothers in the herd—by those who had once welcomed him as a brother, he corrected himself. Mehonvo was dead. Mytaru, Aesor, Pardano, and all the others who survived considered him a traitor. Stories of how the herd dealt with renegades were told around the campfires, to scare the children and to warn others of the utter devastation possible should sentiment turn against them. The herd was all; individuals were tolerated only for what they could do to help the herd prosper.

He had failed the herd because of the Living Armor. Yunnie scratched futilely at the nits working under the armor.

His return to Shingol had gone unheralded, too. His sister and the family fleet of three boats were out scouring the sea for anything edible. Most of the other fishermen were gone with her. Why Heryeon remained behind Yunnie was at a loss to say, and if pressed, he did not much care. What Essa saw in the oaf was a mystery Yunnie had never figured out, nor had he worked much at solving the conundrum. Leaving Shingol had been preferable to dealing with such realities of life.

"You're a walking louse pit," Heryeon said, spitting again. This time the syrupy gobbet flew out the opened door to hit squarely in a brightly painted ceramic pot beside the porch. If he had not been so dejected, Yunnie would have applauded such skill.

"I had scant time to bathe," Yunnie said. "When will Essa get back?"

"Your sister's out with the fleet, I told you a dozen times. You know how it is. They return when they have a full hold, or know there will be nothing more for them." Heryeon looked around their small home and shook his head. "Tried to get her to move a hundred times, I did. Not safe in Shingol, not with war brewing."

"The elves and minotaurs will not bother you. They are too far off, but the—" Yunnie choked when he tried to tell his brother-in-law how dangerous the Niroso were.

Their ambitions would not be limited to the Eln Forest or the valley of the Urhaalan. Coal golems would sally forth to destroy humans, mountain dwarves, ogres, or any who stood against them, until the Stone People gained full dominion over the surface.

Sacumon's curse shoved the words back down his throat as surely as if he had tried chewing the blood-seed himself. The times he had gone out with the fishing fleet, some old salt had always offered him a handful of the crimson seeds. Every time, Yunnie had disgraced himself, much to the delight of the others. The blood-seed burned his throat and turned him sick to his stomach faster than the rolling deck under his feet. Only true sailors chewed it, or so went the tradition.

"Who cares about elf and minotaur?" Heryeon laughed. "It's the *big* war that's threatening the entire coast."

"What's happened since I left Shingol? Have the leer fish decided to return to kill their hunters?" He made no effort to hide his bitterness.

"Nothing has happened. It's as if you returned an hour after you left," Heryeon said sarcastically. "For whatever reason, Essa will be glad to see you."

"Why aren't you with her?"

"Hurt my back," Heryeon said sullenly.

"So you sit all day and rumormonger about war along the coast?"

Yunnie propped himself up. His legs hurt from the long journey and his belly grumbled from lack of food. The initiation into the Urhaalan herd had given him a sense of how long he could go without food, and for that knowledge he thanked them. Their rituals were mostly curious oddities to him, but this one defined his ability and gave him confidence he could continue in spite of extreme hardship. And he had, dragging all the way back to Shingol.

"Iwset fights Jehesic. Lord Peemel offered to marry Lady Edara, and she spurned his offer."

"Peemel is a pig," Yunnie said. He had always wondered how long it would take the egotistical ruler to decide conquering the city-states along the western coast was his destiny. Jehesic would be only the first jewel in what Peemel would consider a royal crown of subjugation.

"He fights from shadows," Heryeon said. "He sent an assassin to kill Lady Edara when she refused to marry him. Killed her chief adviser by accident."

"An assassin mistook an adviser for his true target?" Yunnie shook his head. He knew something of the skill of those kingly killers. They did not make such mistakes.

"Killed Lady Edara's adviser, Ferantia by name. Stabbed her in the back as Edara signaled her harbor defenses to fire on Peemel's frigate. Jehesic sank the ship and the war started for real, though there had been a few incidents earlier."

"Peemel solved all his problems on the land?"

"Heard his generals are having fits with some of the villages along the coast. General Ihesia and the Inquisition troops were turned back up north."

Yunnie shuddered. A defeat elsewhere meant attention would turn in Shingol's direction. A few easy victories would be needed to maintain Lord Peemel's position with his people. Yunnie had never felt any love for the Iwsetians or any of the other nonfishing city-states. Jehesic, on the other hand, shone as an ideal for all seafaring towns, including Shingol.

But Yunnie disliked the sea and being on a ship, no matter where his sympathies lay.

Anger filled him at the thought of war coming to Shingol. With a convulsive jerk, he sent his arm swinging along the top of the table in front of him. Goblets flew and pewter plates broke as his anger soared.

"Hey, now, none of that. You might have gotten used to destroying what you ate on out there in the forest or mountains or wherever you been, but those cost us a fortune!" Heryeon grabbed Yunnie's arm to keep him from smashing more of the dishes. Heryeon had a fisherman's strength in his hands, but Yunnie easily broke free and swung his fist, driven by the power of the Living Armor.

Fury took control of him, and he wanted to kill. He

turned his soaring rage against a man he had never liked. All Yunnie could think of was spilling blood, killing, destroying!

"Yunnie, stop! What are you doing? Otto, Felal, help me!" Essa rushed from where she stood in the doorway and grabbed Yunnie's arms, keeping him from strangling his brother-in-law. The other two fishermen with her pulled Yunnie away, kicking and screaming.

"Outside, get him outside," Essa ordered. She dropped to one knee, saw her husband was furious but otherwise unhurt, then followed her brother. The two fishermen held Yunnie against a pillar used to dry and repair heavy nets. The harder he fought them, the stronger he became, the Living Armor feeding his anger.

"You have changed, and not for the good. Are you no better than Heryeon has claimed all these years?" Essa asked in her gentle voice. She stepped closer and reached out, her hand touching his cheek. Yunnie's rage drained from him, as if she had pulled a plug.

"Essa, I am sorry. I don't know what happened to me. I don't lose my temper like that."

"You were always moody, but such ire is new. And I can't say I approve of your fashion sense, either. This is very poor armor," Essa said, touching the Living Armor. She recoiled in pain and stared at her hand. "It bit me! Or it felt like it did."

"I'm sorry," Yunnie said. The two fishermen released him, but remained wary. Yunnie sank to his knees, shame washing over him. "I never meant to harm Heryeon. I don't like him, but he is my brother-in-law and your husband. I always respected him for that, if nothing else."

"He is a good man, Yunnie. So are you." Essa paused, then said in a choked voice, "So *were* you. What are you now?"

He turned his azure eyes to meet her brown ones. How unlike they were, yet Essa had always seen into his heart. Yunnie worried what she saw there now. If only he could tell her what he knew of the Stone People! Of Sacumon and the coal golems and the danger drifting toward the coast from the forests and mountains.

The words could not arrange themselves to let him give vent to his frustrating message. He sagged even more, his frustration turning to self-loathing.

"I don't know what I am now. I put on this magic armor, and now I cannot remove it." Bitterness flooded him and turned to bile in his mouth. He fit in nowhere, and the Living Armor prevented him from ever doing as he saw fit. Curse Sacumon! Curse her a thousand times over!

"Magic armor?" Essa laughed, and it sounded genuine. Otto and Felal joined in her merriment. "That pathetic fragment of badly cured leather? Yunnie, you were a dreamer and visionary, but never did you delude yourself." Essa's gaiety died, and she turned somber. "Come back. Rest a few days, then join us in our work. I have three boats now. I command one, Otto and Felal the other two, but there is a place for you on my boat. You worked well. Forget your strange obsession to meddle in others' affairs. Sail with me again, as you once did."

"Essa, thank you, I—" Yunnie straightened, then stood. "I cannot. The war must be stopped, and only I can do it."

"Spoken like a madman," called Heryeon from the doorway.

"Go inside, Heryeon. I'll tend to this. He's my brother."

"He's not your brother, and you know it," Heryeon shot back. "He ought to be driven from Shingol and killed if he ever returns!"

Yunnie started for his brother-in-law, the Living Armor fueling his seething anger again. Essa's captains held him in their powerful grips.

"I see I was wrong. There's no place for you in Shingol any longer, Yunnie."

"What did he mean, you're not my sister? I'll kill him!"

"Yunnie, leave the village. We have a hard life here, and there is no need for you to make it worse than it is." Essa glanced over her shoulder in the direction of her home and husband. "Heryeon often shoots off his mouth without giving thought to his words. You know that. Know that I love you as a brother." She stood on tiptoe and gave him a brief kiss, then turned and dashed inside.

"Away from Shingol. You heard the captain," said Otto.

"The captain," muttered Yunnie. As quickly as it had come, the anger left him. This time the void within his breast grew to fill his entire being. Neither Urhaalan herd nor sister wanted him. He pulled free of the fishermen and walked off, limping slightly from an injury to his left leg, dealt him by an elven sword.

Darkness settled on Shingol, masking the town's dreariness with the softness of summer night. Yunnie wandered the dirty streets of his childhood, a stranger now. He remembered his friends and others, wondering where they were and how they would greet him. He became increasingly despondent when he saw no one he recognized. His own family had turned him out. Life had become unbearable in Shingol, forcing him away years before. Now he realized his decision then had been the proper one. Shingol held nothing for him. Nothing.

He walked to the top of Merfolk Vista, a promontory looking out over the Ilesemare Sea. He turned from the sheer plunge of more than a hundred feet to jagged rocks in the cove below to the far horizon, lit by the electrical bedazzlement of Iontiero. Times long gone flooded back to give him a headache, so powerful were the exigencies of fortune driving him.

From here he had waited and watched for the fishing fleet to return when he was only a child. He remembered how excited he had become when he saw Essa's ship coming into view and how he had run pell-mell to the docks to greet her. It had been here he and Nesha, his first love, had watched the moons rise and the stars set. She had died in the Plague Years of some disease born in magic, some vile malady spawned by sorcery gone amuck that stole away her mind and drove her to the point of suicide. With her a part of Yunnie had died, also, that cool, damp spring so long ago.

And so much more had he lost in the years since. He stared across the gently rolling sea and found no peace, only memories growing more disturbing by the moment. He had lost so much. With Mytaru he had lost. With Essa and Shingol and the elf who had brought him here as an infant he had lost everything.

Irrational hatred and rage against himself and the world mounted. The Living Armor fed it. The armor filled him with the necessity to strike out against something, anything, everything.

Yunnie found himself the focus for this violence that knew no bounds. The Living Armor compelled him forward, to the rocky verge of Merfolk Vista. Then the Living Armor forced him to jump.

CHAPTER
33

"WE MEAN YOU NO HARM," MAEVEEN
O'Donagh said, hoping the elven archers would not
develop sweat-slick fingers and loose their arrows
through nervousness. She and her soldiers could never
escape this ring of death except by talking their way out.

"He was a sorcerer," accused one elf, taller than the
others. A finger that had been broken more than once
stabbed in the direction of Coernn's dead companion.
One of the elf's ears had been lopped off, and a deep cut
on his cheek had only begun to heal, leaving the ugly
wound open to the air. His battle record was carried on
his face in a half dozen other pink, ragged injuries. "What
he carries in his sack forces us back to this spot." The elf
jerked his bow in the direction of the fallen lamp.

"We know," Slyfoot said. The scout bent and took the
lantern in his hands, dropped it and squarely kicked it in
a low arc. An elven archer swung smoothly and fired, her
arrow catching the lantern through the center.

Maeveen appreciated such skill, but she did not want it
turned against her.

"That is the object drawing us back here repeatedly.
When he died, he must have been using it to guide him-

self through the forest." Maeveen rubbed her hands on her thighs and bit her lip, considering what to say. "I do not think he was a sorcerer. I do not dispute that he carried a magical artifact, but he was no sorcerer. Would a wizard fall such easy prey to your arrows?"

"Our forest," the one-eared elf snapped. "Our skills are paramount here." He limped forward and studied Maeveen, as if he could sniff out any evil she carried. Whatever went on behind his pale eyes, it was favorable to Maeveen and those with her. He lowered his bow and rested heavily on it.

"You're mere humans," the elf said. "You're not the one who leads the minotaurs, either."

"We are passing through. An expedition intent on reaching the coast," she explained, wondering what was too much to say and what was not enough. If only Vervamon were here! He was a master at dealing with outraged locals intent on denying them passage or worrying over destroyed property.

"We are fleeing from the City of Shadows," cut in Slyfoot.

"Fleeing? A bit strong, for such a fine city," Quopomma said. "And I resent being put in the same camp as 'mere human.' I am an ogre and proud of my heritage, and that's a sureness."

"Should I shoot her, Dalalego?" asked the female elf. "It would be easier than hitting the lantern. She's got so much fat on her, it would be impossible to miss!"

"Fat!" bellowed Quopomma. "You sound like Iro. I will rip your pointy ears off and stuff them up your nose!"

"Quopomma," cautioned Maeveen. To Dalalego she said, "We are explorers, not conquerors. We mean you no harm. In fact, if there is any service we can perform for you, I am sure our leader, Vervamon, would heartily agree."

"Vervamon?" Dalalego pursed his lips. "I've heard the name. He is a pompous blowhard, from all I have read. Vastly preferable is Jenns's description of—"

"Don't let Vervamon hear you say that," Maeveen said, laughing in spite of herself. "Jenns is no friend of his. In truth, they are bitter rivals. It surprises me you have read either of them, much less compare their work."

Dalalego grinned crookedly. Part of his lip had been cut off from a lance thrust.

"We in Forest Eln are not primitives. We enjoy learning of the world beyond our leafy boundaries." He heaved a deep sigh, then coughed harshly. Maeveen thought she heard a rattle of consumption in his lungs. If so, Dalalego had little time left to lead his squad of elven archers.

"I am sure Vervamon would be happy to discourse on his travels. He can tell a fascinating tale, that one."

Dalalego laughed. "From what he writes, I am sure he can tell as tall a tale as the next around a campfire." The elf studied Slyfoot, Quopomma, and the others, then glared at Coernn's fallen comrade. "You are all right, but can you do anything about *his* magic lamp?"

"Your archer already has," Maeveen said. The elven arrow had skewered the lantern, turning out its magical light forever.

"Oji is the best archer in the forest," Dalalego said with pride that went beyond admiring the skill of a comrade-in-arms. The archer smiled broadly, then looked apprehensive when Dalalego coughed a rattling cough. "You are passing through and nothing more?"

"We seek our way to the coast. We are scouting for Vervamon's expedition on its way to Shingol."

"Shingol," spat Dalalego. "We've heard that is where the leader of the minotaurs hails from."

"A human leads the bulls?" This verification of her nightmare vision surprised Maeveen. What she knew of the minotaurs discounted anyone other than one of the herd leading them into battle. They were clannish and a closed society difficult to penetrate, or so Vervamon had thought. He would be interested in any human who had been adopted into the Urhaalan herd and how it had come about.

Dalalego spat and Oji said something too rapidly in elven battle language for Maeveen to understand.

"She says you ask too many questions to be neutral." Dalalego considered for a moment. "She might be right.

There's nothing but your word that you don't conspire against us with the minotaurs."

"You can follow us through the forest. Even better, show us the way through so we don't get lost. Then we'll be gone."

"To Shingol?"

"That's where we head," Maeveen said.

"*You* may go to the human fishing village. Not them." Dalalego pointed to the ogre and her companions. "They remain as our . . . guests. When you and the rest of your expedition have gone through our lands peacefully and without disturbing so much as a leaf on a tree, they will be sent after you."

"You're keeping my lieutenant and the others as hostages?" Maeveen was outraged.

"Maeveen, wait," urged Quopomma. The ogre was seldom the voice of moderation. She quickly outlined their problems and the likelihood of none surviving should the elves attack them. "We can use the rest, Slyfoot and me and the others. And it'll give us a chance to nose about and find what's really going on. I don't believe a human leads the minotaurs. The bulls have too much integrity for that. Besides," Quopomma said, casting a sidelong glance at the leader of the elves, "that one's not too ugly, for an elf. Dalalego, he said his name was."

Maeveen glared at the ogre, then yielded to the inevitable. "I agree. I'll scout the path to Shingol as quickly as I can, then get Vervamon and the others through Eln. Is that acceptable?"

Dalalego nodded, edging away from Quopomma toward Oji, as if realizing he might have made a bad bargain. Oji glanced at Dalalego, smiled wickedly, and said, "Quopomma, I am sure you and Dalalego will enjoy the time together."

Maeveen hefted her pack and hurried on, letting them figure out a peaceful accommodation. The sooner she found a path through the forest to Shingol, the sooner she would reunite her company. It was a loss leaving behind Slyfoot, Quopomma, and the others. But not much. She enjoyed the solitude as she trooped through Forest Eln and even anticipated reaching Shingol.

"A human who leads the minotaurs," she said to herself. It was an intriguing idea.

Shingol appeared no different from a hundred other villages she had seen. The odor of rotting fish rose to assail her senses. She sneezed and wiped away some of the scent, but not enough to matter. Worse was the oily excrescence drifting on the wind, turning her flesh as slippery as if she had wallowed in a trough filled with beheaded fish. Maeveen O'Donagh kept walking, sure this was her destination. Shingol lay on a cove—no doubt called Shingol Cove, or something equally predictable—with a high prominence along the coast to the south where a lighthouse would have stood had the region been better traveled. As it was, the jutting rock provided a good lookout point for approaching ships and little more.

She hiked into town, not sure where to ask for the man who led minotaurs. The few citizens out and about eyed her suspiciously, and well they should. She wore a well-used sword at her side and had the air of a military commander about her. From the snatches of conversation she overheard, the village buzzed with news of the war between Jehesic and Iwset.

This village hardly seemed it could be valuable for Lord Peemel's plans. Why had he spent so much money and sent six observers with Vervamon on a fool's errand? The Sigil of Iwset, Maeveen snorted. It was a pipe dream and nothing more. An excuse. But for what? And why did Coernn decide that the sigil lay in Shingol when Digody was sure it lay inland, in the City of Shadows? Too many questions required answers, and Maeveen was bone-tired and not willing to ferret them out. Not yet.

"Where can I find a place to stay the night?" she asked.

"You from Iwset?" came a fearful question.

"I passed through it as fast as I could. Spent more time in Jehesic," she said truthfully. This lulled the questioner into opening the door a crack more to show a huge, warty nose, watery blue eyes, and a face mostly covered with a tangled, food-encrusted black beard. The man might have been a deep forest bear for all the hair he sported.

"We got no time for those from Iwset," he told her. "Can't say we support Jehesic, but we don't openly speak against Lady Edara. She's one of us, you know."

"She's from Shingol?" Maeveen's eyebrows rose.

"No, no, not that. She's of the sea. She is a mariner, tried and true. Peemel, now, he has a navy, but he hires them away from places like Shingol. Old Rontiquerio, now, he's one what took Lord Peemel's gold to sail in the Iwsetian navy. A fool, Ronti is, but nobody could ever tell him. He'll end up food for some leviathan, mark my depth on that one."

"What do you hear of the war?" Maeveen asked, seeing she was not going to be invited in. The dark clouds gathering out at sea threatened a storm. It would get wet out in the open soon, but she might have no other choice but to find the leeward side of some hill to shelter her through the night and storm. That tall headland, mayhap, might provide protection.

"Lord Peemel's losing it, he is. Tried to kill Lady Edara. Assassinate her, he tried to do. Lady Edara's adviser gave her life to protect her liege. There's a day of celebration for the name of Ferantia. Around here, we don't have much to celebrate, so—"

"So you joined in?" Maeveen guessed. The man's shaggy head nodded once at this. She had no doubt most villagers' sentiments lay with the navies of Jehesic. Hers did, even as she wondered if Ferantia had given her life as the fisherman claimed. Maeveen did not doubt the Ferantia she had seen with Digody was Lady Edara's slain adviser, but the details of that death might have changed with multiple tellings.

"You best find someplace to ride out the storm. Looking to be a bad one. The fleet's already in."

"I'm hunting for someone." Maeveen bit back her description as a "human who led the minotaurs." While it might garner her a prompt response, she had the feeling it would not be favorable. Shingol's residents were provincial and disinclined to favor those from outside. Her chilly reception showed that.

"He live here, or he passing through, like you?"

"He just arrived," Maeveen said, not knowing why she said this. Her dream in the City of Shadows told her of a thread connecting the flaxen-haired man charging down the hill in front of a herd of minotaur warriors and this sleepy, almost defunct village.

"You mean Yunnie?"

"He's the one. Tall, blue eyes, blond hair, high forehead, strong and tan?"

"That's him. I think Heryeon gave him the what-for and chased him off."

"Heryeon? A relative?"

"His brother-in-law," the man said. "Essa is too kindhearted to turn out her own blood, but not Heryeon. The man would eat his own children, if he had so much as a rumble in his belly. Hard man, Heryeon."

"Hard but fair," Maeveen suggested.

"Heryeon, fair?" This provoked laughter. The shaggy man closed the door in Maeveen's face before she could ask where to find Heryeon and Essa. It took her the better part of an hour before she located Essa.

She rapped repeatedly on the door to the shack before Essa's weathered face showed through the crack between door and wall.

"I'm looking for your brother," Maeveen said. The way Essa's face lit up told Maeveen she had found the right shanty at last. Drips from the edge of roof spattered onto her head. Try as she might, she could not find a place out of the wet weather.

"Hush, not so loud. Heryeon might hear." Essa slipped from the hut and stared at Maeveen. "Why's a fancy soldier like you hunting my brother?"

"Can't say." Maeveen didn't want to launch into the nightmare that had ripped apart her senses in the City of Shadows, or the feeling of prophecy wrapped around that hideous dream. The way she spoke misled Essa into believing Maeveen was unable to speak of secret matters.

"I knew he was up to more than he let on. Yunnie was always close-mouthed about everything he did. He didn't even tell me he was leaving those long years ago. One morn I went to bestir his bones to go out fishing and he was gone. Just like that." Essa snapped her fingers.

"If he's not here, where might I find him?"

"Him and his silly minotaur armor?" Essa spat. From the way the red gobbet sizzled in the cold rain, Maeveen guessed it to be blood-seed the woman chewed. The narcotic weed deadened the pain earned through long, back-breaking hours of fishing. "He went on and on about how he was adopted into their herd. Who can believe a fable like that? Yunnie was never one to lie, but—" Essa shook her head.

"Where is he?"

"Gone. Again." Essa thought for a moment, then added, "Maybe he's up on Merfolk Vista. That pile of rock overlooking Shingol Cove."

Maeveen wiped rain from her eyes and thanked the woman, turning into the growing storm before she burst out laughing.

"Shingol Cove! I knew it!" Then she pulled her cloak tighter around her shoulders and lengthened her stride to the rocky promontory. She hoped to find Yunnie there, and if not, then refuge from the driving rain on the leeward side. She did not mind weather, but hated the way rain always drove up and under her clothing whenever she ventured to the coast. It was as if the sea instructed the storm winds on the best way to make her miserable.

Finding the path leading to the summit of Merfolk Vista was simple enough. She tried to decide if anyone had been here recently, but the rain wiped away all trace. She climbed the steep path and came out on a level area going directly to the edge of a sheer cliff. Waves crashed mightily on the craggy rocks below, sending white foam fifty feet into the air. But Maeveen did not notice that as much as the man standing on the bluff. Rain pelted his simple leather armor, but instantly turned to steam owing to a magical blue aura surrounding him.

"Yunnie!" called Maeveen, recognizing the man from her nightmare in the City of Shadows.

She rushed forward as he stepped out into thin air, to send himself tumbling to his death.

CHAPTER

34

"I COULD LEARN TO HATE FISH," MAEVEEN SAID, picking the bones from her fillet and using them as toothpicks. "It's all I've had to eat for three days. At least in the forest I foraged some vegetables."

"You might die of scurvy, but goiter won't bother you," Yunnie said, tossing a severed fish head over his shoulder into the surf. Below him snapped a few bone crabs, eager for the tidbits. Yunnie wrapped the fish in a wad of seaweed and thrust it into the small cooking fire to roast.

"You are a curious sort," Maeveen said. "I save your life and you hardly notice." She fixed him with an appraising stare, but he did not notice.

Yunnie shrugged. He remembered so little of the storm and stepping off the edge of Merfolk Vista. Maeveen told him she had rescued him, but he could not remember—not exactly. The Living Armor had impelled him to walk forward. Where he had gone had been dictated solely by the power of the magical artifact. Somehow, living or dying meant little to him now that he found himself without family or affiliation.

Maeveen stared at him, trying to shake the sensation that she spoke to a young Vervamon. The high forehead, the shape of the eyes, the unconscious gestures, all were pure Vervamon as he toiled over some weighty academic problem.

"Was it in vain that I pulled you back at the last instant?"

"Who can say? I have nothing to guide me." He stared at the Living Armor, then shivered as if a chill racked him. Maeveen tried to decipher his expression and reaction, and found she could not. He had been tight-lipped about returning to Shingol and even more reticent to speak of his days with the Urhaalan minotaurs. She saw tension knot muscles in his throat when he tried to speak of all he had seen during the elf–minotaur conflict.

"I'm not sorry I saved you," Maeveen went on. She watched him carefully, perhaps too closely for comfort. He did not blush, but he looked uncomfortable. Embarrassed by her breach of etiquette, Maeveen averted her eyes. She lacked social graces after being in the field so long. Quopomma and the others were not good proving grounds for genteel manners.

"My sister wants nothing but to be rid of me. My brother-in-law would see me at the bottom of the sea, my flesh bitten off by hungry sharks. My blood brother, Mytaru, thinks I am a coward because I—" Yunnie choked. Maeveen had started to go to his aid when she saw him swallow hard and regain his breath.

"A fish bone in your throat?" she guessed, though he had not finished cooking his fish.

Yunnie nodded absently, as if this was as good a reply as any.

"Where do you go from here?"

"Jehesic fights Iwset. I have no loyalty to either, but Jehesic appeals to me more. Perhaps Lady Edara would accept my enlistment."

"You can accompany us," Maeveen said a little too eagerly. "Vervamon is an adventurer second to none. We find the oddest things, and he writes them all down and—"

"How exciting," Yunnie said in a voice telling Maeveen such travel would bore him.

"We're hunting for the Sigil of Iwset," she said, studying his reaction closely. His eyebrows did not even twitch in response. He had not heard of it. "We came from the City of Shadows. I thought I saw you in a dream there. The city seems to generate dreams—nightmares."

"So I am in your nightmares," he said bitterly. "It is my destiny to bring woe to everyone who crosses my path."

"It is not true," Maeveen said hotly. "You haven't given yourself a chance. With us, you could prove that your bravery is second to none. I can use you in my company. I have only the bravest of the brave, the best fighters, the—"

Maeveen fell silent when she heard a booming voice she knew all too well.

"Vervamon!" she cried, jumping to her feet. The silver-haired scholar strode along the path to their camp, trailing Coernn and his two comrades. "What are you doing here?"

"I came looking for you. Coernn insisted we find the sigil right away." Vervamon strutted around, sniffing at the broiling fish and licking his lips. Maeveen silently handed over her portion of the fish, which the explorer took and avidly devoured.

"What of the sigil?" Maeveen asked, glancing in Coernn's direction. The man stood, gaze fixed on Yunnie as a snake might follow a dancing bird. "Have you located it?"

"There is more to our mission than finding the sigil," Coernn said. "We must also locate the thief who stole it. Peemel is not a gentle master."

Yunnie spat into the fire and boldly locked eyes with Coernn. To Maeveen's surprise, it was Coernn who looked away first, the loser in the battle of wills. She felt the power Yunnie exuded like a miasma. It was difficult not to stare at him, to be captivated when he spoke.

"How did you reach Shingol?" Maeveen asked. "The elves have Quopomma and the others as hostages against my good faith in dealing with them."

"We avoided the elvish patrols," Coernn said. "It was not difficult. We found poor Wesim in the forest. Elves

had got him and somehow shattered the lantern I gave
him."

"An arrow through the middle, zing!" Maeveen showed
how the arrow fired by Oji had skewered the magical artifact and destroyed it. "Those are the elves who have my
lieutenant and scout. I am surprised you eluded them so
easily."

"They all prepare for the great invasion," Vervamon
said, licking his fingers and eyeing a piece of raw fish.
Yunnie silently prepared it for his unwanted guest. "They
march into the Urhaalan valley to kill all the minotaurs."

"But they can't!" Yunnie's lethargy burned away in a
flash. "S-s—" He began choking. Coernn went to his side
and laid a hand on his shoulder, but recoiled when he
touched the simple leather armor, as if it burned him. His
eyes widened, and he motioned to the pair accompanying
him. They backed off, hurrying down the path until they
disappeared at the bend leading back into Shingol.

"Oh, but they will. The minotaurs are not fighting
fairly, not at all," Vervamon went on, taking scant notice
of Coernn's assistants' departure. "They are using magic
to ensnare elvish patrols. Horrible deaths are meted out.
The corpses of a few elves burned beyond recognition. A
painful, awful way to perish, and it is brought on by the
minotaurs and their spells."

"Not the minotaurs," Yunnie denied. His eyes welled
with tears and he fought to speak. Again Coernn
approached, but the Living Armor kept him from touching Yunnie.

"I tell you, I saw it with my own eyes. I am a careful
observer and would never be fooled in such matters. The
elves have no choice but to carry the war to the minotaurs before their magic grows too strong. Of course, I
remain impartial in this contentious strife. I am an observer and nothing more."

"We have to help them!" cried Yunnie.

"The elves?" asked Vervamon. "They are the ones
enduring the brutal onslaught of magic wielded by the
minotaurs."

"No, no, they can't cast spells. Mytaru could never

summon such power. It is—" Maeveen went to Yunnie and touched him, trying to soothe him. She felt an unpleasant tingling that quickly forced her to back off.

"You are wrong. The minotaurs are doing more than dabbling in magic now; they are relying on it. Each encounter leaves more elves burned beyond recognition. Never have I read of such spells being cast. A true novelty and a distinctly different chapter in my journal will be written around this conflict." Vervamon finished the second fish, licked his fingers, and jumped to his feet.

"Gentlemen, you wish to scour the village for the sigil? Then let us be off!"

"Wait," Maeveen said. "Quopomma and the others—we cannot abandon them."

"I told Coernn he has until daybreak to find the Sigil of Iwset. If he has not discovered it by then, we journey to the Urhaalan valley. A lost trinket can be found any day. A war waits for no man to record its tides. I must be there when the elves match force of arms with the minotaurs."

Saying this, Vervamon and Coernn departed for Shingol. Maeveen stared at Yunnie, trying to decide how the news of the impending elvish invasion of the Urhaalan valley affected him. He paced, pale and tense, his blue eyes unfocused and not a word passing his pinched lips.

"From all you say," she began carefully, "there is nothing to hold you in Shingol. But the herd has accepted you as a member. Can you sit in a fishing village while your blood brothers are killed?"

"Can I sit idly when Mytaru uses magic? It will destroy him! He knows he cannot control it, not when she sends coal g-g—" Yunnie gagged.

Maeveen put her arm around his shoulders until he caught his breath. She ignored the electric tingles from the Living Armor. The feel of his strong body excited her, but the force of his emotion drew her more. Here was a man with faith and conviction, who understood friendship and its demands.

"Go back to the Urhaalan," Maeveen said softly. "But

spend the night here. Then you can go back with a clear mind and pure heart."

He turned and looked at her, expression unreadable. For a heartbeat Maeveen thought he would kiss her. Instead, he pushed her away.

"You are right," he said in a husky voice. "Mytaru needs me. He is my brother, more than Heryeon could ever be—or anyone in Shingol. Why did I ever return here? Shingol is my past, not my future. The herd needs me. I must stop Mytaru from using magic, or it will be turned against him. *She* will turn it against him!"

Before Maeveen could ask who "she" was, Yunnie was gone. She heard his footsteps and saw the pale blue aura surrounding his armor for a few seconds, and then he was away.

Maeveen O'Donagh sat and stared into the night after him, feeling loss at first, then disgust with herself later. What did she have to do? She had saved his miserable life! She lay down and pulled her blanket around her shoulders to fight off the encroaching cold. It was not the same as having someone alongside her, and she regretted it every minute of the night.

CHAPTER

35

"I WILL MISS YOU SO, MY DEAREST," IHESIA said, her fingers stroking over Isak's cheek. He reached up, took her hand, and kissed the palm. Her hand had become more callused from swordplay in the last few weeks. Even this minor disfigurement did not mar Ihesia's regal beauty as much as Isak finding she had already taken another lover, a young captain in her bodyguard.

"The others have agreed," Isak said, heaving a deep sigh. "Abbot Offero wants Sacumon killed because she uses magic, and he cannot afford to send a company of sacred warriors—or even a single Inquisitor—to confront her for such mortal and venal sins."

"Peemel now fears Sacumon because Apepei warns him of a powerful force building on the northern border," added Ihesia. "What a strange little man Apepei is. He truly seems to have the best interest of Iwset and its ruler at heart. How curious."

"And you, my love? Do you not worry about the little people?"

Ihesia blinked, then saw how Isak teased her. "The citizens? Most are dolts and need to be taken care of for their own good. Peemel chooses his enemies poorly. I would never have taken on Jehesic so early in a bid to conqueror this portion of Terisiare. Quell those in the south, unite the north, *then* consider alliance or war with Jehesic. Edara is popular among her subjects. It is hard enough waging a naval war without having to overcome a conquered nation's populace who remain fanatically loyal to their former ruler. If she happened to die in the conflict, then a martyr would have to be contended with." She shook her head.

"Ah, dear Ihesia, always the pragmatist," Isak said.

He turned from her and eyed the rusted metal cylinder her troops had discovered. A patrol had skirmished with guerrillas and unearthed this peculiar mechanism a week earlier. Isak laid his hands on the metallic skin and closed his eyes. The mechanism still lived, albeit with a thready heartbeat. His skills in resurrecting ancient mechanisms would be put to the test this time.

"Is this contraption of any use?"

"It is. I can coax it aloft and reach the northlands in a few minutes. How I wish such devices had not been destroyed during the Brothers' War. They prove so useful to ones such as I, desiring to travel vast distances quickly and secretly."

"You will kill Sacumon?"

"I will try," Isak said, hedging his reply. He knew of the threat posed by Sacumon to the rulers and would-be rulers of Iwset. The sorceress commanded an army of unknown beings whose strength might sweep down to depose those who considered themselves the rightful Iwsetian monarchs. For the abbot and Digody, and even Lord Peemel, killing Sacumon was now necessary. Her death removed a dagger at their throats.

But Ihesia also favored the sorceress's demise. That gave Isak pause. When too many vying for power agreed, it was a sure sign to seek different methods, other routes, new solutions. How he would turn Sacumon's death to his own benefit eluded him at the moment.

"You will return soon?"

"As quickly as I can," Isak said, lying easily. As much

as he enjoyed the silken caresses, the warmth of her arms, the heat of her body, and the passion locked within, Isak was no fool. Ihesia wrapped him in love to do her bidding, and he recognized those bonds for what they would become: his death.

The death might not be physical, but spiritual slavery might prove worse. It was time for him to consider other territories, other jobs, and new challenges.

But only after he dealt with Sacumon. In her and the mysterious flame beasts who danced to her tune he saw his opportunity.

"How will you do it? She commands vast magical power," Ihesia said, stepping away from the device. She eyed it with distaste, finding no immediate use for it herself.

"Kill her? I am not sure," Isak said, not wishing to reveal how he had given Digody's letter to Sacumon. Digody had instructed him in the use of the mysterious stone necessary for locating Sacumon—if she had ever touched the envelope and the paper within. Such an edge widened Isak's options in dealing with her.

"It might not be up to returning after it carries me northward," he cautioned Ihesia. He laid his hand on the metal skin of the cylindrical mechanism. "Do not fear. I shall return."

"I love you dearly," Ihesia said.

Isak wondered if his words carried the same feeling of finality that the general's did for him. Somehow, "I love you dearly" might better have been spoken, "Good-bye forever."

He fitted himself into the narrow cylinder and wiggled forward, arms stretched in front of him. He placed his hands in the shallow depressions and pressed down hard, finding the proper method to animate the vehicle. A hissing sounded and the entire cylinder shook as if it had contracted the ague. He craned his neck a little and looked through the transparent plate above him. Iontiero and the greater moon worked their way aloft in the nighttime sky, Iontiero dazzling with its reflected light and the other misty moon barely showing a crescent.

Isak's hands tingled, and he felt control of his body shape slipping for a moment. How he wished he could shapechange into a flying creature! Then he was soaring in an arc high above Iwset, over the Ilesemare Sea, all the way to Iontiero—or so it seemed.

As he climbed higher, his stomach tried to turn somersaults. The metal cylinder nosed downward, and Isak saw nothing but ground rushing at him. He closed his eyes, then quelled his rising fear. The pressure he applied on the hand plates slackened, and the speed of descent slowed. He felt the cylinder shifting subtly.

The ground still rushed at him with impressive speed, but Isak knew not to fear it. When the cylinder crashed into the ground, he was braced for the impact. The force of landing ruptured the side of the transport and spilled Isak to the ground. He rolled and rolled, finally coming to a halt when he smashed into a gnarled bentwood tree. Stunned, it took Isak several seconds to regain his senses.

When he did, the first thing he did was tend to his appearance. Shape-changing into the form he had used with lovely Ihesia, he adjusted himself in time to throw up his arms to shield his face. The cylinder exploded, sending orange flames leaping up into the night to rival Iontiero's eye-dazzling brightness. Then the conveyance melted to a useless lump. Within minutes not a trace of it remained.

"Such is my fate," grumbled Isak. "A decent method of travel lost again." But his outrage was more a reaction to his ignominious disembarkation than to the cylinder's destruction.

Isak sat cross-legged on the ground and spread out his locating stone, a map of the territory, and a long needle. Using the magnetic needle, he aligned it with the map, then rose and hiked for an hour to return to the spot where he had given Sacumon the envelope.

Fumbling in his pocket, he drew forth the stone and held it at arm's length. Even though Isak had been told what to expect, it brought a cry of delight to his lips when he saw faintly glowing specks of purple on the ground. Whatever powder had leaked from the envelope marked a plain path, as long as he held the mysterious stone so that its invisible rays could spark the purplish glow.

"Now, all I need to do is consider what to do when I find the sorceress," he said, starting off through the dark forest, heading in the direction of the Urhaalan's valley and Sacumon. "Assassinate or haggle over paltry details. What *shall* I do?"

Isak laughed. It was obvious what his best course of action would be.

CHAPTER

36

TEARS CAME TO YUNNIE'S EYES AS HE WATCHED
the battle against the elves proceeded with deadly
inevitability. A dozen minotaurs fought a force of elven
warriors three times their number—and the battle went
against the forest dwellers, not because of skill or the
bulls' tenacity, but because of Mytaru's magic. Yunnie
watched his friend casting the spell that rendered the
attacking bulls invisible to the elves.

The elves died. Sometimes Yunnie caught a flicker of a
minotaur escaping the spell at its periphery; at other
times he saw a puff of dust kicked up under advancing
hooves. It mattered little; the elves still died.

Exhausted from his forced march from Shingol, Yunnie
felt no thrill of victory. Rather, he experienced a complete
draining of emotion when he saw the wild expression on
Mytaru's face. The bull's eyes glowed with fanaticism,
and he staggered as he cast one spell after another. The
invisibility of his warriors faded as the minotaurs reached
the main body of the elvish force. Then Mytaru conjured
a new spell, one that slowed the elves as if they were
dipped in sticky syrup. The bulls killed their enemies with
impunity.

Yunnie trooped across the edge of the field and up the rise to reach his blood brother. By the time he arrived, the skirmish had ended, the minotaurs victorious.

"I returned," he said to Mytaru. The minotaur did not even glance in his direction.

"Why bother? You are no longer of the herd," Mytaru said, hurling his cruelest insult. The minotaur turned his hindquarters toward Yunnie to display additional scorn.

"I will always be of the herd," Yunnie said. "It is my destiny."

"Your destiny?" This caused Mytaru to spin about. His brown eyes went wide with anger, and he snorted froth. "Your destiny led away from the Urhaalan when you left. You refused to fight for us. You let your brothers die in battle without helping them, you and your armor." Mytaru cast a dagger at Yunnie.

The Living Armor reacted instantly, forcing Yunnie from the dagger's path. He winced as muscles in his shoulders strained. How the Living Armor had changed! Before, it took the damage for him. Now it forced him to avoid the attack, saving itself even if injury came to its wearer.

"I cannot control it. It forces me to do things I do not like," Yunnie said, remembering how he had tried to kill himself on Merfolk Vista. If Maeveen O'Donagh had not happened by to pull him to safety, he would have smashed against the rocks a hundred feet below. Why had the Living Armor forced him to try to kill himself? Had it chosen another wearer? Or was Sacumon done with him and sought his death?

"Then I am better than you will ever hope to be," Mytaru boasted. The bull strutted around, arms thrust in the air. "See my victory? *My* victory! Without my spells the herd would have never triumphed. Everywhere we turn, the elves outnumber us. We *must* use magic to triumph."

"It destroyed the world. Remember the War of the Artificers," Yunnie warned. "The human Inquisition recognizes the danger, but they take their crusade too far."

"Who cares?" snapped Mytaru. "Our lives are at risk

every instant of the day and night. The elves want our valley. The Urhaalan will never surrender our holy land. We need the Places of Power for our rituals. If we cannot contact the spirits of the departed, what are we other than farm animals?"

"I am not denying the need to fight, but don't use magic. We can win through force of arms!" Yunnie saw from his blood brother's expression, that he was arguing a point already decided. The spells, feeble though they were, worked. This encouraged Mytaru to try ever more complex and dangerous spells.

"You saw our victory today. My victory," Mytaru insisted. "But we lose on other fronts. I cannot be everywhere all the time. The elves burn us out in places we thought they could never reach. Clan Faasir is no more. Did you know that, Yunnie?"

"What happened?" Yunnie's voice choked as it did when he tried to tell of Sacumon and the Niroso. He guessed what Mytaru would say. It still sorrowed him when his friend fulfilled this grim prophecy on his part.

"Burned out, all of them. Adterlo died, set afire and left to die in agony."

Yunnie hung his head. Adterlo was one of the Three Chosen, the spiritual leaders of the Urhaalan minotaurs. His loss represented a major defeat; a new leader could not be selected until the next Celebration of Tiyint. The herd would suffer this lack of leadership for years.

"It is never easy to bear the losses in a war," Yunnie said. "What we need to do is honor Adterlo's memory. Do not embrace magic. Talk with the spirits of the west and let them guide you, as Adterlo might advise." He tried to avoid thinking of the Chosen burned to death, not by elves, but by a coal golem. The Niroso might have tried to communicate with the Urhaalan leader—or they might have simply sent their magical construct out to slaughter any minotaur in the golem's path.

"I have spoken with them," Mytaru said. "I have also talked with the two surviving of the Three Chosen. My destiny is plain." Mytaru turned and walked away, leaving Yunnie to stare after his friend.

"What are you going to do? Wait, Mytaru, what are you going to do?"

"I am going to see the Urhaalan triumph against our enemy!"

Mytaru tried to lose Yunnie the first two days on the trail, then he gave up and set a brisk pace when it became apparent he went to worship at the Shrine of Tiyint. Yunnie kept his distance, not wanting to argue further with his blood brother. Curiously, the Living Armor did not prevent him from continuing along this path.

Yunnie stopped and stared again at the huge stone idol dominating the side of the canyon wall. Whoever had fashioned the image of Tiyint had done an incredible job, imbuing it with life. How stone could seem so alive Yunnie did not know, but Tiyint appeared only to be resting, waiting to continue his life's journey rather than doomed to remain forever in stone. Throughout the stone ran thin white veins, as if blood passed between heart and limbs.

A low drone rose as Mytaru stopped in front of the statue. The minotaur began his chant, the wordless sounds causing Yunnie to grow increasingly uneasy. He started forward, but the Living Armor prevented it. He fought against the leather breastplate, but the magical armor forced him to the ground.

Mytaru's chant ran up the musical scale, and words came to Yunnie now.

"Mytaru, you can't do this. It's not right. You can't control such magic!" Yunnie struggled to reach his friend. The Living Armor prevented it. Slipping his fingers between flesh and armor, Yunnie ripped hard. He shrieked in pain as the Living Armor popped free of his body. He fought to hold the writhing, flailing armor at arm's length. For a moment, he thought he had won his small fight, then the Living Armor whipped around like an attacking panther and tried to flatten against his body again.

Yunnie rolled, as if fighting a human opponent. Only when he pinned the armor with his knees and piled heavy rocks on it did he escape.

Then Yunnie wanted to die. He felt alone in the world, abandoned and so vulnerable. The Living Armor had protected him, even if it had tried to kill him on Merfolk Vista. Or was that the intent all along? Yunnie forced himself to think more clearly. Sacumon! She had compelled him to wear the armor in an effort to control him. Had he come close to something in Shingol that prompted her to order the Living Armor to slay him?

Mytaru's chants grew in power and urgency, forcing Yunnie away from his own problems. Naked to the waist for the first time in months, he ran forward to stop Mytaru.

"Don't do it," Yunnie cried. "Don't!"

A grinding sound echoed from wall to canyon wall. The power unlocked in that noise stopped Yunnie in his tracks. A dozen paces behind Mytaru, he stared past the minotaur to the statue. *The statue.*

It moved slightly, flexing its stone muscles. Then it grew larger, stood, and stretched muscles held immobile for centuries. Tiyint roared, and Yunnie clapped his hands to his ears to hold out the awful sound of rage at being held captive for so many years—and enthusiasm for killing those responsible for binding him.

"What have you done, Mytaru?" he moaned, but his blood brother had eyes only for his idol come to life. Mytaru chanted more fervently now, enhancing Tiyint's power with new magics. The bull began a dance, slow and sinuous, arms moving in tempo with his mesmerizing chant. For a moment, Yunnie thought his eyes played him false. Then he realized the power of Mytaru's magic.

More than Mytaru danced and chanted now. Behind the bull rose others, faint shapes, transparent, ghostlike, all joined to praise Tiyint. In a chain of spectral dancers led by Mytaru, the bulls wove in and out, lost generations joined in a single, prodigious magical effort.

Yunnie edged away, knowing the destiny of the minotaurs had been determined by this conjuration. There would not be a celebration, not with this Tiyint. This Tiyint was a killer and not easily controlled.

As Yunnie stumbled past the rock cairn where he had

buried the Living Armor, he saw a trembling and shaking underneath. The rocks shifted and moved, and the animated armor slid after Yunnie. So shocked was he by the roaring stone god come to life and the sight of the mobile Living Armor, Yunnie stood and stared.

The Living Armor fit itself to him again.

It had the feel of death and awful destiny. Yunnie turned his back on Tiyint and Mytaru, not sure where to go or what to do.

CHAPTER
37

"GO ANY FARTHER AND THEY WILL FILL YOU
with arrows."

Yunnie swung about, sword coming up. He did not
relax when he saw Maeveen O'Donagh sitting in the
shadow of a tall tree. Her sword lay across her lap, but
she made no move to stand and fight. Yunnie had to
struggle against the Living Armor, which impelled him
forward to kill.

Sweat beaded his forehead as he successfully forced
down the impulse to kill the woman who had saved his
life at Merfolk Vista.

"You are not at peace, are you?" Maeveen reached over
and grabbed a thick stem. She plucked it, nibbled at the
red flower, then sucked the juices, watching him closely.
He relaxed a little when he saw how at ease she appeared,
though the pressures within still fought with him.

"Mytaru," he said. Yunnie had spent the last week
wandering aimlessly, somehow turning back toward
Shingol without knowing it. He had not expected to find
anyone, much less the woman soldier, in the elves' forest. The elves had migrated from their leafy kingdom and
massed near the mouth of the Urhaalan valley for an all-

out attack. The summoning had gone out to assemble every able-bodied elf for a suicide attack into the heart of the Urhaalan domain. Too many small battles had left too many elves and minotaurs dead for either side to continue their guerrilla war. Yunnie was certain he had seen every last one of those dead bodies since leaving Mytaru.

"He did something you disapprove of," she said, spitting out the stalk and finding another. "Since you mentioned he dabbled in magic before, he must be doing something even worse now."

"You will tell the elves," Yunnie accused.

"Would it matter?"

Yunnie shook his head. Why did she badger him like this? He wanted to go somewhere he could pull off the Living Armor and find tranquillity. A snort escaped his nostrils, rivaling anything Mytaru—or even old Mehonvo—could have vented.

"It would not matter," Yunnie admitted. He tried to speak of Sacumon and the Stone People's coal golems and found his words once again blocked by the sorceress's spell. Worse, the Living Armor tried to contract around him, squeezing the air from his lungs.

"You would do well to rid yourself of that armor. It carries the stench of evil magic that turns against you," Maeveen said, looking worried for his well-being. "It is wrong to decry your friend's use of simple spells when you are enmeshed in such a powerful one yourself."

Yunnie sucked in a deep breath. "I want to get rid of it, but it isn't that easy. It . . . it is a part of me."

"Are you a part of it?"

"There's a difference?" Yunnie sat beside Maeveen. She was not really pretty, but under her military hardness he saw a person with true concern for others. She might actually care about him, even if he could not figure out why she bothered. He had spent a little time around her expedition leader, and Yunnie decided he did not like Vervamon very much. The silver-haired man was too brusque, too full of himself, too sure he was right. But this woman was something else, someone who listened and heard.

Maeveen O'Donagh did not answer. She leaned against the tree and watched, as if he might explode at any instant. After a while, she said, "You are not well thought of in Shingol."

"That's why I left. Essa tried to raise me after our parents died, but she was not much older than I."

"She's more than ten years older, unless I have lost my eye for such things," Maeveen said. "You hardly seem to share the same blood in your veins."

"Sometimes I wonder," Yunnie said, reaching over to pluck a flower as Maeveen had done. "Memories of my childhood come back to haunt me, more so lately, for some reason." Yunnie knew the reason. The more he struggled to break Sacumon's spell of silence, the more he dredged up from his past. The elf staring at him from his visions proved to be the most enduring of the new remembrances. "These memories seldom have anything to do with our parents or Essa. There is an elf, an old elf, watching over me for years. Perhaps only in my dreams." Yunnie shrugged.

He stared into the forest. Maeveen said nothing, letting him wander aimlessly through his own thoughts. Yunnie was thankful for this. For a take-charge officer used to having her own way, she allowed him to take the lead when he needed. He appreciated her consideration.

"Why are you in the forest?" he asked at length. "You and Vervamon seemed to be hunting for something in Shingol. A sigil, he said."

"For some reason, Coernn decided he could not track it down right now," Maeveen said caustically. "He leads us around like a pig on a leash. We came back in this direction, and we found ourselves caught up in preparation for a huge battle."

"The elves plan to invade the valley in force," Yunnie said, plucking the petals from the red flower and letting them flutter lightly to the ground. He envisioned the petals catching fire and exploding as coal golems touched them, the Stone People laughing. Superimposed over it all Sacumon encouraged all the parties on to their deaths. Yunnie blinked and the petals returned to normal, caught on a gentle wind that caressed both his cheek and Maeveen's short, soft brown hair.

"Where lies your loyalty?"

"Why do you ask? Why do you care?" Yunnie glanced up and saw a half dozen elves, all with arrows readied for flight directly through his heart. He made no move to grab his sword; that would have been suicidal. In spite of the Living Armor, Yunnie knew he could never fight them all.

"Like my lieutenant and scout, you seem to be a prisoner of war. Or perhaps only a guest until after the battle." Maeveen stood and went to the tallest of the elves. "Dalalego, meet Yunnie. He was in Shingol when Vervamon arrived."

"Yunnie? From Shingol?" The elf frowned. He lowered his bow and moved closer. The elf tipped his one-earred head to one side and stared curiously at Yunnie. The desire to erupt into deadly action caused Yunnie to quiver. He barely restrained the Living Armor's urge to kill this battle-scarred warrior.

"You act as if you know him," said Maeveen. She tried to cover her anxiety. Yunnie saw how badly she failed, but the elves were unable to recognize human emotions.

"An old elf, Tavora by name, guarded a human baby for years until she died. A majordomo, she was, in Iwset."

"A powerful position," Maeveen said, directing Dalalego's attention away from Yunnie.

"You might be the one. Tavora was always rushing off to Shingol to be certain her ward was well cared for." Dalalego stared intently at Yunnie, as if he could pry the information loose from him by sight alone.

Yunnie said nothing, for there was nothing he could say. He did not remember Tavora, nor could he claim she was the elf in his dreams—or were they recollections dimly lit because of distance in time?

"Yes, yes, you might be the one. If you are a companion of Maeveen O'Donagh, then you are welcome to walk the forest ways with us She has proven honorable in her dealings."

"Wait, Dalalego, he might be a spy!" spoke up a younger

elf. "He might be the one Tavora nursed, but he could also be the human who leads the minotaurs into battle. He hails from Shingol, too!"

"That one has not been seen in a month or more," Dalalego said. "He is dead or has run away. Will you turn your blade against us in battle?" Dalalego asked pointedly.

"The real enemy lies elsewhere," Yunnie said honestly. Images of the coal golems and Sacumon and the Niroso rushed to bring tears to his eyes. If only he could tell them! The minotaurs would not listen to his inarticulate warnings, but he could not blame Mytaru and the others. They had suffered so many losses to believe in anything but the power of their own war lances. Why believe him when he could not give the warning needed, to provide proof, to bring the Niroso to the light of day so that even the most skeptical minotaur could accept?

"Well spoken," said Dalalego, silencing the elf who again tried to protest, "but you will remain closely watched until after we defeat the minotaurs."

"There is nothing wrong in that," Maeveen said hurriedly. "We can stay together, making the watch that much easier."

"So be it." Dalalego conferred with the others in his band, then said, "We assemble at the edge of Forest Eln. Now."

Maeveen's eyebrows arched as she looked at Yunnie. He closed his eyes and sighed deeply. He had not expected the final conflict to come so quickly. He was not prepared for it, but how would he ever be ready for such slaughter?

"So be it," Yunnie said, getting to his feet. He sucked in his breath as the Living Armor contracted around him, eager for the coming fight.

"So many elves," Maeveen said. "I had not realized they could summon such an army."

"They outnumber the minotaurs ten to one," Yunnie said, sick at heart. Even if Mytaru and the others fought as fiercely as they usually did, sheer numbers might guarantee an elvish victory this day. "They see the futility in allowing to Mytaru choose the battle site and conditions of combat."

"This pits their entire force against the minotaurs," Maeveen said. "Should they lose, they have lost all. A reckless choice."

"Yes," Yunnie said, aware of how reckless it was for the elves, but he understood their frustration and need to end the conflict—or die in the attempt. The real irony lay in that neither elf nor minotaur would emerge the true victor, no matter the outcome on the field of battle.

After the carnage was complete, the coal golems would sneak out from their underground kingdom and do their masters' bidding. The survivors would perish by fiery touch, leaving vast tracts of land open for the Stone People to claim. Or was it Sacumon who would claim the forest of Eln and the Urhaalan valley?

Try as he might, Yunnie had been unable to look past this conflict, although Maeveen had told of even larger conflicts between Iwset and Jehesic. Such massive movement of ships and troops was alien to Yunnie. What he did know and understand was that his friends and blood brothers would die unless he stopped them.

"How can we prevent this?" he muttered. He bit his lower lip hard and tried to tell Maeveen of Sacumon's plot. She was easy to talk to, but even so, Yunnie found it impossible to break the dark-clad sorceress's powerful geas.

"It is like the ancient machines Vervamon finds and toys with as we travel through Terisiare," Maeveen said. "Once set in motion, they cannot be stopped. Or perhaps we simply lack the knowledge of their control. A word, a gesture, who can say?" Maeveen moved closer and brushed against his arm. Yunnie recoiled as if she stabbed him, the Living Armor working to protect him from the most accidental touch.

"There," he said, eyes fixed at the mouth of the valley. "The minotaurs are marching. The herd is confident." Yunnie drew his sword. Behind him he heard arrows being fitted—and aimed at his back. The Living Armor covering his torso quivered with energy and filled him with the need to spill blood.

The sound of the minotaur herd charging filled his ears. The elves were apprehensive, but still confident in their numbers and prowess. The elven commander waited until the minotaurs came even with the first hidden archers before issuing his order.

Dozens, hundreds, thousands of feathered shafts arched upward to fall among the bulls. A few died. A new flight of arrows brought down even more. Singing stirring battle lyrics, the herd moved forward to the edge of the elven fighters. Lances stabbed and swords slashed. A few bulls swung war clubs, and the real struggle began.

"Stay, Yunnie. There is nothing you can do," cautioned Maeveen. She held him, then withdrew her hand when the Living Armor burned with a heat too intense to bear. Yunnie heard her less and the sounds of combat more. Deep within him swelled the need to spill blood, but he held back. For the moment.

"A slaughter," she said. "The elves are fighting cleverly in addition to using superior weapons, tactics, and position. There is no way the minotaurs can hold back the unfolding disaster. They committed their full forces and now find retreat cut off by elven archers. Not even clever spells will help in this—and your friend cannot be everywhere, or protect so many of his fellows with his magic.

"They ought to have done better. A leader who knew tactics," mused Maeveen. "They could have seized the high ground and—what in the name of the seven martyrs is *that*?"

Yunnie blinked as he recognized the huge stone statue Mytaru had prayed to in the valley.

"Tiyint," he said in a choked voice. "Mytaru has brought Tiyint into the battle."

The towering stone monster lumbered forth like some inexorable force of nature and showed no mercy as it slew elves by the fives and tens. Arrows availed the clever archers naught. Swords refused to cut into the stone god's legs, and no amount of attack slowed the juggernaut of death as it turned the tide of battle in favor of the minotaurs.

Yunnie could no longer contain himself. The Living Armor blasted power into his sword arm and drove him to swing around. The blade cut through the archers guarding him. Then he raced into the battle, killing elves with wild abandon.

Even with the blood rage on him powered by the Living Armor, Yunnie's death count was puny compared to that wrought by Tiyint.

CHAPTER
38

THE GROUND QUAKED AS TIYINT TOOK another giant step before reaching down to smash a wounded elf struggling to escape. The idol dripped gore from its rock-hard hands as it drew back, another victim dead. A loud cry to Yunnie's right alerted him of a counterattack led by elves trapped in a small ravine. Eight rushed forward, waving daggers and swinging swords at the rampaging idol. Tiyint paused, as if considering the quickest way to dispatch this minor annoyance, then dipped its head and jabbed with long, stony horns.

Two elves died instantly from the impact; another dangled, impaled, from a huge stone horn. No battle ribbons needed to be hung from Tiyint's horns. The statue brought to magical life used dead elves as its badge of honor, marking battles fought and lives stolen.

Yunnie gasped for breath and looked numbly at his sword. He did not remember having entered the battle, nor could he remember those he had fought—and killed. Had he slaughtered his blood brothers, or had he used his blade against the elves?

He dropped to his knees and held his head. He could not remember, no matter how he tried. His heart pumped hard and the Living Armor tried to force him back into combat. It mattered nothing to the magical artifact Sacumon had forced upon him whether he killed elf or minotaur. All it wanted was blood.

"Mine?" Yunnie asked softly, knowing he would get no answer. Sacumon tried to blind him with her spells of forgetfulness and had only partially succeeded. She tried to kill him using the Living Armor as her champion.

Yunnie's nose twitched when he scented more than the sickening stench of spilled blood. Something nearby burned. He got to his feet and saw a coal golem running down a ravine to the north of the carnage wrought by Tiyint. Tiny spires of smoke rose wherever it stepped on dried grass and set the patch aflame. Yunnie followed, watching as the coal golem duplicated the butchery brought by Tiyint. Any of the wounded died under its fiery touch. It flung tiny lumps of burning coal at its enemies—and anything alive on the battlefield was anathema to the coal golem.

Yunnie turned his energy and hatred toward the coal golem and the Stone People who had sent it forth to do their bidding. He roared and charged, sword held high. The golem spun, saw him, and flung a cloud of coal dust toward him. A flaming blanket blocked his rush, but only for an instant. Without breaking stride, he hit the ground and rolled, kicking and advancing on the golem as the dust blazed merrily in the air above him.

"Die, damn you, die!" shouted Yunnie. He hacked with his sword and struck furiously at the coal golem's leg. The steel blade bounced off, dulled by the magical construct's rocky substance. No matter where Yunnie turned, he faced stone come alive. The Stone People, their golems, Tiyint—and all butchered the living.

"Away, Yunnie. Don't attack it. The creature is magical!"

He saw Maeveen O'Donagh on the far side of the coal golem. Beside her stood Vervamon, silver hair rippling as heat from the golem blew uphill toward the explorer. To Yunnie's surprise, the scholar did not take refuge behind his captain. Rather, he hefted a minotaur's lance and remained at Maeveen's shoulder as they advanced to distract the golem.

"I know it is an artifact," he said. "S-Sacumon sent it!" Yunnie gasped with a dam-burst of relief as he grated out the sorceress's name. "The Stone People. The Niroso, underground, they are the unseen provocateurs! We need to fight them, not the elves or minotaurs!"

"Get back, boy, or you will end up fried like an Argivian oyster in its own succulent juices." Vervamon took two quick steps from Maeveen, then threw the lance with impressive power and accuracy. The war lance struck the coal golem between the shoulders and drove it forward, giving Yunnie the chance to rise to his knees and use both hands on his sword hilt. With all the power locked in his body, backed by the energy from the Living Armor, he shattered his sword against the golem's head.

"Uncle Istvan piss on it," came the curse from the other side of the golem. Maeveen's lieutenant, Quopomma, stared, mouth open, at the destruction. The golem's head exploded into a thousand pieces, leaving a feebly wiggling decapitated hulk behind.

"Don't stand there, help him, help him!" ordered Maeveen. The captain rushed to Yunnie's side. Yunnie dropped the hilt of his ruined sword beside the coal golem. He hardly noticed when Maeveen put her hand on his shoulder.

"I didn't think I could destroy one of them," Yunnie said, staring at the smoldering corpse. His sword had shattered as if it had been made from glass.

"Your armor," Vervamon said. "It gave you power. Maeveen told me of it. A fascinating artifact, left over from the Brothers' War, I should think. May I examine it more closely? I was distracted and failed to note how potent the armor was when we met back in Shingol."

Yunnie stared at Vervamon, all emotion gone now. He tried to get to his feet and failed. Both Vervamon and Maeveen helped him, then the captain supported him as he turned toward the battlefield.

"Tiyint, the stone creature," he said. "Mytaru released it."

"I'd say it worked better than anyone had a right to believe," Quopomma told him. "The elves are running back to their forest, routed. The ones able to run, that is. Too many are dead. They massacred minotaurs until *it* showed up, stomping them left and right. Tiyint, you named it?"

Yunnie nodded, as speech seemed useless.

"What did you mean when you said this coal golem was a minion of someone called Sacumon?" asked Vervamon. "There is far more to whet my curiosity in this provincial warfare than I thought. My hunt for the Sigil of Iwset is nothing compared to the ebb and flow of power as the battles are fought and won. The sigil can remain hidden for another week or month and nothing is lost, but this is history, albeit a small footnote's worth, in the making. I must partake of every detail, or I am cheating those who would read my memoirs."

"Is he always like that?" Yunnie asked Maeveen.

"He has a point. What of Sacumon? This magical construct—" she said, kicking at the dusty remains of the charred golem. "Where does it come from? We have seen strange sights, remnants of magical machines that flew and rolled and moved hundreds of soldiers at a time, but nothing like this."

"Farther south down the coast, across the straits from Lat-Nam," Vervamon said, stroking his chin as he thought, "the land is ruined from the war. We are just beyond the worst of the destruction here. Mayhap something intriguing has been given birth at the edge of influence, something bubbling up from below to fill a void left underground. Too powerful a magical residue might inhibit such growth in Lat-Nam, but here, basking in the dim rays of radiated magic, here might be the spot where new races spawn."

"You make magic sound like warm sunlight," complained Quopomma. "If it were, we'd all be sunburned by now." The ogre glowered at Yunnie, as if accusing him of being the source of their woe.

"Tell me, Yunnie, of these Stone People you mentioned. The coal golems are their minions?"

"Perhaps so," Yunnie said. "Sacumon is a human—at least she is of human shape—and deals with the Stone People." He went on to describe his brief invasion of the underground realm and how the coal golem chased him away after Sacumon forced the Living Armor on him.

"There is more than the rampaging stone avatar?" asked Coernn. His two assistants crowded close behind. All were bloodied, as if they had fought as furiously as any of the defeated elves.

"Who are you?" asked Yunnie, staring at Coernn.

"I must know," Coernn said anxiously. "The Stone People, you called them. They rise from underground?" Coernn's pale face turned paler as he read the answer in Yunnie's expression. He motioned over his two remaining assistants and spoke with them for several minutes, turning angry before dismissing them. They left, one glancing back over his shoulder several times before following his comrade into the forest.

"Things have turned for the worse. I tried to contain the magic and failed. Where else have I failed?" Coernn looked stricken. "My two friends, Feyne and Ehno, carry the message back to Iwset."

"You knew about the Stone People?" Maeveen faced Coernn squarely, hands on her hips. She held down her mounting rage. "What else are you not telling us?"

"There is no time to argue over this. We must stop the Niroso."

"You know of them?" Yunnie staggered and grabbed Coernn's arm, shaking it. "You can confirm all I have said?" Relief flooded him. Not only could he speak of Sacumon, he had witnesses to the coal golems and even the Niroso. If only he had found these people earlier!

"Answer *my* question, Coernn," demanded Maeveen. "Who sent you? First, you claimed that the Sigil of Iwset was inland, then in Shingol. You send off messengers to report back—who receives those reports?—and you carry magical artifacts, the like of which I have never seen before. And in my travels with Vervamon, I have seen plenty."

Coernn licked his lips. "You have guessed I do not travel for Lord Peemel."

"Ha! I knew it!" cried Quopomma. "You are a vile torturer. You spy for Abbot Offero and the Inquisition!"

A look of utter contempt flashed over Coernn's face.
He erased it quickly before speaking. "I have no love for
Offero or his sanguinary passions."

"I saw you feed one of your party to the carnivorous
plant," Quopomma said. "What of that?"

"The good abbot's spy sent back no more reports after
that," Coernn said. "We work against Peemel in that we
seek only what is best for Iwset. His war with Jehesic is
wrong, as is his treatment of his own citizens. We would
remedy that by retrieving the Sigil of Iwset—and especially the pretender to the throne."

"Pretender?" Vervamon's face lit up. "Why, this is
turning into a first-rate mystery. You seek the sigil in
order to overthrow Peemel, not support him? But the
sigil opens the Tomb of the Seven Martyrs. Digody
said—" Vervamon's face shifted as if reflected in a
breeze-touched pond. Realization of how he had been
lied to finally penetrated. "You need the sigil to claim the
throne for your pretender. There is no Tomb of the
Seven Martyrs?"

Coernn shrugged. "There might be, but I know nothing
of it—nor does Digody. His interests have never strayed
far from . . . Digody. He sought the sigil as a lever against
Peemel, not to guarantee the throne for his liege. It is
used only during formal ceremonies, and Peemel has been
lord thirty years or more."

"I hate politics," Maeveen declared. "Always scheming.
They are worse than academics." She cast a quick glance
in Vervamon's direction. He was lost in speculation.

"What are we to do?" asked Quopomma. "The stone
god tramps on anyone venturing onto the battlefield. The
elves are in full retreat, the ones who survived. The minotaurs have seized the day and declared victory. Do we celebrate with them, or do we traipse off to hunt for this
sigil and the pretender to the throne of Iwset?" Quopomma
scratched herself.

"None of those," Yunnic insisted. "We must stop
Sacumon. She is the cause for the war between minotaur

and elf. She roused the Stone People and brought their coal golems to the surface. Without her plotting, the war will collapse."

"This does nothing to solve Coernn's problem of finding the sigil," said Vervamon. "Does the sigil carry any historic value, or is it merely a bauble of state, more symbolic than intrinsic?"

"Never have I seen a man so willing to turn from riches to the pursuit of things you cannot even hold in your hand," grumbled Quopomma.

"Yunnie is right to pursue this sorceress and stop her," Coernn declared. "We must not allow the Niroso to emerge from beneath the surface. They are a force we thought bottled, suppressed, if not entirely extinguished. Digody sought to use Sacumon for his own purposes, but she has proven too ambitious to contain. I was supposed to contact her, but I am sure she would have nothing to do with me now that her plans have succeeded so completely."

"Where have you encountered the Niroso before?" asked Vervamon, stepping alongside Coernn. "You are a sorcerer, are you not? I thought so from the grimoires and other artifacts you insisted on lugging about. You could not have been amateur brewers, no matter what my lieutenants postulated. Now tell me of these Stone People. What do you know of their culture, their mores, the way—"

Yunnie drew Maeveen and Quopomma to one side.

"The battle did not go as Sacumon wanted," he told them. "She sought the destruction of the elves, but not by so powerful an entity as Tiyint. She thought it would be simple pickings to kill off any remaining minotaurs after a huge battle weakened them."

"There might be only a few now," Maeveen said. "What do you intend to do?"

"Find Sacumon. She wields some power over the Niroso. She will try to incite them to send forth their magical constructs. The coal golems will attack both the minotaurs and elves, but she must have more control if she would defeat Tiyint."

"Let the minotaurs finish her. You are one of the Urhaalan, aren't you?" asked Quopomma. "A funny-looking bull, if I may say so, but your sympathy lies with them, not the elves."

"I—" Yunnie closed his eyes as memories flooded him, memories hidden and locked and denied him for too long. "I am Urhaalan, yes," he said. "I was also befriended by an old elf, Tavora. My life has been saved by both. I cannot let them fight one another any longer."

"What are we going to do?" asked Maeveen. Yunnie saw her breathing faster, as she anticipated his answer, half-fearful of what he would say.

"We go underground to stop the Stone People—and Sacumon!"

CHAPTER
39

"I WANT TO SEE IT ALL," VERVAMON SAID
eagerly. He paced restlessly, hands locked behind his
back and his green eyes shining with anticipation.
Maeveen O'Donagh had seen him like this before, too
many times, when confronted with something new and
wonderful, whether it be a discovery or a new love. The
explorer in Vervamon demanded full details of the underground world inhabited by a unique race of creatures.
Their travels across Terisiare revealed new beasts,
mutants from the Brothers' War, which managed to gain
a footnote or two in Vervamon's journals. Never had they
found an entirely new intelligent race spawned by the
deadly magic released during the war, nor had Vervamon
heard of any creature that existed in a semimolten state.
If the Niroso actually flowed through the solid rock as
Yunnie claimed, this would be a discovery far exceeding
anything promised by Peemel and Digody at the Tomb of
the Seven Martyrs.

Maeveen's hand tightened on the hilt of her sword as
she thought of Peemel and his skeletal adviser. Ruler and
counselor had sent Vervamon out to do their dirty work
for them. Maeveen wished the ruler had been more forth-

coming with Vervamon, instead of luring him out with foolish myths and impossible promises.

A quick laugh escaped her lips. There was no other way of getting Vervamon to do Peemel's bidding, she realized. Vervamon had been intent on burial customs in northwestern Terisiare and nothing deterred him except more intriguing academic investigations.

"We can enter their underground realm through a cave not two miles away," Yunnie said.

"Only two miles? Why, after this day's battle, seeing so many elves slain, seeing that Uncle Istvan damned rock minotaur stomp on everyone, only two miles is a mere stroll," Quopomma said sarcastically, puffing out her chest and jutting her chin belligerently.

"I am glad you approve," Vervamon said, missing the ogre's tone entirely. "This will be the crowning glory of my journey. Who else but I can discover an entire species waiting to be studied, recorded, even turned to allies? Consider how useful these Niroso will be exploring buried ruins, under my expert direction, of course!" Vervamon rubbed his hands together, then set out in the direction Yunnie indicated, oblivious to the rivulets of blood draining from the battlefield and the distant quaking caused by Tiyint's heavy footfalls.

"Sarcasm," grumbled Quopomma. "He lacks knowledge of the word, and he calls himself educated." She settled her bandoliers and the heavy sabers which depended from them, then stalked off, her immense boots squishing as she walked in the bloody mud. As she left, Quopomma spoke angrily with her invisible companions, warning them of academics and the trouble such could bring into the world of a simple soldier.

Yunnie trailed the ogre, muttering to himself. Maeveen hung back to speak privately with Coernn.

The pale-faced man looked at her but said nothing.

"You did not fear Quopomma when we first met. Because of your skill with magical spells?" asked Maeveen.

"I would have reduced her to a greasy cinder if she had meant me harm."

"You were not afraid of an ogre, yet you are frightened

now. Of these Stone People Yunnie talks about with such awe?"

"Of Sacumon," Coernn said, surprising her. "I know nothing of the Niroso's intent or ability, so fearing them is futile. But Sacumon? I know her. I know *of* her." Coernn's lips thinned to a line and the set of his jaw convinced Maeveen he knew more than he revealed.

"Who is she?"

Coernn shrugged. "Who can say? She fomented small revolts for a year in Iwset, then vanished. She obviously found more fertile fields for her treachery with the Stone People. Her intentions are simple: kill off the elves and minotaurs, gain control over a huge section of the land, and turn full attention to the Iwset–Jehesic war. If she rules the Niroso, she might control a region the size of Argoth within a year. Peemel thought to use her, foolishly listening to Digody's advice on the matter."

"You know Argoth?" Maeveen was surprised anew by the sorcerer.

"I have traveled, not as widely as you and Vervamon, but I have not dwelled forever in Iwset," Coernn said. With that, he lengthened his stride, forcing the shorter Maeveen to hurry along if she was to maintain the pace. It was not a tiring speed, but one that required Maeveen to expend more energy than was her wont on long trips.

Almost too soon they arrived in the stony arena with its fumarole-protected entrance to the Niroso's underground. Maeveen's pug nose wrinkled at the heavy sulfur fumes rising from the earth.

"All we do is walk down this path and we find the Stone People?" Quopomma snorted in contempt. "They do not guard the entrance to their kingdom? All that would be required is a simple deadfall."

"They do not think in those terms," Yunnie said. "While the coal golems are adequate sentries, such traps are beyond the Stone People's comprehension. Consider. They move through solid rock by melting into it and flowing along. They need no path as they travel from cave to cave. They might not have well-used paths, such as we enjoy, because of their ability to move in and out, up and down, even at angles through the very mantle of the planet!"

"Intriguing speculation," mused Vervamon. "You have a decent mind, if untrained in the ways of particularized cultural investigation."

Maeveen saw Yunnie's body stiffen as the Living Armor asserted itself. Before she could utter a word of warning, Yunnie spun and dashed into the cave entrance. She was bumped from her place by Coernn as the wizard ran after Yunnie.

"What is it?" demanded Quopomma. "Where're they going?"

"Coal golem," called Coernn from down the path. "Yunnie's armor is reacting to its magical presence."

Maeveen drew her sword and raced into the cave, seeking to help defend Yunnie against the coal golem guarding the path. She was pitched into utter darkness, then emerged into a dimly lit area that expanded to the limits of her vision. She paused to take in the grandeur of this cavern, then stepped around Coernn in time to see Yunnie face a coal golem.

The fiery artifact charged—and exploded when it touched his Living Armor. The golem was consumed by the armor, but it left Yunnie stunned and weak.

"Are you all right?" Maeveen asked, her arm snaking out around Yunnie before she remembered what she had just witnessed. She drew back before her flesh touched the armor.

"I feel fine," Yunnie said, his expression distant. Maeveen stepped back as he straightened and backed off, sword swinging in front of him.

She started after him, only to be stopped by Coernn. The sorcerer shook his head.

"He cannot fight alone. We ought to be with him," she argued.

"The Living Armor consumes his good sense. It rules him completely, and there is nothing I can do to stop it. Sacumon's spell—or that of the armor—is stronger than anything I can cast. I was told to end Sacumon's life, should the need arise, but—"

"Who ordered you to do this?" asked Maeveen. She received no answer.

"What can we do?" she asked, worried about Yunnie's safety.

"We can record, my dear, we can observe, we can do what we came here to do! Advance knowledge!" Vervamon laughed and ran after Yunnie. Maeveen blinked. So alike they were in the way they rushed off to do battle, though in different arenas.

"Do you know?" asked Coernn.

"What? Do I know what?"

"Never mind," Quopomma said. "We need to push forward, or we will be left here while they have all the fun." The ogre bumped against Coernn to get him moving.

"The Stone People!" cried Coernn. He dropped to his knees and ran his hands over the dusty track they had just crossed. As if raising the dead, he outlined a creature in the rock. The small lump grew larger and larger as the sorcerer scuttled back on his knees. "One is rising from the bowels of the planet!"

Coernn screamed as the Niroso emerged, reached out, and set fire to his flesh with a burning grip. Maeveen watched in fascinated horror as the Niroso rose to rotate slowly. Its semimolten body spun at different speeds, giving it a twisted aspect. Then she saw its face and screamed. Very little frightened Maeveen; she had been in too many battles and fought too many opponents. Yet she screamed and screamed, and then wondered who the other voice was joining her in terror.

It heightened her own panic when she realized it was Quopomma.

The Niroso clutched the sorcerer to its body and held on to the human for a few seconds, then pushed the mage away, twisting liquidly. Where its face ought to have been glowed small pools reflecting all that went on in Maeveen's terrified mind. She saw herself burned and pulled apart as the lava monster tried to draw her into the rock with it. She saw a hundred different deaths, all cast back from the Niroso's visage.

"Magic—it uses magic instinctively," Coernn said in an

even voice, in spite of the hideous injury he had endured. He cast a spell and some of Maeveen's fright faded. Quopomma gasped and whipped out her sabers, but Coernn held her back with a gesture. "This is a different fight, one you cannot win by force of steel. The Niroso are not entirely corporeal. Part of them seems to be pure spirit, or magic, or something I cannot put a name to. It is that part we must attack. Your sword is useless against its body."

"Uncle Istvan take that!" bellowed Quopomma. She rushed forward, her twin sabers swinging in a silvered curtain of death. Both blades crashed into the Niroso, a cut that would have severed the head of another creature.

Both blades vaporized.

Maeveen dived forward and clipped the ogre behind the knees, knocking her forward and past the Niroso. For all its invulnerability to physical attack, it moved slowly. The cool air gusting down the path from the cave opening gave Maeveen the kernel of an idea.

"This way, rock for brains," she taunted. She threw her dagger at the Niroso to gain its attention.

"No, wait, I can cast a spell to stop it," promised the injured Coernn. Maeveen ignored him. She backed toward the cave mouth, taunting the sluggishly flowing Niroso. The stony mass flowed in her direction, moving faster, since it did not have to change direction. She edged away slowly at first, then danced on fencer's-nimble feet to keep her distance. The cold wind whipping into the cave chilled her.

And it worked its natural magic on the Niroso. The stone creature tried to turn from the opening that would freeze it into immobility, only to find that Coernn had conjured his spell. The Niroso was driven toward Maeveen—and forced to solidify.

"That was close," Maeveen said, wiping her forehead. The Niroso struggled against its hardened exterior. "Is it still molten inside?"

"It will escape, given enough time," Coernn said. "It can flow downward into the rock below us and move from the chilling wind that has solidified it into a stalagmite."

Maeveen looked around her uneasily at the spear-shaped limestone formations jutting up from the cavern floor and dangling down from the high-vaulted ceiling.

"Those are natural," Coernn assured her. "I sense no magic in any of them, save where a Niroso has passed recently."

"How do we fight them? Buckets of water?" demanded Quopomma. "I just lost my two best sabers and have nothing to show for it."

"Water might work," Coernn said thoughtfully.

"How do they intend to conquer the surface world if they cannot exist there?" asked Maeveen. "If they poke out of a mountain face, even the warmest day will begin to harden them. And this far north in Terisiare, why, the Ronom Glacier is hardly more than five hundred miles due east. The winters are cold!"

"A fact Sacumon might have withheld from the Stone People," Coernn said. "This might be her plan to insure control over them. They send their coal golems to the surface to aid her in conquering the minotaurs and elves, then she turns on the Niroso—and what can they do to her?"

"One touch is enough to fry," Quopomma said, hesitantly reaching out to touch Coernn.

"They must be naïve to believe her and not explore for themselves," Maeveen said. "But then, Vervamon thinks they are recently come to sentience, byproducts of the war. They might not have experience dealing with cooler life-forms."

Coernn started to speak, but was cut off by a blast furnace wave belching from deeper in the cavern. His cape began smoldering and his eyebrows were singed from the fierce discharge. He staggered into Maeveen, who supported him until he regained his balance.

Maeveen tugged at Coernn's burned cape. Pieces came free in her hand. Then her eyes went wide. Pieces of the wizard's skin came from his body in charred lumps. She turned in the direction of the blast and cried, "Vervamon! Yunnie!"

With Quopomma at her side and Coernn straining to keep up, they ran down the winding path until they came to a sheer drop into a stony amphitheater. Below, Yunnie stood in front of Vervamon, protecting the older man from three advancing coal golems. Behind them paced a darkly clad figure Maeveen guessed to be Sacumon.

"Look out!" Maeveen cried. "Get out of there! You're trapped unless—" She cut off her warning when all three of the magical constructs advanced on Yunnie. To her surprise, he shrieked, but not in pain. It was a cry of triumph, of victory. Yunnie rushed forward, armor-clad chest thrust out to bump into the golems. The three artifacts blew apart in an explosion that knocked Maeveen from her feet.

Clinging to the edge of the amphitheater proved harder by the second as Yunnie ran forward, the magical energy from his armor drawing in other golems and blowing them apart. He laughed, and it was the titter of a madman. He did not use his sword. He bumped into the golems and let the Living Armor protect him—protect itself—from damage.

"I am invincible, Sacumon. You gave me the power to destroy the golems—and you!" Yunnie laughed maniacally. Maeveen scrambled up and sat on the stony ledge overlooking the amphitheater, wondering what she could do to help him. Then she wondered how she could help herself. Yunnie had passed the boundaries of sanity as he attacked Sacumon.

"I control power you cannot even guess at," Sacumon snarled. Her arms writhed as the tattoos came alive, forcing her hands in intricate patterns of spells to destroy Yunnie. For some reason, she began slicing off portions of her own skin, which puffed away in wispy columns of rising smoke.

"Vervamon, get out of there," called Maeveen, seeing she could not affect the battle between Yunnie's Living Armor and Sacumon. "You will be killed!"

"I cannot move," the silver-haired scholar said. "My feet are melted into the rock. A Niroso tried to come up under me and—"

His words were snuffed out in an explosion as Yunnie crashed into Sacumon. The two rolled over and over, magics dueling for supremacy. The Living Armor sought to protect itself, having gone beyond the control of either Yunnie or Sacumon. The sorceress sought the proper spell to stop Yunnie.

Neither succeeded. Not entirely.

Sacumon cast a spell that sent Yunnie crashing backward into a rock wall. She pinned him there with one spell after another. The spell caused his Living Armor to glow an eye-searing blue. Yunnie fought and moved away from the wall, giving himself fighting room. The actinic glare cast on his face turned him into something more than human—or something less.

"Attend me!" cried Sacumon. "Aid me now that your underground kingdom has been invaded!"

"She's summoning more coal golems," said Quopomma.

"No," Coernn said. "She is calling on the Stone People to come do their own fighting. If they do, Yunnie hasn't a chance. He cannot die! He cannot!"

Coernn vaulted into the amphitheater, muttering his spells as he went. Maeveen and Quopomma exchanged a quick glance, then Maeveen said, "Who wants to live forever?"

They followed Coernn into the pit and immediately regretted it. A new blast of energy thrust them back. Maeveen crashed into Vervamon, and Quopomma ended up on top of the heap. Gust after gust of blistering heat passed over them, then came a softer, cooler period when the cavern was bathed in the blue glow of Yunnie's Living Armor.

"Magic battles magic," Vervamon said, wiggling from under the pile to get a better view. "It has not been this way since the Brothers' War! What an opportunity to witness history as it is made!"

Yunnie and Coernn stood shoulder to shoulder. Sacumon did a curious thing. She drew a golden dagger from her belt and cut off a finger. Then another and another.

The force of her magic tripled as each digit puffed into superheated gas.

"Look! She is sacrificing parts of herself to gain superiority," Vervamon said, intrigued by the process of magic. "She finds it difficult to stand against both Yunnie and Coernn, so needs this added power."

Maeveen drew her sword and launched it like a lance, the blade cutting Sacumon high on the arm. The sorceress hissed like a snake and threw the blade from her, trying to stanch the minor wound. The distraction gave Yunnie the chance to bull forward into the teeth of Sacumon's spell, his arms groping for her. The proximity of the Living Armor caused Sacumon to shriek in rage and pain. Maeveen could only guess what agony might be inflicted by this artifact.

"We can both play this game," Quopomma said, picking up rocks and heaving them at Sacumon. The sorceress ducked and dodged, but one stone struck her in the head, dazing her. This allowed both Yunnie and Coernn to advance, the jaws of a magical vise closing on the woman.

"No, you don't understand. They need guidance. They need *my* guidance." Sacumon shrieked as she tried to hold back the blood gushing from her severed digits. Her eyes went wide and wild, and Maeveen saw instantly what the sorceress intended to do. Using her golden dagger, Sacumon cut off her hand at the wrist. Seeing that this did not give her enough new power to fight Yunnie and Coernn, she sawed frantically at her upper arm. The tattoos responded by writhing as if they were alive.

Sacumon gibbered like a crazy creature, but her power mounted, pressing both men against the rock face. Coernn closed his eyes and started a spell. His hands moved relentlessly, no matter how Sacumon's magic assailed him. The tangible pressure mounted in the cavern until Maeveen wanted to scream. Even Vervamon, usually an avid observer, clamped hands over his ears and turned away.

"Die, you will die!" screamed Sacumon. She hacked frantically at her leg, blood pouring onto the rocky floor in front of her. Every new appendage she sliced off added to her power, but she had not reckoned with another of her creations.

Yunnie walked forward, as if in a stupor. The blue haze surrounding the Living Armor now blazed with a purple light so intense it burned the eyes even through closed lids. Maeveen threw up her hand to protect her face. She saw little of the magical confrontation.

Even as Sacumon whimpered and hacked at her own flesh, Yunnie advanced, but it was Coernn's spell that turned the tide against the sorceress. The small bit of magical energy added to that radiating from Yunnie's armor crushed Sacumon. She had reached the end of her magic.

Sacumon died, inch by inch, piece by piece. But she died.

The sudden release of tension within the cavern was almost as painful as the traded spells. Maeveen blinked and wiped blood from her face. She did not know if it was Sacumon's, her own, or someone else's.

"Never have I seen a fight like this," Quopomma whispered, awestruck.

"I agree. Truly, a peculiar method of casting spells," Vervamon said, staring at Sacumon's body. It had withered into a desiccated husk, as if she had died long years before and had been preserved by the dryness of the cavern.

"She knew that—" Coernn's accusation died in a scream as one of the Stone People emerged from the rock face behind him. Flowing arms circled his body and pulled him backward. Flesh sizzling, he screamed and tried to fight. Closest to him, Maeveen O'Donagh acted.

She hammered at the Niroso's semiliquid arm with a huge rock scooped from the floor. Coernn kicked weakly and died as Maeveen watched helplessly. His lips moved in a message meant for her ears alone.

Then Yunnie pushed her aside and strode forward. The magical energy he had absorbed during the battle with Sacumon now radiated powerfully into the Niroso. The groping rock arms flowed like snow in the spring sun and the creature vanished back into the solid stone.

Yunnie dropped to his knees, panting harshly. The Living Armor now appeared burned out, a leathery cinder. Maeveen saw how drawn Yunnie looked and knew in small part how much this fight had taken out of him. The Living Armor was a harsh and demanding master.

Vervamon bustled about, muttering to himself and taking notes in his journal, sketching quickly so that every detail would remain fresh in his mind.

Quopomma joined her captain.

"You all right?" the ogre asked.

Maeveen nodded, filled with a curious mixture of excitement and exhaustion. She didn't know whether to laugh or cry, shout or fall silent. She stared at Yunnie.

"What'd he say?" asked Quopomma. "Coernn, before he died. He said something to you. I saw the expression on his face."

"I didn't notice how he looked."

"He looked relieved, as if he unburdened his soul to you. What was his confession?" Quopomma asked again.

Maeveen had eyes only for Yunnie. In her nightmare, back in the City of Shadows, she had mistaken him for Vervamon. Now she understood why.

"Coernn told me the secret even Lord Peemel does not know," she said.

Quopomma looked at her expectantly. "Well? What is it, Captain?"

"Coernn magically divined only after we started for the City of Shadows that the one he sought had been raised in Shingol." Maeveen took a deep breath, then said softly, "Yunnie is the son of Lady Pioni, Peemel's wife."

"That means—" Quopomma blinked in amazement.

"Yunnie is pretender to the throne of Iwset. And there is more. He is also Vervamon's son!"

CHAPTER

40

LORD PEEMEL STOOD WITH HIS HANDS
clasped behind his back and chin resting on his chest. He
scowled at the huge map spread on the table, small ships
being pushed about by a half dozen junior officers. To his
right stood Digody and to his left Apepei, but Peemel did
not look at either of his advisers. He glared at the map as
one sublieutenant raked in a half dozen Iwsetian vessels.

"How is it possible Edara sank my fleet?" Peemel
fought to keep his tone level. "You told me it was impossible for her to reinforce her navy in time if we attacked
within three days. I lost eight frigates, eight of my finest
ships, eight ships that cost a fortune to build!"

"And the crews," pointed out Apepei. "You lost almost
five hundred trained sailors."

"Fools be damned! Those ships cannot be replaced
overnight. I can impress villagers into my service, but the
ships were armed and armored! How do I replace them?
Edara lost not a single ship." He leaned forward, still not
looking at either of his advisers. "Jehesic suffered no
casualties in a battle *we were supposed to win easily*."
Menace rippled in his every word. Apepei cringed when
Lord Peemel drew out a silken cloth from his pocket and

wiped his hands angrily, as if this would expunge all guilt
from his heart. When Peemel finished, Apepei watched
blank-faced as his liege spun and looped the silken cloth
around the neck of the nearest guard. A single quick jerk
throttled the man, driving him to his knees as his face
turned bright red.

"You need a better commander of naval action,"
Apepei said quickly to distract his liege. The mountain
dwarf stared straight up at Digody, daring the other to
speak. Digody chose to keep his own counsel, and wisely
so, with Peemel coldly raging at this setback to their
plans. "Ihesia works tirelessly on the land and brings victory after victory. But—"

"Milord," cut in Digody, "it is not lack of strategy or
failure to carry out brilliant tactics that causes such
defeats. I fear there is a traitor in our ranks, a traitor who
tells Edara of our every stratagem. How can we win when
she avoids our strengths and attacks our weaknesses?"

Red eyes locked with Apepei's wide set eyes. The
dwarf bounced up and down as his agitation grew. He
brushed back an unruly shock of red hair and shouted,
"Are you calling *me* a traitor? Speak those words and be
damned! I challenge you to a duel! I am loyal to the
throne of Iwset. I—"

"I said nothing about your loyalty to the throne,"
Digody said, his thin face tight with tension. "However, I
question your allegiance to Peemel."

Apepei sputtered incoherently and grabbed for his dagger. A dozen of Lord Peemel's bodyguards stepped forward, some stepping over the body of their fallen
comrade, ready to defend their liege in spite of the mur-
derous anger directed against one of their own rank.
Peemel waved them back and faced Apepei.

"Enough of that. No one questions your allegiance,
Apepei."

"Digody does!"

"You are too excitable," Digody said smoothly.
"Perhaps we need look farther afield for someone who
has access to all this intelligence." His burning red eyes
scanned the assembled bodyguards, finally fixing one with

his stare. A bony finger pointed at the sergeant of the guard. "That one, for instance. He spends much time dockside. He is a foot soldier, not a sailor. Why do you spend so much time at the pub called the Sunken Treasure?"

"I go there on orders."

"Orders?" demanded Peemel. "Whose?"

"Why, Apepei's. I find out what the drunk mariners are saying, and then root out any who might be disloyal."

"He works at my behest," Apepei explained. "As do others in our service. I take security seriously, while Digody only prattles on, throwing up dirt like some Cape Furious monkey."

"Monkey, who are you calling a monkey, little man?" Digody grew in height and loomed. His stringy mustache twitched, and his goatee quivered as he struggled to find the words.

"Enough!" roared Peemel. "This squabbling serves only Jehesic. You will serve *me*. What do we do to stop that bitch from destroying the feeble remainder of my navy?"

"Not so feeble, milord," cooed Digody, his anger at Apepei pushed aside as he tried to put the best face on his tactics. "A new battle brews, even as we speak. I have taken the initiative to lure her fleet toward our coastal positions. General Ihesia is certain she can lay down an accurate barrage and sink the ships as they sail past Desolation Point. They will go to the bottom and never again trouble us," Digody said.

"You ordered fleet movement without Lord Peemel's approval?" The dwarf jumped to the table, sending small toy ships sailing along random courses. "That is treason!"

"No, it is caution," Digody said.

"Explain yourself," Peemel said. "You have not discussed this with me. I am commander of the armed forces, not you. You serve only at my sufferance. If there is any problem with this tactic, Iwset will be left without a navy, and Jehesic will destroy me."

"There will be victory this night, milord," Digody promised. "Come and watch." Digody spun and pointed a bony finger in the direction of the observation deck.

"We can't see Desolation Point from there," Apepei said, hand resting on his dagger. He suspected treachery. A man as strong and underhanded as Digody could heave both Peemel and a dwarf to their deaths from the top of the tower. Apepei was not sure how Digody could then seize political power, because he would fail quickly without the Sigil of Iwset as symbol of rule.

Apepei doubted the citizens of Iwset would accept Digody on the throne, even with the sigil, but Digody was not the kind who reveled in notoriety. He worked best in shadow, pulling marionette strings, making others jump to his do his bidding. Apepei knew he had to be constantly on guard against such perfidy.

"I have arranged a viewing device for our convenience."

"A scrying mirror?" Apepei stared at the shallow bowl of viscous green liquid, aghast. "Abbot Offero will put you to the question for this blasphemy!"

"We need not tell the good abbot," Digody said, dismissing the objection. "Here, milord, look and see how our fleet will decoy Jehesic's finest ships to the coast, where Ihesia's precision artillery can sink them at leisure before they can turn and flee."

Apepei hooked his chin over the edge of the magical viewing device. The fluid sloshed gently in the bowl, causing the image to ripple. Slowly, the dim shapes took form, and he saw the three fastest ships in the Iwsetian navy tacking toward the land, only to veer off at the last instant, revealing pursuing ships flying triangular Jehesic battle pennons.

"On the coast, see how Ihesia has her batteries positioned?" Digody stood with arms crossed over his chest. Apepei eyed him suspiciously, then shifted his gaze to Peemel. He could not read the ruler's expression easily. Peemel might have been angry with Digody usurping his power, or he might have been pleased. Apepei shivered. He was losing his knack of discerning his ruler's mood, and such a loss meant sailing dangerous shoals ahead.

"She ought to open fire now," Peemel said, leaning

forward. His weight rippled the water, blurring the magical vision from distant Desolation Point.

"Ihesia is capable. She will fire only when the time is right," Apepei said. He fumed that Ihesia had fallen into this clandestine alliance with Digody—and without even a hint reaching Apepei's ears. He prided himself on his spies. They had to do better, or he would find himself shut out of Peemel's most intimate confidences.

Perhaps a whisper in Abbot Offero's ear about Digody and his scrying mirror might shift the balance of power around Lord Peemel's throne. The abbot abhorred all magic with a passion that crossed into fanaticism. Playing such a card in this deadly game might not work to Apepei's benefit, but it could only work against Digody.

"See how they approach. There is no way they can sheer away from the siege engines in time to . . ." Digody's words trailed off when it became apparent that the ships pursuing Iwset's finest were not themselves first-class vessels.

"Those are nothing more than barges. What good is it to sink a barge?"

"Perhaps a great deal," Apepei said. "See how their decks are crowded with marines? They do not sail foolishly into a trap. They sail directly for the shoreline to disgorge troops to attack Ihesia!"

"No, not possible. This is not possible!" It was Digody's turn to disturb the emerald liquid as he gripped the edge of the table, as if he could pull himself into the picture of battle unfolding in front of him. His eyes widened and appeared less menacing now. Apepei took no pleasure in his rival's distress. The Jehesic marines were aimed directly against Ihesia's position, and she was the only one of Peemel's generals more loyal to Apepei than to Peemel—or Digody. Her death or capture would be devastating.

"The barges will be sunk. And if they crash against that rocky shore, they will be destroyed. It does not matter which happens," Digody said, more to convince himself than to relate what unfolded in the scrying mirror. "The ships will be sunk!"

"You fool," snapped Peemel. "Edara has no reason to preserve such vessels. Their only purpose is to launch a landing force against our war engines."

"And Ihesia," Apepei said. "Summon her immediately, Lord Peemel. Get Ihesia to safety, or we will lose our finest field commander!"

"Too late," Peemel said, watching the fronts of the beached barges unhinge and fall forward. Ihesia's siege machines had sunk only one of the wallowing ships, and the marines aboard the sunken ship swam powerfully for shore to join the others in the invasion force.

Apepei fought down alarm for Ihesia's life as he watched the Jehesic forces rushing up the steep cliffs to seize the siege machines. The marines were too well-trained, and the siege engine crews were not trained at all for this kind of battle. They were sappers, not swordsmen or archers. Though they fought gallantly, and Ihesia's personal bodyguards particularly well to save their general, it was to no avail.

"Our engines are captured and Jehesic commands Desolation Point now, denying us access to our own coast," Peemel said, his hot gaze fixed on Digody.

"Worse," Apepei said in a choked voice, "Edara's marines have captured Ihesia. Our finest general is a prisoner of war!"

CHAPTER
41

"WE SAVED THEM, AND NOTHING HAS changed. They will still die," Yunnie said with a despair in his voice that caused Maeveen O'Donagh to shudder. She moved closer to him—to Vervamon the Younger—and studied his strong profile in the setting sun. Gory sunlight cast shadows on the planes of his face, making him look even more like his father. Maeveen held her tongue, though. With his dying breath, Coernn had told her the secret of their quest, gained through magic and death.

The Sigil of Iwset might be important, but more so was the man who could legitimately oppose Peemel. With the sigil, Yunnie stood a chance of ending the war between Iwset and Jehesic, and bringing peace to the entire coast from Iwset to Tondhat. But that war was too distant for Yunnie to appreciate, even if he learned all that she knew or had guessed.

Elves had infiltrated the mouth of the valley held by the Urhaalan minotaurs, ready to launch an attack into the stronghold of their enemy. Diminished numbers and lack of planning after their rout plagued them. They attacked through utter desperation now, realizing they had only one last attempt at battle left in them after confronting Tiyint. If the elves fought well, they might sue for peace.

If the elves lost, all was forfeit. The Ironroots in the Forest of Eln would die—and the victors would also vanish soon enough when the Stone People sent their coal golems to take possession of a land they might never inhabit themselves. Sacumon had set into motion events far beyond anyone's ability to control. She had paid with her life, and even that no longer mattered.

Maeveen knew it mattered little in the scheme of things if the elves triumphed over the minotaurs and somehow defeated their rampaging stone avatar. The Niroso still moved easily through the rock under their feet, ready to rise and assume mastery over them.

Elf? Minotaur? It did not matter to the semimolten Stone People. With Sacumon gone, the underground kingdom might be directionless, but the forces that permitted Sacumon to ally herself with the Niroso were still in place. What need did they have of the sorceress when they could send their minions upward to kill and conquer the struggling elves and minotaurs?

Maeveen shuddered. The dream she had endured in the City of Shadows was proving all too prophetic. The valley of the Urhaalan flowed with rivers of blood. She shielded her eyes against the setting sun and saw that the battle would occur much sooner than she had anticipated.

"We need to get to the rest of our soldiers, Captain," Quopomma said uneasily. "They are hidden away in the forest. With them, we might sway the balance." The ogre carried no certainty in her words, and Maeveen knew why. Even at full strength, rested, and well armed, Vervamon's company would be useless against Tiyint. If they allied themselves with the minotaurs to guarantee being on the winning side, what did they gain? Mytaru and the other leaders knew they required no allies to win this day. Before the Lost Rat hunted his hole in the night sky, or the Arms of Elysium reached out to embrace the land, the fight would be over.

If the minotaurs could not win by themselves, then Tiyint would assure victory for them.

"I cannot watch this," Vervamon said forcefully. "It will be a senseless slaughter of a fine, noble people."

"You would fight alongside the elves?" Yunnie asked. "What of the minotaurs?"

"Their stone god will seize the day for them. You must work to stop the slaughter. I have no bias for the elves—or against the minotaurs. My only disgust is for senseless killing."

"Sacumon's legacy lives on," Yunnie said. Vervamon stared at him, the high dome of his forehead sheened with sweat in spite of the cold wind whipping inland from the direction of the distant sea. Autumn had slipped over the land with no one looking. Soon enough would be winter, cold and lonely and desolate. "She incited this war. The elves had no reason to invade the valley, and the minotaurs sought only to retain their privacy for their rituals on sacred lands."

"Then we must redouble our efforts to convince both sides," Vervamon said with gusto. Maeveen had seen him like this before. A challenge brought out the best in him, a problem to be solved and written about in excruciating detail. She wished that lives did not rest on Vervamon's powers of disputation. Pressing her arm against Yunnie, she nudged him from his deep thoughts.

"I agree that we can no longer stand and watch," he said. How he sounded like his father! Maeveen wondered that none of the others saw what she now did. She did not doubt Coernn's dying words. Why had it not been obvious to her before?

"You talk with your friends in the herd," Vervamon said. "I will see if I can find the one-eared elf, Dalalego was his name, and persuade him that he follows a foolish path to death if he invades."

"And Sacumon, tell them of Sacumon and the Niroso," called Yunnie when he saw that Vervamon was already marching off, oblivious to the lines of warriors already assembling on both sides.

"Quopomma, go along and see that nothing happens to him," ordered Maeveen. "I'll stay with Yunnie." The ogre tipped her head to one side, the braided lengths of coarse

black hair swinging gently in the cold wind, as she studied her commander. A slow smile crossed the ogre's face,
showing the gap between her lower teeth.

"He'll be as safe as if he lay in his mother's arms,"
Quopomma promised.

"His mother sold him to slavers," Maeveen said, looking at Yunnie from the corner of her eye to see if this
affected him. He ignored the comment, but then he did
not know that Maeveen spoke of his grandmother. Even
if he had known, from all she had learned of Yunnie's
childhood, he might not have shown any emotion. For all
his similarities to his father, Yunnie was moodier, darker,
more pessimistic.

"There," Yunnie said, pointing. "There is Mytaru. I can
tell from the group of minotaurs surrounding him."

"I see it," Maeveen said, taking note of the herd drifting from a small grove of trees half a mile deeper in the
valley of the Urhaalan. She started walking, her short legs
pumping twice as fast as Yunnie's longer ones to maintain the same pace. "What drives you to protect the
elves? Why not let Tiyint crush them into the ground?"
she asked.

"I—" Yunnie swallowed hard. "It is difficult for me to
say. Sacumon played with my memory, forced her existence from my mind, stifled the words needed for me to
warn Mytaru and the others, but fighting her geas opened
other memories."

"What other memories? Of your childhood?"

"Yes," Yunnie said. "An elf. Tavora. She watched over
me. I remember so little of her, but the love in her eyes
whenever she looked at me was real. And I remember—
almost—her telling me of my parents."

"You know you were not born in Shingol? Or that Essa
is not your true sister?"

"I had not thought of that before." Yunnie rubbed his
temples and shook his head as if it might clear away the
mists within. "She must be my half-sister."

"Foster sister," suggested Maeveen. "You were brought
to Shingol by Tavora and adopted by the family you think
of as your own." As she spoke, Maeveen put the details

into a coherent whole. "And with you came a bauble, a plaything for a baby, the Sigil of Iwset."

"What? Don't be absurd. I know nothing of this sigil." Yunnie's stride lengthened, forcing Maeveen to jog to stay abreast. She began taking in deep, easy breaths to maintain the pace. Her gently probing had brought other memories to the surface of Yunnie's brain, and they bothered him greatly.

"Ahead, minotaurs," she said, slowing when they reached the edge of the grove. Instinctively, she rested her hand on the hilt of her sword, although she knew it would do no good to draw. She could not fight a hundred minotaurs—or a dozen. The stone idol would not bleed should she hack at it with the sword's sharp edge.

"Mytaru!" bellowed Yunnie. "I would speak with you."

Two dark shapes came from the woods, war lances leveled at Yunnie's belly.

"Aesor," he acknowledged. "Pardano, you have grown. I see three ribbons from your horns that were not there before. A fine accomplishment for one not even accepted as a bull into the herd."

"My son has shown himself to be more of a bull than you," Aesor said angrily. "Why do you return? Leave the valley. You are no longer of the herd!"

"Who disturbs me while I conjure?" roared Mytaru, coming from the grove. Maeveen noted how the bull swaggered and how unlike the others he had become. An arrogance she seldom saw, even in Vervamon, blazed from the minotaur like a beacon in the twilight.

"We have stopped the cause of the war," Yunnie said. "Mytaru, do not attack tonight. Talk with the elves. A sorceress was responsible for your dispute with them. She allied herself with the Stone People and attacked you using coal golems—"

Mytaru laughed harshly, cutting off Yunnie's words.

"Please, I have no standing with your herd," Maeveen said, trying to give Yunnie time to organize his argument. "We defeated Sacumon, the sorceress sent by Lord Peemel to cause all your trouble. The elves want peace."

"Of course they do," Mytaru said. "They are losing. If they were winning, would they talk? No!"

"*You* must seek the peace," Yunnie insisted. "You are a hero, a conqueror. Show that you are also benevolent. They will never invade the valley once they agree to a peace."

"They invade the Urhaalan territory even as we speak," Mytaru said. He turned his head, horns black against the gathering night. Holding up his head, he sniffed as if testing the air. In the distance Maeveen heard the heavy stone footfalls of Tiyint approaching.

"Vervamon speaks to the elves even now. He will get them to stop their senseless intrusion into the valley. They want only to save their own forest, their own families. They do not want to fight."

Mytaru thrust his hands high in the air in a summoning of the idol brought to life. Maeveen gasped when she saw Tiyint's dark silhouette against the sky. The huge stone statue blotted out the stars and seemed to suck in all available light.

"Tiyint, hero of the Urhaalan, guardian of the valley, go and kill the invading elves. Kill them all!" shouted Mytaru. Tiyint reeled and then righted itself, changing direction to attack the elves.

The ground shook so hard it unbalanced Maeveen. She fell to one knee and watched helplessly as Tiyint lumbered past.

"Quopomma, Vervamon," she moaned. "They are with the elves. The rest of our expedition is down there somewhere."

"Kill the elves! Destroy all who would destroy the Urhaalan herd!" Mytaru did not need to send forth such a command. Tiyint already began its destruction. Faint elven voices echoed up the valley. Maeveen wanted to shut out the sound, but she was a soldier. Battle and killing were her métier, but she preferred sword against sword, skill against skill, strength against experience pitted with speed and cunning. To her the fight was something personal.

This was wholesale, mindless butchery.

"Mytaru," cried Aesor's son, Pardano, who thundered up, breathless. Maeveen had not even seen the young bull leave on his scouting mission. She chided herself for not being observant. Such small lapses killed.

"What is it? Tell me of Tiyint's success!"

"Yes," gushed Pardano. "Tiyint has forced all the elves into headlong retreat. They flee, leaving their weapons on the ground. They run like frightened rabbits!"

"Then the battle is over," Yunnie said. "Call off Tiyint. You have won, Mytaru. You are the greatest champion of the Urhaalan since Tiyint himself walked the valley."

Maeveen saw how Mytaru puffed out his massive chest and strutted about, basking in the adulation of the Urhaalan warriors. He beat his chest and let out a bellow that echoed from one end of the huge valley to the other, went down side canyons and found every minotaur's ear to give the news.

Victory. Victory for the Urhaalan!

"Thank you, Mytaru," said Maeveen. "You have shown yourself to be merciful."

"What? What are you saying, human?"

"Recalling Tiyint, not letting the idol kill the elves after they surrendered. See?" She pointed down the valley where the stone avatar plodded back toward them.

"I ordered Tiyint to kill them all, no matter where they ran. I wanted every last elf dead!" cried Mytaru, confused. "Why is our protector returning?"

"All the elves must be dead," Yunnie said, disheartened. "Perhaps even Vervamon and Quopomma."

"No, I see Quopomma's signal. She is all right. So is Vervamon and many of the elves. They . . . they halted their retreat when Tiyint spun around and came back!" Maeveen saw the quick flashes from a battle mirror the ogre used to relay their safety.

"Why is it returning?" asked Yunnie.

They found out when Tiyint began killing the minotaurs venturing out to hail their conquering god.

CHAPTER

42

"PUSH A BOULDER ON IT," GASPED PARDANO, winded from the swift retreat across the glade and up the steep path to the top of a cliff overlooking the battlefield. Yunnie and Maeveen O'Donagh were less tired from the retreat, but no less anxious over the pursuing Tiyint. Throughout the night they had run from the stone creature, stumbling in the darkness. The arrival of sunrise had been a scant help for them; it allowed Tiyint to better spot and kill the scattered minotaurs.

Yunnie stood at the edge of the cliff and looked down sixty feet to where the stone avatar raged unchecked. A wounded minotaur who had taken too long to flee fell victim to the idol's groping fingers.

"He carries three minotaurs impaled on his horns as if their weight meant nothing," Maeveen said, a curious mixture of admiration for such strength and revulsion at the sight tingeing her words. "I thought I had seen and done everything. The latter might be true, but the former?" She shook her head in awe at the sight of the unrestrained carnage being wrought.

Yunnic looked from Tiyint to the woman when she fell silent. He had to admire her strength and courage. Even

Essa would have fled in panic when Tiyint attacked, but Maeveen had held her ground to be sure the others were out of danger before backing away from the deadly statue come to life. Maeveen O'Donagh was a fine woman. Yunnie wished they had met under different circumstances, but if the flow of events had been different, they would never have met at all, he from a poor fishing village and she a renowned explorer. He shrugged off such speculation as a waste of time. He faced a more deadly dilemma: fight and probably die, or run and know forever that he was a coward.

"Tiyint will never stop until he kills all those who worship him," Yunnie said. "Mytaru has summoned death for the Urhaalan."

"Getting stomped by the stone god is no different from being burned by a coal golem or hexed by Sacumon," Maeveen replied. "Most of those with Mytaru got away in time. I saw several of his lieutenants running toward that pile of rocks yonder." Maeveen pointed to a rugged stretch down on the canyon floor where the minotaurs had sought refuge. Even as she moved her arm to indicate the rocks for Yunnie, she knew the minotaurs were doomed. The sharp-eyed Tiyint had spied them and lumbered toward them, every step shaking the ground under their feet.

"Stop, Tiyint," cried Pardano, dancing from foot to foot in fear, looking from Yunnie to Aesor. The young bull tossed his head in unconscious imitation of the idol below. "Father, do something."

"It is Mytaru's fault," Aesor said, limping forward. His leg bled from a deep gash sustained while climbing the steep path to the top of the cliff. "He brought forth the monster. If we sacrifice him to it, maybe it will go away."

"You waged a needless war against the elves," Yunnie said bitterly. "If you had used your head for something more than a rack for your battle ribbons, you would have seen the true enemy came from under your feet, not from the Forest of Eln."

"Always you prattle on about goblins and golems. You have no right to speak. Only those of the herd are allowed," Aesor shot back.

"None of you has any right to speak when your friends and brothers are being exterminated like vermin," Maeveen said in exasperation. She paced along the crumbling edge of the rock and tried to shut out the horrible sounds of minotaurs dying by Tiyint's hand. They had chosen poorly. She had to do better, or dozens more would die, perhaps herself included. She kicked at a few pebbles, sending them cascading to the ground at the base of the bluff. Her mind turned to finding ways of defeating Tiyint.

"Pardano might have a good idea," she said.

"Sacrificing Mytaru?" Yunnie shook his head. He would never permit his blood brother to die in such a useless fashion. Then he saw where she looked and how she evaluated the terrain and he knew what she was thinking. "We can send the edge of the cliff down on top of it, crushing it!"

"Perhaps we can tear off a leg or an arm. Simply wounding it might cause the magic to leak out. I have seen similar results. Vervamon once hacked off the leg of a three-headed dog and, although the wound was minor, the spell giving it life leaked away. It lay dead in minutes."

"Will that work?" Pardano pressed close. His father shoved between his son and Maeveen.

"We must retreat to the far end of the valley and save those there. They must learn of our defeat!"

"Save your family if you must," Yunnie said. "I cannot disparage such a motive."

"You think I am a coward!" raged Aesor.

"Fight the statue, not each other," Maeveen ordered, the sharp edge of command entering her voice. She struggled to work a smaller rock under a larger boulder. Aesor silently joined her. With Pardano's added strength, they rolled the rock a few inches toward the verge.

Yunnie found a thick limb from a tree some distance away and returned with it. The cries of the dying minotaurs faded, only a few whimpers before death assaulting his ears. He forced the tears from his eyes. He had to be more like Maeveen O'Donagh, all military and ready for action. He dared not think of the lives that would be forfeit should they fail.

"There might not be another opportunity as good as this," Yunnie told the others as he forced the limb over the small rock and under the large. "Guide the boulder when I begin levering it."

"Wait, not yet," called Maeveen. She dropped to her belly and stared over the edge. "Tiyint is only now moving toward us. We need him directly beneath the boulder before we send him back to the Hell he came from."

"He is the personification of our greatest hero," Aesor said. "How dare you—"

"He is killing us," Yunnie reminded the raging bull. "The magic that should have saved the herd is destroying it." He grunted as the muscles across his shoulders bulged and strained. The boulder began moving from its anchorage as he applied more pressure. The other minotaurs joined in. Turning his head, he saw Maeveen raise her arm, then drop it.

"Now!" Yunnie shouted to focus his strength on the bending tree limb. The wooden lever almost slid from his grip as the huge rock popped up and tumbled over the side of the cliff.

"Right on target!" yelled Maeveen. She scrambled to her feet as Yunnie reached her side. Her arm circled his waist. He did not notice. He watched in mute fascination as the huge rock, the monstrous weight that would have crushed the strongest minotaur, crashed onto Tiyint's horns.

The stone idol staggered and fell. Yunnie started to cheer, but the sound died in his throat when he saw that the rock had not stopped Tiyint, only slowed the avatar. The stone idol reached around the rock pinning it to the ground and heaved.

"It's got him," Maeveen said breathlessly. "It didn't kill him as I had hoped, but it pinned him to the ground. That might be as good. You can get hammers and chisels and chip away at his legs and arms until there's nothing left. You can—"

Maeveen fell silent when it became apparent they had

not defeated Tiyint. Yunnie searched for a second boulder to send after the first. He saw none that would do more than annoy the stone god. Tiyint's arms circled the boulder holding it to the ground, then began squeezing the huge rock against its chest.

Yunnie closed his eyes when he heard the rock breaking apart like rotted ice falling from a glacier. A dust cloud rose, and when the cold morning wind blew it away, Tiyint remained and the boulder had been pulverized. The statue roared in anger and struggled to its feet.

"Nothing happened," Maeveen said in a small voice. "I thought that would shatter it, or at least break off an arm or leg, disabling it."

"There is some justice," Aesor said. "See? Tiyint has found the one responsible for resurrecting him!"

"No, Mytaru, it's coming after you, Mytaru!" Yunnie shrieked, but his blood brother paid him no heed. The minotaur came up the trail through the canyon, attention fixed only on Tiyint.

"What's he going to do?" asked Maeveen.

"He is going to try to stop Tiyint. There's no way he can do it," Yunnie said. Even as he spoke, he started back down the path to the floor of the canyon. He slipped and slid on the narrow, winding trail, but got to the bottom in a quarter the time it had taken to hike up to the summit.

To his surprise Maeveen O'Donagh was right behind him.

"Save yourself. This is not your concern," he told her. She laughed at him.

"Of course it is my concern. Vervamon and Quopomma are out there somewhere. And you hold the key to more than stopping Tiyint."

"What do you mean?"

"Later. I'll distract rockhead, and you get your friend into a hiding place. Tiyint will get bored eventually and go hunting better game."

"No," Yunnie said, grabbing her arm. He knew how fit she was. The solid muscle under his fingers still amazed him. Maeveen moved easily and quickly for such hidden strength.

"So? You want to get Mytaru to cover while I scare it?" Maeveen grinned wickedly.

"I may come from Shingol, but even there, they aren't fool enough to fall for such an old ploy," Yunnie said. "Tell Mytaru to return to Noadia, that she needs him. Only I have the power to stop Tiyint." Yunnie tapped the Living Armor. It had remained quiescent during the night, after its scorching. Now it shone as if waxed and renewed.

"That might be good for arrows and rocks, but against *that*?" Maeveen shook her head. "It can squash you to a bloody pulp and never notice."

"It will notice," Yunnie said with more confidence than he felt. The power building within fed his confidence. He had to act now if he intended to save Mytaru and Maeveen and the others. Even Aesor and his son deserved to live, to find out that all he had said about their true enemy was right. Knowing he would be vindicated, and that Aesor and the others would have to live with that realization for the rest of their lives, fed something deep inside Yunnie he cared not to examine too closely.

"Whatever you say." Maeveen backed away from the now glowing armor, then dug in her toes and sprinted for Mytaru to stop the minotaur from doing anything more foolish. Yunnie tried to settle his thoughts for the battle with Tiyint, but there was no time.

The avatar saw movement: Maeveen O'Donagh. A deep roar sounded and the stone idol began turning in the woman's direction. Yunnie had no time to settle his emotions, or to compose his death chant. He reacted instinctively to place himself between the idol and Maeveen and the minotaurs, but as he stepped out, he felt the Living Armor jerk him to one side. He fought to maintain his position in the path of the lumbering stone god.

"Get them to safety!" Yunnie shouted at Maeveen.

Mytaru fought with her, pulling away as he tried to conjure new spells. The woman argued with him, but that was only part of the obstacle between them and safety. Pardano had fallen and Aesor fought to pull his son to his

feet. From the way the young bull hobbled, he could
never escape the raging Tiyint—nor could Aesor.

"What of the spell?" Yunnie called, hoping Mytaru had a
new way of controlling Tiyint. He saw this was not to be.

Mytaru seemed confused and unsure. Maeveen pushed
the minotaur toward a cave where they might seek refuge.
Aesor and Pardano trailed them. Tiyint came ever closer.

Yunnie faced the minotaurs' god come to life, only to
stagger. He fought to remain in its path, to present a
diversion for others, but the Living Armor sought to prevent it.

"No, no!" Yunnie cried, fighting against the magical
armor. It protected him well, and now that Sacumon was
no longer guiding it, the armor tried to protect itself in
addition to its wearer. If he fled now, Tiyint would kill
Mytaru, Maeveen, and the others. Yunnie had no love for
Aesor, but he bore him no real ill will, either. The minotaur had done only what he thought right for the herd.

Flesh ripped as he tried to get out of the armor. The
Living Armor's pressure on him to move increased. His
feet marched, marionette legs controlled by the power of
the armor.

"I cannot do this. They will die. I will be responsible."
Yunnie saw the race would be close, should he permit the
armor to dictate to him now. Maeveen and Mytaru might
elude Tiyint, but Aesor and Pardano would die. And coming out of hiding were a half dozen other minotaurs. They
would certainly perish unless he did something to slow
Tiyint's pitiless advance.

Screaming in agony as he yanked off the Living Armor
along with chunks of his own flesh, Yunnie cast it aside,
sending it skittering down an incline and into a ravine,
where a swiftly running stream caught the leather and
carried it away.

Stumbling, staggering, he set himself in the middle of
the path leading toward the others. Yunnie gripped his
sword in a double-handed grip, though he saw no way to
stop Tiyint's advance.

The towering stone god's footsteps shook the ground.
Yunnie prepared to die. For the herd. For himself.

CHAPTER
43

THE PATROLS OF ELVES FORCED ISAK TO GO
to ground for long days. Then he had come onto the battlefield in time to see Tiyint ravage both sides in the senseless conflict.

Sitting high in a tree, watching the carnage, Isak shook his head and clucked his tongue.

"Such bloodshed," he said softly. His fingers moved constantly, shape-changing slightly to prevent discovery from below. The few tight, somber knots of elves passing beneath the limb failed to see him; he melted into the wood, hardly more than a thickening on the ragged bark. Stretching out and squinting, he made out the piles of bodies in the valley and the towering stone god come to life.

"Too little control on *that* magic," he chided, wondering which minotaur had dared dabble in such potent spellcasting. He considered tracking down the poor wight to see if the minotaur controlled any spells that might be of use, then decided against such folly when Tiyint bellowed and began attacking those whom it had fought for only minutes earlier.

Isak lay quiet for the rest of the day and through the

night, getting edgier by the minute. He was a man of action, not patience, yet knew the wisdom of allowing the elves to drag their dead from the battlefield—and for Tiyint to rage farther away. Even the finest wizard could fall victim to those stone hooves and sharp horns. Still, he felt a need to reach Sacumon soon. He had the feeling he missed something, and for someone who prided himself on always knowing the most intimate details, it rankled.

Just before dawn, after Tiyint had swept the battlefield, Isak dropped to the ground, dusted off his clothing, and wondered if he would ever again feel clean. Sap stained his fine garments, and he needed a bath sorely. Returning to Iwset seemed more plausible in the light of such drastic inconveniences—save for Ihesia.

Isak remembered his departure and how the Iwsetian general had bid him safe journey. He shook his head, knowing a return without leverage against her would be deadly. Abbot Offero, Digody, Ihesia, even Lord Peemel, would have no further use for him after Sacumon was removed from the equation of power they all sought to puzzle out.

"I need something more than Sacumon's head if I return," he said softly to himself as he stepped over a puddle of bloody mud. "But why return? I have worn out my welcome in Iwset. Even if Lady Edara wins the war and beheads the entire sorry lot of the Iwsetian nobility, where is the profit for me to the south?" As he walked in the direction shown by the occasional glowing flecks revealed by his mysterious stone, he tried to decide what the profit was for him. A deal with Sacumon?

Possible, but not likely, he knew. Sacumon saw herself as conqueror and had no use for a go-between. From the butchery apparent around him, Sacumon needed no help from his ilk. She provoked extreme slaughter. Isak vowed to spy on Sacumon, then make his decision. A few worthwhile scraps might fall into his lap, should he be alert enough.

Retracing the path Yunnie, Vervamon, Maeveen O'Donagh, and Coernn had already tread, Isak made his way to the entrance to the Niroso caverns. Warnings of

danger assailed him from every direction, slowing his
advance. Isak considered changing form, then decided
there was no reason. He was happy with his current form,
and his clothing fit properly. Why become a fashion
nightmare when all he sought was a paltry wizard who
preferred to burrow underground like a mole?

Slipping into the cave entrance quickly convinced Isak
something was amiss. It took only minutes to locate
Sacumon's severed parts. Isak stared at the charred pile
and frowned. He held out the stone and noted how parts
of the burnt body shone bright blue in response to the
rays from the rock. Beyond a doubt, he had found
Sacumon. Or what remained of her.

"However shall I gain any advantage from you now, my
dear Sacumon?" Isak tossed aside the stone, it having
done its duty. He scratched his chin and then looked
around, thinking there might be something he could turn
to his advantage left around. The sight of a coal golem
moving through the cavern stopped any thought of further exploration. Whatever Sacumon's legacy might be,
locating it would prove futile—and dangerous. The sight
of rocky walls shimmering and slowly taking form as a
Niroso emerged convinced Isak to abandon scavenging.

"So," he said aloud, finally outside in the clear, clean
air, "my mission is accomplished by another. I need not
kill Sacumon. It has been done for me in some vile fashion." Isak shuddered at the memory of the wizard's
burned parts scattered about on the rocky floor.
Whatever happened to her might happen to him.

"How can I profit now? Returning to Iwset is not a reasonable course of action, not empty-handed. So . . . "

Isak frowned as he thought and walked. The Stone
People and coal golems in the cavern below offered nothing for him, but Tiyint might. The rampaging stone minotaur presented both a challenge and an opportunity. Isak
lengthened his stride, finding Tiyint's route easy to follow.

CHAPTER
44

YUNNIE CLOSED HIS EYES, TOOK A DEEP
breath and waited to die. With luck, if not skill, he might
slow Tiyint's charge long enough to let the others find
refuge in the cave. He held his sword over his right shoulder, ready to make a powerful slash. Against a stony limb
animated by ancient magic he could not comprehend, his
sword would do nothing. But hope still raged in his
breast.

Tiyint's slow, deliberate footfalls caused the ground to
tremble. Yunnie stared up at the approaching stone minotaur. It had lost its obscene horn decorations, but dried
blood remained, gleaming dully in the morning sunlight.
All too soon he would be dangling from them, if Tiyint
did not choose to simply crush him between thumb and
forefinger. His heart felt as if it would explode in his
chest, yet he experienced a curious calm. If nothing else,
it felt good being free of the Living Armor and the
strange compulsions it had forced upon him.

For all his composure, he still jumped when Mytaru
spoke from behind.

"I can stop Tiyint. I brought him back, I can stop him."

"Are the others safe?" Yunnie asked.

Mytaru nodded. His brown eyes were bloodshot, and his nostrils flared as he moved to stand beside Yunnie. Tiyint roared at the sight of two mortals daring to block his path. Huge granite hands shoved aside boulders in its way, sending up a shower of gravel and dust to block their view momentarily.

"That will not stop Tiyint, the greatest of our heroes," Mytaru said, indicating Yunnie's sword blade. "Perhaps this will." The minotaur closed his eyes and began a chant, low and compelling. The tempo changed, quickened, became more insistent. Mytaru's hands stirred in slow arcs and drew yellow runes in midair. The magical signs burned briefly and then faded, along with their power over Tiyint.

Tiyint appeared through the dust cloud, more majestic and frightening than before.

Yunnie stepped forward, only to be thrown to the ground as an earthquake hit. Part of the cliff face broke free, whether from Tiyint's rampage or something more, Yunnie could not say. The sudden river of boulders carried Tiyint away with it, sending the avatar stumbling and thrashing into the ravine where Yunnie had discarded the Living Armor.

Yunnie turned to Mytaru, who had fallen to his knees. The minotaur hung his head and shook like a leaf caught in a high wind.

"What's wrong, Mytaru? You got rid of him!"

"I did nothing. I cast a spell to stop him, and it did nothing. Nothing." Mytaru looked up, stricken. "There is only one thing I can do. I thought I knew the magic to control Tiyint. Who can control a god, a force of the world, and a hero of the Urhaalan herd?"

Yunnie started to say something more, but a new quake knocked him to the ground. Yunnie got to hands and knees, his head ringing like a bell. They were cut off from those who had sought sanctuary in the cave. A chasm opened between them. Not a deep one, but Yunnie would never have dared trying to jump it. Beyond rose a wall of tumbled rocks that blocked his view of the survivors—if there were any.

"Maeveen!" he called. "Are you there?" No answer.
Then Yunnie turned his attention back to Mytaru. The
minotaur lay on the ground, bleeding from a dozen small
wounds caused by flying shards of stone. He helped his
blood brother up to a sitting position. Mytaru's eyelids
fluttered and then opened, his gaze fixing on Yunnie.

"I am sorry," Mytaru said. "I wronged you. You are a
noble member of the Urhaalan herd. I am the one who is
to be reviled!"

"I still hear Tiyint," Yunnie said. "We need to find
somewhere safe until you can travel."

Mytaru shook his head. One horn tip had broken off,
leaving a jagged edge, and blood ran down his face, turning it into a crimson sea of despair.

"I don't know what happened to Aesor and the others.
The human with Vervamon, Maeveen O'Donagh, doesn't
answer my shouts. Getting to the far side of the new
chasm is going to be difficult."

"Can you reach them?" asked Mytaru.

"Given time. She can take care of herself, and we both
know Aesor is a warrior of supreme ability. What of
you?" Yunnie checked his friend and found only superfi-
cial damage, though the amount of blood made Mytaru
look more badly wounded than he really was.

"Go, try. They need you."

"So do you. We must get away before Tiyint returns."
Yunnie got his arm around the bull and lifted the immense weight.

"Listen," Mytaru urged. "Hear our stone hero? He is
following the river back to the grassy section of the valley. We are safe for the moment."

"He isn't going away," Yunnie said.

"Help your friend—and your herd brothers," Mytaru
said, standing on trembling legs. Mytaru's stance firmed
as Yunnie watched. Then he nodded.

"You rest. We will tackle the problem together when I
get back. There has to be a way to defeat Tiyint."

Mytaru nodded, then made shooing gestures for
Yunnie to cross the chasm and find what had happened
to Maeveen and the others. Yunnie found it necessary to

scale a part of the cliff face, work his way across, then drop almost fifteen feet to the far side of the newly formed gorge. He scrambled up a slope littered with gravel, then found himself on firmer footing.

His heart sank when he saw that the quake had brought down the roof of the cave where Maeveen and the others had sought refuge. He stared at the tons of debris filling the cave mouth. Anyone inside was past any succor he could offer. Yunnie sat and looked at the curtain of rock until the sun was overhead, then shook off his lethargy, then stood and retraced his path to rejoin Mytaru.

When he crossed the abyss again, Yunnie found more disappointment. Mytaru was gone.

CHAPTER
45

TIYINT'S EARTHSHAKING ROAR AND THE uneasy sense of magic gone awry led Isak Glen'dard through the foothills to a low ravine. He stumbled among the rocks ranging in size from gravel all the way to boulders larger than a Jehesic fighting barge. Only when he came to a tiny ledge above a river did he sit and stare.

"Such power," Isak muttered, staring at Tiyint's stone horns swinging back and forth wickedly as it sought new victims. The stone god found only a few wounded minotaurs, who were dispatched easily. "How do I turn that to my benefit?"

Isak recognized strength beyond his ability to control. A minotaur had foolishly wakened this monster and now could never contain it. Although defeating the elves invading the domain of the Urhaalan might have been worthwhile, Tiyint's continued rampage presented a one-way road to death and destruction more complete than the elves could ever have accomplished.

"Ah, a new player," Isak observed. A battered minotaur with a broken horn splashed in the river flooding the bottom of the gorge and turned to confront his avatar. "How futile, or is it?" Isak scooted from his relative safety and slid down the slippery incline, sending up a cloud of dust and small rocks. He thrashed about, cursing how this fall tore at his precious clothes, then he vented a sigh, reaching the bottom of the gulch without breaking any bones.

Dusting himself off, Isak sought a safe refuge to watch the battle unfolding. He sensed new spikes of magical power being hurled as a minotaur might cast a war lance. Hunkering down, he watched more closely, wondering if he ought to aid the foolish minotaur in some fashion, but Isak's sense of self-preservation prevented him.

This was not a battle the one-horned minotaur was likely to win. Tiyint towered forty feet in the air, blood-stains showing darkly on horns and hands. The small minotaur was no less marked, but Isak never bet on the underdog. Still, a sense of rising energy held his attention. The conflict's outcome might not be as predictable as it seemed on the surface.

"Tiyint!" cried Mytaru. "I brought you to life. Back to stone will you go at my command!"

Tiyint roared, whether in delight at finding another victim or in contempt at such a feeble taunt, Isak was unable to say. He squinted against the sunlight as he saw the minotaur reach into the water and pull out dripping leather armor. He held back a chuckle that such a feeble breastplate could ever deter the stone monster's horn thrust or hammer-hard fist. But as he watched Mytaru don the Living Armor, Isak stiffened. He eyed the armor and sensed the power emanating from it.

"Magic of considerable power," he decided. Was it enough? Isak began to wonder at the hesitation on part of the statue come to life.

Mytaru shivered as he strapped on the Living Armor and jerked with the electric surge of magic throughout his body. He threw back his head and began a deep, soul-chilling dirge. Words twined through the lament, the poetry of a minotaur's death chant. As if sensing opportunity slipping away, Tiyint let out a wordless bellow and attacked.

A thick-fingered hand closed around Mytaru, who no

longer fought. The minotaur uttered his spell as his only defense. His magic was cut off as Tiyint's grip tightened, but blue electricity oozed between the statue's fingers like thick, dripping glue. Tiyint relaxed his grip, but still held Mytaru firmly.

Isak gasped when he saw that the minotaur was not crushed to death. If anything, he appeared to be rejuvenated by the grip around him. The magical energy from the Living Armor held back Tiyint's destroying fist. Small splotches of black marked the stone god's fingers where it tried to squash its victim.

Mytaru continued his spell, casting it again and again. Isak staggered as waves of white-hot heat blasted past him. By the time he regained his usual calm, Isak saw a distinct shift in the fight.

Where Tiyint had been undisputed victor upon grabbing Mytaru, now the statue fought to cast away the minotaur clad in the Living Armor. Stuck to the stony palm, Mytaru now found himself in a position to press his attack. Mytaru issued new spells, woven between the doleful strains of his death chant.

"You give your own life to turn Tiyint back to stone," mused Isak. He marveled at such a trade. Sacrifice was not an unknown concept for him, but not one he considered when it came to his own daily dealings. If the reward did not exceed the risk, Isak was not interested in pursuing that course of action.

But this!

Mytaru died by degrees so that the unpredictable god of his herd would return to immobile stone.

The Living Armor fed Mytaru's power until Tiyint staggered back, almost stepping on Isak. Eyes wide, Isak watched Tiyint stumble into the side of the mountain. For a heartstopping instant, Isak thought the avatar fought back successfully. Then cracks began appearing in its rocky hide. Tiyint leaned against the cliff face as the cracks spread and with them, solidity. As if a liquid freezing, Tiyint hardened and finally became completely immobile.

Hand still outstretched, the rock-hard fingers clutched Mytaru.

Isak ventured from his hiding place and cautiously approached. He stared up at the god, again returned to stone. The bull dangled limply in Tiyint's grip, back broken, desiccated as if left in the sun for decades.

"A worthy fight," Isak acknowledged, touching the brim of his floppy hat in salute to Mytaru's sacrifice. He might not understand it, but he certainly admired such bravery and ability at spellcasting. Rousing Tiyint had been a feat; returning the statue to its quiescent state had proved even more difficult. It had cost Mytaru his life— and the lives of untold others.

Isak stepped back. He started to leave, then thought better of it. A sly smile crossed his lips as he turned his eyes back to Mytaru and the leather armor poking out from between Tiyint's fingers.

It took almost an hour for Isak to scale the statue, crawl out on a rocky limb, and another hour to free the Living Armor from Mytaru's broken body, but it proved worth the effort.

On the ground again, Isak stripped off his ripped and filthy tunic and placed the Living Armor against his flesh. He sighed as energy suffused his body, giving him a sense of power he had never before known.

Isak Glen'dard put his tunic back on over the armor, hiding it from casual examination, then set off toward the east, whistling a lilting, cheerful tune in direct contrast with Mytaru's melancholy lament.

CHAPTER
46

"INTO THE CAVE!" MAEVEEN O'DONAGH CRIED.
She forced Aesor and his son ahead of her, Quopomma
following close behind to make certain, if they got past her
captain, they did not rush back into Tiyint's stony arms.

"This is not a good idea, Captain," the ogre said, eyeing
the cave roof suspiciously. "What if stone-for-brains
decides to bang on the wall outside? The whole cave can
collapse on our heads."

"We have no other choice," Maeveen said. Her mind
raced. What her lieutenant said was true. It was also true
they would be unable to outrace Tiyint, should the minotaur's god decide to come after them. Between this
canyon and the gentler grassy valley lay only rocky terrain, ill-suited for sprinting. The idol's longer strides
would allow him to quickly overtake the party.

And, Maeveen realized, there was little enough agility
left in them, at that. Aesor and Pardano were both still
hobbling. She had no idea how long it would take for
them to regain their feet. Too long for an effective escape
was her guess.

"There's Vervamon to consider, also," Quopomma
said. "Where did he get off to?"

"He can take care of himself," Maeveen said, grabbing the ogre's double bandoliers and pulling her into the cave. She saw that Mytaru had chosen to stand beside Yunnie. She took a deep breath and knew what she had to do.

"Wait, Captain, where are you going? You're not leaving me in this crowded cave with two bovines!"

"I have to—" Maeveen's words were shoved back down her throat as the earthquake struck. She bounced around like a bug on a hot skillet, falling in one direction, only to be tossed in the other before she could get her balance. She clung to Quopomma as the pair of them fell deeper into the cave—and then came the resonant rumbling noise from beneath that sent a cold chill up Maeveen's spine.

"Out!" she tried to cry. Her order was lost in the ominous grinding of rock against rock as the roof caved in. She threw up her arms to protect her head, spun and plunged forward, going deeper into the cave. She bounced off Pardano, then realized how disoriented she was. The young bull lay still, head canted at a crazy angle. He had died instantly when a large section of the cave ceiling fell and hit him on the side of the head.

"Go, go, go!" Quopomma urged. The ogre shoved her along as if she were nothing more than a leaf caught in a fast-moving stream. Maeveen did not object. The ground trembled uneasily under her boots, and she knew secondary tremors were not unusual. Another quake might crush them all.

"My son," cried Aesor, kneeling beside Pardano. "My son!"

"Come along," Maeveen said. "There is no time. We can come back later." She knew this to be a lie even as she spoke. The roof split down the middle, dropping loose dust and gravel. In another few seconds, tons of rock would entomb all of them for eternity. She gripped Aesor's arm and steered him away from his son's body.

"A bigger cavern," Quopomma shouted from ahead. "Looks like the one the Stone People used."

"Can't be. We're too far away for that!" Maeveen burst

into the subterranean chamber and skidded to a halt. For all the world it looked as if Quopomma was right. The dim light from distant, bubbling lava pits caused eerie shadows to move restlessly against the walls and high, vaulted ceiling. The stalagmites and stalactites might have been twins to those in the other grotto. Or they might somehow have blundered back into the same one, even if Maeveen knew it to be miles distant.

"Are you safe?" came a familiar voice. Vervamon strode up, looking as if he had been out for an afternoon jaunt and was quite pleased with himself over what a fine day it was.

"Aesor's son, dead," gasped out Maeveen. "Yunnie and Mytaru are outside. Quake closed the cave entrance. They're fighting Tiyint."

"A pity Mytaru—he is the one who roused the somnolent idol, isn't he?—did not respond with more alacrity to the threat posed by his magical dabbling. Still, it is not all a loss. I have been conducting high-level negotiations with the Niroso. A fascinating people: primitive in social skills and organization, but advanced in other ways. I discovered they know the ancient languages, no doubt from rifling through libraries long buried."

"They cast spells," spat Quopomma. "They're birthed from the Brothers' War, aren't they?"

"They seem to have been spawned in that era, yes," Vervamon admitted. "As such, they are younglings, but developing most quickly for beings forever doomed to remain underground. If they venture out of their fine, sunless realm, they solidify because it is so cold in our world. Or so they find our more pleasant terrain, even in the midst of a scorching summer. The Niroso cannot understand us and seek only to learn. They call us the Cold Ones. Amusing, isn't it?" Vervamon drew out his journal and quickly recorded new observations triggered by his speech.

"Rockhead scholars," said Quopomma, shaking her head. Some of the tightly woven braids on the side of her head had been sheared off during the race through the collapsing shaft. This seemed to bother the ogre more than a multitude of other wounds bleeding on her arms and legs.

"How did you end up with them?" asked Maeveen. "We were together until Tiyint started his rampage and—"

"I saw a Niroso trying to force his way to the surface. I rescued the poor gudgeon. Sacumon had filled his head with all manner of fallacies about life on the surface. It has been quite the chore putting him and his companions straight on the matter of life aboveground. Their reading, while adequate to learn certain old languages, fails in many salient points concerning our lifestyles."

"A chore you are up to, no doubt," Quopomma said. Several of the Niroso approached, smoldering stones in their wake. The ogre looked around and reached for her swords, only to find them gone. She balled her fists, in spite of knowing how futile it would be fighting a molten being that way.

"Ah, they come for another lesson," Vervamon said, rubbing his hands together. He balanced his journal on a rock in front of him as the Stone People gathered in a semicircle, students for his lecture. "They are quite willing to listen and learn." A new quake drove Maeveen to her knees. Only then did she realize that the gathering of so many Niroso triggered the quakes. Somehow, their passage through solid rock caused the tremors that had sealed them all in the cave and killed Aesor's son.

"What of their coal golems?" Maeveen eyed the assemblage uneasily, remembering how they had killed before and sent their minions to destroy both elves and minotaurs. She was not sure she was right about the Stone People causing the quake, but on this point she was positive.

"Sacumon's doing. She had them completely gulled. She used them unmercifully. See, the Niroso travel through rock and find things long buried. What marvelous archaeologists they will make under my tutelage! They have discovered many magical artifacts, including the Living Armor your young friend wears, all of which Sacumon preempted. She was unrelenting in the way she stole. I suspect the Niroso have also found vast ore

deposits, gold, silver, things like that, though they have
not mentioned it. I must find out, but it is archaeological
discovery that interests me most."

"You would trade information and hold them underground?" asked Quopomma, skeptical of any deal with
semimolten creatures.

"Why not?" Vervamon rubbed his hands together
again and launched off on his lecture topic for the benefit
of the Niroso audience, something Maeveen thought had
to do with geological structures. She closed her eyes and
rubbed her temples, trying to get rid of the aching pain
that pounded her eyeballs and threatened to split her
skull.

"Where's Aesor?" asked Quopomma. "He was with us
when we came into the cave."

"Gone back to dig out Pardano," Maeveen guessed.
Her heart weighed more than lead thinking of the minotaur and his lost son, but she had seen too many deaths in
battle for any one tragedy to affect her too much.
Maeveen closed her eyes and swallowed hard. That might
be part of her trouble. Death was her business, even if
she was not a soldier in the way those following Lord
Peemel into battle might be. She protected Vervamon as
he pursued his academic delights, but to do that she often
had to kill.

Her eyes opened, and she stared at the Niroso. Did
they feel emotion? Vervamon said they were new creatures, unskilled in social interaction. Did that mean they
lacked compassion when another died, or were they like
the rock they moved through, forever stolid and unmov-
ing, incapable of learning other ways?

"This is an exciting turn of events," Vervamon said,
turning to face her. "The Stone People speak of secret
passages beneath the ground they have carved out to
transport more solid material."

"That's how they came to store an armory full of
weapons," Maeveen said, remembering Yunnie's tale of
the room filled with human weapons and armor.

"And other artifacts, as well. They find buried cities
and sift through them, keeping only the items they find

more perplexing so they can study them at their leisure. Caverns such as this one provide repositories for their collected horde."

"Is this the same cave we first entered, where Sacumon was killed?" asked Quopomma, ever pragmatic.

"All Niroso grottos are constructed similarly," Vervamon said. "I have no idea how they create such rock beauty, but architecture in stone is definitely the sign they have a budding art community."

"Who'd ever call the tombstone designer a product of civilization?" grumbled the ogre. She hunkered down and glared at the Niroso.

It was impossible to tell where the Stone People's attention was focused. They shifted liquidly as they lounged against their rocky ledges, bodies lacking uniformity, yet refusing to allow any to claim they were not of solid material.

"They use magic in ways I do not understand. My first hypothesis was that they magically transform their bodies to slip through solid stone. I am unsure if this is accurate even after discussing the matter with them at some length. They have a curious outlook on the world," mused Vervamon.

"Best not to let the Inquisition find out about them. Those red-robed butchers would declare the entire underground a stepping-stone to perdition. They'd have all the Niroso put to the question before the sun set." Maeveen stood and paced. She needed to know what happened aboveground to Yunnie and Mytaru and Tiyint.

Mostly, with Yunnie.

"Captain, I don't like the way these diamonds in the rough are looking at us," Quopomma said uneasily.

Maeveen swung about, staring across the wide cavern. Tumbling down a chimney came Yunnie. He dropped fifteen feet from the vault ceiling to the floor, his strong legs bending to absorb the impact. She ran to him, ready to fend off the Niroso should they attack. They shifted fluidly, but remained Vervamon's attentive pupils as he spoke in his damnable ancient tongue.

"Yunnie, are you all right?" She helped him to his feet.

He staggered a pace and rubbed his leg, then smiled crookedly, obviously pleased to see her again.

"It was farther down that chute than I anticipated." He clapped her on the shoulder in a comradely fashion, then turned gloomy. "Mytaru's dead. He gave himself to stop Tiyint."

Maeveen saw tears welling in his blue eyes. He turned so she could not see the sorrow.

"The stone idol is no more?"

"I watched as it was returned to the rock where it was imprisoned for so long," Yunnie said. "Mytaru did not die a good death. He deserved better."

"He toyed with powers he did not understand. Even the most accomplished wizard would hesitate to invoke such elemental force—and those with the ability have long since been killed off." Maeveen added under her breath, "And rightly so."

"He did what he thought was best for the herd," Yunnie said. "I saw him die and could do nothing, nothing but listen to his death chant." He wiped tears from his eyes. Sooty streaks remained on his cheeks.

He pointed at Vervamon's class of Niroso. "What goes on there? I thought to rescue you and the others, but couldn't find any way into the shaft."

"The warrior's son died. He returned to retrieve the body but . . ." Maeveen let the sentence trail off.

"The entire side of the mountain fell in," Yunnie said. "There is no hope for Aesor to ever recover Pardano from under that rock slide." He heaved a deep sigh and stared across the cavern, eyes seeing nothing. "I don't know what to do. Mytaru is gone. Most of the herd is dead. The Urhaalan are almost extinct after their war. And the elves? I don't know about them, but I suspect it is the same for them. What's left for me?"

"Shingol," suggested Maeveen, thinking of the lost sigil and all she had learned of Yunnie's heritage. "Return there. The elf who acted as your protector over the years left you a legacy."

"Tavora? What do you mean? What legacy?"

"The Sigil of Iwsel," she said earnestly. "Recover it.

Vervamon hunts for it, also. We can do it together. You know where it is. You must!"

"I know nothing of any sigil," he said, but a tiny smile crept across his lips as memories flooded back. "My only toy as a child was a likeness of an old man etched on a metal disk and a chain."

"The Sigil of Iwset," whispered Maeveen. "Where is it?"

From Yunnie's expression she knew he remembered that, also.

CHAPTER
47

"I FEEL LIKE A COWARD RUNNING FROM BATTLE,"
Yunnie said distantly. Maeveen O'Donagh knew he
longed to be back in the Urhaalan's valley, but there was
nothing remaining for him there. Mytaru had died returning Tiyint to its stony eternity, Aesor was lost in the maze
of caved-in tunnels hunting for his son's body, and everywhere lay rotting corpses in once peaceful lands. There
was no way to give all a decent funeral; there were too
many bodies.

"There is more to this than meets the eye," Maeveen
said. "Coernn told me your mother was Lady Pioni, Lord
Peemel's fourth wife, if I remember Vervamon's history."

"Why didn't Vervamon come with us?" Yunnie stirred
from his lethargy and looked around. They had been trav-
eling for a week, and now that they approached the fishing village of his childhood, Yunnie was asking questions.
Maeveen took this to be a good sign that the shock and
sorrow were wearing off.

"He's still with the Niroso, trying to learn more about
them. He thinks he can convince them of the error they
made believing Sacumon and that he can forge a bond
with them which might prove useful." Maeveen spat a

gob of gumweed. She didn't know if Vervamon really believed this possible, or if the scholar simply took the chance to engage in pedagogical curiosity. Vervamon considered himself not only a masterful explorer and researcher, but also an instructor second to none.

Teaching a race of rocklike beings would be a real credit for his curriculum vitae. That he might be bringing peace to a war-torn area was incidental in Vervamon's universe of facts and research publications.

"I don't want to go back to Shingol," Yunnie said, staring at the quiet fishing village. "There is nothing there, nothing. I am adrift in a world without purpose."

"You don't have purpose, or the world doesn't?" asked Quopomma. The ogre grunted when Maeveen elbowed her in the ribs. She frowned and wandered off, grumbling to herself.

"She meant nothing by it," Maeveen said. "Quopomma gets bored easily, and when she does, she turns argumentative."

"She's a good warrior," Yunnie said. "A fighter. I saw how she fought in the cavern and before."

"I'm lucky to have her as my lieutenant," Maeveen said. "There might be a spot for you, also. I have to rejoin my company, but I have no good feeling that my other lieutenant has recovered. Iro's wounds were more mental than physical."

"Are you offering me an officership?" This seemed to amuse Yunnie, making Maeveen a little irritable.

"Yes," she said curtly.

"I belong with the Urhaalan," he said. "What happens elsewhere in the world holds little concern for me. There is much to be done to soothe the ill feelings of both minotaurs and elves, and if Vervamon brings the Niroso to an acceptable harmony with the others, then there is rebuilding to be done." Yunnie sucked in his breath. "Noadia deserved more than she received from Mytaru."

"His wife?"

Yunnie nodded once and rushed off, leaving Maeveen to hurry along behind. Her irritation grew by the minute as she lengthened her stride. He was not the only one to have lost friends and family in the pointless conflict. She fumed, remembering how her own family had been sacrificed to the Inquisition to prevent additional outrages—and how the atrocities had occurred anyway. He was not the only one to suffer loss in a war.

"There is more conflict than between elves and minotaurs," she called to him. "There's the war between Iwset and Jehesic."

"You believe I can do anything to sheathe that bloody sword?" Yunnie laughed without humor. "All because of memories that might be false and a muttered confession by a dying wizard?"

"Coernn had no reason to lie. You are the pretender to Iwset's throne. With the sigil you have legitimate claim."

"I don't want it."

"Stop the fighting. It is as meaningless a conflict as that between elf and minotaur. Stop it, then do what you choose." Maeveen felt a flush rising to her cheeks as Yunnie turned to stare down at Shingol. The sun caught the fine lines of his face in precisely the same way it would Vervamon's chiseled features.

A catch came to her throat. She and Vervamon had been lovers for a short while, until it became obvious to her that his experience, his drive, his ambitions were completely alien to her. He had a personality that drew men and women like a lodestone pulling iron, and it had attracted her. He had an easy, charismatic command to him. His world was also filtered through egotism so great it overshadowed mere human concerns.

But Yunnie was different. He had the same air about him. He commanded attention in the same way. He was a leader, but without the overweening vanity that characterized his father. Maeveen might have made a mistake getting involved with Vervamon, but it would be different with Yunnie.

"I don't want to see my sister again. It would serve no purpose," Yunnie said.

"Why bother?" asked Quopomma. "The fleet is out fishing. If your belongings are stored in her hut, fetch them now."

"Heryeon might be there," Yunnie said, "I would avoid him, also. He would ask questions I have no desire to answer."

"I can send him on his way," Quopomma said, strutting off down the dirt lane to Essa's home. The ogre banged on the door, spoke at length with Heryeon, who answered, and then went off with him, the man occasionally glancing up at her as if in wonder. The way he wiped his lips told Yunnie that Quopomma had found the man's weakness and had overcome any uncertainty he might have had accompanying an ogre.

"What did she say to him?" asked Yunnie. "Heryeon is a suspicious sort at the best of times."

"Quopomma can be persuasive, especially when she has a real thirst. It has been too long since she downed a few pints of ale. I hope your brother-in-law can hold his drink. If not, he will have one fine hangover in the morning."

"Heryeon gets more practice bending his elbow than he does pulling in nets," Yunnie said. He stopped at Essa's door, a worried expression clouding his face. "This does not seem right."

"Your belongings, your right to fetch them," Maeveen said, anxious to see if the toy Yunnie remembered from his childhood was truly the Sigil of Iwset. Too many had died for it. The sigil ought to end up in the proper hands.

"I buried everything under the floor before I left," he explained.

"We dig, we put the dirt back. Essa might notice, but she might think Heryeon has finally chosen to do some work."

"That thought will never cross her mind," Yunnie said, laughing. He sobered quickly. "There is something more." He rubbed his hands over his bare torso. "Since shedding the Living Armor I have felt naked, vulnerable. And I have experienced feelings of dread that grow worse daily."

"It was a powerful spell Sacumon cast on you. The Living Armor saved your life and you came to depend on it. You can act on your own, without it, without another's magic forcing you to do things you don't want."

"Pawns," he muttered. "We are all pawns who rely on magic," and then he entered the small home. Yunnie walked to the far corner of the main room and used his dagger point to dig. In ten minutes he had dug down three feet to reveal a small box constructed of Ironroot wood. Strong fingers pried the box free and dropped it onto the floor. He stood and backed away.

"What's wrong?" she asked.

"I fear what I will find there. What if I *am* pretender to the throne of Iwset? I remember nothing of my mother or father."

Maeveen started to tell him of his father, then stopped. The time did not seem right, not with Yunnie racked with such uncertainty.

"If the old elf put me in this foster home, there had to be a reason for taking me away from Iwset."

"You are a provincial," scoffed Maeveen. "Lord Peemel would have killed you if the elf had not protected you." Yunnie stared at her, the question in his eyes. "You are not Peemel's son, but you are a threat to him and his plans for expansion along the coast."

"Let him do as he sees fit," Yunnie said, turning and leaving the hut.

Maeveen started to call to him, then her eyes fell on the wooden box. Some of Vervamon's curiosity had worn off on her. She had to know if Coernn really had discovered the Sigil of Iwset. She pried open the lid, using the edge of her sword. Unoiled hinges creaked in protest, then slowly yielded the contents to her anxious gaze.

Pieces of cloth, bits of metal, old toys from an impoverished childhood, those were the items she saw on top. But under it all, wrapped in a moldering cloth lay wrapped the Sigil of Iwset.

She pushed away the dusty material and held up the gold medallion, letting it swing back and forth. The sigil carried a power of its own, possibly magical, but more likely only driven by the knowledge that the bearer held claim to the throne of a prosperous and powerful city-state.

Footsteps behind her caused her to call out, "Yunnie, I found it. The sigil!"

The knobbed hilt of a sword crashed into the back of her skull. She pitched forward, stunned.

CHAPTER
48

MAEVEEN O'DONAGH CURLED UP TO KEEP THE man from kicking her in the belly. Still stunned, she tried to focus on something more than the pain in the back of her skull and the booted foot seeking her ribs.

As quickly as the attack began, it ended. She sat up.

"Feyne!" she cried, recognizing one of Coernn's two surviving assistants. Ehno and Feyne had been dismissed by their leader before Coernn entered the Niroso underground with Yunnie, Vervamon, Quopomma, and Maeveen. She had thought Coernn had sent them back to Iwset and now regretted her false assumption. Feyne wrestled with Yunnie, the Sigil of Iwset swinging like a golden pendulum between them. Maeveen pushed to her feet, ignored pain, judged distances, then aimed an accurate punch that crashed into Feyne's temple. The man staggered and quickly fell to Yunnie's continuing strong onslaught.

"What's going on?" Yunnie demanded. "I came back, and he was kicking you. What happened?"

Yunnie grunted as Feyne rolled over and drove a dagger straight up, intending to gut him. Yunnie strained to keep the point from his belly, but he had been caught off balance. He crashed into the wall; Feyne hooked a heel and pulled him to the floor.

Before Maeveen could come to Yunnie's rescue, a chill filled the air inside the hut. From the open door came a whistling and a silver blur moving like a small tornado toward Feyne. Maeveen tried to move, only to slip in loose dirt from the hole. The thrown knife sank into Feyne's back.

"Yunnie!" she called. "Out, get out. Run!"

"That will not be necessary," said Ehno. At the door Maeveen saw Coernn's other assistant enter the hut, limping heavily. Ehno's left side was covered with caked blood, and his face showed great strain at every movement. After thrusting an unthrown spare knife into its sheath at his belt, Ehno dropped heavily into a chair and stared at Feyne, a sneer on his split, bleeding lips.

"You betrayed us," Ehno said in a low voice laden with menace. "You are a traitor!"

"No," grated Feyne, forcing himself up, the knife trembling in the center of his back. "I am loyal to Lord Peemel! It is you, you and Coernn and the others, who are traitors."

"I have only the best interest of Iwset at heart," Ehno said. He tugged at his stiff shirt front and peeled back the cloth to reveal a deep, dangerous knife wound. "It is a good thing you were in too much of a hurry to stab me properly. Like all of Peemel's minions, you lack attention to detail. Therein lies your downfall."

"A pox on you and Coernn!"

"A pox on you," Ehno said, his tone cold. He sat and watched Feyne shudder and collapse, the last breath riven from his body.

"I thought Quopomma had a mean streak when it came to dispatching enemies," Maeveen said, staring at Ehno, aghast.

"I had thought Feyne to be my friend. Betrayal always hurts more than a mere flesh wound." Ehno winced as he shifted weight in the chair to reach down and pick up the Sigil of Iwset. "Coernn died for this, didn't he?"

Maeveen nodded, not able to find her voice.

Ehno turned to Yunnie, looking as if he reflected on some deep thought, then tossed the pendant to him. Yunnie caught the gold disk easily.

"Wear it," Ehno said. "You are better suited to the throne than Peemel."

"You are not Peemel's sycophant," Maeveen said. "Are you Digody's henchman?"

Ehno smiled, then winced in pain. "Hardly. There is no secret to Digody's rampaging ambition, save possibly in Peemel's case. He trusts Digody, the fool. Iwset needs better than those two. Iwset needs you, Yunnie."

"Me?"

"I bring official declaration from Lady Edara, ruler of Jehesic, asking for your hand in marriage."

"What? This is insane. I don't know Edara. Why—" Yunnie's mouth clamped shut into a grim line as he realized what this meant. "Politics. She wants to forge a union with a ruler of Iwset because she cannot defeat Lord Peemel in battle."

"Iwset is mighty. It has riches and commands a vast territory filled with potential soldiers. Jehesic might win at sea, but it can never win a war of attrition. Lady Edara wants to end this. A marriage—"

"Of convenience," Yunnie cut in.

"Call it that, if you wish. You can be ruler of Iwset. From all I have seen, you would be a good one. You have common sense, and your efforts to bring peace to both the elves and minotaurs shows compassion. Your peace effort need not be limited to Forest Eln and the Urhaalan's valley. Bring peace to Iwset and Jehesic, then rebuild the minotaurs' valley. Help the elves using the wealth of Iwset. Rule and you will achieve what you cannot as a simple citizen of a fishing village."

"Why does he need to marry Lady Edara?" demanded Maeveen. "All he need do is claim the throne of Iwset and do these things on his own. He would not press the war with Jehesic. Isn't that what she seeks? Peace?"

Ehno closed his eyes and nodded slowly. When he opened his eyes, they were hot with fever—or was it fervor?

"He will never achieve the throne without the alliance
with Lady Edara."

"She seeks marriage with someone other than Peemel
to send him the message she will never surrender,"
Yunnie said, understanding coming to him. "That I have
claim to the throne of Iwset stirs internal unrest in
Iwset."

"Turmoil in Iwset will break apart a rich city-state and
ruin it for ages. What does Yunnie know of rule? He
might have some of the citizens backing his claim to the
throne, but Peemel's faction would fight at every turn,
blood or no, sigil or no. Lady Edara desires peace, and
not from a fractured Iwset. Such a civil war within Iwset
would adversely affect Jehesic for years to come. No, she
seeks this marriage and the abilities to rule in order to
settle a war."

Maeveen started to protest, but saw the expression on
Yunnie's face and knew she could never compete with
Lady Edara, a beautiful woman and ruler of a prosperous
city-state, who offered him his heart's desire. Yunnie
might not seek pleasures of the flesh, no matter how gor-
geous Edara was, but he could bring peace and prosperity
to the Urhaalan herd.

How could she ever compete with that? Unless . . .

CHAPTER
49

"THEY ARE SLOPPY FOR ALL THE RUMORS OF being well-trained," Quopomma said, studying how the Iwsetian soldiers guarded the road into their city-state. "I would have posted four with crossbows on either side to catch any traveler in a barrage."

Maeveen muttered half-hearted agreement, but her thoughts were miles away. Before leaving Shingol, she had traded messages with Vervamon, only to find he could not be pried free from interrogating the Niroso and learning all he could about the Stone People. The surviving members of her company—the rest of the expedition—had slowly reunited after wandering through Forest Eln. Vervamon had quickly put them to work, not helping the minotaurs or elves, but in building a small village at the mouth of the Niroso cavern to serve as his headquarters.

She was not sure why she had accompanied Yunnie and Ehno rather than staying to aid Vervamon. She was Vervamon's captain, not theirs, but she had no indication that Vervamon required her services. Iro was hardly able to command, but capable sublieutenants easily kept the discipline and followed Vervamon's imperious orders as well as she could.

"I want to see the outcome," she lied to herself, staring at Yunnie. Vervamon the Younger, she mentally corrected. How like his father he was! The passion was banked for the moment, but she saw flashes whenever Ehno spoke of how Yunnie could aid the minotaurs and elves. Yunnie might be concerned less for peace between Jehesic and Iwset than his blood brothers and their suffering, but he cared.

Damn him.

"What now?" asked Quopomma. "We reach Iwset and then sit on our thumbs? We could do that back in the City of Shadows, or in Shingol, for all that." The ogre growled deep in her throat as a small band of Jehesic marines popped up alongside the road to attack the slovenly Iwsetian sentries. The skirmish lasted only seconds, the Jehesic soldiers fading back into the countryside to leave a half dozen Iwsetians dead or wounded, sustaining no injuries to their small band.

"That's the way they fight," Ehno said. "Lady Edara lacks enough troops to launch a full-scale attack, so relies on guerrillas. Iwset has lost its navy—and its best general. Worse, I fear unrest in the city saps its will to fight against its real enemies."

"Ihesia has been captured?" This caught Maeveen's attention. She did not like the woman. If Jehesic had captured or killed her, it would shorten the war and might force Peemel from the throne without Yunnie needing to go through the charade of a marriage to Lady Edara.

Even as this thought crossed her mind, Ehno dashed her hopes.

"Edara refuses to ransom Ihesia, but Peemel has other good generals who, while lacking her brilliance, are capable sorts. If only I could communicate with those who command me, but I grow weaker daily." Ehno seemed to collapse in on himself, the travel and the conversation too taxing for him after Feyne's dagger had almost robbed him of life.

"Quopomma, stay with Ehno. Guard him."

"What of you, Captain? You thinking of sneaking into the city?"

"Yunnie . . ." Maeveen said, her mind racing as she ignored Quopomma's question. She knew what she had to do and had a plan for accomplishing it so they would all benefit—all, perhaps, save Ehno and whoever pulled his strings. "I need you to use the Sigil of Iwset. Rouse the citizens, rally them to your cause."

"What? No, you can't," protested Ehno. "We must see the dockmaster. He will get us to Jehesic, where the marriage can be performed. Try to seize power too early and all will fail! The city is in turmoil!"

"Ignore him," Maeveen said, leading Yunnie to one side. Coernn had not given her any help when she needed it, and she doubted Ehno would. The politicians played their own games—or the games of those who wound them up and set them on the table to peck and bob like magical automata. It was time for her to think of her own happiness. If all worked according to her scheme, everyone would win.

"He is right. To reveal myself now would mean increased danger. Even from here, I can see gangs of citizens sniping at one another. Iwset is tearing itself apart."

"How do we know Ehno is telling the truth about getting to Jehesic? Who gives him his orders? He is not working alone. He might be leading us directly into Peemel's clutches. Or Digody's," she said.

"I know little of such double-dealing," Yunnie complained. "Finding the dockmaster seems a reasonable approach if we want to sail to Jehesic."

"We could have sailed to Jehesic from Shingol," Maeveen pointed out. "Rather, Ehno insisted we come to Iwset."

"His contacts might be here. If we sailed into Jehesic's main harbor on an unknown vessel, they might think we were spies and kill us," said Yunnie.

Maeveen shrugged this off. "I have a plan. Rouse the guard, get them stirred up, don't let yourself be caught—but use the Sigil of Iwset to see if any of the citizens recognize it and are inclined to accept its wearer as their liege."

"If they are not, then we return to Shingol," Yunnie

finished. "However, if the citizens are truly as disgusted with Lord Peemel as we believe, they will at least listen to me."

"The guards and the Inquisitors are the two groups we need to distract," Maeveen said. "Mostly, I need to learn of the various alliances and who we might trust. Vervamon was lied to consistently while we were in Iwset before."

"He wanted to be deceived," Yunnie said. "I spoke briefly to him about Peemel and Digody. Vervamon is a difficult man to hold a conversation with, I must say. Anything involving his expedition serves as bait for his intellect."

As anything dealing with the minotaurs is bait for your heart, Maeveen thought, studying him. He had never looked more like his father. She fought down the urge to tell him his true parentage, but held back. It did not suit her purposes. Not yet.

Yunnie pulled the sigil out from under his torn tunic and held it, as if staring at it might solve all the problems. He suddenly shivered and turned his blue eyes to Maeveen.

"I got rid of the Living Armor, but this burdens me in the same way." He shuddered again. "There is no magic locked within the sigil, not as there was in the armor, but the weight is still here." He balanced it on his fingertips as if considering how far he could throw it. "So many years it remained buried. Why not a few more?"

"Destiny can be strange," Maeveen said.

"You don't believe in a flow of time and events that carries us along like helpless leaves in a stream, do you?" He speared her with his gaze.

"We can change our course through life," she said simply.

"Let's do it, then. I shall draw attention from your mission, whatever it is," Yunnie said. "How long do I have before they either stone me or imprison me for the question?"

"Not long, but it won't take me long, either." Maeveen settled her weapons and pulled the cloak around her broad shoulders to hide sword and dagger. While her brown-and-green splotched clothing was not a military uniform, she did not want any to mistake her for a soldier battling against Iwset.

Side by side they set off to find the way into a war-weary Iwset.

Maeveen O'Donagh pressed into a doorway as Yunnie jumped on the back of a dead wagon. He stood on two corpses, deceased through action other than combat from their poxy appearance. He sucked in a deep breath and began his rallying speech. Maeveen felt herself stepping from the door, drawn to him, just as she found it impossible to ignore Vervamon. Words flowed like honey, stabbed like a knife, grated like sandpaper, and slid past smoother than any silken caress. Yunnie knew all the tricks his father used.

"How do they do it? Instinctively?" She shook her head. Yunnie launched into the faults of Lord Peemel and his advisers, then drew forth the Sigil of Iwset. Maeveen took this as her sign to withdraw. Her short legs pumped fast as she worked her way past the red-robed Inquisitors' roadblocks and the occasional military patrol set to maintain order or track down Jehesic spies.

Not surprisingly, Yunnie was right about other trouble in the city. Small bands of roving citizens looted stores and fought among themselves for their pitiful spoils. Maeveen saw a city coming apart, and its ruler apparently did little to quell the internal fighting. Yunnie would have more to deal with than marriage to Lady Edara.

She was slightly out of breath by the time she reached Peemel's palace, not so much from exertion, but in anticipation of what she must do.

In a way she felt as if she betrayed Yunnie, and this left a sour taste in her mouth. But there was no other way to peace. Maeveen strode forward through the opened doors into the courtyard, aware of dozens of archers training their poisoned arrows on her.

She stopped and made clear her request to the captain of the guard. Then Maeveen waited to see if she would be killed on the spot.

CHAPTER

50

"YOU HAVE LOST THE WAR," MAEVEEN O'Donagh declared forcefully. Lord Peemel straightened on his throne, staring at her, his chin resting on tented fingers. She tried to read his expression. The statement had given him pause, but Maeveen could not determine the exact effect it had on him. She preferred dueling with swords rather than words. The cut was more obvious, the blood always debilitating. Wounds could not be hidden and advantage increased as the opponent weakened. She was unsure of Peemel's strength.

"Why waste your time with her, milord?" asked Digody. "She is a rabble-rouser. Why, she even brought back an agitator from Shingol to badger you. I have sent troops to arrest him before discord spreads."

"Spreads?" Maeveen laughed harshly. "Your people riot in the streets. They kill each other indiscriminately. There is discord already in Iwset. Yunnie has the Sigil of Iwset, the one you sent Vervamon to fetch—and more. *You* wanted Yunnie returned to Iwset with the sigil, did you not? *He* can restore peace to Iwset!"

"Why would I—" Digody tried to look inoffensive,

even shocked at the idea that he churned public sentiment to shake Peemel from the throne.

"You wanted a pretender brought in so you can kill
Peemel *and* the pretender," accused Apepei. Maeveen had
only vague memories of the feisty mountain dwarf, but he
apparently still sowed seeds of dissent among Peemel's
other advisers. There was obvious animosity between
Digody and Apepei.

"Enough bickering," Peemel said, cutting short the dispute, which obviously had its roots in personal antipathy
rather than Maeveen had presented this afternoon. "You
tell me I have lost the war with Jehesic? How do you
know? I sent you—and that fool Vervamon—to fetch the
sigil for me. Now I find you gave it to a man claiming to
be my bastard son. Is there reason I should listen rather
than ordering your immediate execution?" Peemel
reached down beside the throne and drew forth a white
linen cloth, daintily dabbed at his lips, then vigorously
rubbed his hands.

"Your hold on Iwset fades by the minute," Maeveen
said, wishing Vervamon were here to plead the case, but
she knew her leader would never bother. Such political
maneuvering was beneath his dignity, even if he were not
currently engrossed in learning all he could of the Stone
People. For all that, she wished Yunnie could do it for
her. He had the flair she lacked. She was only a military
commander, not an orator.

"Why does that concern you?"

"You were generous," Maeveen said, "in supplying
Vervamon's expedition."

"Which generosity you repay by treachery," cut in
Digody, red eyes lit with balefire. "You find the object of
the search, then return to overthrow our liege!"

"Quiet, Digody," Peemel said, amused. His humor
chilled Maeveen. She had hoped to convince him to stop
the war against Jehesic in return for the Sigil of Iwset and
Yunnie's promise never to lay claim to the throne.
Prosperity and peace along the coast benefited everyone,
especially if Yunnie could also get much-needed food and
other provisions for both the minotaurs and the elves.

With Iwset on the side of the elves and minotaurs, they stood a chance against the Niroso, should Vervamon fail in his negotiations and the Stone People chose to pursue their war.

If only she knew who Coernn had served—and who Ehno swore allegiance to. The wizard and his five assistants had divided loyalties which proved increasingly treacherous to her and Yunnie. Maeveen swallowed hard as she caught movement in the corner of her eye and saw Abbot Offero enter the audience chamber to stand patiently, waiting like a vulture for his dinner to die.

The storm gathered around her, crushing her.

"There are powers stirring beyond your capacity to defend against," Maeveen said. "Beneath Iwset rise the Niroso, the Stone People, intent on destroying all surface dwellers. They have lain waste to the elves of Forest Eln and the Urhaalan minotaurs." Maeveen bent the truth slightly, but felt it gave power to her argument. "Vervamon can stop them—and you cannot, if you continue to fight both Jehesic and those within your own ranks."

"There are none here disloyal to me," Lord Peemel said haughtily. Again humor curled his lips, giving Maeveen a sinking sensation. She had played her only card—the sigil—and felt her grip slipping away. She was unable to stop the conflict between Iwset and Jehesic. All she wanted was to depose Peemel and allow Yunnie his freedom—to be with her rather than Edara.

"There are none disloyal to me *for long*," Peemel amended. He laughed. "I care nothing for the sigil now. It would be nice to have it returned to my vault, but it is not necessary. The war with Jehesic will end soon. In Iwset's favor!"

"But, milord, the Jehesic navy hammers our supply fleets. Not one in ten ships penetrates their blockade. Soon, the merchants will not dare to enter Iwset harbor, no matter how much we offer. This lack of food causes riots within our walls. We need to transport everything into Iwset overland," said Apepei. "If the woman is right, these Stone People might cut off even that supply. We would be in dire straits, then." The dwarf tossed his head, sending red hair flying in a wild spray. He bounced about as if someone had set fire to his feet as he tried to jockey for position in front of Digody.

Maeveen experienced a surge of confidence after hearing Apepei's evaluation of the war. Then the confidence died when she saw how truly amused Lord Peemel was by the outburst.

"We need fear neither Jehesic's navy nor the lost sigil," Peemel said with more than a hint of arrogance. He snapped his fingers. From one side of the large audience chamber entered a small knot of soldiers. Penned in by the half dozen guardsmen walked a slender woman with copper hair and emerald eyes that flashed fire. She wore a sleek, sea-green gown that clung to her figure—and heavy manacles at her wrists clanked like buoy bells as she walked.

Maeveen had never seen Lady Edara, but she knew instinctively that the ruler of Jehesic stood before her in chains, no longer a threat to Peemel. She glanced back and saw the play of emotion on his advisers' faces. It came to her like a bolt of lightning that Peemel had not told Digody or Apepei or any of the others that he had captured his archenemy—or was that *betrothed*?

"What is the meaning of this?" raged the dwarf. Apepei was the first to regain his tongue as the shock passed. "You cannot kidnap the ruler of another city-state. This is against the rules of war!"

"Rules of war," mused Peemel, as if trying to understand such an outrageous notion. "What might they be, Apepei? Rules for killing? How absurd! She sends her fleet to kill me. Is it not more humane if my spies creep up on her and spirit her away from her stronghold with no loss of life?"

"Kill me now," raged Edara. "I will never marry you. Sooner would I take you to the grave with me!"

Peemel frowned as he considered those listening to this outburst. Maeveen read the ruler's expression accurately. Any who might speak of this to another would never leave the audience chamber alive. Since she had blundered in trying to forge peace without knowing Peemel had already captured his enemy, Maeveen knew her own life would be forfeit. She easily came to the conclusion that Peemel's guards were to be sacrificed in the name of secrecy. With them she might find an uneasy alliance lasting long enough to escape.

"You have no choice, milady," Peemel said, rising to smile down at her. "You will be my wife. We shall rule both Iwset and Jehesic, the most powerful alliance on the western coast. Together we will bring peace to this sorry land."

"You intend to rule in her name," cried Apepei. "The people of Jehesic will never accept that. The war will turn even more vicious. Lord Peemel, I beg you, this is wrong. Either defeat her navy or—"

"Silence," Peemel snapped, glaring at the dwarf. Maeveen wondered at Apepei's agitation. The small man bounced nervously from foot to foot, more frightened than outraged.

"You will marry me, Edara, and the world will know how powerful your navy and my army can be. We—"

"There is more than the Sigil of Iwset," called Maeveen, knowing she had to seize power before it slipped away entirely. "Yunnie is more than Lady Pioni's son. Yunnie is *not* your son. He is the son of Vervamon, the man you sent to retrieve the sigil."

"What is this?" Peemel spun about, his face a mask of pure hatred. "Pioni had a bastard with that pompous ass? How dare she!"

"You had her executed, milord," pointed out Digody. "She never cared for you. That was the reason for her execution."

"This son of Vervamon. Kill him. And Vervamon, too."

"Vervamon even now deals with the Stone People living beneath your feet. Never again will you be safe if you murder his son."

"His bastard son," sneered Peemel. "I do not fear these Stone People you prattle on about. My generals can fight any creature. And for a dowry, Lady Edara will undoubtedly offer the return of all captured officers, including Ihesia."

"You're not thinking, Lord Peemel," Maeveen shouted again. Soldiers grabbed her arms, ready to drag her from the chamber. "Kill Yunnie and Vervamon, with all his connections across Terisiare, and you will never rest easy again until vengeance is taken on you!"

"What do I care of an academic who is so easily duped?" Peemel waved the soldiers away. "I will have an army and navy able to fight any war. And my loving wife will sit beside me on the throne." He patted the low stool beside his black wood throne.

Peemel had turned to reach out to the chained Edara when his eyes went wide. He stepped woodenly from the throne and then his legs turned boneless, sending him tumbling down the steps in front of his throne. Lord Peemel lay facedown at the base of his throne with a long, slender knife sticking from his back.

CHAPTER
51

SILENCE FELL ON THE ROOM. MAEVEEN O'Donagh heard only the pounding pulse in her temples. The guards holding her stepped back a pace, unsure of their duty, and the others in the room held their breaths. Only Abbot Offero moved, gliding forward silently to kneel beside the Peemel's still body. He turned the body over, drew out a thin purple-and-gold grosgrain sash and laid it ceremoniously over Peemel's shoulders, first left, then right, then over the closed eyes, and finally began the slow, mournful prayer for the dead.

"He did it!" shouted Lady Edara, lifting chained hands to point at Digody. The bony, fierce-eyed adviser threw back his head and let a thunderous laugh erupt from his throat. The sound combined evil and triumph such as Maeveen had never heard. She wanted to clap her hands to her ears in an attempt to shut it out, but instead reached for the guard nearest her. She clamped her hand over the hilt of his dagger, drew and spun about. In a flash she held a sword, also.

She was armed and felt better for it, but the situation in the audience chamber had yet to resolve itself to her satisfaction.

"I killed the fool," cried Digody. His red eyes burned with manic fury now. He flung back his cape and showed two more knives, mates to the one sunk into Lord Peemel's back. "He worried over trivial matters. He had no sense for rule. I shall change that. Follow me, soldiers of Iwset, and I will give you the world. Everyone in this room will be made a general, a baron ruling his own city-state. We will fly across Terisiare and—"

As Lord Peemel before him, Digody staggered before tumbling down the steps. This time the assassin did not leave the murder weapon buried in his victim's back. Apepei stood with a bloody blade held ready to fend off any of Peemel's bodyguards foolish enough to attack him.

But the dwarf's action was less startling to Maeveen than what followed. Edara shoved aside her captors and rushed forward, arms outstretched. For a heartbeat Maeveen thought the ruler of Jehesic was trying to impale herself on Apepei's knife. Instead, the dwarf dropped his weapon and threw his arms around her in a loving embrace.

"Get the chains off her. Immediately!" the mountain dwarf snapped. His commanding tones caused the captain of Edara's guard to obey without thinking. The heavy shackles fell to her feet and were kicked aside. The lovely woman spun and stood familiarly beside Apepei.

"You," Maeveen exclaimed, puzzle pieces fitting together into one small, perfect picture. "Coernn and Ehno were your spies."

"Mine," Apepei said, staring defiantly at Abbot Offero, who still ministered to the fallen Peemel. In a few minutes he would ensure the dead ruler's soul proper transit and move to Digody's body. Maeveen thought that act of salvation lay beyond even the good abbot's doing.

"All save for Feyne," she said.

"He was Peemel's pawn," Apepei said. "And another— I cannot remember his name—swore allegiance to the Inquisition. He died quickly."

"Fed to a carnivorous plant," Maeveen said, remembering how Coernn and Ehno had performed the savage task early in their expedition.

"He deserved no less," Apepei said. "But there lies the worst of them all." Apepei spat on Digody's corpse. Edara took Apepei's wrist gently and drew him closer, whispering urgently to him. The dwarf's anger faded.

"As always, my darling Edara is correct. Guards, release them. Fetch Yunnie from the plaza, or wherever he is speaking to the citizens of Iwset. Promise him safe passage and amnesty. The time has come to talk, not fight."

Apepei's positive control edged a few of Peemel's lesser advisers in the dwarf's direction. The few who openly opposed him—and Lady Edara—huddled to discuss new alliances. Maeveen doubted those loyal to Peemel would find any succor from Digody's partisans.

She also doubted they would be effective against Apepei and Edara. The dwarf had taken control and held it firmly. Maintaining that control would no doubt fall on Lady Edara's able shoulders, but for the moment Maeveen felt danger had passed.

But how would the people of Iwset react? Would they follow an assassin of their ruler's assassin and the leader of an enemy city-state?

The war had robbed loved ones from every home in Iwset.

Maeveen followed them into a smaller conference room, cautiously hopeful that she might witness an end to the Iwset-Jehesic war.

"I can't believe Abbot Offero is giving in so easily," Maeveen whispered to Yunnie. Vervamon the Younger sat silently, as immobile as a statue, while Peemel's former advisers hammered out a new power structure in Iwset. His hands were clenched into fists and only iron will kept him from shaking. Maeveen reached out and laid her hand on his. Yunnie did not move away, nor did he respond to her touch. He had taken her revelation of his paternity stoically, but inner turmoil was obvious from his distant expression.

"He doesn't have much choice," Quopomma said. "He opposes all magic, but he supports more in this proposal

than he opposes, it seems. If he is to keep any power, he
has to allow people like Apepei and Edara to have a few
of their minions armed with spells." On the ogre's other
side sat a bandaged Ehno.

"For all his militant tendencies, the abbot favors peace
between Iwset and Jehesic," the man said, "although it
means giving the likes of Ihesia and me an indulgence for
our sins." He turned to the freed general.

Maeveen stiffened as from across the chamber Ihesia
smiled her wicked, knowing smile. That one was trouble,
Maeveen knew, but she said nothing about her concern
over the general's ambitions. It was up to Yunnie to
decide how best to deal with Peemel's former military
commander. For Maeveen's part, she would have banished Ihesia to the Ronom Glacier with the sincere wish
that she freeze to death.

"Then the Inquisition agrees that our greater problems
will be resolved, in return for diminished activity against
our citizens, and that this is the true meaning of the sign
given Peemel before the war," Apepei said, his wide-set
eyes fixed on the abbot. Offero inclined his head slightly
in the dwarf's direction. Lady Edara whispered to Apepei
for a few seconds, then sat back, her face pale and drawn.

"This leaves the greater issue of conflict between
Jehesic and Iwset to be dealt with," Apepei went on
grimly. "Lady Edara has no desire to press the matter,
will cease hostilities immediately, and will not sue for
damages. In return, there must be similar resolve on the
part of Iwset." Apepei closed his eyes. Maeveen saw tears
form at the corner of the dwarf's eyes. A quick brush of
his hand hid the tears before they rolled down his cheeks.

"Who rules us?" demanded a subadviser, one of
Digody's supporters. "I will not follow a dwarf born in
distant mountains!"

"Why not?" asked another. "You jumped like a frog
every time Digody croaked. Who can say where he was
birthed?"

"Silence!" bellowed Apepei, his baritone command filling the small room. "There is no need to lower yourself to
bickering. The decision has been made." Apepei closed

his eyes and ran his hands through his unruly hair in a vain attempt to compose himself.

Maeveen sucked in her breath as Yunnie pulled away from her. From the drawn expression on Edara's face, Maeveen knew what was coming. That did not mean she liked it any more than the others involved.

"Vervamon the Younger, known as Yunnie, scion of Lady Pioni, Lord Peemel's fourth wife, and holder of the Sigil of Iwset will rule our city-state."

"He's a bastard commoner, no matter his mother!" Digody's subordinate jumped to his feet and pounded on the table. "How can we expect the people to follow a fish-monger who has not lived even one day in our fair city? The people riot, demanding a firm hand on the rudder of state! He cannot give it to them."

"He will not be a commoner after his marriage to Lady Edara," Apepei said, his voice level. Maeveen saw the effort the dwarf expended to keep from blurting out his true feelings. He pointedly did not look at Edara, nor she at him. Yunnie closed in on himself more and more as Apepei detailed how peace would be forged.

Maeveen sank back in her chair, aware that Quopomma stared at her as she did at Yunnie. How perfect was Apepei's plan! She gloried in its devious maze of implications. Yunnie and Edara married would fashion the power-ful dual city-state Peemel had sought, but without animosity. The Inquisition would be weakened, peace guaranteed, and prosperity rising on the horizon for years to come. For Yunnie, it also meant the opportunity to aid both the mino-taurs and the elves. He need not even remain in Iwset. Lady Edara could rule in his stead, after the populace came to accept her as an ally rather than a conqueror.

With his father dealing with the Niroso, that threat might be put to rest, also. Yunnie need only appease Vervamon the Elder with new funding for another expe-dition, perhaps a return to the City of Shadows, perhaps to discover other lost treasures.

Maeveen reached out to Yunnie again, and again he drew back.

She was not the only one sacrificing personal happiness

for this peace. Apepei and Edara loved one another. It was obvious in the way they spoke and stood close and touched and simply looked at each other. Apepei was willing to give up his love for the sake of Iwset, as Edara gave up her love for Jehesic. And Yunnie gave up his freedom to enjoy the solitude of the Urhaalan valley and the joys of the herd for a people he did not know, at least for the immediate future. He could never be true to two lives, not when one demanded daily attention. Yunnie might be a bull of the Urhaalan, but he was now also the promised husband of Edara and ruler of Iwset.

"That is possible," Digody's lieutenant allowed reluctantly. "There exist many who will argue against it, but their voices can be stifled." He did not need to add, "For a price." Apepei understood the unspoken words, as did the other powerbrokers in the room.

"I, for one, shall enjoy serving under him," said Ihesia. Her tongue made a slow circuit of her red lips. Maeveen wanted to give her a new mouth, starting under one ear with a sharp dagger and finishing under the other ear with a quick slash.

"I pledge fealty to Lord Vervamon the Younger," spoke up Ehno, responding to an almost imperceptible nod from Apepei.

"He legally carries the Sigil of Iwset as his emblem. May he wear it with dignity and honor at his coronation," Abbot Offero intoned, finishing the authorization for Yunnie's ascension to the throne. Military, civil, and religious factions agreed. Maeveen knew Yunnie's earnestness and honesty would win over many of Iwsetians when he addressed them.

On his wedding day.

"I agree to these terms," Lady Edara said, eyes straight ahead. Her drawn face spoke more eloquently than her words.

Maeveen thought Edara could do far worse than Yunnie for a husband, and Yunnie had won a woman of beauty, integrity, and intelligence for his bride. And power. Vast power and wealth, unlike a captain commanding a scholarly expedition's company.

Yunnie rose and waited for the hubbub in the room to die. He held out the Sigil of Iwset and let it spin slowly. It caught and reflected light from the lamps placed around the room.

"By this sigil I claim power in Iwset. As a baby I was stolen away by Peemel's elven majordomo, Tavora by name. She carried me to Shingol, where I was raised by a foster family, but my heart was never with Shingol—or Iwset." Yunnie let this sink in. "I have been accepted into the Urhaalan herd and consider myself a minotaur."

He ignored a few snickering remarks whispered behind shielding hands.

"The war between elf and minotaur is at an end. Vervamon—my father, by all accounts—works with the Stone People to hold them in check to prevent further strife. Now Iwset and Jehesic are at peace—if only I marry Edara."

Yunnie stared at Edara.

"You are lovely, Lady Edara, lovelier than any woman I have ever seen. You are brave and loyal to your people, true to the pursuit of peace. Any man would be delighted to accept one such as you as bride." Yunnie held up the Sigil of Iwset even higher, then dropped it on the table.

With a quick movement, he drew out his sword and lifted the pommel above the golden disk.

"I follow my own path, not one lit by others, no matter how decent and honorable their intent."

The pommel crashed down on the sigil, smashing it into a dozen pieces. Yunnie threw down his sword and walked from the chamber, head high.

He left behind only stunned silence.

CHAPTER

52

IWSET WAS AGLOW WITH WEDDING BONFIRES
and filled with boisterous, joyful singing. It was not every
day a marriage of such import was performed within the
city's walls. As if giving its benediction, above in the dark
night sky the Spiked Serpent writhed in stellar glory from
the zenith all the way across the sky to curl around the Pole
Star. The gauzy white patch of the Maiden's Curls and the
distinctive pattern of the dozen stars forging the Broken
Sword of Ennea rose, late, much later since autumn now
held the land in full grip. The Lost Rat found its hole, and
the Two Dryads preceded the Arms of Elysium, but would
never allow those blazing stars to blot out lesser patterns
after it rose above the eastern horizon. Instead, they
embraced the twin moons of Iontiero and Fessa.

"Fessa," Yunnie said, still uncomfortable naming the
greater moon with its misty shroud.

"What's that?" asked Maeveen O'Donagh. She held a
pewter goblet in both hands to keep from spilling any
more. She tried to remember how many times she had
emptied it and couldn't. Every time only a little heady
wine swirled in the bottom, a reveler staggered by and
offered her more. She always accepted.

For all the festivity, she felt no joy. A wedding ought to be cause for celebration. She endured emptiness as she stared at Yunnie, whose gaze fixed on the rising moons.

"The moon. The minotaurs call it Fessa. I was raised not to give any name to it."

"As were many along this coast," Maeveen said. She drained her goblet and waited for another jug-bearing celebrant to offer more. Maeveen had to hold herself in check when she saw a half dozen Iwsetians beating up a solitary man for some real or imagined slight. The rioting had died down, but too much unrest remained, a festering sore amid all the merrymaking. Before true peace could reign, the dozens of factions within the city's walls would have to be united.

"What do you see up there?" Maeveen turned her attention back to the sky, trying to figure out his fascination, and failed. The lesser moon shone with a reflected light that bespoke of utter unnatural smoothness. A moon placed in orbit by an ancient mad wizard, some said. Artificial, she was certain. It had the look of magic to it, rather than the natural craggy peaks visible on the misty greater moon. But what did this matter to her, with her feet on solid ground?

"I see trouble for Edara and Apepei," Yunnie said.

Loud music drowned out his words, but she saw his lips moving and read them clearly.

"You could have been the center of the ceremony. No one is pleased with your rejection of a perfect solution to strife along the coast."

"Perfect? Not for me," Yunnie said. "I cannot sit on a throne and make haughty decisions affecting the lives of others."

"Yet you tried to stop the war between the elves and minotaurs," she pointed out.

His glumness infected her and turned her own dour mood even more somber. Yunnie had rejected the plan and insisted that Apepei and Edara marry. The festivities would rage for weeks, Maeveen guessed, but that only covered the ill-will bubbling beneath the surface with a brittle veneer of forced joy. Iwsetian prejudice would eventually force Apepei to take stringent measures to maintain the peace. To many, Apepei had married the enemy who had killed relatives and friends. Even his well-liked bride might have difficulty with the marriage back in her more accepting Jehesic.

The pair faced considerable unrest, personally and politically. But this was nothing new for either Iwset or Jehesic. Maeveen thought the two were capable of dealing with the obstacles as long as they trusted each other.

"I'm a fool. I did nothing to stop the war. Mytaru summoning Tiyint. The Niroso and the coal golems. It only stopped because there was such slaughter no one was left to fight. I did nothing."

"You were the only one who tried," Maeveen pointed out. "You alone stood against Sacumon until Coernn joined the battle. There is considerable rebuilding to be done, both in Eln Forest and the Urhaalan's valley."

"Yes," Yunnie said. Maeveen was unable to decide what thoughts rambled through his brain.

"The offer to be my lieutenant stands," Maeveen said, knowing what Yunnie—Vervamon the Younger—would say. "We move on when Vervamon gathers enough information for a monograph on the Stone People. He thinks he has learned where the Tomb of the Seven Martyrs might be and hopes to enlist their aid in rifling it."

Yunnie nodded but did not speak. He was too engrossed in Iontiero tumbling wildly across the constellations.

"All Terisiare would be yours to explore. Vervamon knows no limit to his inquiry or curiosity."

Maeveen fell silent when she realized she might as well be talking to a brick wall. A drunken vintner pushed his wine cart past, stopped and spilled potent wine into her goblet, gave her a sloppy kiss, and stumbled on, singing off-key as he went. Yunnie did not even notice.

"Quopomma and the others from the expedition will be ready in a few days. We sail for Shingol, then go overland to the Urhaalan's territory to rejoin Vervamon."

"I leave soon," Yunnie said. "But I cannot spend my life as a subordinate." He turned and hastily added, "No offense meant to you. Never have I seen a more capable captain. It is Vervamon. I cannot tolerate him, even if he is my father. Being under his authority would drive me to rash acts." Yunnie paused a moment, then smiled crookedly. "Mayhap I cannot go because he *is* my father. I would hate to become like him."

Maeveen wondered if she ought to tell Vervamon that Yunnie was his son. The knowledge had come as a shock to Yunnie, but he had endured so much else it hardly seemed to affect him now. She snorted, knowing this morsel of paternity would hardly stick in Vervamon's throat. He had lived well not knowing. His indifference to such things would ferry him on through his intellectual studies, still not caring.

"Come with me," she said, making one last plea.

"I have done all I can here. Apepei and Edara will succeed. They have already forged good, strong alliances."

"Ihesia? Abbot Offero?" Maeveen scoffed at the notion of them being good, much less strong allies.

"They are expert at political infighting and maneuvering. I am not." Yunnie vented a deep sigh. "I am not sure what I am good at."

"Caring," she said. "You care."

"My destiny lies with the Urhaalan herd. I have known that for some time. Good-bye," he said, placing his goblet on the ground. He stared down at her, blue eyes aglow from the light of the stars and moons and his concern for the Urhaalan minotaurs.

"Wait," Maeveen said, putting her goblet on the ground beside her. She wobbled as she came closer. "I am not going back to Vervamon. There is no need. Quopomma will make a capable captain." Maeveen tried to stem the flow of her words, but found the wine lubricated her tongue too well. "My travels with him are at an end and I must find new territory to explore."

"I understand why you would seek your own path. Are you going to stay here?" asked Yunnie, studying her with sober eyes. "I heard Lady Edara offered you a position at Jehesic, and I am sure Apepei would welcome you as a high officer in the Iwsetian army."

"I . . ." Maeveen cursed herself for being such a fool. "I seek more, as you do."

"Where does your fortune lead, or can you say?" asked the man who looked so much like Vervamon but acted so differently.

Maeveen started to tell of her plan to accompany him, then fought down the tongue-loosening effect of the wine to say, "I will sail on the tide. Quopomma and the others go north. I am sailing south, perhaps to Lat-Nam."

"What is there to draw you?"

"Adventure," she said. "The unknown. Somewhere far from Vervamon."

"I understand," he said. He bent and kissed her lightly. Then Vervamon the Younger walked away from Maeveen's life.

"And somewhere even farther from you," she said softly to his back. Then Maeveen O'Donagh hoisted her goblet, drained it, and went off in search of revelry that would make her forget. For a while.

EPILOGUE

Two shadows stretched from the rocky cairn he had built for Mytaru, Iontiero illuminating it from the east and Fessa from the west. Yunnie stared at the monument, his heart heavy. He wiped away tears before they ran down his cheeks and left dusty tracks.

"Mytaru, my brother, I wish I could have done more." He received no reply. He watched the shadows shift silently and finally merge as the faster Iontiero overtook Fessa. Then both moons dipped under the lip of the world and disappeared from the sky. In the darkness lit only by the sprawl of stars overhead, Yunnie knew it was time to give honor to his friend.

Vervamon the Younger lacked the deeply resonant voice of a minotaur, but he began the dark lament that told of honor and rage, magic and heroism—and his love for a fallen brother.

Enter the World of
Magic: The Gathering™

Adventures Based
on the Bestselling
MAGIC: THE
GATHERING™
Trading Cards

MAIL TO: **HarperCollins Publishers**
              P.O. Box 588 Dunmore, PA 18512-0588

Yes, please send me the books I have checked:

❑ ARENA William R. Forstchen 105424-0 .... $4.99 U.S./$5.99 Can.

❑ WHISPERING WOODS Clayton Emery 105418-6 .... $4.99 U.S./$5.99 Can.

❑ SHATTERED CHAINS Clayton Emery 105419-4 .... $4.99 U.S./$5.99 Can.

❑ FINAL SACRIFICE Clayton Emery 105420-8 .... $4.99 U.S./$5.99 Can.

❑ THE CURSED LAND Teri McLaren 105016-4 .... $4.99 U.S./$5.99 Can.

❑ THE PRODIGAL SORCERER Mark Sumner 105476-3 .... $5.50 U.S./$6.50 Can.

❑ ASHES OF THE SUN Hanovi Braddock 105649-9 .... $5.50 U.S./$7.50 Can.

❑ SONG OF TIME Teri McLaren 105622-7 .... $5.50 U.S./$7.50 Can.

❑ AND PEACE SHALL SLEEP Sonia Orin Lyris 105619-7 .... $5.50 U.S./$7.50 Can.

❑ DARK LEGACY Robert Vardeman 105697-9 .... $5.50 U.S./$7.50 Can.

❑ TAPESTRIES: A MAGIC: THE GATHERING ANTHOLOGY 105428-3
   Edited by Kathy Ice .... $5.99 U.S./$7.99 Can.

❑ TAPESTRIES: A MAGIC: THE GATHERING ANTHOLOGY 105308-2
   Edited by Kathy Ice (Trade Paperback) .... $12.00 U.S./$16.75 Can.

❑ DISTANT PLANES: A MAGIC: THE GATHERING ANTHOLOGY
   Edited by Kathy Ice 105313-9 (Trade Paperback) .... $12.00 U.S./$16.75 Can.

SUBTOTAL .... $_____

POSTAGE & HANDLING .... $_____

SALES TAX (Add applicable sales tax) .... $_____

TOTAL .... $_____

Name _____

Address _____

City _____ State _____ Zip _____

Order 4 or more titles and postage & handling is **FREE!** For orders of fewer than 4 books, please include $2.00
postage & handling. Allow up to 6 weeks for delivery. Remit in U.S. funds. Do not send cash. Valid in U.S. &
Canada. Prices subject to change.   http://www.harpercollins.com/paperbacks   P03111

Visa & MasterCard holders—call 1-800-331-3761